A Brief Life

Juan Carlos Onetti

A Brief Life

TRANSLATED FROM THE SPANISH
BY *Hortense Carpentier*

Grossman Publishers
A DIVISION OF THE VIKING PRESS
NEW YORK
1976

Assistance for the translation of this volume was given by the Center for Inter-American Relations and the New York State Council on the Arts.

La Vida Breve *by J. Carlos Onetti*
© 1950, 1971 Editorial Sudamericana S.A.
English language translation Copyright © 1976 by The Viking Press, Inc.

First published in 1976 by Grossman Publishers
625 Madison Avenue, New York, N.Y. 10022

Published simultaneously in Canada by
The Macmillan Company of Canada Limited

Printed in U.S.A.

Library of Congress Cataloging in Publication Data
Onetti, Juan Carlos, 1909–
  A brief life.
  Translation of La vida breve.
  I. Title.
PZ4.0557Br [PQ8519.059] 863 75-28197
ISBN 0-670-19069-1

O something pernicious and dread!
Something far away from a puny and pious life!
Something unproved! Something in a trance!
Something escaped from the anchorage and driving free.

—Walt Whitman

Contents

Part Two

Part One

1

Santa Rosa

"Crazy world," the woman said once again, as if quoting, as if she were translating.

I heard her through the wall. I imagined her mouth moving in front of the refrigerator's cold vapor and vegetable odors or as she faced the curtain of brown slats that hung rigidly between the afternoon sun and the bedroom, obscuring the disorder of recently arrived furniture. I listened, absent-minded, without thinking about what she was saying.

While her voice, her footsteps, the dressing gown, and her thick arms, as I imagined them, moved from the kitchen to the bedroom, a man was agreeing with her in a continuous string of monosyllables that held only a hint of scorn. The heat that the woman parted as she moved coalesced again, filled every crack, rested heavily in every room, in the space between stair treads, in the corners of the building.

The woman walked up and down the only room of the apartment next door, and I listened to her from the bathroom, standing, my head bent under the almost silent shower.

"If my heart breaks into little pieces, I swear," the woman said, slightly sing-song, catching her breath at the end of each phrase as if a persistent obstacle arose each time to block her from confessing something, "I'm not going to beg him on my knees. He's got what he wants now. I have my pride, too. Although it hurts me more than it hurts him."

"Come on, come on," the man said consolingly.

For a short time I listened to the silence of the apartment, in the center of which ice cubes were tinkling now, spinning in glasses. The man must be in shirt sleeves, heavily built, pug-faced; she, grimacing nervously, dispirited by the sweat on her upper lip and chest. And I, on the other side of the thin wall, was standing naked, covered with drops of water, feeling them evaporate without deciding to pick up the towel, looking, beyond the door, at the gloomy room where the gathering heat hovered over the clean bedsheet. I thought, deliberately now, about Gertrudis, dear Gertrudis, with her long legs; Gertrudis with an old and whitish scar on her stomach; Gertrudis silent and blinking, at times swallowing her bitterness like saliva; Gertrudis with a small gold rose on the bosom of her party dress; Gertrudis, known by heart.

When the woman's voice returned, I thought about the task of looking without disgust at the new scar Gertrudis would have on her breast, a round area, complicated, with a pattern of red or pink lines that time would perhaps transform into a pale entanglement the same color as the other scar, delicate and smooth, quick as a signature, which Gertrudis had on her stomach and which I had explored so many times with the tip of my tongue.

"He'll break my heart," the woman next door said, "and I'll probably never be the same again. How many times Ricardo made me cry like a madwoman during those three years. There are plenty of things you don't know. What he did to me this time wasn't any worse than other things he did to me before. But now it's finished."

She must have been in the kitchen, crouched in front of the refrigerator, examining it, cooling her face and chest with the cold air that had the greasy smell of vegetables hardening.

"I'm not going to do a thing, even if it breaks my heart. Even if he comes crawling on his knees . . ."

"Don't say that," the man said. He had moved noiselessly, I suppose, toward the kitchen door. Leaning on the frame with one hairy arm, the other bent, holding a glass, he would look down at the squatting body of the woman. "Don't say that. We all make mistakes. If he, let's say . . . If Ricardo came to ask you . . ."

"I really don't know what to say to you, believe me," she confessed. "I've suffered so much because of him! How about another drink?"

They had to be in the kitchen because I heard the ice hitting against the sink. I turned on the shower again and moved my shoulders under the water while I thought about the morning some ten hours earlier, when the doctor was carefully making cuts, or a single incision, no less careful, on Gertrudis' left breast. He would have felt the scalpel quiver in his hand, sensed how the sharp edge had passed through the softness of fat, then to a dry, immediate hardness.

The woman snorted and burst out laughing; the phrase reached me blurred by the murmur of the shower.

"If you knew how fed up I am with men!" She moved toward the bedroom and struck the balcony doors. "But tell me, when is the storm that comes on Santa Rosa Day going to get here?"

"It has to be today," said the man without following her, raising his voice. "Don't worry, it'll break before dawn."

I discovered then that since last week I had been thinking the same thing, remembering my hope for a vague miracle that would bring springtime to me. An insect had been buzzing for hours, confused and furious, between the water from the shower and the last light from the small window. I shook the water off me like a dog and looked toward the dark part of the room where the entrapped heat throbbed. It was going to be impossible to write the film script Stein had spoken to me about while I could not manage to forget that cut breast, shapeless now, flattened out on the operating table like a jellyfish, offering itself like a wineglass. It wasn't possible to forget it, even if I persisted in telling myself over and over that I had played at sucking it, that thing. He would have to wait, and poverty with me. And on Santa Rosa Day everybody—the unknown chippy who had just moved into the neighboring apartment, the insect circling in the air perfumed by shaving soap, everybody living in Buenos Aires—was condemned to wait with me, whether they knew it or not, gasping like idiots in the menacing and portentous heat, trying to catch a glimpse of imminent spring and the brief grandiloquent storm that would open a passage from the coast and transform the city into a fertile land where happiness would appear, sudden and complete, like an act of memory.

The woman and man had turned into the room again, out of my hearing.

On leaving the kitchen, she had said, "I swear there's never been madness like ours."

I shut off the shower, hoping the insect would come by so I could whack it with the towel, flatten it against the drain, and I went into the bedroom naked and dripping. Through the blinds I saw night beginning to darken from the north, I counted the seconds between streaks of lightning. I put two mints in my mouth and threw myself on the bed.

. . . Breast amputation. A scar can be imagined as an irregular cut made on a rubber cup with thick walls, containing a motionless substance, pinkish, with bubbles on the surface, and that may give the impression of being liquid if we make the lamp that illuminates it sway back and forth. Also to be considered is how it will look in fifteen days, a month, after the incision, with a thin layer of skin stretched over it, translucent, so fine that no one would dare look at it for more than a moment. Further on a hint of wrinkles begins, changing and taking shape; now it may be possible to look at the scar on the sly, surprise it naked some night and predict what depressions, what configurations, what tones of red and white will prevail and endure. Besides, some day Gertrudis would laugh again, carefree, on the balcony in the spring or summer air, and look at me steadfastly for a moment with her radiant eyes. She would lower them immediately, permit a smile with a trace of defiance to appear at the corners of her mouth.

Then the moment for my right hand will have arrived, time for the farce of squeezing in the air, exactly, a form and a resistance that are not there and that have not yet been forgotten by my fingers. 'My palm will be afraid of swelling up abnormally, my fingertips will have to graze the rough or slippery surface without promise of intimacy, strangers to the round scar.'

"Understand, it's not because of the fiesta or the dance, but just the idea of it," said the woman on the other side of the wall, near and above my head.

Perhaps, like me, she had thrown herself on the bed, on a bed the same as mine, which could be buried in the wall by day and exhumed at night with the desperate creaking of springs; the man—stocky, with a dark bristling mustache, always drinking—would be doubled up in a chair or sweating, next to the woman's bare feet, prisoner of an imaginary respect. He would look at her, agreeing, saying nothing; his eyes at times wandering, fascinated by the toenails painted red, the short toes that she would be moving in rhythm, unconsciously.

"You can imagine how little the carnival matters to me. Now, at my age, I'm not going to go crazy about a dance. But it was the first dance of the carnival and we were going to go together, Ricardo and me. And I tell you straight out, as I told him, he behaved like a son of a bitch. He could easily have told me he couldn't come—'Look, I have something else to do,' or 'I don't feel like it.' If he can't trust me, tell me, who can he trust? A woman's never fooled; sometimes we pretend to be—yes, often—but that's not the same thing." She laughed without bitterness, between two coughs. "I could even give names; he'd fall over backward if he knew what I know about him and keep to myself. He hasn't any idea! But tell me if this isn't something special—carnival night, the first dance that we're going to. And eleven o'clock comes, twelve o'clock comes, and the gentleman doesn't appear. I even told La Gorda I felt it was a shame Ricardo couldn't get away until so late. Sorry for him, can you imagine, thinking he'd lost out on a good time! I was going as Madame Pompadour, but in black with a white wig."

The woman laughed in three bursts of laughter; her laugh was the reverse of the anxious voice that stopped unexpectedly to mark the end of each phrase; it seemed to have been restrained, developing for a long time and then breaking out suddenly, falteringly, like a weak whinny.

"La Gorda, poor thing, was green with rage. She lost the night because of me, and finally she left. It was daylight already when I woke up still sitting in that big chair—I don't know if you've ever seen it—that we had in Belgrano, with my wig falling off and the enormous bouquet of jasmine on the floor. What with the heat and everything closed up, it really seemed like a wake."

'. . . And Gertrudis is going to come here half dead,' I thought, 'convalescing, if all goes well. With that loathsome beast on the other side of the wall which seems thin as paper. Nevertheless, when I see her tomorrow in the hospital, if she can speak, if I can see her, if I see that she isn't going to die yet, at least I'll be able to squeeze her hand and tell her, smiling, that we have neighbors already. Because if she can speak or listen to me and isn't suffering too much, I'll have nothing more important to tell her than the news that someone's moved into the apartment next door, apartment H. She'll smile, ask questions, improve, return home. And the moment will come for my right hand, my mouth, my whole body; the moment of duty, pity, terror of humiliation. Because the only convincing proof, the only source of happiness and confidence I can provide her, will be to raise and lower over her mutilated chest, in full light, a face rejuvenated by lust, to kiss and go wild there.'

"I'm not just talking," the woman was saying now in the doorway. "This time it's for good."

I got up with my hot, dry body; slipping and drooping in the heat, I went to open the peephole in the door.

"You'll see how it all works out," the man repeated, calm, invisible.

I saw the woman; she was not in a bathrobe, instead she wore a tight dark dress, but her bare arms were white and thick. As she continued to smile at the man, who was now showing me a gray shoulder and the dark brim of the hat on his head, her voice, hesitant, as if pressed into cotton to withstand the tenderness of pain, rose again and again to repeat that nothing could be changed.

"That's how it goes. In the end you just get tired. Isn't that so?"

Díaz Grey, the City and the River

I stretched out my hand until it entered the small circle of light from the table lamp next to the bed. For some minutes I had been listening to Gertrudis sleep, covertly watching her face turned toward the balcony, her mouth half open and dry, almost black, her lips thicker than before, her nose shiny but no longer wet. I reached for a morphine ampule on the bedside table, picked it up with two fingers and turned it over, for a moment agitating the transparent liquid, which threw off a bright and mysterious reflection. It must be two or two-thirty; since midnight I had not heard the church clock. Some noise of motors or streetcars, some unidentifiable rumble, occasionally mingled with the room's odor of medicines and cologne.

She had vomited before midnight, she had cried, pressing the handkerchief soaked in cologne against her mouth while I gently patted her shoulder, not speaking to her now because in the course of the day I had repeated as many times as I could, "It's all right. Don't cry." While I played with the ampule, I thought I continued to hear—like old echoes in the corners of the room—the resolute, almost desperate sounds with their palpable shades of hatred and shame that she had made with her resigned head over the basin. I had felt the dampness of her forehead increase against my hand as I thought of the film script Julio had spoken to me about, and recalled Julio smiling at me, hitting me on the arm, assuring me that very soon I would leave poverty behind like an old lover, convincing me that that was what I wanted to do. 'Don't cry,' I thought. 'Don't be sad. Everything is the same for me, nothing's changed. I'm not sure yet, but I think I have it, just an idea, and Julio is going to like it. There's an old man, a doctor, who sells morphine. Everything has to radiate from that, from him. Perhaps he isn't old, but he's tired, dried up. When you're better, I'll start to write. A week or two, no more. Don't cry. Don't be sad. I see a woman who suddenly appears in the doctor's office. The doctor lives in Santa María, near the river. I was there only once, hardly a day, in summer, but I remember the air, the trees in front of the hotel, the placid way boats came down the river. I know there's a Swiss colony near the city. The doctor lives there, and suddenly a woman enters his office. The way you went back and forth from behind a folding screen to take off your blouse and show the swaying gold cross suspended from its chain, the blue spot, the lump on your breast. Thirteen thousand pesos, at least, for the first outline. I'm going to leave the agency, we're going to live in the suburbs where you'd like to be, and maybe you'll have a child. Don't cry, don't be sad.'

I remembered talking, I saw my stupidity, my impotence, my false words filling the space occupied by my body, taking its shape. "Don't cry, don't be sad," I repeated as she quieted down on the pillow, barely sobbing, trembling.

Now my hand overturned the morphine ampule, overturned it again near Gertrudis' body, near her breathing, knowing that one thing had ended and another was beginning, inevitable; knowing it was necessary that I not think about either and that both were only one thing, like the end of life and the beginning of putrefaction. The ampule was moving between my thumb and index finger, and I imagined the liquid had a perverse quality insinuated by its color, its capacity for movement, its ability to become still the moment my hand stopped moving, and then to shine serenely in the light, pretending it had never been agitated.

Slightly maddened, I played with the ampule, feeling my growing need to imagine and to draw close to me an indistinct doctor of forty years, the laconic and despairing inhabitant of a small city located between a river and a colony of Swiss farmers. Santa María because I had been happy there years ago, without reason and for twenty-four hours. This doctor must possess a past both convincing and revealing—though of no interest to me—and the fanatic resolution, based in neither morals nor dogma, to cut off his hand before he would perform an abortion. He must wear thick glasses, have a small body like mine, strands of blond hair mixed with the gray; this doctor must move about in an office where glass cabinets, instruments, and opaque vials occupy a subordinate place. An office with a corner shut off by a folding screen; in back of this screen, a mirror of good somber quality and a nickel-plated clothes tree that gives patients the impression of never having been used. I saw, for certain, two large windows above the square: cars, church, club, market, pharmacy, coffee shop, statue, trees, dark barefoot children, quick-moving blond men; overlooking unexpected deserted places, hot afternoons, and some nights of milky skies into which piano music from the conservatory unfurled. In the corner opposite the folding screen was a wide desk in disorder, and shelves holding a thousand books about medicine, psychology, Marxism, and philately. But I wasn't interested in the doctor's past, his life before arriving the previous year in the provincial city of Santa María.

I had nothing more than the doctor, whose name was Díaz Grey, and the idea of the woman entering the office during the morning, near noon, slipping behind the folding screen to undress, smiling as she mechanically examined her teeth in the immaculate mirror in the corner. For some reason that I still ignored, the doctor wasn't wearing his white jacket at that moment; he wore a gray suit, new, and was stretching black silk socks over his ankles as he waited for the woman to come out from behind the screen. I also had the woman, and I thought I had her forever. I saw her advance into the office, serious and, swaying slightly, in rhythm with her walk, a medallion with a photograph that hung between her breasts, breasts too small for her full figure and the solid confidence her face reflected. The woman stopped suddenly, a smile lengthened her lips; unconcerned and patient, she heaved her shoulders. Her composed face was directed toward the doctor for an instant. Then the woman turned on her heels and retreated without haste until she disappeared in the corner with the mirror, from which she would reappear almost immediately, dressed and defiant.

I threw the ampule onto the night table, between the bottles and the thermometer case. Gertrudis raised a knee and lowered it again; she made noise with her teeth, as if to chew her thirst or the air; she sighed and was quiet. All that remained of her, alive, was a contraction of painful expectation in the skin on her cheeks and in the small wrinkles encircling her eyes. I let myself fall back gently, face up.

. . . The torso that the woman showed Díaz Grey, and the small breasts that did not move when she walked, were excessively white; only in relation to them, and their evocation of milk and glossy paper, did the doctor's tie appear gaudy. Very white, astonishingly white, and contrasting with the color of her face and throat.

I heard Gertrudis moan and I sat up in bed in time to see her purse her lips and become still. The light couldn't be bothering her. I looked at the whiteness and the blush of Gertrudis' ear, too fleshy, very round, visibly suited to hearing. She was asleep, her face always toward the balcony, hermetic, showing only the edge of a tooth between her lips.

. . . More about the doctor, Díaz Grey, and the woman, who disappeared behind the folding screen in order to reappear with her breasts naked, then impatiently conceal herself again and return dressed. I already had the city where both were living. "I don't want anything really bad," Julio had said to me, "not a story for a women's magazine. But not too good a script either. Just enough to give them something to ruin."

Now I had the city in the provinces above whose main square the two windows of Díaz Grey's office faced. Silently, slowly, I left the bed and turned off the light. I walked about in the dark until I came to the balcony and touched the slats of the Venetian blind, pulled up halfway. I was smiling, amazed and grateful because it was so easy to see clearly a new Santa María in the spring night. The city with its slope and its river, its brand-new hotel, and in the streets, men with dark faces who exchanged jokes and smiles without spontaneity.

I heard the door of the neighboring apartment slam, the woman's footsteps as she went into the bathroom and then began to walk back and forth, humming, alone.

First I squatted with my forehead resting on the edge of the blinds, breathing the almost cold night air. White linen fluttered and flapped occasionally on the flat roof across the street. An iron skeleton, rusty, dark brown, with decayed bricks and mutilated plaster moldings. Behind me Gertrudis continued to sleep, snoring gently, forgetful, freeing me. My neighbor yawned and pushed a chair. Again I leaned my head toward the barrancas and the river, a broad river, a narrow river, a lonely and menacing river with fleeting reflections of storm clouds, a river with festive ships, with multitudes in fiesta clothes on its banks and a paddleboat riding the current with a cargo of barrels and timbers.

To my left, the woman lit a bright white light on the balcony. 'Not the best thing to do, but not unpardonably foolish either. Furthermore, it could mean she's calming down.' The woman was humming, more audibly now, and tapping against the parquet floor with her brilliant and high heels. There were no man's steps; still singing, she walked to the blind and raised it so that the thin white light would extend toward the east into the dark night. She continued humming with her mouth closed; her almost motionless shadow lengthened across the balcony tiles and shattered against the iron grating; her raised hands moved precisely and lazily, touching the clasps on her clothes or undoing her hair. Then she dropped her arms and breathed aloud. A harbor smell came on the wind. The woman walked to the middle of the room, then began to laugh into the telephone. Gertrudis murmured a question, then snored again. The woman's laughter grew high-pitched and powerful, stopped abruptly, died, leaving a dark silence, almost round, filled with a familiar kind of hatred and desperation.

"Tell him he's got to have patience, Gorda. He'll live. Tell him he's not acting like a man." The woman's voice was hardly audible. "He should ask himself about it. . . . No, I haven't had anything to drink. . . . Tell him to let us talk. Listen to me, Gorda; he's not going to cry because it cooled off. Listen to me. He spent the night saying, 'My two little white pigeons,' and then he fell to driveling, I swear. Finally, of course . . . But he's a gentleman, Gorda, I'll tell you later. Are you coming tomorrow? No, I don't want to speak to him, don't give him the phone. I was so hot! All I could think about was getting out of my girdle, and now I'm cold. I don't even think of calling him, it's as if he was dead. That's what I told Ernesto . . . Yes? Tell him if he wants, I'll give him lessons. Listen to me, Gorda, tell him to knock it off. Don't forget tomorrow, we have to arrange about Saturday. Tell him he knows where. *Ciao.*"

The woman took up the song again, nasally, and made several turns around the room, barefoot now. She returned to the balcony, and before she switched off the light, the smell of perfume reached me, an aroma I had breathed before, long ago, in a confused mélange of unpaved streets, ivy, a tennis court, a street lamp swaying over an intersection.

'La Gorda must be the fat woman who helped her wait and sweat out a carnival night in the Belgrano apartment, sitting in the chair that perhaps Ernesto has never seen.'

'Gertrudis' breast can still ooze blood if she moves too much, according to what the doctor said, the doctor made of rings of fat, with the voice and manners of a eunuch, tired watery eyes, protruding, but that nevertheless reveal unmistakably the habit of modest retreat from what bores him, regardless of his best intentions. His eyes, looking at Gertrudis, have observed enough to last a lifetime of inner surfaces of thighs, folds, bulges, temperatures, ordinary and abnormal places. For this we sing, for this we struggle. The drooping face inclined over improvements and failures, the smell of fresh meat and cooked meat that rises and separates itself from the perfume of bath salts or of cologne previously dispensed with a single finger. Overwhelmed at times by the involuntary obligation to analyze the chiaroscuro, the shapes and baroque details of what he was looking at, and trying to imagine what it had meant, or could mean, for any ordinary man in love.'

"Come on, a plot," Julio Stein had said, "something we can use, something that'll interest idiots and intelligent people, but not the geniuses. You should know that better than I, like a good Buenos Airen." Julio had unobtrusively spat into his handkerchief. And like the kind and sad doctor who had looked at Gertrudis with his sudden distilled smiles that vanished rapidly like ripples on water, Díaz Grey must have tired eyes in the fleshy drooping head, eyes with a small steady flame, cold, that remembered the passing of faith into wonder. And perhaps just as I was looking at the night of slow cool wind, he could be leaning on his office window, facing the square and the lights of the wharf. Confounded and not understanding, just like me, listening to the sound of clothes beating on the flat roof across the way, to the irregular rhythm of Gertrudis' snores, and to the small silence around the head of the woman in the neighboring apartment.

I heard Gertrudis cry, certain she was still asleep. 'My woman, full-bodied, maternal, has wide hips that make me want to sink into them, my eyes and fists closed, my knees drawn up to my chin, and to sleep there with a smile.'

Through the windowpanes and his eyeglasses, Díaz Grey would be looking at a noon of powerful sun melting into the winding streets of Santa María. His forehead would be resting and sometimes slipping on the smoothness of the window glass next to the corner cabinets or the half-circle of the disorderly desk. He was looking at the river, neither wide nor narrow, rarely agitated; a river with lively currents that did not show on the surface, crossed by small rowboats, small sailboats, small motor launches and, according to an invariable schedule, a slow, broad ferryboat that cast off in the mornings from a coast of *ombú* trees and weeping willows, to plunge its prow into the unruffled water and, rocking, to approach Dr. Díaz Grey and the city where he lived. A ferryboat loaded with passengers and a pair of automobiles fastened with cables, bringing the morning papers from Buenos Aires, perhaps carrying hampers of grapes, demijohns wrapped in straw, farm machines.

'Now the city is mine, together with the river and the ferry that moors at siesta time. Beyond is the doctor with his forehead leaning on the window; thin, sparse blond hair, the curves of his mouth worked by time and boredom; he looks out at a timeless noon, not suspecting that at any moment I will put a woman against the rail of the ferry. She already wears, moving between her skin and the cloth of her dress, a fine chain holding a gold medallion, a type of jewel that now no one can buy or make. The medallion has tiny claws forming a petal that holds the glass over the photograph of a very young man with a full, closed mouth, and clear eyes that extend toward his temples, shining.'

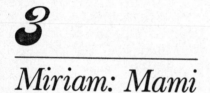

3

Miriam: Mami

From the back of the vast room sparsely furnished with desks and drawing tables, from behind the white light in the glass of the swinging doors with the inscriptions *Manager, Assistant Manager, Media Chief,* came Julio Stein raising his arms.

It was seven in the evening and no one was in the office except me and the strange woman. I waited standing in the semidarkness, looking at a half-finished drawing on one of the tables: a woman sunbathing in a beach chair on a flat roof, drinking from a bottle. The bathing suit was going to be green, the sun yellow, the chair already had a beautiful reddish color. It was no business of mine; for almost two months now I hadn't written the ads. It must be Stein's campaign, and Stein would recommend "Summer without Money," or "Bring the Summer to Your Home," or "January on a Rooftop," or "You Can Do It without Luggage." In the manager's office old Macleod would have shaken his head, half closed his eyes, then suddenly shouted with his hoarse voice, "Weak, very weak! It's been done. Have a few drinks and come up with something that's got punch."

And Stein would have some drinks, he would be missing from the

16

office in order to summer without money with some woman, or to take some woman to his apartment, or to devise a January between the sheets, or to show some woman it could be done without luggage. Later he would convince old Macleod of the sales power in any one of the former phrases, and convince him simultaneously that the idea was his, Macleod's.

On the other side of the metal counter dividing the room, over where the shadow of approaching night was thickest, near the sound of arguments and the corridor being scrubbed, the woman was smoking, waiting for Stein. It was Miriam, I was sure: I was seeing her for the first time. Her face and bare arms, still beautiful, shone in the shadow; her dress was black and low-necked, her hat audaciously slanted over her forehead, perhaps dragged down by the excessive adornments of flowers and feathers, possibly fruit.

Stein advanced rapidly, heels clicking, arms outstretched.

"It's incredible! And I have to find out through the old man! If Macleod hadn't told me, I wouldn't have known they operated on Gertrudis. And perhaps it happened one day when we were discussing the budget for underarm deodorant! You were worrying about her, and I was bothering you about the best way to grease an armpit in the summer! Or underarms, because Mami is over there and in her presence I'd never allow myself . . ."

The woman rested her elbows on the counter and laughed in a swift diminuendo, with a grotesquely aged smile.

"That Julio!" she murmured.

Stein turned between the desks and bent over, searching for something.

"And I only knew through Macleod. Because it seems the old man is a better friend of yours than I am. Inasmuch as he has a refined sensibility to the tune of three thousand monthly and the three per cent commission I laboriously earn for him."

He straightened up with a dark leather portfolio in his hand; over my shoulder he smiled at Miriam, bold and tender.

"It's right that you open your heart to the old man. The Jew Stein knows only how to make money. But how is Gertrudis? How is she now?"

'Very different from how she was when you went to bed with her in Montevideo,' I thought without bitterness, feeling that Gertrudis was a stranger to him now. I picked up my hat and turned to look at the drawing of the woman in the bathing suit, drinking and smiling on the roof.

"She's fine. A dangerous operation, but now it's all right. We'll talk about it later."

"Poor little thing!" the woman commented from the counter; she turned, looking around with half-closed eyes. Then she tossed her cigarette to the floor and stepped on it quickly. "Poor little thing! Brausen wouldn't want to talk about it, Julio. Just imagine . . ."

"He wouldn't want to talk with me, of course," said Julio, hitting me on the shoulder as he led me toward the small door in the counter. "But it's not important. Every seven minutes I celebrate a day of forgiveness. And now let's drink and break bread together, and if Mami's somewhat twilight beauty can console you . . . She's generous and understands everything. Mami, this is Brausen." He went close to her and touched her round smooth chin; Miriam smiled with her head tilted to the side, her half-closed eyes fixed on Stein's mouth. "Twilight, I said. . . . She's marvelous! A glorious twilight, with more colors than a subway poster! Macleod Publicity. Complete with slogans and phrases that we're sure Brausen the ascetic didn't write—he who can't open his heart to true friends."

"That Julio!" she repeated, laughing, trying to see Stein's face in the dim light.

Stein kissed her three times on the forehead and cheeks; his worn faced moved smoothly, his tongue quickly moistened his lips.

"Yes, dear," Stein said without releasing her, holding the fat of her chin with three fingers. "If calling on Mami's beautiful maturity can help you in some way, here we are, she and I and our proven spirit of sacrifice."

"That Julio . . ." For a second she directed her steadfast smile toward me.

"Let's go down," Stein said. "One drink, only one drink for the ascetic."

In the elevator I looked at the round, powdered face of the woman, the lines that life had etched from childhood to old age, without decisive changes, the bones that conserved the beauty under the devastated flesh. I looked at the small round chin, the large blue eyes, myopic, and the short doll-like nose.

"Brausen-without-trust," Stein said. "Perhaps afraid that I might offer him money. Preferring to ask the old man. Brausen thinks twice before asking: he keeps his thoughts under his hat. But what did you tell the old man? Because I also know you didn't ask him to take your IOU, or to give you a few days off, or to raise your salary."

"I asked him for two days off."

"And why him? Aren't I here with IOUs in one hand and days off in the other?"

We moved slowly through the narrow, crowded street, Miriam in the middle, separating us with her enormous hips, shrinking a little each time she put a foot down, as if distrusting the ground she walked on; beyond the silky black breast of the woman, her smooth round chin and the threatening ornaments on her hat, I saw Stein's profile, always smiling, his jaw jutting out in front of the line of his forehead. In the light from store windows I could inspect Miriam's dyed yellow hair, the wrinkles around her right eye, the fine veins below the layer of powder or rouge on the cheek that was beginning to sag. Fifty, I thought; Jewish, sentimental, selfish and good, with many values saved from shipwreck, still hungry for men or needing their attention. Stein paused at a corner, took her by the shoulders, and leaned over to talk to her.

"I swear to you, you're wrong. It's not so. You know yourself that I'm right."

"Yes, Julio. Yes, dear," she said, and extended a veined hand to straighten and caress Stein's tie. "But you're too good and they take advantage of you."

"Too good!" Stein repeated, winking. "They can't take advantage of me because it doesn't matter to me."

"He's not going to give you back the money."

"Even if he doesn't give it back . . ."

Miriam turned toward me and smiled with a slow sadness; the white round face was touching, coated with her compassion for Stein.

"You know how Julio is," she finally sighed.

"Yes," I said. If they hadn't spoken about money, that night I would have asked Stein for fifty or a hundred pesos. "But you're not going to change him. It's too late."

"No, no," Stein protested, laughing. "He doesn't know anything. He's an ascetic; worse still, he wants to be one. Only Mami knows me." He patted the woman's cheek, and pressed up against her to allow a couple to pass.

"This Julio . . ." With her head thrust toward Stein's chin, Miriam allowed a worn-out, poignant laugh to be heard.

"Only Mami," Stein insisted, walking again, holding her by the arm. "And now, before I get drunk, I'm going to tell you both a story. I heard it last night and immediately thought . . ." He handed me Miriam's purse and took me by the arm. "Let's go two blocks down the way, where there's no music. When they told me this story, I thought, 'What a pity there can't be a woman like that in this world.' But then I remembered you could have said it. Only Mami could have said it."

"It's best you don't tell it, Julio," Mami begged.

"Because of the ascetic? Oh, he'll like it. All my clashes with Brausen take place on coarse practical ground. Outside of that . . . On the other hand, with Mami . . ."

"Mami is an old woman, Julio," she murmured, and I understood it was her custom to say that, sigh, and then shake her head.

Stein was serious; he bent over to kiss her.

"We're going to have a drink, dear. Brausen is coming with us. Can you let Gertrudis know if it gets late?"

"Yes," I said, and thought again of the hundred pesos I needed. "It's no problem; she's with her mother in Temperley."

I would have a few drinks, forget their discussion about money, and ask Stein for the hundred pesos. Miriam chose a table in the bar and went to the ladies' room with a heavy and cautious walk, her head held high, a freshly lit cigarette between her fingers.

"You didn't know Mami, right?" Stein asked me. He smiled at the waiter. "No, no, we won't order until the lady decides. I talked to you a lot about Mami. Well, that's Mami. Old, yes; and no words could make you see in the face she has now, the face she had before. The bitchiest bitch, the most fantastic and intelligent I've known. And I'm not lying when I say I love her like a mother—all licenses permitted, naturally. I told you, didn't I, that she worked in a cabaret, and I was twenty years old, and we went to Europe?"

"Yes, often," I said. While she was returning to the room without a cigarette, looking into her compact mirror, and the waiter was clearing the way, coming toward us, I hastened to ask, "Could you lend me a hundred pesos for a few days?"

"Of course," Stein said. "Do you want it now?"

"Now or later."

"Can you wait until tomorrow? Or perhaps they can cash a check for me. I can lend you that and much more. But tonight is an exceptional night, since I'm with Mami and you. It makes me feel good that I have plenty of money, that there are no limits. And she isn't old or ugly; she's delicious." He got up to help her into her seat. "Mami, I didn't dare order a gin fizz with a dash of sugar for you. Women never order the same thing twice. I was telling Brausen that up till today I've been the most faithful man you ever had. A special fidelity, but a lasting one; a fidelity full of holes, it's true, but thanks to that, it can go on breathing."

She smiled, agreeing and coquettish, throwing me looks that were friendly and faintly apologetic. She sighed in homage to things conquered and lost and quickly lit another cigarette with her elbows leaning on the table so no one could see her hand tremble.

While I was in the empty office waiting for Stein to end his discussion and the exchange of lies with old Macleod, Miriam tapped with her nails on the glass window of the door; she had entered immediately, advancing with the swaying motion that cost her some effort to control. Between solemn and smiling nods she asked for Mr. Stein.

"I think he'll be out soon," I said to her. "I'm waiting for him, too."

"Thank you. It's just that we didn't arrange to meet in any particular place. We were to meet downstairs by the door at six-thirty, and I thought he had already left. Because it's late . . . Thank you. There are so many people on the street. And waiting downstairs, with everybody passing . . . Thank you."

She didn't care to sit down; after walking back and forth in the grayish light, half closing her heavy eyelids to scrutinize the advertising posters pinned on the walls—glorious trophies of Stein and Macleod campaigns, some of the slogans mine—she leaned on the counter and lit a cigarette. Stealing a glance at her, I saw her smile, briefly surrendering her head to a tremor that seemed to announce she had read some affecting phrase. But she said nothing; she smoked with two fingers outstretched, rigid. A moment later someone laughed behind the lit windows of the door at the back of the room; the fresh night air and a feeling of nocturnal resignation passed by and then remained hovering in the empty room; the fat and old woman smoking in the dim light began to evoke a nostalgic story for me. I saw shadows descend around her without touching her, incapable of covering her, making it evident that darkest night would lack sufficient force to annul the ridiculous ornaments on her hat or the softened whiteness of her puffy baby face.

As she moved back and forth in front of the unfinished poster where the woman in a bathing suit reclined smiling and clutching a bottle, I realized, helped by the memory of Stein's energetic and persistent confessions, how she, as an adolescent and even earlier, had walked the streets—painted, adorned, and encouraged by her mother (who herself was nothing more than an enormous flour-covered mask, a noxious emanation of fried fish)—to the taxi stands on the squares. I also knew how she came to meet Stein, when Stein was twenty, at a dance. And I also knew that they had slept together that night; that they had fled the dance hall, fingers entwined, murmuring to each other, cheek to cheek, aroused, words to which they attributed unmentionable dirty meanings, in order to live for one week in the hotel at Tigre. Seven days that ended on Saturday, the evening when Stein called for the bill, then threw himself, laughing and naked, on the bed, and asked between hiccups, "But don't you know, my dear, I haven't got a cent?"

I discovered and remembered how, to look at the naked boy, she had gone close to the bed, near a window overlooking the water, the yacht club, the sailboats, the long sleek launches, the heavy barges loaded with fruit from the north. At first she leaned her then slender body against a bedpost in order to look at him with hatred, to bring close to him a prostitute's puckered red mouth, swollen with insults. Then she looked at him with thoughtful eyes that swiftly saddened, and paid the bill, and continued paying until the day—it was also evening—when Stein returned to the apartment on Congreso Plaza and woke her with kisses, then waited as she went smiling into the bathroom. He filled two glasses, took a drink, always waiting, walking up and down the room, looking out of the small window at the movement of cars and people on the corner of Rivadavia. Miriam was fifteen years older than he, but she was still young. He didn't tell her at once, he made her drink as she sat naked on his knees, and before saying it, he pushed her onto the bed and waited for it to be over, waited for the sigh and the blind smile, to tell her that he was going to leave her. And she, raising her eyebrows, her mouth open and incredulous, sat up in bed effortlessly.

"You're leaving me? Me?" she had asked, full of laughter and amazement—the same broad, heavy woman now smoking on the other side of the agency counter, staining her dress with cigarette ashes.

She allowed him to go on talking and reasoning, to show his fear and gesticulate. And when Stein was finished and exhausted, so abased that he began to invent moral justifications, she finished dressing and uttered, without looking at him and without taking him into account, the most beautiful phrase life had destined for Stein's ears: "We're going to Paris on the first boat. You know how I earned enough money for the trip. I'm going down to order food and a few bottles for a celebration."

From Miriam's black silk skirts there came to me a caricature of Stein's scruples on that evening fifteen years ago, the lies he had forced himself to believe not only for the sake of self-justification, but also to justify himself to others, and above all to some corpses he could imagine lying, more severe in death, beneath the earth of some cemetery in some Austrian village.

After the trip and all the complex absurdities and sudden explanations of surprising cunning, what Stein had had left as justification and defense of his personal austere past—which he had also imagined—was nothing more than the phrase *"Oh, la Butte Montmartre!"* delivered with a smile that he thought apt to express the ineffable, the mention of Aragon and *"Ce Soir,"* a bleached-out "That's the life!" and trivial anecdotes without national character. Without explanations, incapable of ever understanding the need for explanations, she had returned to Buenos Aires two years after Stein. She had searched him out, offered him half a bed, two daily meals, liquor and cigarettes, a little pocket money and, at times, counsel and cautions, a vigorous and playful backing that Stein would almost never be able to acknowledge. So when Stein said, *"Oh, la Butte Montmartre!"* across a restaurant table and needed to reach for her hand to stroke it, smiling and winking to insinuate some memory of past bliss from which Miriam was excluded, he was instantly transformed and became, in relation to her, a contemptible Stein. In relation to her—who had begun to grow fat, to calm down and to relax her eyes since the day of her return to Buenos Aires. In relation to Miriam, Mami, who—when after many drinks and with a tolerant and confidential smile, she referred to *la Butte Montmartre* or evoked and poeticized the sound of the bells of Saint Jean de Briques—was alluding without recriminations to her own unalterable destiny, which she probably would not have changed at any price.

4

Salvation

I convinced myself that I was simply planning to save myself in that night that was beginning beyond the balcony, exciting, with its intermittent gusts of warm wind. I kept my head bent over the lamp on the table, occasionally glancing behind me and looking at the lampshade's reflection on the ceiling, an incomprehensible drawing that promised a square rose. Under my hands I had the paper necessary to save me, a blotter, and a fountain pen; to one side, on the table, a dish with a bone on which the fat was hardening; before me, the balcony and a spacious night, almost silent; on the other side, the inflexible gloomy silence of the neighboring apartment.

The woman would arrive at dawn, alone or with someone; Gertrudis would return from Temperley during the morning. From the moment she opened the door and entered the elevator, from the moment I woke up to wait for her, the room, once more and worse than ever, was going to be too small to hold both of us and Gertrudis' sighing sadness, her eyes in a fixed stare above the handkerchief that she did not take from her lips. The room was going to be too small for her long slow steps, for the sobs timidly shaking the edge of the bed in the early hours of dawn

24

when she thought I was asleep. Too small to hold, besides, the hopeless movements—a brief frenzy, now, at such irregular intervals that they never seemed related—with which I was trying to extirpate my knees from the spongy ground of pity and disaffection, of unpaid bills, of intimacy that was leading to promiscuity, of long-planned smiles that failed, of the persistent odor of medicines, and the odor of Gertrudis, separate now, with recognizable origins.

But I had the entire night, this Saturday night, to save myself. I would be saved if I began to write the screenplay for Stein, if I finished two pages, or at least one, if I captured the woman who would enter Díaz Grey's office and conceal herself behind the folding screen; if perhaps I wrote only a single sentence. Night was just beginning and the warm wind whirled on the roof; someone was going to laugh furiously in a window close by; the woman next door, La Queca, would enter quickly, singing, escorted by a man with a deep voice. Some sudden simple thing was going to happen, and I could save myself by writing. Or perhaps salvation would descend from the picture Gertrudis had had taken in Montevideo so many years before, hanging now on the darkened wall to the right, beyond the dish with the gnawed bone; perhaps from over there, from the spot of light on her forehead and cheek, from the points of light on her lower lip and eyes. Perhaps from the fleshy, almost horizontal ear, from the slender neck, the blouse from the Lycée Français, her hair dominating the small forehead; from the photographer's signature or the age of the picture.

The wind was moving its hot eddies, scarcely touching the curtains and the papers; and it would also be moving for Gertrudis in the trees of Temperley. She in bed, and not sobbing yet; her mother going up and down the stairs to take care of her, repeating the two or three phrases that advised resignation and promised joy, phrases with which her mother had managed to arm herself between endearments and apprehension, and which she would shuffle like cards and deposit indefatigably on Gertrudis. And she, despite the flood of tears at dawn, would end by sleeping, only to discover in the morning, as she hastily rid herself of dreams, that the consoling words had not overflowed into her breast during the night; that they had not germinated in her chest, had not accumulated—firm, resilient, and triumphant—to shape the missing breast.

There it was in the photograph, the profile, a little silly in its forced immobility, marking the end of her adolescence, the moment that had begun to demand firm ground under her feet, a single bed for rest and pleasure. The profile, beautiful and without meaning. But she had also been in Montevideo five years before, wearing a silk blouse and dark pleated skirt, her hair knotted at the nape of her neck, leaving the school building between boys, carrying books and notebooks under her arm from September to June, walking in the center of the troup, laughing and talking down 18 de Julio to the corner of Ejido, where she disappeared.

Leaning back in the chair, I looked at the picture; I waited, relying on the images and phrases essential to my salvation. At some moment of the night Gertrudis would have to leap out of the silvered frame to wait her turn in Díaz Grey's waiting room, to enter his office, causing the medallion to tremble between both breasts, too large for her reconquered girl's body. Not a sound in the apartment next door. She, the remote Gertrudis of Montevideo, would end by entering Díaz Grey's office; and I would keep the weak body of the doctor, I would furnish his sparse hair, the thin and dejected line of his mouth, in order to conceal myself in him and open the office door to the Gertrudis of the photograph.

"A girl," Stein had said to me. "What more can I tell you?"

I recalled the café in Montevideo, at the corner of a square. I recalled Stein's changed face, his stained old suit, too big for him, the neck of his shirt with wrinkles that the dirt underlined and emphasized.

"A girl who isn't important to you, who doesn't care about you, whom you can't touch because of our friendship. Very beautiful, of course. We met in the Party, because I'm trying to teach Spanish to Germans who are just off the boat, and she comes along—why, I don't know. I was never so crazy in my life. When you see her face of pensive sweetness, you'll be fooled. She's alone because her family left Montevideo. We have to telephone her. I talked to her about you, I invented an incomparable Brausen. She doesn't want to see me, things are complicated. Loyalty obliges me to confess that you're not the first marvelous type I've invented for her and carry with me like a passport, so that she'll allow me a few hours at her side to try my luck. She doesn't want to see me again."

She would enter smiling into the office of Díaz Grey–Brausen, this Gertrudis–Elena Sala whom I met that night, who had looked at me closely as I drank and talked with Stein, and who had slouched in her chair, patting her head, bashful and absorbed and always smiling. In order to bring Díaz Grey to life, this girl dismissed Stein, and when she was alone with me came near until she touched me, closing her eyes.

"I don't know what's happening and I don't care. Unlock the door and turn off that light. Close the door."

She didn't stop following me with her blind and marvelous smile.

I knew then that I wanted to be resurrected now with the name of Díaz Grey. I knew the girl's potent force, her ruthless way of cutting out inessential prologue, phrases, and gestures.

A moment more, any slight event, and the same Gertrudis would descend from the picture to save me from discouragement, from the climate of soiled love, from the fat and mutilated Gertrudis; she would come and lead me by the hand so I could write a new beginning, another meeting, describe an embrace that she would go on seeking, stupefied and smiling, with closed eyes and that old aggressive style, imprecise and dreamy. An instant more, anything, and I would be saved: a cup of coffee or tea, a bottle of beer forgotten in the refrigerator. In the picture of Gertrudis I went to look for Montevideo and Stein, to search for my youth, for origins imperfectly seen of late and still incomprehensible, for everything happening to me, entrapping me, and that had made me as I am.

As I got up to go to the kitchen, I saw the envelope. It was on the floor next to the door, crossed with a crude handwriting in blue ink. It had the full name of the woman next door, La Queca; three initials on the back, and an address in Córdoba. I found only some wine; I drank a glass and sat down at the table again without letting go of the envelope, holding it in my fingers against the light, certain that I wasn't going to open it and that the letter wasn't worth reading.

I still had not touched the pen again. I was thinking about the woman next door, La Queca, about her almost forgotten profile, her voice and smile; I was thinking about each of the things I knew about her life. When night ended, when I could stand up and accept without bitterness that I had wasted it, that inventing a skin for the doctor from Santa María and putting myself in it could not save me; at some moment at the end of the night, when it could only be prolonged by closing the windows and the balcony doors, La Queca, Enriqueta, was going to return from the street, murmuring words and performing nocturnal acts, alone or with a silent man whose footsteps accompanied hers. Returning home from whatever sort of company she kept, a little drunk, singing in a low voice as she undressed. She was going to be there, almost next to my ear, undressing her hot, perspiring body covered with a dampness created hours earlier when she was dancing, or in some improvised corner—fly, garters, lace, and the orchestra on the record suddenly muted.

I went out to the corridor and slipped the letter under the door of apartment H. 'All is lost,' I repeated without conviction.

La Queca woke me at dawn, laughing and gasping on the telephone. She was telling someone a story about two men and an automobile; a bottle of brandy, some woods with a lake; again the two men, covering up their mounting cowardice and indecision with arrogance. The story of an automobile parked under dense branches and the perfume of flowers. The slamming of the car door was the solitary conventional resonance of the ride.

I heard her get into bed and switch off the light, putting aside the memory of the night's small mishaps with a quick mutter. Then I smiled and crossed the edge of sadness, now widened, practically infinite, as if it had grown during my sleep and the woman's short monologue on the telephone. I wasn't able to write the screenplay for Stein; perhaps I would never save myself by drawing out the long initial sentence that would return me to life again. But if I did not struggle against that suddenly perfect sadness; if I succeeded in abandoning myself to it and tirelessly maintained the consciousness of being sad; if I could examine it closely each morning and make it leap toward me from a corner of the room, from a fallen garment on the floor, from Gertrudis' complaining voice; if I loved and each day deserved my sadness with desire, with hunger, filling my eyes with it and every vowel I pronounced, then I was certain I would be saved from rebellion and despair.

In my sadness I buried the tall strong figure, secretly damaged, of Gertrudis rising toward me in the elevator at eight o'clock in the morning; I closed my eyes in the fading darkness to see, at an hour close to noon, toward the north and near the river, in Díaz Grey's waiting room, a fat woman with an impassive and offensive expression, holding a child between her knees. A flimsy table with a majolica flowerpot and a pile of magazines separated the fat woman from the other one, tall and slender, her blond hair combed back, who waited examining her fingernails, a restrained hint of a smile on her face. I saw the blond woman yawn and smile as she waited, alone now in the waiting room, hearing the child's wail in the office and the mother's commanding

voice; looking without curiosity, with faint disgust, at the empty
flowerpot, the colored glass window, the staircase and its bronze
handrail. Later—when the fat woman left, dragging the child behind
her, and a sweet odor of soap mingled with the depressing sensation
emanating from the light and objects in the waiting room—it was
myself, wearing a long white jacket not properly buttoned, who held the
office door open until the unknown woman brushed past me, walked
ahead to the middle of the carpet, stopped, and began turning her head
in order to calmly observe my furniture, my instruments, my books.

5

Elena Sala

I opened the door to allow her to enter and I turned in time to catch her smile, the unguarded scorn that she was projecting onto the furniture and into the noon light shining through the window.

"Excuse me one minute. Have a seat," I said without looking at her. I leaned over the desk to write a name and a sum of money in the account book; then the doctor, Díaz Grey, coolly approached the woman who had not cared to sit down.

"Madame . . ." he invited with a tired voice.

She smiled frankly, searching for the doctor's eyes, and slowly looked him over from top to bottom. She wore a white tailored suit, no hat or purse, and the fair hair—reddish now in the stronger light—was gathered at the nape of her neck.

"I'm staying next door at the hotel," she explained. Her voice was indifferent, somewhat brisk, softened by an old habit of courtesy. "Perhaps I was right to come. But probably you'll laugh. . . ."

Díaz Grey was almost interested in this prologue. He looked at the woman's dilated pupils and supposed that she was lying, that she had come only to lie.

"Why?" he answered. "In any case, even a mistaken suspicion has to be dealt with. . . . You thought you should consult a doctor."

"Yes." The woman spoke rapidly, as if she didn't want to hear any more. "It began on the trip. True, I'd felt the same thing before, briefly, at times. But never as strong as now. I'm very brave or I don't scare easily. Anyway, to consult a doctor is the same as accepting that you're sick, authorizing sickness to insinuate itself and progress."

"If it were so simple . . . Why don't you sit down and tell me all about it."

"Thank you," she said, and she pushed back her shoulders as if making a decision. "You're right. I don't want to waste your time." She leaned on the examining table and began to move an arm in front of her chest, mechanically, without relation to what she was saying, as if she were only trying to make her hidden bracelets jingle. "It's my heart—nerves, probably. Sometimes I believe it's dead, I think it's stopped beating. I have to leap out of bed and force myself to shake my head, to say no. Or it's just the opposite: I'll wake up and find myself sitting up in bed with my mouth open so I can breathe, afraid of dying."

"A feeling of suffocation?" 'If she had felt herself suffocating, she would have said so, she would describe it as her outstanding symptom. She lies; but she's very beautiful, she doesn't suffer for want of men. I don't understand why she goes on lying to me.'

"Suffocation, no. I feel as if my heart is going to stop beating."

"Tired?" Díaz Grey asked, almost mocking.

"Tired?" she repeated indecisively, as if it were difficult to choose an answer. "Not that either. I feel—in fact I'm certain—that my heart is going to stop. Sometimes I spend an entire day waiting to die at any moment. There are other periods, weeks, when nothing bothers me. I almost forget about it. But now, with the trip, since I left Buenos Aires . . . I couldn't sleep at night. For two days I've been in the hotel and I feel worse. I went out for a walk, I saw your name plate, and it occurred to me to come in; finally I decided to do it."

The doctor agreed with a nod and smiled to calm her, to create friendliness and confidence, just as he had smiled a moment before at the woman and the child with sick bones, just as he had smiled throughout the morning at five pesos a client.

"Neither suffocation nor fatigue. I don't think it's anything, but in order to reassure ourselves . . ." He looked at her narrow waist pinched in by her girdle, her hip resting on the examining table. "If you will undress . . ." He raised his arm, indicating the corner with the folding screen.

He went to glance quickly into the waiting room; it was empty. He stood with his forehead resting on the windowpane, wondering if she had come by ferryboat or had taken the roundabout course through the north by car, and if she were alone in the hotel. He tried to guess what she had felt on seeing the city from a distance for the first time; what impression the plaza had made on her, with its footpaths of sand and the reddish stone at the edge of the gardens; what significance the church in ruins had had for her, covered by scaffolding, with the dent of a cannon ball in the tower.

The woman came forward in an easy manner until she resumed her place on the carpet. She was serious without severity and although she wasn't looking at him, neither was she hiding her eyes. Her torso was naked, and her full breasts still remained erect, almost rigid, with unusually large nipples. Díaz Grey saw the chain and the medallion, the sudden shine of crystal over the tiny photograph. Forgetting her, he took a few steps, went to fetch the stethoscope, and had bent over to adjust the lever on the examining table, when he saw the nude calves and the high-heeled black shoes retreating toward the folding screen. He heard the rustle of the clothes she was putting on again while he tried to remember, faithfully, if he had or had not looked with desire at the woman's breasts. 'She's not going to pay me the ten pesos, the rate for guests at the hotel; or she'll pay me insolently. Behind the screen she's straining to provoke the miracle by which her face and body—obviously used to men—can justify this sudden attack of modesty.'

He sat at the desk and opened the account book. He heard her approach, saw the hand resting on the pile of books, clutching a glove.

"I'm going to ask your pardon." She was dressed, her eyes looking at him politely when he raised his head. "You'll think . . . I see you have a lot of work."

"No, not much." 'It's not the way it looks, there's something more; the real lie is just beginning.' "At least, not much interesting work. What happened?"

"Nothing. I was ashamed. But not because you saw me naked." She was smiling with an ease more irritating than impudent. 'I was right; a long familiarity with men.' "It was a farce; I don't know how it occurred to me, it's so stupid, so coarse, so incredible. I thought of the scorn you would feel, believing I wanted to seduce you when I undressed."

"That's absurd," he said. He looked at her, trying to measure everything about her that was worth believing, that existed under the lie. 'I wish to God she had never come. I wish I had never set eyes on her. Now I know I was frightened from the first moment, I feel that I'm going to come to need her and that I'll be willing to pay any price. And she knew it with the first glance; this certainty was inside her even before she herself realized it.' "That's absurd," he repeated, searching for phrases in order to detain her. "For me, you have to understand, scorn is a dead sensation. At least, from nine to twelve and three to six. And outside those hours, for a long time now I only feel scorn when I think about myself."

She did not protest; seated on the arm of a chair, without taking her eyes off him, she pulled a cigarette case from her pocket and began to smoke. 'I'm confiding stupidly, without any object except to gain a few minutes, to the loyalty I see in her eyes; despite the fatigue of being loyal, which they also show.' From the chair, above him now, she patiently smiled, as if she were looking at a child.

"I'm in no hurry. Go on talking."

"There is no scorn, just as there can be no pity. Now all that is finished. But I don't want to bore or detain you. You don't know what it means to me to suddenly find a person I can talk to. Although it almost always turns out that I have nothing to say and no great interest in listening."

She agreed with excessive enthusiasm, too easily, almost contemptuously.

"That's so. But go on talking. Perhaps the more certain we are of being understood, the more difficult it is to say anything. I, at least . . ."

'Familiar with men, yes, but no need of them. No true need of anyone or anything, I'd swear. A full-blown egoist with an experienced sense of selection, and a recently acquired laziness in the face of omens, temptations, new faces, one's own dreams. And it's not because of getting older.'

Díaz Grey stood up and unbuttoned his white jacket as he moved toward the farthest window. From there he turned to smile at her, ready to defend himself.

"You spoke of a farce and a lie."

"Yes, I have to tell you." She was looking down at the floor, smiling. "A farce and a lie. Everything I told you about my heart is what my husband tells me. What happens to him. He'll arrive from Buenos Aires before the weekend, and then you can examine him. I'm going to convince him that he must come. I carried the game too far because it amused me, and I got undressed. Suddenly I realized what you would think when you knew I was lying. The idea that you might think me idiotic shamed me. May I speak?" She smiled again, pursuing the doctor's face minutely with her smile. "We're taking this trip for many reasons, we'll talk about that later. But when I decided to come to Santa María, I knew you were here and that I was going to meet you. I knew almost nothing about you. One afternoon, a Sunday, I saw you at the hotel bar. Don't be angry with me. I don't know why I'm telling you this. I could keep quiet about it. . . ."

"I'm not going to be angry. Tell me, it's better that you tell me."

"Don't be angry. I wondered about a village doctor. Do you understand? Sulfa, poultices, laxatives, some abortions. Member of the club, the school board, friend of the pharmacist, the judge, the chief of police. For some years engaged, perhaps to a teacher. If I'm right about anything, please forgive me. The way you walk, the clothes you wear. All that, you understand? But when I was here, suddenly I knew I was mistaken. You didn't say a word. I looked in your eyes, nothing more, and I knew I was mistaken. Then—it's hard to believe—I was ashamed and suddenly ashamed of being ashamed. A small-town doctor, I thought. And I went to undress in the corner. Then I saw your face, your hands, heard your voice, and realized that it wasn't possible. I was afraid you might laugh at me."

"It's all right, I think I understand. But what was the farce?"

Suddenly the woman composed her childish face and laughed uncertainly as she slipped from the arm of the chair into the seat; she crossed her legs and with effort put her hands into her jacket pockets.

"I came to you on the advice of Quinteros."

"Quinteros?"

"A doctor. He's a friend of yours. He told us he was your friend from medical school."

"Yes, I remember," Díaz Grey said.

"And that when you were in Buenos Aires, you had cared for some patients together."

Then Díaz Grey left the window, passed close to her with the walk she had found ludicrous and clumsy in the hotel corridor, and sat at the desk again. He believed he understood everything, although vaguely; believed he understood the woman, had understood her from the moment he saw her bending over the old magazines in the waiting room; thought he understood all that had occurred during the interview: the smiles, the intelligent cold face, the pupils that did not become smaller when they looked at light, the exhibition of her breasts, the menacing atmosphere that, resolute, rocking her leg back and forth, she had now created.

"Certainly," Díaz Grey murmured. "Quinteros. Is he still in Buenos Aires?" 'It would be so sad to have to admit that the fear I remember feeling when I saw her was nothing more than this fear of blackmail, a fear that in reality has nothing to do with me.'

She raised her eyes and then began to rhythmically press the fingernails of each hand into the palm of the other; but her eyes were steadfast, searching for those of the doctor, patiently waiting for them, confronting them at last. She shrugged and leaned toward the desk.

"He's not in Buenos Aires. He went to Chile. They were going to put him in prison." She remained silent, looking at him with a soft expression of pity, her mouth half open.

'So that's what it's about. But what can it matter to me? I suffer, if I do suffer, because I don't care what the key to the enigma is. Cocaine or morphine: I have to guess which.'

"Quinteros," he said. "Yes. We were good friends. I knew he had specialized in nervous disorders and was a member or the head of a clinic. He was lucky. Furthermore, he was willing to stay on in Buenos Aires, and had the courage or insensitivity necessary to endure so many things. I'm speaking of young doctors like Quinteros and me, at that time, without money or a university big-shot to take us under his wing."

He was talking to the familiar objects arranged on the table in their familiar disorder, sure that she—with her face now toward the ceiling—wasn't listening. The woman got up and again composed the pious expression. With only one step she was alongside the desk, and leaned there on her right hand.

"I need a prescription. Or better, an injection and a prescription."

"Yes," Díaz Grey murmured. "What?"

"Morphine. You can also give me a prescription. Or sell it to me, if you have it."

"Yes," he repeated.

"For some time now, my husband and I have been treated by Quinteros."

She was calm, leaning on the desk as if it were a shop counter, as if she were waiting to buy stockings or talcum powder.

"Intoxification, detoxification. As you wish," she said.

"Didn't Quinteros give you a letter for me?"

"He went to Chile without notifying us. You understand. He had spoken to me about you."

"And if I were to tell you that I cannot, simply on your word?"

"Oh, for God's sake! For God's sake!" she said with a controlled sneer, shaking her head, which was again held high, patient and maternal.

The doctor thought of getting up and embracing her; he was compelled to remember the large breasts, her waist where the ribs visibly ended, the medallion suspended from her neck, the yellowish photograph. 'But I'm beginning to suspect that that isn't the price, for the moment. The only possibility is not to let her go, to adopt a passive manner, a deliberate submissiveness.'

"Morphine . . ." he said. "I should explain that I attend those sick persons because they want to get well, or because I want them to get well. Give me your name. Don't lie, because I'll know it from the hotel. I'm a town doctor."

"Elena Sala. S-A-L-A. I have no reason to lie to you."

"There was a husband. Is your husband's name Sala?"

"Elena Sala Lagos."

Díaz Grey reflected, looking at her hand on the glass-covered desk, at four phalanges set there firmly and consciously, four hard knuckles over which the taut skin was whitening.

"Ten pesos for the consultation," he said at last. "It's not my doing. And twenty pesos for the prescription. For every two ampules. I have no intention of giving you an injection."

"Make it four."

"For four. But now it occurs to me to charge you twenty pesos per ampule. I have no interest in treating you. Does that suit you?"

She hesitated to speak for a moment; her hand, her knuckles on the desk, remained still.

"Twenty per ampule," she said, neither protesting nor submitting.

"Twenty," Díaz Grey repeated, and quickly wrote the prescription, tore it from the pad, and moved it closer to her. "In all, ninety pesos. So perhaps you'll think you made a bad deal and not come back."

She picked up the paper to examine it, put it away, and took out a hundred peso note from the same pocket. She opened her fingers to allow the bill to fall on the desk.

"We're going to spend some time here," she said. "We'll rent a house, if we find one." Díaz Grey took some bills out of his trouser pocket and handed her ten pesos. "We think we'll stay for a while. That is, if my husband likes it. I can't imagine him outside of Buenos Aires. Perhaps we'll get—do you know of one?—a furnished house near the river. And I want you to examine my husband."

"No," the doctor said. "I don't know of any house. It's very pleasant here, especially in spring. Bring your husband. It's probably nothing more than nervous upset. There's a nerve that stimulates and another that slows one down. We'll see."

6

Old Cronies: Misunderstandings

Through the window of the restaurant we could see the people leaving theaters and movie houses and filling Lavalle, blinking as they entered cafés, lighting cigarettes, shaking brilliantined heads as they looked for cabs in the heat of the street. From the table we watched the groups as they came in, the women yawning yet animated, the men frowning, arrogant, mistrustful.

"Those are my people," Stein said, "the material entrusted to me for building the world of tomorrow."

'Twelve-thirty,' I repeated to myself. 'Stein isn't drunk yet and he won't want to leave before he is. I still have to wait; I can't go home if she's not asleep in a dream impervious to the door's noise and the light of the lamp. When we finish the wine, Stein will suggest a cabaret. I'm going to refuse, but if he insists, if I see he's determined, I'll say yes. Now he's starting to look at the women with moist, insulting eyes.'

Stein was glancing toward the rear of the room, touching the wall with the back of his chair; he had his jacket open and was smiling, moving his head from side to side, observing the women as they arrived or left. Light flashed in the wineglass that he covered with his palm; it flashed in his smile, in his hot eyes; it lengthened and disappeared, absorbed like water, in his white silk shirt.

"It's not asceticism, I won't believe that," Stein grumbled. "Hypocrisy. Or perhaps a vicious degeneration of pride. Any complicated and repugnant thing could be the explanation. Would you give more than money to sleep with the one in the white hat? All I do is look at them, but I do look. If only to please me, you'd do well to turn that gloomy face of yours and look at them."

'Perhaps it's twelve forty-five now,' I thought. 'I don't want to arrive if Gertrudis is awake or just falling asleep. I can touch her with my right hand open, without suffering; I can convince her nothing has changed and at times feel that in reality nothing has changed; and I also can sustain the immediate deceit in dignified ways and trick her with only the memory of herself. I can do it with this hand lighting the cigarette. But I can't look at her mouth or know that she is staring at the wall or at the ceiling or at her hands with empty eyes that no longer seek anything. She now takes care of her hands desperately, as if they were children. I'm reasonable, I know there are things I can do and others I can't. I can, for example, not listen to her, not understand what she says; I can't endure the desolation and tears that alter her voice when she talks to me. Death would be worse, but it would be final; dead, she would not be at my side more than twenty-four hours before I understood, in silence, that she had died to prevent me from forgetting it. She would come to repeat it to me in memories, but not every day, or at least every day only at the beginning; and never she herself, attesting to her misfortune and mine in a monotonous and unchanging manner.'

"What's the matter with you?" Stein asked. "I saw immediately that you were gloomy, and with a nasty kind of gloominess, but the kind that can be relieved by company. Is it Gertrudis?"

"Among other things. But I don't want to talk. Let's ask for another half bottle."

"A half bottle, please, Solícito. A servant ought to be called Solícito. Last night I was thinking about that year and a half that we wasted so foolishly in Montevideo. Does Raquel still write to you?"

"I no longer remember Montevideo," I said, and drank some wine. "It's been a while since I've had a letter. I knew through Gertrudis that she was going to marry. I believe to a fellow named Alcides."

"She was marvelous," Stein said; he tried to say it tenderly. "The fundamental Eleusinian mystery concerns the ascetic and his young sister-in-law. In my moments of depression I believe we'll die without resolving it."

"We will die."

"An attitude that demonstrates gentlemanly reserve is a double-edged sword. We can imagine anything. Imagine, for example, what would have happened if I had taken the place that destiny assigned to the ascetic."

"We can imagine that," I agreed. "But nothing happened. Perhaps an indecent game on my part, without my quite realizing it. When I understood what was going on, I came to Buenos Aires."

"Without a final explanation? Without at least exploiting your touching sacrifice?"

"Perhaps I began to love her. One never knows. But I came to Buenos Aires and the story ended. Now she's getting married. She was hurt for a time, imagining that she hated me. Later she began to write me. Gertrudis reads all the letters."

"All right, that's the end of it. But there was that so-called indecent game. Only you're sad and it bothers you to talk. She must be eighteen or nineteen now. And considering it's been five years since the performance of the sonnet of Arvers . . . For an ascetic, it's not too bad. The last half bottle of wine?"

'I don't want to suffer the sight of Gertrudis lying on her back, watching in turn the two sides of a scale; on one side, the intensity of pain that at any moment can give her a new warning of her illness, this time in the lung, and on the other side, her chances of living again, of participating, of being interested in things and successful, of feeling compassion for others. And she and I have discovered, to our dismay, with a horror now diminished by experience, that every subject can lead us to the left side of her chest. We're afraid to talk; the whole world is an allusion to her misfortune.'

"Instead of feeling sorry for me," Stein was saying, "they have the delicacy, those beasts, of pretending to envy me. You belong to another species, you wouldn't envy or pity me. If they knew what I have to go through, the tortures I endure . . . ! We can use the last affair as a symbol of my martyrdom. Married, thirty years old, two children, a husband dedicated to things I could never understand, a country club."

'But there's no sense in this waiting,' I thought, 'because she can wake up at any hour and I'll have to smile at her and joke, and make her happiness mirror mine, increasing as mine increases. I'm going to pace up and down the room, talk in a loud voice, and snatch in turn from one corner and then another, the future, trust, joy, a few immortalities. I'll find the way we laughed in the early evening, standing there desiring each other in Montevideo, right on the corner of Médanos and 18 de Julio. In the doorway of the Lycée five years ago, nothing could prevent me from caressing her cheek with just one monotonous finger. I'll force her to believe that an anecdote can contain life but cannot alter the sense of it. Perhaps she'll sit up in bed, ask for a cigarette, exhale the smoke in a slow, sure breath, provocative, fluttering her eyelashes as before and murmuring any obvious lie in order to make me confront her.'

"And I kept smiling and agreeing," Stein was saying, "averting my eyes so she wouldn't guess what I thought of her and her seven generations of ancestors. Distorted by translation, her conversation went like this: Look, I had to take the kid to be vaccinated because of school, and there was an endless line, right? And then the doctor passes by, he looks at me once and I look at him, not for any reason, but just in case he can hurry up the vaccination, and the doctor passes by again later, and he doesn't take his eyes off me, and as I have a bandaged wrist because I twisted the tendon, like I told you, with the swing at Tigre, he came and questioned me on the pretext, imagine, of wanting to know what had happened. And I go and tell him that I was in Tigre where every Sunday we go to an island with the family and the fellow from the factory, and I was pushing a friend, Luisa, in the swing, mind you, and suddenly I got such a pain that I thought my wrist was broken. It was a pulled tendon and they prescribed bandaging it very tightly, and he tells me he'd like to have taken care of me, and he has me come in before anyone else. He vaccinates the kid and begins to joke around and wants to make a date with me, but since the nurse had given me the certificate already I told him no, absolutely not, and I left with the kid."

'She ought to be asleep,' I thought. 'She's not going to wake up, she won't ask me for a cigarette, she won't know I've come home.'

Stein paid and we got up. We went out into the street and reached the corner where the early morning papers were unloaded. It was almost two by the café clock. Now I was certain Gertrudis was asleep and that she wouldn't wake up. I invited Stein to have a drink at the bar, and I emptied mine in one swallow, suddenly feeling peaceful, while a desire for the sleeping Gertrudis began to stir.

"It's easier when I pay money instead of being humiliated in installments," Stein said. "Much easier when I have half of a hundred peso bill with my telephone number on it sent over to a woman in a cabaret. My office number, because I live with Mami and it's no longer worth while making her jealous."

'The long thick legs, the wide sunken stomach, the animal movement with which Gertrudis, between dreams, makes sure of my presence in bed.'

"Let's look for a woman," Stein proposed.

"No, I'm leaving."

"But not just any woman. A woman who can anticipate our fantasy and show us that reality surpasses it, who can give us cosmic totality—till the next one comes along—with only three holes and ten tentacles."

"I'm going to bed," I insisted.

"At home, I suppose. Maybe I'll follow your example and go see Mami. She must be playing rummy with old Levoir, poor Mami's penultimate flirtation. She cheats so that the old man wins and then they put a map of Paris on the dining-room table and play the famous game of telling, without looking at the map, if their walks or a tryst or a business appointment drew them to the intersection of Rue St. Placide and Rue du Cherche, and if you need a v.d. checkup at the Broussais Hospital, what bus must you take? It's thrilling, I understand. And each time Mami can't stop her tears from falling all over the Seine. Poor Mami! Every once in a while she goes out at night and sits at a sidewalk café, especially now that the weather is nice. She imagines she's there. Her eyes become large and pinched at the corners because she doesn't want to take her glasses out of her purse. I know, I've watched her from another table without her seeing me. She does nothing more than let men look at her, she fancies that they see her as she sits there for an hour or two, weary or deep in thought, with that Mona Lisa smile that seems to say, 'If you only knew!' Naturally, there's nothing to know, if we exclude the twenty unwritten volumes of Mami's memoirs, which go from the end of one war to the end of another. What's more, there are our Saturdays. I invited you a thousand times but you never came. And you should meet *Monsieur* Levoir."

"I'll have a last drink," I said.

"Two more, please. . . . He's a loathsome fellow, body and soul. I believe at some time he paid Mami's rent. Now he's a fat old man with an enormous rose-colored head. Twice a week they play cards and lose themselves in the streets of Paris; sometimes he brings a bottle. It's all very proper, as she would say; an old engaged couple. But naturally, Mami has to imagine a serene friendship, something like Disraeli and Madame de Pompadour. Because the tiresome beast gives her two or three lectures on free trade, the idiosyncrasy of the atom, and the true Ballet Russe, which he saw, I believe, in Vienna. But I'm not going to waste the charge from this atrocious brandy talking about old Levoir. Before they throw us out: have I told you about Mami's Saturdays?"

"Yes, many times."

"Did I tell you about the gatherings, the piano, the *chansons*, the little theatrical group?"

"Yes," I said. "But it doesn't matter."

"I'm sure I haven't explained it to you properly. Impeded by the vertigo of modern life . . . Now you're going to hear the real truth. Better still, you're going to see it—right here, between the bar, the head of this Galician waiter, and the shelves of bottles."

"I'm beginning to see," I said. "*The Merry Wives of Mami*. If we agree there are no real women any more."

"Profoundly, lamentably wrong," Stein said. "That's how it seems to you because you never wanted to be involved, because you resigned yourself to a secondhand culture. Right now I happen to know Mami's Saturdays are different from anything you could possibly imagine. A little room of the Veterans' Center, only open to the chosen few. Because if it was ever true that many were called but few were . . . Anyway, here there are only veterans—retired, of course. More than once I've told Mami she should put an R in parenthesis on her calling cards. And all were in the war, all members of the club were in at least a half-dozen campaigns; and the memory of so many operations on different fronts . . . But I don't believe you capable, tonight, of imagining so much. We'll leave it at that. It will be enough for you to think about the words: Marengo, Austerlitz, Borodino. And the Hundred Days. Once thought about, the words can substitute for Armenoville, Casanova, Switzerland, Boulevard, or those appropriate to a limited ascetic repertoire. Do you see it?"

"I see it," I said. "But that's also how you told it."

"I spoke of the veterans of Napoleon? You're sure? Before tonight?"

I felt not only peaceful but happy, no longer worrying whether she slept or not, trying in vain and without enthusiasm to suffer directly for her, for the story of the cut breast, for the memory of the round scar, for the virile sensation that the left side of her body sometimes gave me.

"I don't know exactly," I said, filling my mouth with little mint wafers and waiting for them to soften in the sip of brandy. "I can't be sure. But you did speak of the retreat from Moscow—I'm positive."

Stein shrugged his shoulders slowly and lit a cigarette without taking his eyes from the row of bottles behind the bar.

"Don't worry," I added. "One of these Saturdays I'll be there."

"That's better," he replied nonchalantly. "This is a night of failures. The mistake is to persist. Nothing frightens me more than this series of small failures. None serious enough to hurt, but all showing that there's a tendency that directs them. Faithful to experimental methods . . ."

He threw a bill on the counter and walked toward the telephone; I spat out the mints and went to wait for him on the corner.

'Now surely she's asleep. And tomorrow I have to get up early, pay my respects to Macleod, guess by his voice in what month he intends to fire me, and walk all day long. Talk, smile, take an interest in things, not touch on the point that does interest me or else touch on it with a friendly and cynical expression, a slap on the shoulder, an invocation of human brotherhood. I'll remember that Gertrudis' body, in spite of everything, is longer and stronger than mine; I'll have to remember her as I walk with the brief case under my arm. I'll sit in a café imagining myself with a full blackish beard. I'll wait a quarter of an hour, a half hour, hiding my worn shoes under the seats in outer offices, until Perez cigarettes, Fernández razor blades, and Gonzalez maté are ready to receive me. And when I return home I'll enter the apartment without looking at her, trusting that the air in the room will let me know if she was crying or not, if she succeeded in forgetting, or sat near the balcony looking at dirty rooftops and the sunset.'

"Another failure—two is more like it," Stein said, coming out of the café. "I'm going to play strolling the streets of Paris with Mami. I'll walk a few blocks with you."

'Gertrudis, and the filthy work, and the fear of losing it,' I thought, arm in arm with Stein. 'Bills to be paid and the unforgettable certainty that nowhere in this world is there a woman, a friend, a house, a book, not even a vice, that can make me happy.'

"Decidedly unjust," Stein exclaimed, letting go of my arm. "I'm referring to the little failures. Because just this afternoon I had come to consider my general failure with joy. The big failure, that of the individual Julio Stein. And the good will I've demonstrated, the spirit of acceptance I've shown, should be taken into account."

"It doesn't work that way," I replied. "It would be too easy, also unjust, if it did."

"What does it matter to me?" he was saying. "I never did anything and presumably I will die. I have, naturally, a certain impersonal remorse; but it hasn't kept me from being content. If you're going, this is your corner. In the other world Mami will thank you."

I waited until Stein had walked away; though sure I was going to take a streetcar, I flagged down a cab. I leaned back against the seat, eyes closed, breathing the air deeply, thinking, 'At my age, life begins to be a twisted smile,' admitting, without protest, the disappearance of Gertrudis, Raquel, Stein, all the people who were mine to love; admitting my solitude as before I had admitted my sadness. 'A twisted smile. And one realizes that, for many years now, life has been nothing but misunderstandings. Gertrudis, my work, my friendship with Stein, the feelings I have about myself—misunderstandings. Outside of this, nothing; from time to time, some opportunities to forget, some pleasures that in the end are poisoned. Perhaps every existence I can imagine must be transformed into a misunderstanding. Perhaps, but no matter. Meanwhile I am this small, timid man, unchanging, married to the only woman whom I ever seduced or who ever seduced me, not only incapable of being otherwise, but of possessing the will power to be otherwise. A little man despised to the degree of pity he inspires, a little man confused amid a legion of little men to whom the kingdom of heaven was promised. Ascetic, as Stein says, because of my incapacity for passion and not because of the absurd belief in a conviction that in time becomes mutilated. This person, me in the taxicab, nonexistent, a mere incarnation of the idea of a Juan María Brausen, the biped symbol of a cheap puritanism, made up of refusals—no to alcohol, no to tobacco, an equivalent no to women—not anyone, in reality; a name, three words, a minute idea constructed mechanically by my father, without opposition, so that his similarly inherited refusals would continue shaking their conceited heads even after his death. The little man and his misunderstandings—in short, like everybody else. Perhaps this is what one learns with years, insensibly, without realizing it.

Perhaps we feel it in our bones and when we are determined and desperate, shut in by the height of the wall encircling us—so easy to leap over, if it were possible to leap over it—in short, when we are on the verge of accepting that only one's self is important, because it alone has been indisputably entrusted to us; when we perceive, however slightly, that only our own salvation can be a moral imperative, that only it is moral; when we succeed in breathing the natal air that vibrates and calls from the other side of the wall through an unforeseen chink, and we imagine the joy, the scorn, and the release, perhaps then we will feel the weight of the conviction, like a lead skeleton placed inside the bones, that all misunderstandings are bearable until death, all except those we discover outside our personal circumstances, outside the responsibilities that we can reject, impute, or trace to their source.'

Still Life

October was beginning when I resumed the nocturnal ways of the past—nights with old cronies and the misunderstandings that followed —returning home to Calle Chile in a taxi, pulling away from the corner where I had left Stein and Mami arm in arm, smiling at me, her hand raised to wave good-by.

As I went up in the elevator, I looked at my eyes and mustache in the mirror, thinking, 'She's asleep, she's not going to wake up, and I love her and must not forget for a moment that she is suffering much more than I.' La Queca's apartment door was open, the key ring was hanging in the lock, the light from the hallway streamed in and died against the legs of an armchair and the design of the small carpet. I didn't know what I was doing until it was done. In the silence I listened and raised an arm to ring the bell. I was sure no one was in the apartment, but I continued waiting, motionless. No one was on the stairs, there was no sound from the ground floor. I rang the bell again and waited; I put out a hand and turned on the ceiling light. Leaning against the wall, I looked around and smelled, across the opening of the door, the room's indefinable air, I inhaled until I felt my throat closing and my whole body longing to abandon itself to sobs that I had repressed over the last few weeks. I waited until I became calmer and then the air of the empty apartment gave me a sensation of tranquillity, filled me with a special friendly weariness, induced me to press my shoulder against the door and to enter, slowly and in silence.

At the far end of the apartment, the bathroom door was open and the greenish color of tiles gleamed smooth and liquid. I looked at the drawn blinds and quickly discovered that the disorder began there. Somewhat confused, I contemplated the disarray reflected on the horizontal wooden slats, painted white. She had spoken from there the afternoon I had first heard her voice complaining about Ricardo and the heat.

There was a crumpled girdle on the floor between the balcony door and the table, and some woman's garments were hanging on chairs. On the blue tablecloth and white lace doily, near a Chianti bottle wrapped in straw, amid some fruit and some full packs and crushed packs of cigarettes, a large picture frame slanted upward, old and massive, empty, with a broken glass that still seemed to tremble. I listened again, my back to the door; I waited for the sound and the silence of the elevator arriving at the floor. I waited to see if I could recognize La Queca's quick walk, her unmistakable short steps.

'I can tell her I saw the door open with the keys dangling, that I heard crying inside.' The elevator remained still; far away, someone was cautiously dragging a piece of furniture.

The big bed, the same as mine, placed like an extension of the bed in which Gertrudis was sleeping, seemed prepared for night; but over the yellow, almost golden bedspread lay a pile of fashion magazines, some freshly pressed clothes, and a handbag, open and empty. I began to move across the waxed floor, without noise or anxiety, feeling contact with a small happiness at each slow step. I was calm and excited each time my foot touched the floor, believing that I was moving into the atmosphere of a brief life in which there was not enough time to become involved, to repent, or to age.

I tried to examine the inside of the bottle without touching it; I sniffed the wineglasses. Standing near the small bookshelf, I looked at the colors of the books, but not the titles. Then, with my body inclined, I pressed an ear against the wall, crushing my hat, and probed the silence with my eyes closed; I stopped breathing for a moment to be sure I had heard Gertrudis stir and sigh, to envision my apartment in shadows, the space between pieces of furniture, the shape of the solitary body in the bed. I moved away from the wall and understood without effort that I was forbidden to touch any object, to move even one chair.

In the bathroom I tried in vain to detect some aroma of soap or talcum powder; I remained motionless before my face in the mirror, scarcely able to distinguish the shape of the hat, the hollows around the eyes, the shine of the nose and forehead. Presently I stopped looking at myself and contemplated, alone in the mirror, free of my eyes, a flat look, peaceful and without curiosity. Perhaps my heart would beat, unconcerned, and the special happiness that had filled my lungs would move inside my body, up and down, coming and going like brush strokes, without enthusiasm or purpose; perhaps the noises would recede into the night's distant borders, leaving me alone in the center of the silence. When my gaze extended from hat to chin and settled there like a hot flush or pallor, I left the bathroom, approached the table, and again bent over it.

The light fell vertically from the ceiling and after touching the objects arranged on the table, gently penetrated them. The edge of the fruit basket was crushed in two places and the handle across it was clumsily braided; three tiny apples, visibly sour, were grouped against the edge, and the bottom of the fruit basket showed slight, almost deliberately made, depressions, and old stains that had been scrubbed without result. To the left of the bulky base of the fruit basket, there was a little gold clock with only one hand that seemed to weigh intolerably on the lace threads of the doily, which in turn had some vague interrupted spots, some holes that briskly altered the intent of the design. In a corner of the table, still on the left side between the clock and the edge, on the most luminous slightly wrinkled section of the blue felt tablecloth, another pair of apples threatened to roll and fall to the floor; one dark and reddish, already rotten; the other green and beginning to rot. Nearer, on the carpet of coarse weave, just between my shoes and the edge of the table's shadow, there had fallen, crumpled, a small pink silk girdle stiffened with a rubber lining, with metal and rubber hooks; shapeless and soft, it expressed resignation and indolent protest.

Without moving, I discovered a small bottle knocked over under the table, and shapes of apples that had just stopped rolling. On the center of the table two dried lemons, wrinkled, sucked in the light with white circular spots that smoothly went on growing larger under my eyes. The Chianti bottle was leaning over, supported by an invisible object, and in a glass with a residue of wine, some greasy violet-colored lines were drawn out in a spiral. The other wineglass was empty and clouded, retaining the breath of whoever had drunk from it and who, in a single swallow, had left at the bottom a drop the size of a coin. To my right, at the foot of the empty silver frame with the splintered glass, I saw a one-peso bill and the shine of silver and gold coins. And in addition to all that I could see and forget, in addition to the worn-out tablecloth and its blue color affecting the glass, in addition to the large rents in the lace doily that recorded old acts of carelessness and impatience, there were, to the right near the edge of the table, the packages of cigarettes either full and intact or open, empty, and crumpled; and also loose cigarettes, some stained with wine, bent, the paper torn by the swollen tobacco. And finally there was a pair of women's fur-lined gloves resting on the tablecloth like half-opened hands, as if the hands they had warmed had melted gradually within them, abandoning their shape, which a precarious temperature, the sulphurous odor of sweat that time would modify, was transforming into nostalgia. There was nothing more, nor was there a recognizable sound in the night or in the building.

I walked from the table knowing that time had expired, that I had to leave; I put out the light and went into the hall. Gertrudis was sleeping; the balcony was open to the black sky. I undressed and got into bed; I stroked Gertrudis' hair, felt her tremble and sigh. Moving a mint candy with my tongue, making it hit noiselessly against my teeth, I abandoned myself to sleep, thinking of Mami and Stein, remembering what Stein had said to me with a sad smile as he looked at the glass in his hand: "I remember two years ago, at Necochea. Mami used to get up very early to go to the beach and I stayed in the hotel, sleeping until noon. I believe she got up early because by then she had accepted the fat old woman that she was, and at that hour she met very few people on the beach. I woke up and looked out the window; I saw her below, moving around. But no one can describe how she moved. There were fellows painting the hotel walls and there was a sandy path down which people were returning for lunch. You'd have to be an animal to remember and understand how the female moves to attract the male. But Mami, naturally, needed pretexts: she went from one side to the other, picking leaves from trees, calling a dog, smiling at children, examining the sky, stretching, running a few steps and then stopping as if someone had called her, or bending over to pick up things from the ground that weren't there. All this along the path between the beach and the hotel, and with the masons on the scaffolds. It occurred to me—and I still believe it—that it was the last attempt, the desperation to hunt and fish, whatever happens, as long as there's a chance you may catch something. Poor Mami! I understood all this and started saying 'Poor Mami!' as I watched her from the hotel window. There was nothing but her there below me; her and the possibility represented by the masons, or a hotel employee, or someone driving back from the beach. That noon in Necochea I got wildly drunk and forced myself to make love in the afternoon until I was exhausted. No one in the world could grasp the purity, the humility with which I would have offered just about anything to those painters or the masons, if one of them would come close to Mami and proposition her in brutal, dirty language, as a man does when he can no longer control himself."

8

The Husband

Many days passed without Díaz Grey's getting to see the husband, so that he began to believe the man was another of her lies, and that there would be nothing more than his own story with Elena Sala, a predictable story with no complications other than those she personally brought to it. He believed, or resigned himself to believing, that this story was about to begin immediately—in each hour following the moment he remembered the woman—when he would embrace her and push her toward the examining table, or when she would telephone him one night from the hotel, or when they would walk near the pier and he, with the obdurate clumsiness, the bewildered impatience of a lustful aging bachelor, would lightly touch her breast and tickle her under an arm. However it started, they would understand simultaneously that the story had begun the moment she entered the office the first time—the noon that both would commit to memory and reconstruct so as to free it from time, to make it unforgettable.

And although it was possible for me—often when I could scarcely go much further—to place, near the windows of the office door, a changing face that gave no idea of the man's height—indeed, seven or eight faces that would suit the husband—Díaz Grey lost all interest in the matter. When the presence of the other was somehow announcing its indefinite threat, the doctor approached the door slowly and disinterestedly, or moved his head very slightly in its direction. Meanwhile, and without my having to control events or even pay attention to them—while I thought about money, Gertrudis, or advertising slogans, or persisted in arranging the situation between the woman and Díaz Grey, and the inflexible matter of the husband, so many times drawn with hazy lines and so many times but one step away, a detail, full grown from the moment of his birth—meanwhile Díaz Grey had continued receiving visits from Elena Sala, had repeated the first meeting hundreds of times, trying hard not to look her in the eyes. And during each of the visits he had given an injection to the woman, no longer looking at the essential area of skin on her thigh or buttock; he had signed prescriptions and when she disappeared, he went to the table to gather the bills she had left there, crumpled and carelessly abandoned.

So it went, without variation, once or twice a day, without my having to intervene or being able to avoid it. I had to find the exact inevitable husband so I could write the screenplay at one stroke, in a single night, and put some money between me and my worries. And these same worries blocked me from writing, discouraged and distracted me, forcing me to draw out of dreams, out of the blank nights and sudden flashes in the working day—fatally—the wrong, unusable husband. It was very difficult to find him because that man, whoever he was, could only be known firsthand.

9

The Return

In the first cold days when spring seemed to launch itself from the dregs of winter—appearing as unexpectedly as rocks, moss, dead crabs, and sand laid bare by a sudden receding of the waters—Gertrudis seemed to have discovered the superstition and hope that she could be happy again simply by taking a step or two backward. She seemed to feel sure everything would be as it had been if she could accept the circumstances and control her feelings, in order to go back in years and, imitating memory, live the days of the Gertrudis with two breasts.

She pictured herself, first, confronting her misfortune, as if it had taken form and would try to harass her, to make itself present in the cloudy sky, the grimy light, the gurgling sound of rain on the roof and balcony. I, a man, was abandoning her in the morning and leaving in her the first hatred of the day by killing—with a noise or movement of comings and goings meant to be stealthy—the dream in which she had immersed herself. Every morning I killed faces, unknown rooms, incomprehensible assembled landscapes, dialogues separated from any mouth, little changing worlds in which she—small, young, or somehow

54

different—could place herself and laugh, conquer, move about naked.

Awakened, accepting wakefulness after a moment's struggle to deserve oblivion again, she felt herself coincide immediately with the concave shape of her affliction. She remained awake in bed, motionless, her eyes closed so I would think her asleep, so I would not talk to her as she waited impatiently for the slow cautious noise I would make when I shut the door as I left. Awake and motionless, stretched out, heavy, leaning toward the warm center of the bed, facing up with one leg doubled under and an arm encircling her head, with lips parted and breathing deeply to reconstruct a convincing image of her own sleep, she listened to me move about the room as I began preparations for leaving her alone until night. She sensed me consulting the clock and sitting on the bed—not me, but this shape, this weight, this body— clumsily putting on slippers (this back of a man in pyjamas), wrenching myself from sleep, accepting the distasteful start of the workday. She heard me go toward the bathroom in the meager light, avoiding the chairs, the table, the large basket of magazines; perhaps she heard me pause to examine the look of the morning unfolded in the balcony window. She heard the loud noise of the shower, imagined me, a sexless shape, bent over the toilet; she divined the scratching of the razor on my beard. Then she heard me come back, shaking myself, invading the room with the smell of soap. She listened to me sigh as I dressed, tolerated the moment of silence when I knotted my tie in front of the mirror. After that—I would be moving my swollen eyes to search for my hat—she would harden her thighs to change the statue of the sleeping Gertrudis into stone, and the energy from her contracted body would reach out to my back and force me to leave. Then, separated from me, from anyone—from a presence, a body, the thickness of that body, the memory of its odors and temperature—imitating the docile and hypocritical posture of a corpse, she joined her hands over her stomach, drew her knees together, and prepared to receive the smooth voices that proclaimed her misfortune, her defeat, the size of the piece missing from her body and that would have to be missing, proportionately, from all her future happiness.

She lay under the images of her failure, under the cold that withered her cheeks, under the perpetually gray light of the foggy day. And she sought to save herself with the memory of another winter, with the evocation of a young and whole Gertrudis who was waking up, who had awakened confident and energetic in the cold mornings of yesteryear, separated from today by incalculable time.

I began to see her recede, to see her trying to take refuge in the past with prudent movements, walking backward with cautious steps, her foot testing each of the days she trod. I saw that the windy days of spring and the first warm dusks following the weeks of rain were allowed to cross the balcony and settle down in the room. I saw her smiling, emotional, and repentant, fastening her gray silk dress before the mirror. 'Thank God!' I thought, free of Gertrudis' sadness, free to embrace my own sadness and surrender to it.

She began to move around the room practicing laughs that could match exactly the echo, so confused now, of her old familiar laugh. She put flowers and wine on festive tablecloths, and when I returned at night I often found her humming around the table over the clinking wineglasses. And suddenly she began talking of her misfortune, smiling and insistent, as if she hoped to wear it out and forget it.

"It's not important to me any more," she repeated with an emphatic smile, impudent, bewitched.

"It's not important," she confessed cheerfully after dinner, and in bed she tried to convince me that it didn't matter to her through imprudent movements, defying the light, lying naked and eager beneath me, pushing those powerful hips, slipping away from any suspicion of shadows, turning toward the light and my eyes. She looked at me without distrust, without scrutiny, searching only for the happiness she could extract from my excited face, following the movements of my mouth that harshly repeated the coarse familiar words suited to the ritual. I came to look at the round scar without disgust, to see in it a barbarous sign whose meaning remained indecipherable but possessed sufficient power to arouse my anger and jealousy.

It was between this period and the following one that the idea of killing her occurred to me, vaguely, without resonance, always superficial, like a whim of spring. Perhaps not even that; merely the distraction, the game of imagining her dead, of making her disappear by shoving her, with a smooth movement of my hand, toward her origin, her birth, her mother's womb, toward the very eve of the night when she was conceived, toward nothingness. She is not here; that place she occupies in the air of the room has remained empty; what I seem to remember of her is purely imagination. Now that she had stopped tormenting me, when her disappearance could in no way benefit me and my liberty was of no use whatsoever, it was possible for me, permitted and legitimate, to amuse myself with the idea of her death, to create a gracious and mourning Juan María Brausen, courageous, bearing his misfortune with dignity, not allowing himself to be bowed by destiny, discovering the comfort of being humble and resigned, submissive and penitent before the designs of Providence that were not his to judge.

After having rehearsed in the confinement of the apartment; after having transferred her new happiness to the main streets of town in quick emotional excursions, Gertrudis began to search for happiness apart from me and in the time before she had met me. She revived the youthful days before our marriage, remembering and imitating the girl with the proud head and chin, the carefree teen-ager who walked with long strides. She tried to be the former Gertrudis and to place her on a corner in Montevideo, in a month when it was possible to breathe, in the simple air of the city, with the promise of months of vacation, of the country, of lunches near a small stream, friends waiting, letters received and answered.

I had already stopped playing with her death, I wasn't pushing it. But with a new-found anxiety she thought one day of her mother, the old lady mulling over her own uselessness in the house at Temperley, and she was sure of the comfort and of the everlastingly young Gertrudis she would find there, near her mother, alone now with a servant older than she, alone with a telephone to wait for Gertrudis' calls, with a window from which she could see, beyond the small garden of dried rose bushes, the sharp-pointed fence, the mailbox, and the small bell the mailman used when, once or twice a month, he left his bicycle for a moment to deliver a letter from Raquel.

She saw herself, more and more often, until it became an obsession, drinking tea with her mother, chatting and munching toast. There—on returning to the familiar smell of the house, the smell of infancy transported from Montevideo to Temperley—she would be placed in a beginning, strong, safe, and friendly, with the sips of strong tea, the cigarettes smoked without anxiety, the marmalade, the intimate smell of roquefort. She imagined herself reclining in a weak, innocent voluptuousness, as if exposing her back to warmth; she imagined herself listening to water boiling on the stove, which would only be taken from

10

The Real Noons

I was resigned to the disappearance of the face of Elena Sala's husband, the disappearance of Gertrudis, the loss of my job, vaguely intimated by Stein. And yet I was trying to hold on to all this, to prevent Díaz Grey from vanishing. I was resolved to tolerate and almost provoke the repeated arrival of the woman at the doctor's office, exactly at noon, when the waiting room was empty and she could announce herself and be admitted by only rapping at the door with her knuckles, scratching her nails over the corrugated glass plaque and permitting herself to be surprised by the doctor with a nostalgic and malicious smile; as if she could guess that I, in Montevideo, had repeated the same gesture innumerable times, the same brief, hopeless sound made years before in the hallways of brothels, when I lifted my hand reddened by the light high on the ceiling.

Elena Sala had chosen, almost at once, the small armchair against the office wall with its back to the window; the cabinets were to her left and the examining table was in front of her. After greeting the doctor, she would advance from the door to sit down, offering a half smile with her profile, as if she were returning home after a pleasant but tiring walk, and would try to relax for a few minutes in the easy chair, without talking, without the attention of Díaz Grey, who would go to his desk, review papers, and make notes of payments, pretending to be busy and oblivious of her. Then it was as if I myself could see her, as if I were transformed by the doctor's controlled curiosity, and I would spy on the abandon of her body as she crossed her legs, as she touched the beads of her necklace with her teeth, her brilliant and thoughtful eyes directed toward the screen, toward the space between the examining table and the screen, where she had stood with her arms at her sides, half her body naked.

It made me happy to confirm that they faithfully maintained the tacit rites of their platonic relationship, insincere, businesslike. The ritual began with her fingernails scratching the glass, with the smile that she partially offered and Díaz Grey neglected to accept. It continued with the lowering of her body until she was accommodated in the armchair, with the crossing of her legs, with the nibbling on the necklace, with the distracted expression aimed at the screen; two or three minutes later she let her necklace fall in silence and crossed the other leg. Then the doctor understood it was necessary to end the farce at his desk, to raise his eyes and look at her. She kept her body still, softly drumming on a side of the armchair with her fingernails painted red. He looked at her and understood, reencountering each time the understanding reached the day before, that she did not have the first visit in mind, that her thoughts were not related to him. Now he had to wait only a moment for her to turn her head to look at him and smile again sweetly, fluttering her eyelids as if apoligizing for having succumbed to an old reverie familiar to both of them.

Then Díaz Grey stood up—'it's as if she had come by to ask me for a cup of tea, to ask it of an old friend, a father mellowed by affection, a respectable Díaz Grey, an adviser, inoffensive, proud of his art in preparing tea'—and walked slowly toward the corner where she was. He lit the alcohol and disinfected the syringe.

They almost never spoke before the farewell phrases, accompanied by small gestures at the appropriate moment; the doctor would close the door and take a slow look, needlessly furtive, at the nape of her neck, at her hips, calves, hips, back; he vaguely desired her, and for the first time, at noon. Then he picked up the peso bills and went into the house for lunch. Nothing else could happen until the husband appeared, and Díaz Grey did not have the courage to evoke him with questions.

In that way, one noontime or another, docilely, and without memory of the immediate past, without enthusiasm but still without disgust, Díaz Grey came to the end of his impatience when Elena Sala scratched the glass and showed him her nostalgic lewd smile that he could not understand. Always at noon she crossed the doctor's office and went to sit in the armchair next to the window farthest away, put one leg over the other and without avidity gently sucked the largest bead of the necklace, then smiled at the doctor, vaguely entreating his pardon. Time and again both imagined—because at that hour the noises from the town were quieter—that the office had risen to an impossible height of solitude and silence. Díaz Grey imagined it with such force that he thought, "Now, without noises and so far from everything, so alone, and as if forever alone, she can uncross her legs in the armchair, stand up—she doesn't have to take the necklace out of her mouth—and walk toward the corner with the folding screen. It would be convenient to bring the leather couch in from the dining room; but it's broken and stained. If only she felt this solitude, I would see her naked, coming toward me from the screen, even though we would have only our legs, the carpet, or the examining table; the light is too bright, that's true; but it would remain in memory above me, above her, convincing me that it happened here and in this way."

As for her, Elena Sala, she might have a sense of the extraordinary quality of the noon silences, and murmur from the armchair, a second before the moment would come to turn and smile at him: "Listen. If the train doesn't blow its whistle or the pianist from the conservatory doesn't go mad, we won't hear anything until the ferry arrives. We're alone in this silence. You can come close and kiss me, you can do whatever you and I want and it will be, in this silence, like something happening out of this world."

Always at noon, because it was impossible for me to see the husband's face; repeating without variation the style of the visit, so I would not lose it all when I detached myself from what I already had: the small, aging doctor; the tall blond woman who waited looking at her nails in the gloomy waiting room, examining the coat rack with disgust, the majolica flowerpot stained and empty, the handrail of the staircase. So many things, definitely mine, and that were beginning to be the most important and real; all the city and its people, the doctor's office, the square, the greenish river, the two of them at noon nurtured by the magnitude of the vast solar whiteness, made concrete by the dark, sharp-edged shadows in the streets—all of it storing itself in my memory, thanks to the silence and special solitude of the hour.

11

The Letters:
The Fortnight

I thought with indifference that I hadn't been mistaken when I returned home one night and found a note, not on the table, but on the uncovered bed pillow, that said:

"Dear: I was sad to tears thinking about Mama and I'm going to Temperley for a few days. Call me or come. I didn't have the heart to tell you (although it's not important, don't think crazy thoughts) or to call you on the phone. It's very possible I'll get a job, we'll talk later, and everything will be better then. After a few days in Temperley I know I'll be happier and everything will again be as it was."

I called Temperley and listened to the mother's voice, so old and resigned, yet so confident when it sounded for him, not the best of the males who could have married her daughter. The voice explained that Gertrudis was visiting some friends who did not have a telephone, that perhaps she'd gone to the movies and might not return until very late. I ate in the nearest restaurant and hurried back to the apartment to stretch out on the bed where the smell of Gertrudis hung in the air, imprecise. Rereading her note, I confirmed that the invitation to telephone her preceded the request that I see her in Temperley. I confirmed that the phrase, "I'll be happier and everything will again be as it was," sprang from the same fierce resolution that, in the same bed, led her to make a left breast grow on her chest, to offer it to me, to oblige me to believe in its reality, and above all to gain the assurance that she could offer to any man in the world an identical sensation, even and symmetrical.

Lying on the bed, while on guard against stirrings of sadness and joy, while moving my tongue in a mouth full of mints, I admitted that our mutual love was no doubt lukewarm and sullied, as far from its origins as an immigrant whom life had furiously dragged around; that, protected, it was getting restless in the refuge of bed sheets, common meals, and habit. I thought about that phrase, "It's very possible I'll get a job," how it would simplify everything if this possibility were realized, if that was what she wanted and succeeded in doing. It would let me make scrupulously small cynical justifications in order to accept my failure—though not failure for some nonexistent inflexible goal, or for any particular form of life—and to accept it with the resignation suitable to a man of forty years. If for the great liberation of her death she was substituting the lesser one of not in any sense needing me, it would be possible for me to face my failure without melancholy, to speculate impersonally about how life would have been—not that it matters, I'm going to die anyway—if instead of coming to Buenos Aires with Gertrudis, I had left Montevideo alone, gone north to Brazil, or tried to get a job on a cargo boat when there was still time, when I still had the small faith necessary to do such a thing.

I would set everything aside to feel myself alone and complete once again, to incubate a certain curiosity for what the days might bring. Stein had hinted that they might throw me out of the agency at the end of the month, and old Macleod had bought me a drink and spoken to me in a muffled voice, with his throat full of fog, about advertising's golden years in Buenos Aires, comparing those times with today's restrictions, absurd competition, indecision. And since then I had been fluctuating between abject fear and the idea of relative freedom for three or four months; I had wanted and dreaded the check that would accompany the dismissal, the hundred and twenty days of unconsciousness, of being on my own and alone in the streets where the spring wind was stirring, to at last allow myself to think about myself as I would about a friend to whom I'd never given proper attention, and whom it might be possible to help.

Another letter from Gertrudis arrived by mail, suspect from the address on the envelope, suspect for having been written. I read it at breakfast, half asleep, feeling that each item of stupidity I had discovered in her and put aside—for five years, from the first time that I saw her until now—was reappearing behind my back, piling up with others, so that a dull inescapable atmosphere of stupidity was beginning to surround me.

"I'm sure I will recuperate much faster and everything will be the same again if I can stay a few days more, I don't know how many, in Temperley with Mama. Don't see in this, because it would be absurd, anything against you, my poor dear. No one could have had more understanding or delicacy, given so much comforting and helpful attention. I'll explain it all to you later. We're a few minutes away from each other, but I don't insist you come, not even for Mama, who has made me feel that very soon I will be free from the atmosphere of pessimism and renunciation into which I was sinking. We're a half hour away and there is a large bedroom here in which we could live comfortably. But you'll understand, you who have always understood everything, that I want to be alone for a while. I was determined to tell you this, and wanted you at the same time to know that there is nothing in this, absolutely nothing against you, on the contrary. Anyway, I want you to telephone me and I think you should have done that already, since the first night when I simply had to go out."

I called her and tried to console her, assuring her once again that everything would be fine; leaning on the corner of the counter where the phone was, as I waited for the connection to be made, I remembered the time when Gertrudis' letters had been reduced to an intricate and obscene sentence without explanations or questions, and with no need for reply.

She remained in Temperley and I went to visit her twice a week, sleeping with her on Saturdays, holding her in my arms until she fell asleep, convincing myself without jealousy, without suffering, that some man was hidden in her decision to live there, was responsible for the firmness of her resolve. The other nights I locked myself in the apartment, disconcerted by not having Gertrudis' big body near me like a dam to contain my sadness. I pledged myself to remember her because now, night after night, I was discovering my capacity for forgetfulness as I remained alone, without her warmth or breathing, my head lying next to the confusion of La Queca's bedroom.

And so a fortnight passed during which I went out into the street every morning. I went to the agency; I went from one client's office to another until evening; I felt myself give in to sudden miseries as I stretched my legs in waiting rooms in order to look at my new shoes, as I almost jumped out of my chair when the indifferent voice of a heavily made-up secretary announced me, as I talked—transformed into a jovial imbecile, smiling, loquacious, polite, and animated—with fat imbeciles and skinny imbeciles, old ones and young ones, deliberately boyish, all well dressed and sure of themselves, cordial for the moment, all with the same patriotic and social affinities confessed behind doors with opaque glass, facing the backs of posters with slogans about pay days, time, and productivity, and calendars, maps, photos of landscapes, and colored lithographs.

At dusk I returned to the agency to submit reports and explain patiently and humbly how I had spent the day, without relaxing my vigilance over the firm tone of voice with which I expounded promises of future accounts and foreseeable successful transactions, followed by explanations of how and why the refusals of today would be reversed by the contracts of tomorrow. I spoke stroking my mustache, lifting it so my lip showed a smile of infectious confidence, always listening to the voices, the bells, the doors slamming, trying not to be taken by surprise by the invitation "Mr. Macleod would like to see you in his office before you leave," the first in the series of tender, protective, false sentences with which the old man would have me know I was fired.

And although there were many other things in that fortnight—drinks with Stein, another dinner with Stein and Miriam, wind, a smell of the sea in the streets, a misty glow in the sky—I was only concerned with remembering the attitude of my body's forlornness in bed, alone, as I sucked mint candies in the dark, as I fastened my hold on the doctor's office in the city next to the river, as I envied Stein for having gotten into Gertrudis without remaining a prisoner. The sole importance of the fortnight was my body flung across the bed, my face raised against the wall with my mouth open so the noise of breathing wouldn't disturb me, the pain in my shoulder and waist, my ear recognizing voices and sounds on the other side of the wall.

The fortnight was left behind—probably lost along with my forced and persevering attitude in bed; but in some way, what La Queca did and said through the wall endured. And the feeling of the fortnight remains and reveals itself in confusion, in the round shape of memory, in the possibility that memory can begin or end in any of the elements that comprise it. A door slamming, a woman's laugh in the silent moment between the crackle of frying in the kitchen and the man's voice reciting lyrics of a tango. The three apples from the fruit basket that had rolled a few inches, crushed and wounded, smelling foul. Drunk, the man repeated the words of the tango to himself, hands on his waist, wondering if he could drink another glass of wine without getting sick. "Don't tell me you're afraid!" the woman shouted. Someone less drunk picked up the silk and elastic girdle and threw it onto the bed. "All men are alike," La Gorda said contemptuously, with fatigue. Someone banged the closet door, and approached barefoot to jump onto the bed, placing a foot on either side of the girdle. From a distant corner in the rear, as if the apartment had three or four rooms and they were in the last one, four men took turns repeating poker phrases. La Queca raised the broken gold watch from the table and began to kiss it, while the one who was barefoot on the bed moved his body and made the springs creak. The first drunk shook his head, made an effort to think whether he should or should not lend the fifty pesos; the risk of losing them was not what worried him. "You're afraid, don't tell me you're not!" La Queca said again. She put the watch down on the table and was laboriously pulling on the fur-lined gloves. "There's always something for friends," affirmed the man who had picked up the girdle. The doorbell rang and a woman's voice, more lively than the others, very high above the sound of her footsteps, announced from the door, "Messenger for you. Flowers or candy." The first drunk raised the bottle of Chianti and tipped it until a single acid drop fell on his tongue. "It's a purse," La Gorda said. "He could've put some money in it." To end the silence that was increasing above sounds of tissue paper being shaken and a metal ash tray crashing and vibrating against the floor, the lively voice said, "It seems he really got hit hard this time." Although apparently distracted, La Queca heard her and replied bitterly, "And you're afraid!" She repeated it three times, more smoothly, more hopelessly, and then, drawing herself up, leaned to the right and gave an unexpected open-handed smack against her buttock. Everyone gathered around her, the women clustered and in their slips, the drunken men with smiles that showed the wish to not get involved, the unshaven poker players, drowsy, counting their chips. La Queca began her tirade, stopping to laugh every three syllables, every nine, every eighty-one. But it wasn't a happy laugh: it heralded difficult times, it carried an unmistakable note of warning and alarm. "Why don't you grow up?" La Queca said. "In my time we weren't so afraid. After all, it had to happen sometime. Or don't you think so? And why not admit we wanted it as soon as possible? And I mean *you*—don't play dumb—you want it more than you're afraid of it. Pure pretense, acting afraid. We know it. No, don't cry. If that guy falls for it, that's fine, but not us. Eh, Gorda? I'm pretty fed up with her yelling, and the last few times we didn't bring her against her will. She came all by herself, nobody forced her, freshly bathed and wearing more lace than a princess. They're all the same, all the same, all the same! They're only interested in one thing, the same thing, all of them. Looking at the ground as if they'd lost something! I swear to you, if I could help you find it . . . I knew it—I knew it so well, the other night I said to Roberto that maybe at the last moment . . . But it's one thing to cheat him and another to cheat me. Take a drink, you'll feel better." The wine bottle, naked without its straw wrapping, rolled under the table and stopped with a small clink next to the other bottle. "Admit he was a brute," La Gorda said. "I know how to forgive." After taking the place of the man who was bouncing on the mattress, the cool voice of the woman told the story of the impotent recruit. Four of them were dancing, two were working in the kitchen; from the bathroom La Queca advised, "Give it to him good and don't worry. I'll take care of it. I'll give you a signal, you leave me alone and I'll talk to him." When the man stopped sighing, La Queca stood in the middle of the room and said, "I'm going to die soon, nobody can tell me different. A life of sacrifice. That damn Ricardo wanted to smear me. Kill me, I don't care. You're unique, unique, divine creature!" She sobbed with the last syllable of the last word and everyone disappeared without slamming the door. She was alone in bed, crying, walking on tiptoe through the empty room with her hands stretched out to reach for bodies and small lost happinesses; to caress the head of the pensive drunk, to pick up the money she had asked to borrow, to lean against the wall, to have the impulse to run barefoot, leaping and tossing her choked laugh into the air. She began to bounce on the mattress fast, grinding away there as if forever attached to the precise movements of the man, until the messenger knocked on the door, and in the kitchen eggs were sputtering in the oil.

12

The Last Day of the Fortnight

In the middle of the second week I spent a half hour with Gertrudis in Temperley between trains. I thought that for her I was dead or had not even been born, and that, in her retreat in time, she was also finally passing beyond the period of the clandestine meetings in Montevideo. Guided by the familiar bold expression in her eyes, by the shade of disdain and expectation in her movements, I placed her, approximately, in the period when she first met Stein at Party functions—possibly some weeks before Stein appeared in her life, when she was living impatiently but without rushing, so sure was she of the abundance and the extraordinary quality of what she would come to know.

Precisely on the last day of the fortnight, when the date of Gertrudis' return was already settled, La Queca tossed out a tender laugh after a silence, after a half hour of quiet. It was Sunday afternoon. I heard her laugh and talk with the thick-tongued voice that women have when they lower their body over a man in bed. I was sure her fists were sunken in the sheets, her hair hanging down, tickling the other face;

certain that the outburst of laughter had left an unfathomable intimate smile on her face, a smile that simultaneously cherished and scorned her past, a smile that had nothing to do with the brief jealous ardor of whatever man was stretched out beneath her.

"Why should I cry, tell me?" she exclaimed. "One leaves and another shows up. I'd have to be dead not to have a man. I knew it was going to be like that since I was a little girl—I remember, incredible as it seems. I'm not going to cry. Men come to me easier than a breath of air."

I leaped out of bed, suddenly sweating, shaken by hatred and the need to cry. It was as if I had just awakened from a fifteen-day nightmare; as if the woman's sentence and the fortnight's confusion had ended in the same moment, terminating the sum of hours in which I was immobile, close to the scandal but outside it, stretched out in bed, my head against the wall to listen.

I went close to the light from the balcony to look at the time; I had to remember what day it was, think of the name of the street where I lived, the 600 block of Calle Chile, in the only new building on that one winding block. "San Telmo," I repeated, to finally wake up and know where I was: at the beginning of south Buenos Aires, the remains of yellow and pink cornices, iron gratings, watchtowers, back patios with grapevines and honeysuckle; girls promenading down the sidewalk, taciturn young men on street corners, a sense of enormous space, the last iron bridges, and poverty. Old and young filling the hallways, a familiarity with death.

'Here I am,' I said, believing I understood the statement. La Queca was moving about, humming as she tidied the room; the man came out of the bathroom and asked for a drink.

"Now you're working me for a last taste. . . ." she said cheerfully. She went to the kitchen and returned, whistling.

As I shaved and put on my tie, I saw shame in my face; I carried it with me as I went down the stairs; I waited for it to fade before the face of the doorman who detained me to talk about a broken waterpipe. Then I walked slowly down the warm, noisy street, where the lights had not yet been turned on. I entered the Petit Electra Café at an hour when fellows were returning from soccer matches and the races, from outings with their girls, the hour when they gathered there shoulder to shoulder, laconic, the disappointing Sunday spent, helping themselves endure the prospect of Monday morning.

The owner greeted me and had the small cup of coffee brought to me with the little pitcher of fresh raw milk. From the table next to the window I could watch the street, the door of my building, see the white jacket of the doorman in the sky-blue shadows. A man would come out of the door from time to time, and walk toward me or start to walk down the street. I played at stirring the top of the milk with a spoon, slowly modifying its whiteness, letting drops of coffee fall into the pitcher, happy and alone, dissipating my shame, waiting for the happiness that needs solitude to grow. I watched the men walk from the doorway to the corner of the Petit Electra, and I imagined that each in turn had been with La Queca; I tried to guess what amount of suffering they took away with them or lamented having left with the woman.

As far as I was concerned, only joy and innocence could suit me, the willingness to not think, to dust the past off my shoulders, the memory of everything that might serve to identify me; the willingness to be dead and contribute to the world's perfection just the right husband for Elena Sala: an anxious man, a mythomaniac, indecisive, an immortal son from my miserable past, from the wombs of Gertrudis and La Queca. At last he was there, distant, a little rigid, deflecting his eyes; docile, after all. Condemned, from the beginning of time, to be born during my waiting and my absurd vigilance in the noisy room of the Petit Electra, during a moment of dusk when the smell of aperitifs and soups circulated. Again, as far as I was concerned, I too had been condemned to this birth, to be dragged along by this strange audacity that I did not dare resist; to contemplate a quick farewell to Gertrudis, the way one salutes a flag, symbol of the country from which I was expatriated.

Condemned to leave my coins on the café table, rewarding the owner's smile with a movement of two fingers, and to go back home as if leaving stale air, atmospheres, appearances, and habitual misgivings behind me forever. Not different or changed, as I walked back under the first evening lights and the bells of the Iglesia de la Concepción; no different, no other Brausen, only empty, closed, faded—in sum, nobody. Crazy, terrified, driven, I was drawing away from refuge and sustenance, from the maniacal job of constructing eternities with elements made of fleeting moments, transience, and oblivion.

I rang the bell twice; I heard steps on the carpet, on the wooden floor; I heard the silence. I must have been smiling in front of the door while I straightened up my body as much as I possibly could and thought about cancer, apoplexy, a stroke; Chaldeans, Assyrians, and Etruscans.

"Mrs. Marti?" I asked the woman who opened the door. I believed I saw my voice sketched in the air between our faces, with calligraphy identical to the marks on the envelope that came to her from Córdoba.

"Yes. Who . . . ?" She was younger than the profile I had seen on Santa Rosa Day; smaller and more fragile than the woman I had imagined. But the voice was the same.

"I'm Arce. I'm here on behalf of Ricardo. Ricardo must have spoken to you about me."

She didn't recognize me, she had never seen me entering or leaving the building; the top of her head came to my mouth, perhaps to the middle of my nose. She seemed to understand all at once that someone had knocked at her door, that she had opened it and was being spoken to. It was impossible for me to recognize the room behind her back: the bed was hidden; only the tablecloth of blue felt and the fruit basket were on the table; the bookshelf was higher and narrower than the one I had examined. The woman's dark eyes narrowed, not with curiosity or distrust but merely steadfast, simply resting on mine.

"On behalf of Ricardo?" she repeated, raising her voice as if she were talking to someone behind her. Nothing happened inside the room.

"Yes, a friend of Ricardo's. Arce . . . Perhaps he mentioned me. You're Queca, aren't you? I don't mean Ricardo asked me to come."

I spoke slowly, as if things might improve by choosing the words, as if impatience were not already visible on the small pursed mouth.

"I only want to talk to you for a moment," I added. "But if I'm bothering you . . ."

Amused, La Queca smiled, raised a hand and let it fall; she moved aside to permit me to enter. I don't know if the smiling, tilted head was mocking. She went to the table, leaned on it, and offered me a chair.

"For only a moment," I repeated, already cooled off, repentant.

Leaning against the table, she looked at me, hands concealed behind her back, repeating the hospitality with a gesture of her head.

"Sit down," she said. "Do you want a drink?" Rapidly she murmured an excuse and walked toward the kitchen. The white door swung back and forth.

I turned my head, noting each change in the room, remembering my first visit to the apartment, its appearance of disorder, of accumulated experience. But some unknown element continued to impose itself, emanating the same inexplicably joyful atmosphere, deceptive; the sensation of a life outside of time and redeemable. She returned without haste, reflective, a bottle of gin in one hand and two glasses in the other. The glasses were not clinking; silently also, La Queca made room for them on the table and bent over to serve.

"Please sit down. You don't have to be formal," she said without looking at me.

I tried to place and appraise, from the chair, the sudden hint of hostility and coarseness that I discovered in her voice.

"So you know Ricardo very well," she said, handing me a glass.

"Some time ago, yes. We were very good friends. Is he in Córdoba now?"

"He never spoke to me about you. Arce, you said?" She raised the glass, never taking her eyes off me. "I don't know where he is. And I'm not interested. Cheers!"

I handed her my empty glass, she offered me another, I said no. Stretching her lips until they almost disappeared, she laughed without looking at me, as if she knew my past, my absurdity, my life of only one woman, mocking all that but not mocking me, full of wonderment and without wickedness.

"But these aren't glasses, they're thimbles," she said, and again hid her hands behind her back. "What's the rush? I swear, if you've come to drag up the subject of Ricardo, we'll never finish. What have you got to tell me?"

I failed each time I tried to relate to her now, mixing it up with what I had heard through the wall. 'This mouth did and said . . . those eyes watched . . . her hands touched . . .' And from the impossibility of separating the woman of flesh and bone from the image formed by voices and sounds, from the impossibility of getting the excitement that I needed from her, a growing rancor swelled up until it overwhelmed me, a desire for revenge on her and at the same time on all the insults I was able to remember. And the insults had existed; although I might not remember them, they had shaped this small man, no longer young, from the feet that just reached the floor to the disproportioned head that was unable to lose respect for a whore.

"So you want to talk about Ricardo. . . ."

"Yes. I'll have another drink, if it's no trouble."

"Why not?" she said, and turned around quickly to serve it; the calves of her legs were low and strong; their movements erased the impression of a petite body that had attracted me. 'And not only not knowing how to treat her, but really as intimidated as a child, afraid she'll become too daring and repeat to me the filthy words I've heard her say so many times.'

"Cheers," she said.

"You don't know me," I began. "It must seem strange to you. . . . Ricardo doesn't know I came to see you. It's been a while since I saw him. But he mentioned you often and I know he cared for you and that something happened between you. I don't want to say more. If you're separated, no doubt you have reasons."

I kept still then, suddenly tranquilized by the conviction that I could not go on talking, that I was going to give it up, sit silently in the chair, and force the woman to take the initiative. 'She's much younger than her voice, she's simple in spite of everything, only in her half-closed eyes can I find the egoism and cowardliness that defile her. She can do what she wants. It's up to her and she'll make up her mind without knowing what she's doing.'

She waited, attentive to my silence, confused.

"If you're such a friend of Ricardo's," she said finally, "you'd know the reasons. He would've told you no one could stand me, that I deceived him, that no one could live with me. Right?" I smiled from the back of the chair, equivocal and proud of my cunning. "You see! That's what he tells everybody. Is that a man? If he didn't tell you that, you're the only one. I've known Ricardo for more than six or seven years. Or is it ten? Oh, how I know him! No one was ever more patient than I was, believe me!"

The familiar voice rose now, sharp, firm, impetuous, supported by a skeleton of roughness and cynicism. At times I stopped listening in order to study the hard, inevitable movements of her mouth, the steady shine of her eyes between the eyelids.

"I know Ricardo loves you," I said in the pause, controlling my urge to laugh. "Perhaps it can all be fixed up. It's been a while, a month and a half, since I saw him and he talked to me about you."

"You don't know. That's all over. Whatever happens, it's over. . . . I'm going to have another drink, even if you don't want one." She drank and began to laugh; she scarcely allowed her mouth to tremble, hiding it as she dried it with her hand. "And what's all this to you? If Ricardo didn't ask you to talk to me . . ."

"It occurred to me to do it. He's a friend." I felt the irresponsible air of the room moving forward to encircle me; and, dangling in the frivolous atmosphere, a grotesque sensation, almost comic, to console me for my failure before the woman.

"You must be half crazy," she said amiably; with her lips, she made a quick, decisive gesture, as if she were erasing Ricardo and the reasons for my visit, as if she were setting up a casual encounter for us. "Well, don't talk to me about Ricardo any more or about any of that damn business. I've already told you it's over. Have another drink, come on. Tell me how you knew where I lived." She smiled with her eyes shining, wide open, waiting for the surprise.

'Now I'm also in the scandal, letting my tobacco ashes fall all over the place, even if I don't smoke; drinking, moving eagerly between furniture and objects that I shove, drag, change around; immobile, I carry out my timid initiation, help to construct the appearance of confusion, to erase my tracks at each step, to discover that each minute leaps out, shines, and disappears like a newly minted coin; I understand what she was saying to me through the wall—that it's possible to live without memory or foresight.'

"That's it," I said. I raised a finger to point it at her, showing the resignation in my smile. "You would have to ask me that question, everything has to get complicated. But how do I tell you the truth so you'll understand me, without getting the wrong idea or thinking badly of me? That's why I took a long time making up my mind to come."

"You're crazy," La Queca said, laughing, searching for someone with her eyes. "Crazy . . . Now what are you trying to say? You must know I can understand anything, everything."

"Don't interrupt me." One more drink and I would be drunk. "I came to your door a thousand times and didn't have the courage to come in. I want to explain to you; I want you to hear me without getting angry."

She shook her head slowly with a happy expression that seemed fixed, inseparable from her face, as much hers as the skull bones under the flesh; she raised a hand imperiously to stop me, turned toward the table, showing me her buttocks, very large, very rounded now. She gave me a glass and drank hers in one swallow, spilling it into her trembling mouth.

"Go on," she said, laughing. "I think I'm going to laugh. You didn't have the courage to see me? But don't talk any more about Ricardo.

Men are disgusting." This was said with a brief, radiant smile that separated me from the rest of men, that succeeded in isolating me, sitting there pure in the chair. "Go on. You're not in a hurry?" She had a small gold wristwatch; she looked at it and came closer, resting a leg against the arm of the chair. She was bending toward my head, attentive and maternal, without any other trace of happiness on her face but the shine of moisture on her lips; pensive, dilating and contracting her nostrils, as if she were smelling me and trying to understand my odor.

"It wasn't for Ricardo that I came," I said.

"Don't speak to me about Ricardo."

"I came for you, I wanted to see you."

La Queca sprang up and moved backward until she touched the table. We both heard the noise of the elevator, the sound of keys, a door closed. She had tracked the sounds with her mouth open like a third ear, then she closed it with a dry smack, parting her lips to smile at me, and came to settle on the arm of the chair. With a fingernail she touched my hair, the nape of my neck, followed the shape of my jaw, while I remembered her face absorbing the noises in the corridor, the look of cruelty and terror, the mask of cowardice so quickly put on and removed.

"Don't leave yet," she said when I turned to look at her. It was impossible for me to comprehend the meaning of her perplexed, questioning expression, her eyes' impassioned examination, frenetic and without calculation. The thin lips moved forward, immediately disintegrating the sadness, lengthening in order to smile.

"Tell me, why did you come?" she murmured.

I breathed the air again; it was enough for me to open my mouth slightly for it to be present and fill me. I remained at her side in the chair, abandoned and happy, suddenly feeling as if it were an old habit for me to be with La Queca, to see and use the furniture and objects in the room. I wasn't obliged to lie to her any more, to excuse myself; I felt instead the pleasure of lying and the need to lie.

"One night we were in the same restaurant," I began. "You wouldn't remember, you didn't see me. You were with a man, I don't remember his face, a young man. Your hands were touching on the tablecloth. I don't remember either if I was happy or sad; I had eaten alone and after I paid the bill I saw you, with your hair combed differently than the way it is today—it was wound around your head. Don't say no, you don't know, you don't remember. I already told you I don't know who the man was, he had his back to me. A restaurant, not in Corrientes, but nearby, one that's busy at night. You were serious, you had your heads close together over the plates, you didn't do anything but look at him. I can still see you. You were looking at him with such intensity, with eyes that could burn, so open and steady. At times you blinked and squeezed his fingers on the table; your hand was white, it went slack, and then the blood began to race. Then he pressed your hand, first one, then the other. I thought you wanted to cry and couldn't. To shake your head and cry. Later I followed you here in a taxi. On another day I found out from the doorman which was your apartment."

"When was that?"

"I don't know. Maybe a month."

I felt her shake her head, denying, and she moved away from me; standing, her mouth darker and smaller, she looked at me thoughtfully, incredulously, determined to defend herself.

"It's true I had my hair that way," she said after a moment; again leaning on the edge of the table, she renewed her expression of doubt. "But why can't you tell me what restaurant it was?" She bent over the table without waiting for my reply. "Let's have a last drink."

I got up from the armchair and took two steps toward her and pressed my hand against her arm; I saw her calm down, then raise the glass and drink. She swayed a little without looking at me, without drawing away from my hand. 'I want to know, really, if she lowers her eyelids or raises her open eyes. Could it be so easy, was it so easy during all these years, since forever?' I took her other arm and she moved back, trembling, with a grimace of suffering; I heard her make a sound that seemed to be a sob, she swayed, knowing she was supported, and came close to me as if she were crumbling. I squeezed her, sure that none of this was happening, that it was nothing more than one of those stories I told myself each night to put myself to sleep; sure that it was not I but Díaz Grey who was squeezing the body of a woman, the arms, the back and breasts of Elena Sala in the doctor's office at noon, finally.

13

Mr. Lagos

From the windows of the doctor's office, it was possible to see the square with its whitish empty pedestal surrounded by the obvious geometry of trees in the center of the deserted landscape, near and unreal as a dream. Farther down, near the sun-whitened pier, groups of people could be seen growing larger and smaller.

'I'm not waiting for her with a feeling of love; it's just that she destroys my solitude, keeps me company, and then goes away, vanishing in the course of the day. It doesn't occur to me to kiss her when I first see her, when she lifts her skirt for the injection. But when she rests in the armchair for a moment and nibbles on the necklace, her cautious eyes continuing a hidden, unchanging thought; when I am free to imagine the thickness of her legs and the intensity of their heat when she crosses them; when, without looking at her but needing her presence to do it, I add to, modify, exaggerate, suppress, attenuate the form and weight of her thighs flattened against the chair, and think of the possible shine of silk and hair, excessive perfumes, the sudden and servile youthfulness that she would lend me for a few minutes in restitution, it occurs to me to choose her as the reason for my death and to die immediately. Without love, without even true desire.'

From the second window he was looking at the sharply defined black and white form of the ferry, surrounded by foam and reflections, which distance made seem an excrescence. The boat was moving close to the wharf, slowly and steadily, as if its flat bottom were gliding over a solid greased surface. Díaz Grey moved away from the window when he heard a steady knock at the door.

The man was short and stocky, with a round face and animated features obscured by the incessant rapid waves of expression that descended from his forehead and made his eyes shine—his eyes, the only dark area, the only part of his face that seemed made of hard matter, with deep wrinkles around them. Helped by the delicate pallor of the mouth, his eyes were shaping ephemeral contempt, provocations, insinuations, jokes, melancholy, reticences, astonishments, doubts and furious affirmations, definitive yeses that teemed on the lips.

"Do I have the honor of greeting Dr. Díaz Grey?" asked the man, bowing and drawing his feet together. He kept his head erect behind the closely scrutinizing eyes, his face fluctuating between reserve and the offer of indestructible friendliness.

Unsteady, quick, without rudeness, the man stepped forward until he reached the middle of the carpet, the center of the office. Then he turned with the promise, already decided by his frank and friendly smile, that nothing would be hidden, no matter what the future might hold.

"Dr. Díaz Grey," he now affirmed.

He bowed again, with his curved, mirthful lips, the gleam of his small eyes overflowing, one hand against the side of his trousers, the other against his chest to hold the gray hat and a pair of unnecessary yellow gloves. The doctor smiled without moving his head.

"Lagos," the visitor explained. "Elena Sala Lagos is my wife."

He finished saying it and moved forward with a smile, his mouth open now, jubilant, as if he had made an astonishing revelation, as if the names he pronounced were enough to create an ancient intimacy that would last until the hour of death.

"My dear friend . . ."

He embraced Díaz Grey, smoothly forcing him to take one step backward and another forward; then he returned to the exact center of the carpet from where he could contemplate and admire the doctor.

"Lagos?" Díaz Grey said, pretending. He only wanted to gain the time it took to separate and unite the woman with this chubby mature man who seemed to be waiting for his smile and gratitude.

"Yes, now I remember. Mrs. Lagos. I treated her until she returned to Buenos Aires."

"Exactly. I'm her husband."

He approached again and they shook hands. Lagos examined the doctor's face, lowered his eyelids, and went to leave his gloves and hat on the bookcase.

"Exactly," he repeated, walking around. "But now we've returned. We came back by train yesterday."

He was in profile, talking to the backs of the books. He interrupted himself to look with distrust at Díaz Grey.

"She's a little indisposed, nothing serious, don't concern yourself. That's why she hasn't come. Oh, nothing that warrants your professional services, doctor. And we trust you will excuse us if, even though we've been in Santa María since yesterday . . ." With an apologetic grimace he chose the armchair next to the window. "I needed many hours of sleep to recover from the trip. And she did, too. I can assure you that she wanted to come visit you herself last night. And I confess that this suggestion met with my firm refusal: not only was she very tired then, but she still is. However, she will come, we will come. Elena's indisposition is—you'll understand me better than anyone—transitory and nonexistent. Meanwhile we're sure that your honor as a gentleman will make you behave as if . . ."

"Don't worry, please," said Díaz Grey from the desk. 'Again the lie, the need for the exaggerated farce. Husband and wife!' "It's absurd. Why did she feel obliged to let me know she's back?"

"No, no, no. By no means," the other persisted.

'So this oppressive rubber-faced imbecile seated now, unalterable, in the very armchair that remembers her body, is the husband. And everything I constructed and imagined bit by bit in my feeble noontime lusts is ancient history for him, known by heart, already forgotten. So she had been approaching me, the city, treacherously. She arrived by train at night, she got into the hotel and separated this imbecile from the sheets so he would come, exactly at this hour, to give me the good news of her return, to lie and implore that I look at and treat her thigh or backside in exchange.'

"No, no, no," Lagos insisted. "She should have come. Or I myself, the

moment we arrived. I know you two are friends and I dare to believe I
will be admitted into that friendship."

"Naturally. But forget the rest. Precisely, between friends . . ."

Lagos smiled, his face gave thanks in silence, and he moved his head
until it touched the back of the armchair. In the pause he continued to
smile, his eyes almost in the direction that she preferred.

"Have you had lunch yet?" the doctor asked.

"Yes, yes. Thank you. But have you? You haven't even eaten and
here I am stealing your time. I don't know how to excuse myself." He
got up carefully, as if afraid the smile might spill over, and gathered up
his hat and gloves. "My dear friend . . . An untimely nuisance, you
must be thinking. I'm holding up your lunch. Let's see . . . Could I win
your forgiveness by inviting you to dine with me tonight? In the hotel.
You've already had occasion to discover that the food there is
acceptable. If one has good sense and a little intuition to guide him . . .
We'll be alone and able to talk comfortably. Though there's a chance of
having coffee with her. But I'm not promising. You'll come, won't you?
At eight-thirty, for a cocktail? Is eight-thirty convenient? Many thanks.
Until later, then."

He bowed—again with an undecided expression coming and going
on his face, joining his heels, his eyes friendly as he stretched out his
hand to the doctor. And when Díaz Grey again shook Lagos' hand at
exactly eight-thirty in the entrance to the hotel bar, he forgot the time
that had passed between both identical greetings, and the small
personal events contained in it.

"If it's all the same to you," Lagos said, patting him on the back,
"and better still if you prefer it, we'll stand at the bar. It's a symbol of a
stage in life. Youth, bachelorhood, friends . . . I guarantee that this
man makes a first-class dry martini. Unless you prefer whisky or
sherry . . ."

Díaz Grey winked to the man smiling behind the bar.

"Good evening, doctor. Two dry martinis, then?"

"Yes," the doctor answered. "Two—very dry and very fast."

"Fine," Lagos said. "I join you in your haste. We suffer the same
thirst. Here we are together at the bar, through your kindness. Or
perhaps you're not used to drinking this way, standing?"

"I'm not used to it," the doctor said with a smile. "I very rarely
drink."

"You're a Quaker. That's bad. I can't approve of that." He spoke hardly moving his lips, searching for the smile, the approval of the barman. "As I was saying, this is the stage of youth and bachelorhood. We're going to drink to it. After that comes the stage of café tables and private dining rooms. There one drinks without the feeling of camaraderie, one goes through an unconvincing imitation of drinking. There, in spite of everything, we drink facing a pair of critical eyes. In spite of love, which I don't rule out. A pair of eyes that remain lucid on the edge of our abandonment and appreciate it. And if we say that, aren't we also saying contemptuous eyes? That's why I please myself when it's possible, and today it is, thanks to your kindness." He smiled, then moved the smile to the glass, which he emptied almost without throwing his head back. "It pleases me to step over the dividing line and return to the bar stage. Would you like to talk about Elena?"

"I don't want another, for now," Díaz Grey said to the bartender, and turned toward Lagos. "Not especially. Although it's not only as a friend that I'm interested in knowing . . ."

"Yes, yes," Lagos replied. "I quite understand. I'll have another drink—if possible, a little drier. . . . Yes, I understand. But let's wait a little, I beg you, for exactly the most propitious moment. With respect to my theory on the bar stage, one could argue that it's not extraordinary—at least in Buenos Aires—to find couples drinking, standing at the bar. But no . . ." He raised a finger to reinforce the negative, then the same finger pointed to both empty glasses.

"May I fix you another, doctor?" the bartender asked. Díaz Grey shrugged yes.

"But no," Lagos insisted. In profile, head lowered and reflective, perhaps a little drunk, he now seemed older than fifty. "No, no. If you're drinking at a bar like this one, with its brass rail where each foot must rest in turn, and you're accompanied by a woman . . . If the two of you are standing here like that, with drinks in front of you, it's because you're courting the woman. . . . I think we'll have a last drink. I've taken the liberty of ordering dinner, since you're not accustomed to eating in the hotel. I have investigated. You won't regret it. I've taken the fluvial character of the city into account and I'm favorably disposed toward it. I confess—why not, since you'll discover it soon enough. I'm inclined toward fish. Then, my friend," he said to the bartender, who was waiting, following the movements of his mouth with a fixed look, respectful and cheerful, "then we'll drink, with your collaboration, the last two drinks of the night. And if I were to see you in similar company and in similar places, my dear doctor and friend, I would express the opinion that you are courting a woman, I would refuse to believe otherwise. And in that situation, believe me, you wouldn't let yourself relax. And to what fuller happiness can we aspire when standing at the bar, if not to relax? To always start a night of drinking with a friend who listens and talks to us. I allude—you don't need explanations—to the spontaneous surrender to a moment we have always longed for. When we repeat the same sentence, and this sentence doesn't lose its novelty and serves to explain everything."

He faced the doctor directly, smiling like someone who has won at cards and is apologizing for his good luck. And only when liquor was served again, this time in snifters after dinner, together with the coffee—for Díaz Grey did not want wine and had watched the excitement of the other mount in proportion as his bottle of sauterne emptied—only then did Elena Sala's husband remember his offer to talk about the woman. He rested his head on the back of the chair in order to calm down and regain that gentle quality that contained all possibilities.

"Now, yes, now we'll talk. Elena is sick without being sick. I'll mention, since we're not talking over dinner, the monthly female indisposition. I mean to say that this and that other thing depriving us of Elena's company right now, are inevitable, regular, common, and not sicknesses. Right? She—permit me, do you call her Elena?"

"No," said the doctor. "Mrs. Lagos."

"Good—she, then. For some time, let's say a couple of years, she knew a man. I'm not going to conceal anything from you—that would be an offense to your intelligence and the fact that you're a gentleman. I hope, moreover, that this night, these drinks we're having, may be the beginning and consecration of true friendship. Well then, as I was saying—and now I come to the part that's so difficult, if even possible: to define a man. Right? I could tell anecdotes, formulate observations, then venture my definition or let you find your own. But I'm going to employ the opposite method. I'm going to tell you who that man was and then I'll show you why. And there's no need to mention professional confidence." He smiled, excusing himself.

"Of course not. But I don't think it would help me professionally to know that story."

"No, no. Allow me to disagree with you. Presently you'll see. That man—his name is Oscar, Oscar Owen, the Englishman—I defined what he was: a gigolo. And he'll be that until he dies, come what may. Not only because he lived for a time on my money and hers. A gigolo, even if he hadn't taken a cent from us; even if he had given us money, food, and clothing. A born gigolo, as others are born mathematicians or painters. A question of spirit, not circumstance. Am I boring you? Thank you. Another coffee and cognac? Permit me . . ."

He spoke with the waiter and took a thick notebook from his pocket. He tore out a sheet and wrote on it quickly; when the waiter returned with the coffee and cognac, he gave him the folded note and said a number. "Thank you. As I was saying, he was a gigolo, as I vaguely suspected the first time I saw him. In the same way that a disease might have infected us, he transmitted this habit of drugs to us, though not the need for it, fortunately. And basically, on my part, it's more the desire, out of loyalty, to keep her company in her misfortune. I could renounce this habit at any moment. But why? It hurts me no more than tobacco. That man appeared suddenly in our life. Was he successful? Yes, from his point of view, I must admit he was. Yet there was never a hint of intimacy between them. I'm certain of it. His victory consisted in bewitching her, in making himself as indispensable, say, as the habit he transmitted to us. He was young, beautiful. That type of boy without shame who insists on talking about his virility—so much so that in the end we suspected a certain hidden femininity. I repeat, physical relations are not involved in this case. And aside from that, what does the gigolo give in exchange for money? Those thousand attentions, that attitude of constant servitude. Flowers, cheap timely gifts, help when she sat down or got up, or put her coat on or stepped into a car. Constant company to go shopping, to the theater, to movies, for a cup of tea. In exchange he was getting something more than money. He was getting her admiration. A man until then nonexistent, not capable of arousing lasting interest, still less of being dazzling, unexpectedly finds himself—through the goodness of my wife, who was inexplicably and irresistibly charmed by him—at last allowed to be in a way complete, to enjoy like others what we call a personality."

A young boy came out of the elevator and delivered something to the waiter; the latter approached the table. Lagos slowly unfolded the paper, read it, and put it in the pocket where he kept his wallet. 'He's not an imbecile. He's lying; this whole story is fantastic and I can't imagine why he's telling it. But he's not an imbecile.'

"I understand," the doctor said. "But such a man seems harmless."

"Yes and no. Presently you'll see." He drank, his small half-closed eyes staring at his hand. "We're not discussing that, if you'll permit me. I was telling you he could exist for the first time in his life because he found two people—infinitely superior to him in culture, education, means, and social position—who showed him affection and admiration, who treated him as an equal. But we'll continue with this later, there'll be plenty of time. My wife just let me know she can receive us for a moment. She even says she'll be pleased to see you. So we shouldn't linger."

"Very well," Díaz Grey said, and he smiled frankly at the reddened face of the man who was bending over the table, solemn and authoritarian. "But you were going to tell me something about your wife's illness."

"That's true, excuse me. I could sum it up in one sentence, since it seems to interest you. I'm very grateful to you. . . . It has to do with memory. Regularly, every two months, let's say, she suffers thinking about that man as if she had loved him, as if his disappearance meant something more than the annoyance occasioned by the dismissal of a valet. . . . Permit me. Did you have, in your adolescence, those crises when we think only of death?" He stood up and waited for the doctor to leave the table. Lagos smiled at him again while pressing his arm. "Insomnia and nightmares. Cold sweats, unrelieved depression. Memory that comes and goes. . . ." He paused again when they reached the elevator.

Díaz Grey thought of the quantity of memories that suited and shaped, for Elena Sala, the memory of the vanished man. He thought of his own poverty, he recognized himself abandoned by life in that provincial town, a man without memories.

"It was a mistake," Lagos said. "No bedazzlement in the first meeting. Not even a special interest. She can still remember that she saw, with better perception than mine, all the defects, the total weakness of the boy. It was I who came to his defense. Pure pity. It was I. There is no sickness, then," he said on getting out of the elevator. "Only these memories that come, oppress her for a few days, then disappear."

The woman heard the voices, the knuckles rapping on the door, the pause. She said "yes," and had time to decide to take off her bathrobe, and to advance smiling in the heavy nightgown that looked like a party dress, the silk grazing her knees. 'But I'm sick; Lagos has already told you that I'm sick, although not so sick that you can see me naked again. You smile, but you don't want to look me in the eye; you persist in showing me your affability and scorn. My poor dear giver of enemas. And Lagos spouting sentences endlessly to explain nonsense or not explain anything, and the country doctor smiling, interested, amiable, contemptuous. Keeping his nostrils open to sniff the trap, the demand for ampules or prescriptions that it may present. Now they talk about fishing and exchange stories, fishermen's jokes; occasionally he sneaks a look at me to see if I'm amused. Already Lagos is talking in a loud voice, laughing and moving around, ordering drinks on the telephone. And right now I can see him naked, his belly, his weak legs; I can remember all the symptoms of old age he's had to show me without realizing it. Life in common, doc. And you're thinner and paler than when I left you; you're not a youngster either. In Lagos' comedy of mirth—he's laughing again and talking in his loud voice—there's always a facial muscle that doesn't function quite properly or move in time, and shows clearly that there's nothing so decrepit as his display of good humor, of joy in life, of oh! carefree youth. At least, doc, you don't make the effort; at least I don't know your fears, I haven't heard you lying to yourself, I haven't heard you tell the same story a hundred times. I've never had the need to save my respect for you by betraying you with another man; I've never felt your caution at my side, I've never received words from you instead of a slap in the face.

'Now we all laugh again at the excellent story of the cardinal and the ballerina that we just imported from Buenos Aires. "It's excellent," Lagos repeats, trying to laugh the way a boy would, rocking himself in the chair with touching good will. Here we are, the three of us, you looking at my legs occasionally, trying not to lower your guard, not to be taken by surprise when we ask for a little morphine, for charity's sake. You saw me naked, doc, you should have touched me to keep me from becoming like a mother to you. What's wrong with life isn't that it promises things it never gives us, but that it always gives them and then stops giving them.

'You needn't laugh at Lagos, doc; he's more complete than you, more intelligent, more difficult. He always lies, lies so much that he'd only get to know himself if he died alone. And he doesn't even lie for my benefit; he does it because he's afraid. In the final analysis, a possibility for oblivion. We're not going to ask you for anything and you're going to leave, doc, tossing greetings to the hotel employees, the one with

14

Ernesto and "Them"

We barely spoke, and what was said was unimportant; it can be forgotten and omitted. She, the man, and I made the indispensable gestures without a superfluous movement, as if we had rehearsed the scene night after night.

While we were alone La Queca drank, stretched out on the bed, laughing, between refusals and promises, mulling over the secret she had never told anyone, her half-closed eyes facing the prospect of being laid out in her coffin without ever having betrayed it. I was insisting dispassionately and cautiously, with a muffled voice for fear Gertrudis might have returned and might hear me. Often I drew near to caress La Queca's head and put my ear against the wall for a moment, trying to discover sounds in the silence on the other side.

"No," La Queca decided. "I'm not telling you or anyone. Why should I tell you, when I've only seen you five or six times in my life? It's not because I'm drunk; it must be that face of a saint you put on when you look at me. But on second thought, no. You'll think I'm crazy, too. Arce, your name is Arce, that's all I know. Crazy world. And it's to you, and not to others I know better, that I feel like telling it. I'm not going to tell you."

"As you wish," I said. "I didn't ask you to tell me anything." 'Arce . . . I mustn't forget myself; I'll have to visit her without papers, without documents. Although some day, for all the care I take, she'll see me coming out of my apartment or she'll find out everything from the doorman.'

"No, it's better not to talk. Why don't you want to drink today? I'll tell you one thing: their name is 'them.' Lots of times I say to La Gorda, 'Good-by, I've got to go home to them.' God knows what she thinks. I'm always afraid, because there's nothing I can do. The minute I'm alone, they appear. But if I drink enough, I can fall asleep right away."

"Who are they?"

"No one. That's the thing," La Queca said, and she began to laugh, raising her head to mock me. "They're made of air. You already know enough."

She emptied her glass with a mysterious and prudent smile; she approached until she reached the chair, then bent down to bring her laugh close to me.

"Who are they?" I asked. 'If someone were to listen attentively on the other side of the wall, they would find out who she's with. The sound of her laugh and the words she says would slowly cordon off my silence and my composure; they would finally make a cast of my face, my hands, and my body in this chair.'

"So you want to know?" She shook with the laugh, bending her waist in rapid bows. "It's a riddle. Them. Only I can see and hear them. You don't know anything. La Gorda doesn't understand either, even though I've talked to her and almost told her about it. Maybe someday you'll sit on one and not even know it! You'll say I'm drunk or crazy. . . ." She became serious, raised her body, and moved her head away, the laugh disappearing quickly. She moved back until she placed herself as she had the first night, standing and leaning against the table, her hands hidden. Saddened, younger under the loosened hair-do, she scrutinized me.

"Now go bring me a glass and give me a drink." I examined the wall stethoscopically while I was handling the bottle of gin; Gertrudis had not arrived. "Without spilling a drop, not so fast, wait a minute, over here. Give me a little kiss. Your name's Arce? I like it, but Juan María is a woman's name. Don't get mad. You carry it off real well, but I'm not going to tell you anything. It's a secret I better take with me to the grave. Don't laugh; give me another kiss. Look how crazy I am; often I fall asleep before they come, because I begin to think it's raining in a forest, and on the ground under the rotted leaves there's a little broken mirror and a penknife, all rusted. Listen, I don't know if I saw that when I was a kid or if it's a dream I'm remembering. But if I think about it a lot, about the forest and everything, I can sleep without having to face them. But I don't have to think as if I'm remembering. No, you can't understand me, don't say you can. I have to think as if it was happening that very moment, as if it was raining in a forest someplace and somehow I just knew it."

Then when I approached to kiss her she heard, before I did, the sound of the key fumbling and twisting in the lock. She squeezed my arm, pulled her hands away, and let them fall; her face, turned toward the door, was again wearing that mask of terror and cowardly decision that I had seen during the first encounter. But not in profile now, not constructed with only one eye, a cheek, a black half mouth opened in order to swallow the noise. She backed up against the table, forcing me to guess what was about to happen with no data other than her expression, her backward movement, the sound of a fallen glass. Still, for a second she showed me her drawn face, three times pierced by fear; I saw her eyes try quickly to explain, but immediately give up. She raised her arms, forcing me to turn around, to stumble and stop in front of the bookshelf. A fist beat the door as she ran to open it; I saw La Queca disappear into the corridor and heard a masculine voice rise and suddenly die, lost in the indefatigable, spiteful buzzing, as of an insect, that she was making.

'A man, another man. I am Arce.' I righted the overturned glass, filled it with gin, and tried to wait with my back to the bookshelf, drinking. She entered first, the moisture of tears over the mask of nervousness and fear, faking the triumphant, joyless smile that she showed me. The man closed the door and advanced. He was taller than I, younger, bony; he wore his hat pushed far back on his head, and it was impossible to imagine him wearing it any other way; his jet-black hair began to shine very close to his eyebrows, and the freshly shaved face presented, as if deliberately, its impassivity and whiteness. They approached slowly, abreast now, and in silence. I walked toward the table, toward them, toward the middle of the room, while searching for the adequate smile, at last showing something of a smile that I split between the two of them. They didn't seem to see it; I watched them take a last step and stop at the same time; she raised the tip of her chin to point me out, to defy a foreseeable regret, her cheeks burning, the small mouth moving smoothly as she sampled and chose a final expression. The silence lay there between us, triangular, covered by the sudden, remote murmur of drizzling rain. Then La Queca shook her head toward the newcomer, not looking at him, as if she had left the hard bright glance, directed at me, hanging in the air. He was waiting for something, without understanding or deciding what, his shoulders a little stooped; the dark lines of his mouth and eyebrows saved his white face from becoming a mere smudge. A second before she could move her head again, dragging with it the decorum of her mouth but not her eyes, I understood that she was waiting for the man; I blindly put the glass down and imitated the posture of his body, arms hanging deceptively, shoulders hunched.

"There he is," La Queca said. "He says he came on Ricardo's behalf, that I've got to go back to him. I've already told you, I'm tired of this persecution. . . ." She didn't want to look at me, she raised an arm and let it fall against her leg. "Always with threats. Thank God you came."

"Why don't you talk now?" The boy's voice was coarse and old; as soon as it sounded, his white face became molded, acquiring form through planes and shadows suggesting insomnia and sorrow. "Talk to me now about Ricardo. Why not?" He spoke with dismay, as if he were thinking of something else.

La Queca backed away step by step, moving close to the violin music that languished on a radio. She leaned against the wall, her head touching a painting, motionless.

"I don't understand," I said. "She can't say that . . ."

She didn't want to, or perhaps she couldn't, look at me or hear me. She was out of the room, far away, under the noisy bell of rain. I saw a movement, the shadow sudden and lengthened; I felt the bang of my ribs against the back of the chair and, immediately, the preceding blow to my face; I realized that I was sitting on the floor with my legs and arms apart.

"Ernesto," she whispered without implying anything.

Ernesto's hat remained pushed back on his head; I heard him

breathe audibly, saw his mouth agape, as if he had run a few blocks, as if he enjoyed hearing himself breathe. He took a step back, arms at his sides again, blocking out La Queca. There was a noise of a door; I knew, and immediately forgot, what was happening. Standing, I stretched out one arm, and with the other struck a blow to Ernesto's chest. Again I felt the pain in the left side of my jaw, again I collided with furniture. A raging pain was extending circularly from my stomach when, alone and facing the ceiling, I was aware of a world consisting only of my open mouth and my desperate need to breathe, of nothing else but the clothes crinkling up between my back and the ground, sliding along the floor, and the coolness of the corridor tiles.

Slowly she drew close to the man's gestures; from his body my hat came spinning at me, hitting me in the chest. Then the door slammed in my face and there was nothing more than the sound of rain. I sat down on the staircase, waiting until I could breathe, hunched over and patient, looking at my apartment door, unconcerned that Gertrudis might open it and look out. I straightened the dents in my hat, and cleaned off my dirty wet hand that was covered with sawdust from the spittoon in the hall.

For a split second I experienced again the meaning of the recent scene, of La Queca's body and her past, of the resolution that had brought me to visit her and lie to her. I believed that I could decipher all the former enigmas of my life, that I could gather together the most minute everyday sensations and wring from them the answer, a single one, for all the important doubts; one joyful answer, as useful and convincing for me as for all other blind, enraged, or desperate men who were with me on earth at that moment. Later I smiled with abandon, hat in hand like a beggar in a doorway, smiling as I felt that I had preserved the essential so long as I continued calling myself Arce.

15

Small Deaths
and Resurrections

At dusk Gertrudis came into the room from the balcony; face up in bed, I was thinking again about the recently acquired revolver that I kept in my desk at the agency. The twilights were longer now; often I returned home before dark, and from the balcony Gertrudis would transmit to me, with or without words, the phases of the waning day. I couldn't go out on the balcony; it was necessary to protect Arce. From the big melancholy silhouette, from the profile turned toward the river, the vision came to me of gray houses, blue shadow, the last fringe of light in the sky; through her I succeeded, sometimes, in intuitively perceiving a happiness, a gentleness, a particular curiosity about the idea of death.

Now we were talking, and in a pause I thought again of my brand-new revolver, I saw it in the desk drawer between papers and notebooks, next to bits of glass and iron, the screws and springs that I picked up from the ground when once a week I visited a potential client near the harbor. I stopped listening to Gertrudis in order to recall the revolver's serial number and to think about it as if it were a name. Her bare feet apart, she was smiling at me, playing with the cord of her bathrobe.

"And later what?" she asked, jokingly.

"Oh, later nothing," I answered. "I can't conceive, I don't feel the need to think about later. Unless you . . ."

"Me neither. Not a single thought."

She twisted her head, smiling and obscured by shadows, then raised her shoulders, turning her back to the twilight. She was playful and happy, her body again assuming the gently provocative attitude characteristic of her adolescence. Looking at her from the front of her bathrobe, no one would guess which side of the brassiere was false.

"I believe we're talking theoretically," I exclaimed, and stopped looking toward her and the sky beyond the balcony. "At least I owe you loyalty. Even if with others I allow myself . . ."

"Or loyalty is the least you owe," she said, interrupting the sentence I was about to finish. "Isn't that more accurate?"

"It's not more accurate. It's idiotic." I stretched out on the bed and half closed my eyes, hands joined at my groin. I saw the inexplicable shine of the revolver barrel. 'If I could smell the perfume of flowers, I'd be dead; each silence she accepts would signify not only my solitude, but also my inability to hear. That's how I'm going to be; my father and my grandfather were that way, and for that reason I force them to forgive me.'

Through lowered eyelids I saw her approach the foot of the bed; the last light of dusk touched her eye, it extended, joining the fraction of a smile that she was determined to retain.

"It's so absurd, Juanicho," she said softly. "That idea is idiotic. I know it by heart: 'Each day further from me. All wrapped up in herself, preoccupied. Ambivalent, sustained by my heat.' Am I wrong? It's so idiotic!"

I was thinking about the need to carry the revolver away with me, to find a place in the apartment, the kitchen or bathroom, where I could hide it.

"But it's not so," I said, coming away from death. "We're not talking about doubts or denials—none of that really matters. I didn't ask any questions, nor did I try to guess; I told you what I see, what I feel, what I have to think without meaning to, automatically."

"Good. But wouldn't it matter to you?" The smile, now invisible, was present in her voice. "Not a bit?"

"It's not that," I said quickly. "It's not that." 'By this path we ended up in bed and now I don't want it, now I'm happy. I could be dead.' "I said you were strong and happy. I said your face is the face of someone thinking of someone else, remembering something or other—whatever may be the source of your happiness. I said that I feel you to be distant, remembering it, when we embrace."

"Yes. But does it matter or not? If I were sure . . . Would it matter to you? How much?"

"All right. It would be hard to bear. Is that enough? I don't know if I could stand it. . . ." Perhaps the imprecise threat would be enough; perhaps it's enough for her to hear me assert that any form of her infidelity would make me suffer; perhaps she'll stop talking and get dressed. "We're going to be late."

But she didn't move; I was surmising the sparkle of the smile in her eyes, in the shadows above. I began to die again in the silence, dispirited, losing consistency under the darkness of night. To my right, someone dragged his feet down the corridor, stopped perhaps at La Queca's door, disappeared. Almost against the bones of my skull, the room from which they had thrown me out, dragging me by my feet, continued desolate and silent. Near my left temple the sounds of night's beginning were converging and inspiring awe; an ancient inoffensive sadness, the stirring of spring wind.

'Far beyond my father and my unknown grandfather, to the unimaginable beginning behind my loins, crossing through terrors and brief shapes of hope, blood and placentas; me, here, dead, the momentary apex and last of a theory of dead Brausens, of heels, buttocks, and shoulders, indifferent, flattened, hardening themselves, impersonal prologues of carrion and, nonetheless, of Brausens. Raised to earth level by all of them—without generosity, without hate, without purpose—for this, for nothing, to rehearse my death and discreetly observe its face; to be stretched out and in peace this night, obliterating myself, being myself at last in annihilation, when I am helped, as silence spreads over my precarious beatitude, by this woman who looked with longing and conventional nostalgia at the last reddish light of my last false day, and who now sits erect and overflowing with things alien to me, *stabat mater, stabat mater,* as the living always have been, alongside the deceased; a little overwhelmed by the mystery, the fear, and the remains of an old curiosity that questions have exhausted.'

"Ay, ay!" Gertrudis said, singing *do* and *sol.* "What does it matter if we get there late? Can we talk? Yes, naturally we can talk. Trust and understanding, et cetera. But if we can talk, I'm no longer interested. If I can say it all, nothing has any destiny other than your mind. If I talk to you and you comprehend everything, you're not going to understand what I would want you to understand. So that to understand me, really, you'd have to be so furious you couldn't understand. And I don't care either, I seem to be talking to a corpse, but a corpse who can reason faultlessly. Love is over, Juanicho. We already know, we've said it so many times, that love is understanding. And yet it lasts only as long as we can't understand everything, while we can anticipate with alarm the surprise, the confusion, the need to begin to understand again, from the beginning. Juanicho, I'm beginning to feel, with the passing of years, that my feet are getting cold. Is it because the source of my happiness isn't here and isn't you? Is it because at night I curl myself against your body to remember the reasons for happiness that I invented during the day, apart from you? That's not true, Juanicho. It's not true yet. Shall I get into bed or shall I get dressed? I'll come stay with you for just a bit."

I felt her draw near and stretch out, her icy feet resting against my ankles; curled into a ball, she gave a warm laugh, touched my ear with the tip of her nose. Someone had probably moved on the other side of the wall, careful not to make noise. Gertrudis' voice and breathing were obliging me to return to life, unwillingly, regretfully.

"Don't move, Juanicho. I can see you from head to toe. I don't want to touch you. I love you so much and everything you said is absurd. May I touch you? I know that I may, but I want you to say it. I'd like you to ask for it. There's no one, there's no other man, there's not even the shadow of a possibility. Is that good? Are you pleased that there's no one? You are pleased. If you think I'm lying, I don't understand why you don't hit me. It would be good if you were furious and hit me. But don't talk to me; don't talk. If it's true but also may not be true, how can we understand each other with words? But Juanicho is good, he has principles. I no longer have any; if there's a change, it must be that."

Then I jerked my head away to rid myself of the innumerable sacred wounds, the harsh and sweating Brausens who had preceded me, the periodically repeated Juan, José, Antonio, María, Manuel, and Carlos Brausens who had gone from bone to dust, decomposed under the humus and clay of Europe and America.

"Don't touch me any more!" I said.

"All right." The fingers slackened, the mouth was withdrawn from my ear and neck. "I only wanted to know if it would matter to you. I'm going to get dressed."

'It could be true that it doesn't matter to me. But she's also going to need my jealousies, the slyly measured amount of bitterness that doesn't quite show, the absorption in thought, the eyes averted without stubbornness, but never an explosion that might make her retreat. She's going to need my jealousies and also the assurance that I'm not suffering too much, so she'll be able to wallow in it with the other man, if there is one; an assurance that can also sustain her when she's in bed with me, moved to pity, tender and excited by repentance.'

"But I don't believe you'd suffer. If I could believe it, I'd be happy," she said in a loud voice toward the ceiling. She waited; in the darkness now complete, I felt she was rigid and expectant.

La Queca's door was closed with a bang and four feet were advancing; I heard an unfamiliar laugh, a winding, interrogating sentence. In the desk, so small and light it seemed a school child's, the revolver would be sleeping, understanding now why once a week, near the dock, I leaned over close to the narrow train track to pick up glass and useless, rusted pieces of machinery.

"I'm going to get dressed," Gertrudis said at last; I heard her open the closet, lower the blinds, go into the bathroom. Nothing from next door, not one sound, when the silence came. I didn't know when, nor was I interested in finding out why, I would return to La Queca's apartment and kill the man, Ernesto. I knew, on the other hand, that I was ready to pay a hundred adolescent Gertrudises with two breasts, plus the totality of this Brausen, to reexperience the moment when La Queca was under my chest or bent over the table or helping me with her hands, or to see again on her face, solid, palpable, the humiliation and cowardice.

I heard Gertrudis singing inside the murmur of the shower, I imagined her body, I understood that her presence and all we might do or say would be mere graceless, tedious repetitions of moments that had a place in my past. Useless to make efforts and be saddened. Alternately her voice rose above the sound of the water and descended like a leaf in the rain.

From that moment and forevermore I avoided the possibilities of discussion; impassively I admired her new dresses, in silence I breathed unexpected perfumes. When dusk fell on the street, I became accustomed to throwing myself onto the bed to listen to the sounds in La Queca's room and wait for Gertrudis to return at dark.

While I was waiting without impatience, without desire, with nothing more than anticipated compliance at the announcement that the time had come to go knock on La Queca's door with the revolver in my pocket, I got used to imitating dozens of Brausens, disinterested and prostrate, while with respectful trust I put the back of my neck in the place where theirs had been, accommodated my height to heights familiar and alien, and scarcely smiled as I repeated with my lips the form of soothing and in the end inefficient refusals invented as a defense against the existence and death of the Juan, Pedro, or Antonio Brausens who had preceded me.

16

The Hotel
on the Beach

Díaz Grey dragged the boat over the sand and straightened up, exhausted and ridiculous; he looked at his bare feet, the trousers rolled up at the cuffs, his forearms burned by the sun and aching from fatigue. The woman, Elena, was already fifty feet from the shore, her head wrapped in a bright colored scarf, her shoes already on, smoking a cigarette as she waited, looking back over the invisible track they had made while crossing the river. The last hour of sun was striking against the dark lenses of her sunglasses.

The doctor put on his sneakers and picked up an oar. 'That's enough; it's too clumsy, too grotesque to walk along the shore dressed this way, next to her and her slacks, with oars on my shoulder. Too bad if they're stolen.' He left the oars against the side of the boat and moved ahead over the heat stored in the coarse, dirty sand. Elena resumed her walk slowly, allowing herself to be overtaken, exaggerating the difficulty of her steps on the beach.

"Are you tired? Of course you had to do all the rowing! But don't forget your promise: to the end of the world. Past the rise there must be a road—I just heard a truck. We'll find a hotel there or someone to ask."

"All right," replied Díaz Grey. "I'm a little tired, perhaps from the sun. But I'll get over it."

"Let's go up here," she said, as she began to climb the banks. "We'll get something cool to drink at the hotel. How wonderful if we can have a bath."

They were climbing in silence, bent over, again perspiring freely. From the top of the dune they discovered the road, winding and narrow, running between wires and new posts. They paused, trying to conceal the panting, their faces jutting into the still, burning air.

"Shall we rest a bit?" she suggested.

Díaz Grey shrugged, but crouched until he was squatting. He took off the knapsack to lean against it.

"It must be to the left," Elena said. "There's a big building and a tennis court. I don't see anything but farmhouses on the other side."

"Sit down and we'll smoke a cigarette."

"No, my legs are cramped from the boat. But hand me a cigarette." He felt happier; he would rest, smoke, look at her backside. "We're at the foot of the walls," she said jokingly. "Think back to the time of walled cities, with portals and embattlements and guards."

"I'm thinking," he mumbled. 'Oriental Story. Ali Díaz Grey, the eunuch.'

"If you want to rest some more . . ."

"No, it's better to make use of the light. At the hotel, if there is a hotel, it'll be more comfortable."

They descended the slope, allowing themselves to slide in the sand. They settled on a slow, steady pace down the silent and deserted road bordered by plains of dry reddish earth absorbing the last heat of the sun.

"I don't understand Lagos," Díaz Grey said.

"It's something to worry about. But why? Because of this trip. Because he isn't accompanying me?"

"That, too. I know the answer already: he has to be in Buenos Aires and he can trust me like a brother. But I didn't ask him something important. When did you receive the last letter from Oscar?"

"Less than a month ago. While I was searching for him in Santa María, he was there in the hotel. I found the letter when I returned to

Buenos Aires. Then Lagos and I decided to come back to Santa María, find out the exact address of the hotel, and look for him. With your help, naturally."

"Thank you. It's proof of solid trust and not to be forgotten, as your husband would say."

"Don't joke," she said, laughing as she glanced ahead, unconcerned with the doctor.

"I'm not joking, I couldn't—I'm afraid of him. It's been a month, then. It's possible he's no longer here."

"It's possible. He said he'd found a cheaper and more isolated hotel."

"Hotel is the word used here. Oscar, the Englishman, could be in any house where they take in boarders. There are many in the summer, all along the river."

"That's also possible," she said dryly.

The bend in the road where the building stood seemed to recede against the serene and darkened sky at the same pace they were walking. 'Don't trouble yourself, I don't want you to bother. Here I am full of aches and pains and stiffened by the gymnastics of handling the boat, carrying things step by step, by hand, with humility, toward the refuge of that inescapable Priapus, and doing it with your husband's permission.'

"I was unfair to you." She turned so she could smile at him, without slowing her pace. "You have the right to know. Ask whatever you wish. What did Horacio Lagos tell you?"

She walked faster, looking toward the right of the landscape, toward the spotted cow, the dog moving away at a trot, the colored clothes laid out on the grapevine.

"I already told you all Lagos said to me. An inexcusable indiscretion."

"But about this, his flight to Santa María, to that hotel that we still haven't found. What did Lagos say?"

"Oh yes," Díaz Grey said, stopping. "Excuse me."

He took a thorn out of his heel, then wiped his face with an open handkerchief. 'They can't say his name, either one of them.' Ahead on the left, they spied sterns and masts against the sky: a small bay filled with sail and motor boats.

"The hotel must be near—facing the Yacht Club, they said at the dock. What did Lagos tell you?"

Díaz Grey looked at her with a little hatred because he did not desire her, because without realizing it she was quashing desire with her hunched-over body, the stiff corduroy overcoat with shoulders hard as metal, the fitted slacks, the dark glasses.

"Different versions, as was expected," the doctor answered. "You can imagine them. If we put them in order, it turns out that, first, the fugitive robbed you of something so he could sell it and pay for a deserved vacation with a woman whose name is not mentioned; second, he stole money from the place where he worked, he collected and kept money that belonged to his bosses, noble folk who put up with him through charity and at Lagos' request; then, more simply, he tried to disappear in order to get away from you, from the nymphomania—purely spiritual, of course—that his youth had awakened in you. Is that enough?"

"Go on, it doesn't bother me. Go on, provided it's everything Lagos really did say."

"It is—I lack imagination. There's another version: it seems that the sexual tendencies of the fugitive were at a crossroads, and it was more than likely that Lagos—or another younger Lagos—would in the end be favored, to your detriment. And there's even another, the last, which has the merit of being twofold: simultaneously, he fled from his love of the needle and fled also to surrender to this new love in solitude, until death might overtake him. If that's the case, he's not going to have a happy time, I assure you. And if it *is* so . . . Anyway, I don't understand why he didn't come to see me, as you did, when he was in Santa María."

"He's cured. What's more, he didn't know you exist. He had left already when Quinteros spoke to us about you."

"I understand. Quinteros never told you I went to jail because of him?"

"Never."

She stopped for an instant and stood on tiptoe to look at the building on the highest point of the sloping terrain, where bare bricks shaped the rectangular patch, the beginning of a grove.

"It's curious," the doctor murmured. "I was sure you knew that and somehow were using it to blackmail me."

"I didn't know a thing!" she said furiously, and began to walk again.

"Also . . . because from the first I smelled blackmail and deceit.

Then you tried to do something like applying pressure through diplomacy; you gave full powers to your breasts. Apropos, did you ever have problems with your nipples? Burning, irritation?"

"Well . . ." She stopped again, with a resigned and tolerant smile. "You know what I think of you sometimes? Would you like me to tell you?"

Díaz Grey nodded. She put her hands on his shoulders and looked at him with superiority and tenderness.

"It's not worth the trouble, doc. We have to be friends. The fault is mine, if there is a fault. But there's no need for you to suffer; I can end your suffering whenever you wish, this very night, in the hotel."

Díaz Grey thought of slapping the face encircled by the scarf whose color the dusk was darkening; to slap her, only once, under the round black glasses directed at his eyes.

"Yes," he said at last, submissively. "Don't worry."

Appeased, she rapidly pressed his shoulders in a fraternal gesture. They started to walk again, now on the gravel path, toward the trot of a horse and the circular movement of the rider's arm, which approached and passed them.

"That must be the hotel," Díaz Grey said. "I've told you Lagos' versions—all false, or all but one. However, you haven't told me the truth about this chase and this fugitive. Lagos in his style waited until the train was moving to ask me to go with you 'to visit the area.' And he knew what it was you intended to search for, and you knew it, too. No, it's not that; I'm not asking anything, I have no curiosity. I prefer to remain outside of this. I only thought that with more information I could be of more use to you. Don't thank me; if you asked my advice or made confessions, for a moment I could have—or nurture, as Lagos would say—the illusion that you depend on me. Here's the hotel. Good luck."

The flight of stairs, also brick, climbed very gradually from the sandy terrain. Above the small wrought-iron tables in a garden with irregular clumps of grass, they saw a large sign on the roof, and the wooden veranda, already in shadows, where indolent forms were resting, where a little dog barked, where the island of cool air would be an invitation to close one's eyes and smell the end of the day.

"Good," she concluded. "I'm not hopeful or desperate, I'm not even nervous. Can you believe it?"

They began to climb the stairs, and Díaz Grey at each step felt the unbearable awareness of his weak, stooped body increase, dressed in drenched trousers and the brown shirt stained with circles of sweat; the awareness of the knapsack swaying back and forth against his kidneys, of the undeniable company of the woman who was, nevertheless, free of him as in her tight slacks she climbed up two steps ahead, independent and secure, mounting agilely and steadily toward her need, wanting to forcibly re-create the past, she herself now transformed into nothing more than the anticipated sensation of the meeting in a warm hotel room, already living the fictitious hostility of the first minutes, the phrases of explanation and reproach, the unsurpassable epilogue.

Díaz Grey was already halfway up the flight of stairs, beginning to understand the design of the hotel in the shape of an L, part wood and part brick; he saw the old building adjacent and its large door painted green, probably a storage room for luggage or vacationers' cars and bicycles; he could already distinguish the guarded curiosity in the faces of men and women drinking or simply resting in the coolness of the veranda, in the growing shadows, all silent, with tanned inexpressive faces turned toward the high brick staircase joining the hotel to the road. Elena had reached the level of the veranda and had paused here, straightening her body, when the doctor remembered with surprise an old dream, a fantasy so many times repeated, the only thing that linked him to the future. In the dream he saw himself seated on the decrepit wooden terrace of a hotel closer to the water than this one, damper and more decayed, with the blackness of mussels clinging to the half-rotted beams supporting it; seated, alone and without desires, almost horizontal, looking with the placid curiosity of well-being toward the high steps up which an unfamiliar couple were returning from the beach, not suspecting that the man and woman were bearing, along with the colored bags, parasol, and camera, the destiny of the lonely Díaz Grey, bemused drinker of cool refreshments, facing a marine dusk. In the dream it was the beginning of autumn.

But now he himself was climbing the stairs, perhaps helping to change the course of another's destiny, exposed to faces maintaining their indolent expressions as they watched him. With Elena he arrived at the veranda, and searched in vain for the unprepared Díaz Grey at some table. They sat down without speaking, she unloaded the knapsack from his back, and asked if he felt tired; smiling, she waited for the negative, removed the scarf from her head, and from the pocket of her slacks withdrew a hand holding a mirror and lipstick.

17

The Hair-do

I knew it by late afternoon, when I had finished my work at the agency and was chatting with Stein in the lavatory.

"I'm earning a lot of money now," Stein said, soaping his hands. "And I could earn much more, as much as I want, I'm sure, if I were my own boss. But even if one's made a happy mess of one's life, in the opinion of the most severe biographers, ascetics, teetotalers, and monogamous—"

"Not so happy," I replied, looking in the mirror, indifferent to Stein and his confession, anticipating in an impersonal way what was going to happen, guessing that Brausen-Arce would return to his desk in order to carry away the revolver. "Perhaps not so happy as appearances suggest. . . ." 'Today Gertrudis is sleeping in Temperley.'

"Go to hell," Stein said, laughing as he grabbed the paper towel. "It's that I can't, for now, accept the idea of having employees, of exploiting people. I was sincere all the time I lived in Montevideo, and I'm still sincere, although I try to forget my faith. The difference between the value of goods produced and the salary paid to workers for its production continues to be more than a phrase. It's much more comfortable to be just a cog in the machine, I can ease my conscience when old Macleod swindles me out of a commission. Then I tell the story to Mami, the only person on earth capable of believing me. 'You see how they exploit me,' I say to her. 'Do you realize how monstrous this social structure is?' "

Leaning back on the tiles of the lavatory wall, Stein laughed in a loud outburst.

'I'm going to feel like master of the world with the weight of the revolver against my leg; I'm going to force my way in, wait for the guy, and kill him. It's going to be very easy, disappointing; but at some point I'll realize I've done it, I'll feel the full meaning of what I've done. But for the moment, that's not my concern.'

"Shall we go?" Stein asked, touching my arm. "And Mami agrees with me, she's convinced that capitalist society is monstrously organized in order to take a percentage of my earnings; she becomes indignant and admires me, when she manages to understand the social question. That is to say, everybody conspires to inflict injustices on Mami's poor, good, incomparable Julio. That's how it is, I shouldn't laugh. When I think that, at bottom, money doesn't interest me. I'd be happier if—"

"One minute," I interrupted. "I forgot a paper I'll need tomorrow."

I went for the gun. Without turning on the light and with my eyes closed, I entered the office where my desk was; without fumbling, I reached the drawer and took from it, in addition, a piece of green glass, very dark, very sharp, that I had found the previous day near the harbor. Perhaps it was Arce, that sure, slow man, who advanced with a smile, hands at his sides, along the linoleum strip that wound between the desks and tables of the empty room, as he hummed in his mind the melody of the only foxtrot he knew.

Stein's head was lowered, his furious finger on the elevator bell. We greeted the elevator boy and I entered behind Stein.

"Furthermore," Stein continued, "one doesn't know how long it will last. Right now it's easy to put off the problem from one day to the next. But the day has to come when you say to hell with everything."

With the brim of my hat bent against the elevator mirror, I looked at his voracious jaw, his bland, shining eyes.

"Yes," I said automatically. "Money doesn't interest you. In the end you'd be much happier if you were back in Montevideo again dying of hunger, working for the Party, occasionally compensated by some Gertrudis of eighteen."

He looked at me with distrust, pushing his smile forward to win me, his lips protruding in an infantile pout.

"I'm sure I would be happier," he said, his voice also childish.

I stood motionless in front of La Queca's door, without listening, calculating the movements necessary to scratch an obscene phrase in the dark wood. I rang the bell and counted odd numbers in the interval; I entered, pushing aside the woman who opened the door, repelling her surprise, fright, hate. Pounding the floor with my heels, I advanced toward the place where I had stood the last time. I breathed the air, looked slowly at the shapes of the furniture, at the spaces that vaguely separated them, at the gradation of light on the walls. Then I turned toward the woman, cheerful, almost peaceful. It was La Queca.

"Here I am," I exclaimed. "Close the door."

She smiled at me without fear, latched the door, and bowed. Leaning against the door, she looked at me without question, her eyes steady and half-closed, calculating, her open mouth simulating surrender.

"Don't be afraid," I said. "You don't have to be afraid of me. I wanted to see you again."

She didn't answer; she had arranged her body—one leg bent, hands behind her back—in a position of repose, and she waited without anxiety, scarcely curious.

"You knew I'd be back," I said. "I only knew it tonight, a while ago."

I turned my head toward the wall separating her room from mine; I thought that the woman who had been humming in the distant eve of spring had nothing to do with this one, motionless, stuck to the door like a figure painted in pastels, an advertising poster image appropriate to the pornographic text I had thought up to write. She continued to wait, pondering the advantage of smiling again; she wore an old bathrobe, firmly closed from the neck down; the one foot visible showed her red toenails between the leather straps of the sandal. Indecision had remained on her face, without conflict, as if forever.

I smiled at her again, unable to ignore the joy and friendliness, but I didn't speak to her; I tossed my hat onto the bed and set about leafing rapidly through the movie and fashion magazines that lay in disorder on the table.

"You're crazy," La Queca said in an unfamiliar tone.

"You talk to me as if I were a stranger," I replied sadly.

She seemed to suffer as she tore herself away from the door; she went to take the hat off the bed and put it on the arm of the chair.

"You're nuts," she said, watching me.

"Such a curious story . . ." I interrupted myself with laughter, I looked around, searching for the presence or traces of "them." "Is your friend going to come? Ernesto? He's going to come and throw me out. He has a temper, you know. The three of us are going to have a good time tonight."

"Do you want a scene? Because if you think that . . ." Her voice struck against the suffocation and faded.

"In any case, things have to be done properly. We could begin with a little gin."

She looked at me, incapable of anger; later—sweetly—a joy, a limited and sufficient understanding, an easy kindness brightened her eyes, showed itself in the gesture of the open mouth.

"What a guy!" she said. "Crazy world . . ."

I sat down in the chair on which she was resting an arm; my hat fell to the floor; I felt the hardness of the revolver against my thigh and relaxed, smiling, with the woman's vertical silence at my back, the tiny sound of one of her fingernails scratching the fabric almost next to my ear.

"Why don't you get the gin? It was all a lie, I never knew Ricardo. You spoke of him that night in the restaurant, when I followed you. You wore a dark red dress."

"Maroon," she corrected with precision. "But I never wore my hair the way you said I did. I was thinking about it, and I haven't worn my hair that way since I was a little girl. You know, I feel like laughing and I can't? I never knew a guy like you. The other night wasn't my fault. I was dreaming up ways to find you and explain."

"Why don't you get the gin?" I asked, stretching my legs. "Isn't there any gin in the refrigerator?"

La Queca's perfume began to spread; the light from the lamp was weak and fell on the tip of one of my shoes, on the violet-colored triangle of the tablecloth that hung over the edge, on the empty cigarette pack on the floor. I heard the sound of the elevator doors; each time I remembered it, the breeze entered from the balcony and receded; the fingernail was scratching the fabric, secret and tenacious.

"I left my table and went to the bar to listen. You never came back to eat in that restaurant."

"I don't remember wearing my hair in braids wrapped around my head. Only as a young girl, in a photo."

Her thoughtful voice slightly altered the face that I imagined behind the chair.

"We can drink a little gin and later Ernesto may come," I said. "There are dreams like that, they repeat themselves; you know what's going to happen, but you can't change it."

Her finger stopped scratching; the curtain of coarse fabric rustled on the balcony like a branch in a bonfire.

"That one won't come here any more," she said. "Never again. How did you get in after they locked the door? I'm sure you waited until someone was coming in; sometimes I forget my key and have to wait forever. . . . I have gin in the kitchen."

"I didn't wait for anyone. The door was open; I knew it would be open."

Her laugh tumbled out, remote, suddenly smothered, identical now to the one I had heard from the other side of the wall.

"I almost believe you," she said. "I'll get the gin. Give me a light. Ernesto isn't going to come any more. We had a fight and I threw him out. You won't believe me, but I wondered how to find you to explain. I know I've got no excuse. Wait a minute."

She crossed the room with a surprisingly quick step, dragging an unfastened sandal; she bumped into the kitchen door. I was alone in the room again; the irresponsible air filled the space, rested on objects like slight scratches and stains from long ago; an unconquerable freedom, capricious, was rising from the dusty rug, descending from the shadowy ceiling. Next to the bathroom door the sagging shelf was still there with the secondhand books picked up in the room of a corpse; I was looking, smiling, at the reddish bindings that protected the novels' happy endings and the sad odor of time.

La Queca returned without haste, carrying a bottle of gin and glasses.

"Better pick up your hat," she said as she served. "Put it any place, but not on the bed. Though the floor is clean."

I saw her hair rearranged in thin braids encircling her head, and her belly jutting out, grazing the tablecloth.

"So you were lying about Ricardo. Don't think you fooled me, I didn't really pay much attention. I know a liar when I hear one."

Her laugh and the wind were trembling, they ended suddenly,

mingling. I thought of undressing, laughing in silence, naked; I loosened my tie and unfastened my collar.

"I'd really like to know where Ricardo is. But not for the reason you think."

She turned suddenly, steadying the glasses while she laughed.

"Cheers," she toasted, insistent, waiting for me. "Let's have another. These glasses are bigger."

I drank the second glass very slowly, looking at her stomach, somewhat swollen, which rose smoothly under the sash of the bathrobe cutting into her waist.

"No one's going to come," she insisted calmly. "Crazy world . . . You're thinking the worst of me. I want to explain."

'It isn't possible that she's pregnant and I didn't notice it before. Too late for an abortion if she is.' Like the smile and the conjecture on La Queca's face, like the wind in the cretonne curtain, rage and laziness were passing through my body, taking off, running away without leaving tracks. 'I want to shed my clothes like a winter skin.' Then, playing with the empty glass, she began pacing from the wall where she had leaned to watch him hit me, to the foot of the unmade bed.

"I can't figure out who I could have been with that night in the restaurant, talking about Ricardo," she said. "I don't know who the man was. Almost always at night I go to the restaurant with La Gorda. A friend. What can I say? I'm getting more fed up with men all the time. I'd like you to meet her. If it hadn't been for her once . . . I could always count on her. One night we'll go out together and you'll get to know her. I talk and talk, and you say nothing. All right, you blame me for what happened that night and you won't let me explain."

"I'm listening. Talk."

I got up to fill my glass and approached La Queca with the bottle. She had two rings on her hand, a small hand with big fingers, mannish, a cared-for hand with aged knuckles; her belly seemed smaller to me, insignificant, but hardly the symbol of a Gothic virgin. I waited for her to raise her glass and smile: "Cheers." The new hair-do attenuated the bestiality of her face; the thin lips were trying to be fuller, the eyelids were slipping down like thick, calloused membranes, like valves whose dry click could be imagined. We drank and I relaxed in the chair again, smiling at the memory of the young Gertrudis: 'I think about your hatred of lies, your rage; how you became exasperated and your voice failed you when you tried to salvage the meaning of life, digging down into the roots of a subject, persuading, breaking your fingernails to grub up and destroy like insects those ubiquitous lies that are always there, even though nobody mentions them.'

"Why won't you let me explain?" La Queca asked, seated on the bed.

I turned my head to look at her frenzy, her conviction that it was possible now, once and for all, to explain what could not be believed.

"It doesn't matter," I said to her. "You don't have to explain."

"What do you want to know? You see? You don't let me talk. You thought I liked what happened that night, that I was a free agent. You came here with a lie and I listened to you; you seemed like a different sort of man—half crazy, I thought at first. I thought that tonight too, when I was behind the chair, hearing you speak without knowing if you really meant what you said or if you were crazy. Believe me, that night it was great listening to you and it was your fault that I forgot the time. Ernesto swore he'd kill me if he caught me with another man. Laugh if you want, but I know him. I was in terror when I heard him arrive, and I couldn't tell him anything except what came to mind, because I was afraid of him, more than afraid, scared to death. That was all, I swear it on the Virgin Mary. Now you laugh at me for having been afraid of him. I threw him out and it's finished, he made life impossible. You don't believe me? Why not?"

Remote and apathetic at the end of a long day, as if inaugurating the hours of dawn, the elevator slammed its doors and was silent. Without compromise or future, the air was sliding over my body, making itself hollow to contain the belly that La Queca rested on the edge of the bed between her parted legs. The air brought me the memory of the miserable phrases, the simple and sordid male-female relations that the phrases had roughly modeled, clumsily accentuating the dependence, the mutual egoism, the petty sacrifice, a farewell.

She got up, went toward the table, and filled her glass without offering to fill mine.

"You don't believe me, you'll just go on thinking, of course. Men are all the same." She ended with a timid defiance.

"I just don't care," I said, straightening up in the chair. "You and me, that's all that matters."

"Darling," La Queca answered, after turning and looking at me, lengthening her lips and moistening them, "you've got to believe me."

"Better close the balcony."

I saw her look at me and hesitate, with the glass in the air; she swallowed her drink and put her hands behind her body, searching for things to say but finding nothing.

"Darling . . ." she repeated before moving; she was drawing away over the sound of the unfastened sandal, with her body contracted, not humbling itself, but made smaller like any woman being caressed. I heard the balcony door and the blinds close. I looked at her stomach and hips, the face that I had spied on one suffocating afternoon long ago, the same profile with its short curved nose, the thin line of the mouth.

"Yes," I said in a low voice as I got up.

She remained motionless near the closed balcony doors, bent over as if she were supporting a weight, her ear clinging to the noises of the night, to the story of the wrinkled, faded birds and branches in the design of the curtain fabric. I took off my tie and jacket, I returned to the table for a drink. As I undressed, I whistled a waltz I had heard her sing. She didn't seem to hear the noise of my shoes hitting the floor, she couldn't guess that I had hidden a revolver under the pillow. When I stood up again and looked at the bookshelf ('I remember, Gertrudis, you used to hate the endings of old novels; perhaps you just guessed that you'd end by being afraid'), La Queca began to straighten up her body as she turned; she gave me a small smile of despair and again her mouth fluttered without finding words. She moved forward immediately, her face telling me of her need in advance; she collided with the table and leaned on it, looking at me constantly, breathing heavily. She shifted her waist to avoid the blue rectangle of the tablecloth and continued walking toward me, her hands in the air as if she were groping carefully in the dark.

"Darling," she said hoarsely as she stumbled, her knee crushing the empty pack of cigarettes on the floor. Her head swayed blindly; she tried to smile, the thick fingers were fondling the braids twined around her head, and she began to kiss me.

18

A Separation

By now I had accepted the death of the film script, I mocked the possibility of getting money for writing it, certain that the vicissitudes I had planned coolly and precisely for Elena Sala, Díaz Grey, and the husband would never be realized. The four of us would never arrive at that conclusion of the plot that was awaiting us hidden in my desk drawer, sometimes near the revolver, sometimes next to the box of bullets, between greenish glass and useless screws.

But in spite of the failure, it wasn't possible for me to lose interest in Elena Sala and the doctor. A thousand times I would have paid any price to be able to abandon myself uninterruptedly to the fascination, the absorbed attention with which I followed their absurdities, their lies, the situations they senselessly repeated and modified; to be able to see them come and go, to circle an afternoon, a desire, a discouragement, time and again; to be able to change their confused adventures, to take pity on them, to stop loving them, to confirm, as I looked at their eyes and listened to them, that they were beginning to know they were getting nowhere with their efforts.

114

That afternoon Gertrudis came back to the apartment before me and usurped my corpselike pose on the bed. As I entered the room taking off my hat, I thought that if I were she, I would not have moved from bed all afternoon, I would have stayed there, horizontal and still, while I imagined myself hurrying down streets, visiting offices with windows opened to a spring more profuse than any I could find outdoors or observe from the balcony of my house. She smiled at me, half closed her eyes to greet me as if our pasts had never crossed, as if she had appeared before me suddenly, long and ample on the bed, emerging from depths whose origins were unknown to me.

"I would like to seduce you," she said when she stopped looking at me. She was studying her fingernails, holding them up to the light from the balcony. "It could happen. But I don't want to. I can't. Just now, this afternoon, before you arrived, I was remembering your naked body, your hands, your breathing. Then I wanted to. But not now when I see your face, when I remember the whole story, know it's been exactly so many hundreds of days that we've been together. And I know your face, the mixture of firmness and weakness in your chin; your eyes that confess nothing, your mouth that always seems eager but isn't. I know you're never going to give me anything. Not you or your face. So I can't seduce you."

"Yes, I understand that," I answered, seated near the wall, between her and the balcony, while I remembered that, according to Stein, old Macleod had decided to fire me. "But the importance seducing me may have for you . . . Without saying it's impossible, if we're speaking of true seduction . . ."

"No, no," she said stubbornly. "It's that I don't want to, I can't want to. Why impossible? Because we know each other so well and have slept together for five years? If my sister wanted to seduce you, I'm sure she'd do it. Why? Because Raquel is twenty, because she hasn't lived with you for five years? That interests me: to know if, for a man, there's a sense of mystery in all intimacy he doesn't know, or if it's enough to know the intimacy was given to others—and what woman after twenty doesn't give it, how could she live without giving it?—so that mystery vanishes. Putting aside the possibility that Raquel did seduce you. You never wanted to talk about it."

"She never did," I replied. The telephone was ringing next door with no one to answer it. 'Maybe she's not there, maybe she's in bed.'

"Seduction is impossible; now it's not important why, it can be for all those reasons. Fundamentally, it seems to me, it's because we can't play any more."

"We can't?" said Gertrudis, getting up. "I can play; I'm going to play."

In the weak light from the balcony, I saw the shine of her dress, the ornaments, her hands with rings.

"Were you just out?" I asked.

"No. I stayed in all day. I was thinking and I got dressed to wait for you. When I thought I'd like to seduce you. Juanicho, did I seduce you at any time?"

"Yes, entirely, body and soul."

"And can I do it again?"

"We can't play. When you did it, you weren't playing."

"One always begins by playing a little; suddenly we realize we're not playing. But I did it and I can do it again."

I thought she was going to walk toward the balcony, but the big dark body bent over and she sat on my legs. She kissed me gently, her mouth following my jaw line.

La Queca entered singing. Someone was walking around behind her on the other side of the wall.

"I don't understand that you don't understand it," Gertrudis continued. "I put on a new dress, silk. I guess it's all over—I admit it."

"Why should I be sad?" La Queca said, then laughed, separated from the back of my neck by the wall. The voice of the man was rising and falling, indifferent. On sitting down, one of them had made the bedsprings creak.

"Yes, Juanicho," Gertrudis murmured, nibbling my ear. "I even fixed my hair this way. It must have been five in the afternoon when I thought I wanted to seduce you; I thought I wouldn't go out tonight. I have a date, not entirely firm, with a friend, Dina—I've spoken to you about her—and some other people."

"Don't you worry," La Queca's voice was saying. "I'm as bad as they come, but I don't play around with religion. When I have a little money, I'll light a candle for you."

While Gertrudis kissed me again, sweetly, now on the chin and the neck, I imagined the patience of the man opposite La Queca as she began to undress herself.

"Like a little girl," Gertrudis went on. "When I remembered your face, I knew you were never going to give me anything, that I'd never be able to seduce you completely, and that I never have, not even back then in Montevideo. I could hold you fast, lock you in my fist, and what I want would always fly away."

"I don't live with my eye on the clock," La Queca said firmly. "But we have to go eat, and I'd like to see La Gorda tonight—it's been ages since I've seen her."

"It's not so," I said to Gertrudis. "I tell you it was complete, body and soul."

We got up and I looked at her face, pale in the approaching night and slightly higher than my own, while I smelled a weak perfume that did not remind me of anything specific.

"The mistake is wanting to talk this way, without spontaneity."

"It's not possible to talk," Gertrudis said. "It doesn't make sense any more."

"Yes, yes, yes . . ." La Queca began to repeat behind the wall, each syllable a little higher than the one before, the last one interrupted as it descended and died.

"It seems they're amusing themselves," Gertrudis said without smiling. "At least you're going to kiss my hand."

I kissed her hand, took her by the shoulders, and pushed her toward the bed.

"No," Gertrudis said. I smiled and pushed her again. "No," she repeated gravely without resisting; I looked at her and lowered my arms. From the wall I heard silence; I imagined that the syllables of affirmation were returning to the open mouth, and at last I could imagine La Queca under the weight of the stranger.

"I'm going to go out tonight," Gertrudis explained rapidly. "I have to see Dina. Now nothing matters to me, I don't want to lie to you. I know I can play."

"Play and forget it's a game?" I asked.

"Yes, I'm sure. It's sad, but it's marvelous."

She moved away from me to switch on the light; we looked at each other, pale and puzzled, and smiled at the same time.

I sat down near the wall again. 'Perhaps it's the truth and she, at least, may be happy again.' I saw her go to the kitchen, return, and set the table. Watching her, I was motionless, my mouth full of mints, until I heard the farewells, the door's slam, and La Queca's laugh into the telephone. Then I got up and imposed the obligation on myself to desire

Gertrudis and to suffer for her. She was leaning over the table, handling the plates and salad bowl, with a smile that expressed only tranquillity.

"I'm not going to ask questions," I said.

"Yes, it's better that way. We can sit down."

She paused a moment to look at me, without animosity, curious, free of me.

As we ate, I observed in Gertrudis' round face a calm, triumphant expression and a glow that flooded it like a vapor, like the resolve to guard and taste her victory in silence. That mask of happiness was already too mature; it was so perfectly adjusted to the lines of her face, to the color of her cheeks, to the shape of her eyes, that it could not have been born recently, that evening. It had been growing at my side daily, for one or two weeks, without my seeing it. I could hardly imagine it, the face screened in shadow only an hour ago, commenting on seduction in a tranquil, inadequate voice. But now it was actually here, slightly inclined over the plate on the other side of the table; and for days had been exhibited, but not quite apparent. Perhaps the mask had been born during the time she lived in Temperley, the child of a look, a phrase, a restless knee, and had been nourished during successive afternoons in coffee shops, suburban streets, and hotels. I looked pitifully, with desperate curiosity, at that face so irremediably strange in profile, which threatened to climb into the photograph on the wall and be joined to it, in spite of everything, by a sudden perishable resemblance; that dignified expression, anxious and placid, invulnerable to the threats of the world, that happiness that was trying to overflow in retribution.

There was life again, docile, in her hands and youthful legs, vibrant with the old, powerful energy that I had supposed extinguished forever. It wasn't possible for me to desire her, to feel jealous, to suffer for her. But I looked at her with an impersonal excitement, an obscure and diluted pride in the species; I saw her, tall and strong, shut the closet door and stand whistling in the drafty area near the balcony as she tied the apron to her waist. 'If I forgot her, I could desire her, make her stay and infect me with her silent happiness; press my body against hers and afterward leap out of bed to feel and look at myself naked, harmonious, shining like a young Greek god, from the youth transmitted through skin and mucus, overflowing from my thirdhand vigor.'

Sitting on the couch, I asked her from behind the newspaper if she was going out. She approached silently, walked directly to my side, carefully folding the apron before she put it away.

"Don't you want me to go out?" she asked.

"That's not the point," I said. "I want you to do whatever you wish."

"Whatever I wish?" she repeated.

I got up and walked to the balcony; there were neither lights nor voices in La Queca's apartment.

"I mean," I said, "whatever makes you happy."

"Oh that . . ." she began.

She was motionless for a moment, gazing at me, attentive and patient, as if I were reminding her of something. Then she looked for her coat and began to pull on her gloves, holding her hands away from her body, her head inclined to one side like in the old days in Montevideo. I said her name, trying to smile.

"And that takes care of everything," she said. She buried the gloved hands in her pockets and straightened up almost defiantly, attributing to me some unknown offense.

"It doesn't take care of anything," I said. "But since we can't live without acting . . ." I looked at her smiling, mocking me, but she didn't stop me. 'Anything is preferable to her knowing I pity her.' ". . . and as the greatness necessary fails us, we can put another objective in place of happiness. . . .

Now she was smiling without scorn, slightly bored. She seemed to make up her mind, offering me a confused apology.

"And you're happy," she said.

"I don't matter now," I answered cautiously. 'It would be funny if the pity were reversed.'

She glanced at me quickly, then moved her hands together to take off her gloves, and immediately regretted it. Sitting on the couch, she smoked with just a little smile showing on her face, the allusion to a trivial secret. Leaning on the table, afraid of ruining everything, I continued to look at her in silence.

"I don't want to speak of us or of the years, Juanicho. I suppose that each of us did what he could, gave the best he had."

Amazingly, she was talking to me with a visible fear of hurting me, she was beginning to practice the delicate administration of pity.

"You do understand, Juanicho, all it means, my going out now; not for tonight, but for later."

A door had been slammed on the other side of the building, not in La Queca's apartment. We were alone, playing our parts, squeezing everything out of it, trying to understand a simple human situation. She was smoking, determined to continue smiling while the cigarette lasted, carefully keeping her gloves from touching the hot tip and the ashes. 'You used to hate violent noises, loud voices. I can remember your girl's body only if I lay it face down, support it on my elbows, let your hair hang down, and direct your pensive face toward a distant, tiny light. I don't know if you remember everything that is destroyed, that row of books, the picture on the wall, the phrases of any idle conversation. I myself can only remember what is destroyed, and try to re-create it according to vague, imperious patterns.'

Gertrudis allowed the cigarette to fall and rubbed the fingers of the glove for a long time as she got up, her body swaying. 'And it's so difficult, above all because the infinity of things around us is even less meaningful, almost alien. I have to re-create the small destroyed world with only a stain on a new dress, a broken fingernail, feverish days, sudden drizzles, cold feet, the air from the coast, the waist your body used to have.'

"Then I'm going to Temperley," she said, as if chiding herself now, as if feeling somewhat sorry for herself.

I offered her money and went to look at her up close: I saw that she had not freed me from pity and responsibility, that this new Gertrudis was in reality more vulnerable than the previous one who had been submerged in a concrete sorrow that in the end was familiar and protected her.

The Gathering

The small vestibule of Miriam's house was hot and perfumed. 'It's not only because of the get-together,' I thought, looking at Julio's face; 'he didn't invite me just because the old cronies are going to be here, that ridiculous group. There's something else; perhaps old Macleod has decided, in view of the hardly encouraging prospects the new year presents . . .'

"I thought you weren't going to come," Julio said. "But, as always, Mami sustained my faith."

It was a somewhat different Julio: he spoke in a higher voice, needed to move around more, and wouldn't let me look him in the eye.

"Don't go in yet," Julio continued. "Let's talk about the weather, let's have a drink by ourselves. They're not all here, but you'll have enough with those who are. It would be terrible for you to go in and see them without a little alcohol in your brain." We were drinking over the bouquet of roses on the small table; I could almost see them wilting in the heat. "Are you ready? But first, you have to wipe the dust off your sandals, renounce your press agent sensibility. Patience is required here, and a desperate attention to all nuances."

The window behind Miriam, at the back of the room, had its shades drawn. Next to Miriam's chair a lamp was lit, a rosy globe. I preceded Julio through the heavy air, trying to smile at the three women lined up in the shadows to my left. Julio walked past me so that he arrived first in the area of soft light surrounding Mami; he removed the small knitting basket with wool and needles, and moved out of the way to offer me the sight of Mami adjusting her body, fondling her hair and the cameo on her chest, raising a hand to be greeted.

"I've wanted to see you here for such a long time!" Mami murmured, holding my hand. Her half-closed eyes showed a rapid glance of desperation and love more powerful than her will and natural reserve—hidden, nevertheless, from all others during the half minute it lasted. "But as I was saying to Julio, I understand that an old woman isn't very interesting. . . ."

"Don't take her literally," Julio said. "This is simply an intellectual preoccupation, and in a certain sense honors her. It's the product of comparing present days of peace with feats of heroic times. A dried-up subject from the point of view of statistics."

Good-natured, Miriam smiled without understanding. "That Julio . . ."

"Now that this part of the ceremony's over," Stein said, "can I introduce him to the girls?"

The three of them were fat, and they were making lively sounds, discreet and overlapping, while the feather on the hat of the one seated in the middle swayed back and forth.

"This is Brausen, the pure one, the stylist who refuses to write a column because he's a coward, through mere fear of future remorse. Chaste, ascetic, but inexhaustible in love," Stein said. "For the same reason, ergo . . ." He turned around as he pointed with his half-full glass. "That will be verified by whoever deserves it. This woman with the shy eyes . . ." She was the fattest; the damp powder on her face had a grayish color in the revealing clearness of twilight, and was beginning to crack and sag. "This is the beautiful Helena, immortal as the other one. Everybody complains about it. This"—the woman with the feathered hat nodded with a patient face, looking at Stein's mouth—"this is Lina, Lina Mauser, an automatic weapon. And don't I know it! For years now she's been automatically rejecting me, in spite of my generosity and my fantastic propositions. Perhaps in your case . . ."

From the moment her name was mentioned, the woman had fixed a wide smile under her long nose, and caressed my hand without banishing the distrust from her eyes.

"You know him well," Lina Mauser said. "Then you know he's crazy, you don't have to pay any attention to him."

The last one wore a white dress, her round arms were bare; she was smiling with her mouth open, and an infantile expression covered her face from the narrow forehead to the loose and trembling chin.

"Now we come, such is life, to Buggy," Stein began.

"Buggy . . . Pleased to meet you," she hastened to say.

"Buggy," Stein repeated. "Always impatient, like a virgin. She ends up botching all artistic purpose because of her mad haste. But perhaps, perhaps—I don't want to mislead you—with the years . . ."

"Julio, stop teasing," Mami intervened from the easy chair; she had recovered her work basket and was directing her myopic eyes in the general direction of the gathering.

"*Missa est,*" Julio said. "Let's have a drink. Perhaps later Mami will have the goodness . . . You're not too tired, dear?"

"Too tired for what?" Mami asked.

"To sing something in honor of my friend."

The three women interrupted Mami's modest laugh to approve and beg, alternating monosyllables.

"Oh come now!" Mami exclaimed, shrugging her shoulders, holding high her apologetic head, eyes wide open, blinking her humility. Taking up the knitting needles again, she changed the subject. "A drink for your friend and the girls, Julio. I'm not going to drink yet."

"Perhaps she'll want to sing later," said the woman with the fat arms.

"I'm so hot. . . ." the immortal Helena said slyly.

Seated on a stool on only half a buttock, I could see, under a large bunch of roses, a small piano of pale wood.

"We'll have to wait until they get drunk," Stein said, passing the glasses around. "Not for Mami, who doesn't need it, whose heart eternally . . ."

Mami had raised her head and was lavishing smiles and glances at random, intuiting, and thanking Stein for, his gallantries.

We drank again; I wondered if I was sweating a lot as I examined the blurred surface of the glass. The woman with the feather in her hat ended up talking in a whisper; nostalgia was suggested in her voice, a superstitious trembling, tears.

"Haven't you recognized that all ghost stories are the same, only one story," I began to say, feeling that everyone was looking at me, that Stein was moving away laughing, that it was impossible to stop myself. "One tells them as if each were different, as if the same thing hadn't been told ten times. Think of the importance we give to details: whether the ghost is a gentleman or a young lady, whether it starts as an old ghost or a young one, whether it has a look of anguish or one of superhuman happiness. . . ."

"Superhuman," Stein echoed.

"Not all the same, it seems to me," Lina Mauser responded, her face toward the floor, the feather toward me. "Besides, this happened in broad daylight."

"They only tell ghost stories," Stein whispered at my side. "But the other stories are much more interesting. More macabre, though they don't suspect it."

"It's true," said the immortal Helena. "She said they were just finishing lunch. And in the country, lunch is eaten early."

"It wasn't even noon," Lina Mauser agreed. "And I not only saw it. I touched its hand, its ring. I would know that ring anywhere!"

Stein said something, Mami raised a radiant face, ready to approve or just wait. Lina Mauser softly fluttered her head and the feather; she spoke with a tolerant smile.

"And you think he wasn't dead?" she went on. "I was a very young girl, but I still remember, as if it happened yesterday. In the early afternoon someone came from the ranch, one of the hands, to report that he had died during the night. My father said to me, 'I'd whip you for lying, except that it might be a warning.'"

"And why were you to blame?" Buggy asked, laughing. "Still, if that were me—I who always lie . . ."

"There she goes, playing innocent . . ." Mami said, moved, shaking her soft fingers in the air.

"My father was very righteous," Lina Mauser replied.

I saw an honest, almost austere country-girl expression flash under the make-up on her face, under the years of life in cabarets or as a prostitute. I said, "Besides, you were too young to invent such a thing."

"I can still see my godfather with a black handkerchief around his neck; he was tapping his mouth with the whip."

I rejoined Stein, drinking alone in the small gloomy vestibule next to the bathroom, its ocher walls covered with photographs, pictures of people whom I'm almost certain were dead, a charnel house of lovers and friends, chapters from years of promiscuity, follies, and tears, reduced now to discolored heads with hair parted down the center, profiles that held an expression of ardor and languor during the long minute of the pose, the invisible eye threatening to show itself and register, for the benefit of posterity, a rotund glance—all the possibilities of love and communication. A solitary mistaken moment, an illusion of complete understanding isolated on a unique occasion and perpetuated in sepia against the wall, sustained by the promise and memory of pleasure that the dedications implicitly contained. Stein, in shirt sleeves, had tapped his fingernails against his glass, then stretched out uncomfortably on the small wooden sofa in the vestibule, smiling under the exhausted testimonials of Mami's bygone happiness.

"So there's nothing to worry about," Stein insisted. "Old Macleod committed himself to keep you on for two months. And after the two months he'll give you a check, which is what we're discussing. He and New York, they're talking three thousand, and I talk six, clearly with the intention of making generous concessions. You'll have—well, at least you'll be able to manage for eight months. And in eight months . . . All this, without considering that within sixty days cancer may leave the old man forever speechless. Trying to justify himself in hell, muted. Which personally I don't like, since I've always got on very well with the old man."

"I'm not worried," I said. "In a certain way, I'm glad."

"In time we'll find something better. When I can help you and we can set up our own agency."

"Of course Gertrudis . . ." I hinted in order to strengthen his pity, so he would continue fighting for the six thousand pesos. Who knows if the phrase hadn't been dictated to me by the three faces smeared with sadness that were contemplating me from the wall.

"Yes," Stein said. "In your place I wouldn't tell her anything for now."

I withdrew, thoughtful over my glass; I saw Stein's sleepy, happy face suddenly diminished, attenuated, coinciding with the other faces on the wall, changed into another testament of Mami's existence, of her place on earth, in beds, sofas, automobiles, corners, parks.

"In the end, I'm not worried. Really," I said. "Thinking about Gertrudis is like a reflex, inevitable."

But I wasn't thinking of her; I was trying to appraise the possible threat that the news of my dismissal held for those secret needs: to continue being Arce in La Queca's apartment, and Díaz Grey in the city on the edge of the river. Otherwise perhaps it never would have occurred to me. In that moment—disagreeably imprisoned between the friendly, inquiring, evocative expression of Stein on the sofa under the array of dead faces of his comrades in a cause, and the gathered darkness at the far end of the narrow vestibule, where I thought I saw, sinking, the words of the women in the parlor—I understood that I had known for weeks that I, Juan María Brausen, and my life, were nothing but empty molds, mere representations of an old meaning maintained through indolence, of a being dragged along without faith among people, streets, and hours of the city; routine acts.

I had disappeared on the indeterminate day when my love for Gertrudis ended; I was subsisting on the double secret life of Arce and the country doctor. I was resurrected daily on entering La Queca's apartment with my hands in my trouser pockets, my head exaggerating a youthful arrogance, almost grotesque, inflated by the smile of pleasure with which I moved to the exact center of the room in order to slowly turn around and verify the permanence of furniture and objects, of the air in eternal present time, incapable of nourishing memory or offering points of support to remorse. I was reborn on breathing the room's changing odors, reborn when I threw myself on the bed to drink gin while listening to the comments and news that La Queca's voice uttered, and the now familiar laugh, interrupted as if it were collapsing against a yielding softness.

I was Brausen when we took advantage of a pause to look at ourselves and change that pause into a particular silence that ended with the sound of La Queca's breathing, with an affirmation and a dirty word. And I lived again when, far from the small daily deaths, the fatigue and the crowds in the streets, the interviews and the never-mastered professional cordiality, I felt a little fair hair grow, like down, on my head, as my eyes looked through glasses and the window of the doctor's office in Santa María, in order to allow my back to be caressed by the waves of an unknown past, to look at the square and the harbor, the sunlight or the rain.

The Invitation

La Gorda, not very fat but massive, stood upright, arms akimbo, laughing from the door of the kitchen.

"Will you lend her to me a minute?" she asked sweetly. "I forgot a bit of gossip."

"Take her, she's yours," I said to her.

"What more could I want!" La Gorda laughed. "And don't you dare come listen."

Neither the head, the voice, nor even the laugh of the woman suited the radiant depravity of her bold, guarded eyes.

La Queca went into the kitchen and I remained alone with the aroused consciousness of my body in trousers, bare-chested, lying on the bed. I could move my arm and reach the glass of gin. I could switch on the small table fan. I could remain still and smell the bed and my body, recently used, I could breathe the warm air.

Spring was already well advanced and there were hot, dry days; twilights were falling, compact, from excessively clear skies, spreading between buildings, filling the city, grazing the walls and streets, palpable as rain. I could breathe the air that had isolated and nourished sweaty vanished shadows, momentary furies, brief resolutions, oaths of penance and love, the breath of drunks. It was possible for me to reconstruct faces and figures, to listen to sentences that had sounded in the room, the oral traditions bequeathed by Shem to Arphaxad, by the latter to Salah, by Salah to Eber, by Eber to Peleg. It was easy to distinguish their low voices despite the deafening noise of the world; to capture with the ear: 'I suffer so much and you make it more difficult'; 'I'd kiss God's feet if he killed me when we're in bed'; 'Anyway, come what may, even if everything falls to pieces . . .'; 'Why are we so lucky?'; 'At times I could kill you, and at others I wish you'd tear me to pieces.' Phrases, voices wanting to shout from the dust of the carpet, the walls, the shadows under furniture, afraid of loud laughter and drafts, resolved to endure until their rebirth in the mouth of some other pathetic face, until being discovered and invented by new bedazzled eyes and mouths.

"They," the diminutive, unconventional, fleeting, elusive monsters who cornered or lured La Queca as soon as she was alone—"I know there's no one, I know they're not here or talking; but as soon as I'm alone at night, they begin to chatter and move around so fast they make me dizzy, without ever noticing or referring to me, but it's because of me that they're in the room; and if I listen to them, they don't go away or shut up, but they calm down"—"they" must have been left there together with the sweat, phobias, and lies of her visitors. Perhaps the presence of two or three men and women were needed to form a small monster, give it a voice, a characteristic way of moving about. Perhaps it was essential to add an attack of animal terror before death, repentance for some filthy thing forgotten in La Queca's past or that she had done outside this room. Maybe the life and consistency and murmur of each of "them," to be engendered, also needed a crisis of total despair, moments when La Queca was capable of understanding life as a pitiless joke planned for her personal humiliation.

In any case, each one of the moving, speaking dwarfs sprang from numerous parents. Lying down in the hot late afternoon, listening to the constant noise of water dripping in the kitchen sink, I recognized one by one the insecure well-dressed fat man, that cautious smoker of cheap Havanas who knew the right time to retire from business; I saw the good-looking one, shoes with spurs and thick soles, the latest style suit and matching tie. I saw the fifty-year-old with his gloves and pearl, the paltry pay, the romantic discourse murmured in darkness after making love. I saw the young boy of political convictions, almost always Jewish, closing in with impatience or with a method, a manifesto, a platform on which to rest his need for unloading himself in La Queca. I saw the man with the smile, graying temples, the single luxury of a silk shirt, the expert on life and women. I saw the one who smoked next to La Queca's quiet body, making decisive oaths to himself, trying to believe in his right to an act of justification before the end. I saw the methodical, the jovial, the resolute, the resigned, the incredulous, I saw the sad; I saw all those who will die without knowing themselves.

I knew that La Queca and La Gorda were kissing and caressing in the kitchen; they would leave spaces of long silences so that conventional sounds of innocent activity would reach me, an abundance of reality that they intended to create, but only clumsily and unimaginatively imitated. The water fell furiously in the sink, they opened and slammed the refrigerator door, the wicker curtain was raised and lowered against the window. Hardly curious, with the strange sensation of being half betrayed, during the pauses I guessed that their skirts and blouses were pulled up, that La Queca's small breasts were searching blindly and avidly for the large nipples of the other. 'But they never took so long,' I thought. As I looked at my bare feet hanging over the edge of the bed a foot and a half off the floor, stretched out and sweating, I again was aware of breathing the air of the room, the inefficacy of dead memories, their transformed faces. Submerged in this air, I could laugh without cause, free from pity, from duty, from any other names given to dependency.

"At nine," La Gorda breathed audibly—a mistake, for the sound of water was already stilled.

I took a drink and waited; the suggestion of a spacious warmed landscape was saddening against the windows, of a plain with short yellow grass flattened by a sudden dry wind. Broad and laughing, La Gorda was the first to appear, blocking and then revealing, as she advanced, La Queca's inexpressive reddened face.

"At last," I said, sure that that would please them, that they would not suspect I knew.

La Queca came closer to the bed and clasped her hands on her stomach while she looked at me, friendly, maternal.

"What a lazy guy!" she exclaimed. "What a man I have—he lives in bed!"

On her knees she began to kiss me on the neck, talking in turn toward my ear and toward the white linen back of La Gorda's dress, as La Gorda put on make-up. She almost sang as she spoke, almost buried what she was saying in the music of a childlike tune, while her breath was refreshing me and warming my skin.

"I'd better leave," La Gorda said. "When you two begin . . . I'll call Monday."

"Monday or Tuesday," La Queca replied, nibbling my ear now; she spoke without moving her teeth away, making her tongue and the words dance inside her mouth.

"So you're going to the movies . . ." La Gorda said, straightening her hat in front of the mirror.

"We don't know yet if we're going," La Queca replied.

"Everything I put on makes me look fatter," La Gorda said coyly. "Today I saw, mind you, three women fatter than me. I was shopping and the butcher tried to cheat me with the change. I forgot to tell you."

"We're going to eat out because we don't have food here." She let go of my ear, laughed, and went on kissing my jaw from one temple to the other.

"At this rate you'll never get to the movies," La Gorda said protectively. "It's seven o'clock already. I'm going to fly."

La Queca sat up in bed to kiss her friend's powdered cheeks. 'They're meeting at nine o'clock today or tomorrow. If it's today, she's still got two hours. What will she think up to get rid of me?' They kissed again in the doorway.

"Shave, and learn to say hello and good-by to guests!" La Gorda shouted to me.

"How that woman talks!" La Queca said on returning from the door; she unfastened her bathrobe and was fluttering it to cool her naked body. "She's a good friend, she really is. If we're going to the movies, I want to clean up here first. You could phone the place on the corner and have them send a bottle and cigarettes. We have wine for dinner, if we've got enough food. Gin, if you want it. But we're out of cigarettes. Do you have some in your jacket?"

She turned smiling, getting my smile in response; she began to fan her legs with the ends of the bathrobe. It was a bathrobe that had green and pink stripes, good to see in the morning, cheerful bands of chalk in the sunlight. She went to the kitchen and came out again; I tried to see her eyes, her mouth, the left knee that peeked out when she moved; I wanted her jealously. Behind the curtain the afternoon had died; in the upper part of the balcony an intense, fleeting blue was announcing the beginning of night. Without stopping her chatter, La Queca switched on the floor lamp, scratched her head to help her contemplate the disorder, then decided to spread a sheet of newspaper on the floor so she could empty the ash trays there.

"You figure when he says he likes pregnant women, he must be a degenerate. La Gorda was telling me about him. So you thought I was pregnant? It must have been my clothes or I was bloated. I'm never going to have a child. And since she lives in a room with a grown-up kid, La Gorda said, she invents stories for him, telling him the guy is the doctor. But at the age of six or seven, the kid must realize. . . ." She carried the pile of rubbish to the kitchen and returned with a rag to dust the furniture. "It's all right if you like men, it's the law of life. But there are things that . . . Imagine the little angel. Crazy world, this life. Don't laugh because I always say that. Imagine. Because being a mother is something, isn't it? Even if the fellow is the father of the child she's carrying—seven months, I think. But that's how it is. . . . Don't think I'm ever going to have a child. It's too much slavery. Did you phone the corner? I have to do everything because the gentleman can't be bothered."

Perhaps the date was for that night and La Gorda was already consulting clocks and beating the powder puff against her shiny nose. La Queca ordered over the telephone while sitting on the bed and nibbling me on the chest.

"Why do I like gin so much?" Her loose hair, a little dirty, had a bitter smell mingled with perfume. "I think I got used to it because of you and now it seems I can't live without it. What can I do? Since I know you, I'm crazier every day. The only thing I don't like is that you don't want to smoke. Sometimes I think how my life was before."

She tipped the boy who brought the bottle and the cigarettes, then began to pull out the few books from the shelf and clean them with the rag. I looked at the curves of the stripes around her buttocks, the small head from which her hair dangled; I pitied her servitude to falseness and deceit, I admired her capacity for playing god to each untranscendent, dirty moment of her life; I envied that gift which condemned her to create and direct each circumstance through mythical beings, fabulous memories, characters who would turn to dust before the threat of any glance.

She brought me the new bottle of gin, opened, and made a grimace, still holding a book and rag in her hands.

"I never meant to tell you," she said. "But were you ever in Montevideo? I've never been there. I have a friend—don't make anything of it—an old man who wants to take me to Montevideo to spend a few days. As friends, nothing more. He needs my company, he says. I always told him no because it doesn't interest me to go that way, and also because I didn't know what you would think. But he has a lot of money and he always goes there on business. So you could come, too, and we could spend some great days together. You won't have to worry about the expense. He's an old man who doesn't even touch me, you understand. Not right away but sometime, if you want to. He goes every two weeks, but if you don't go, I won't either."

I shrugged, smiling; she drank from my glass and slapped me on the chest.

"Sometimes I could kill you. We could go when you like, if you could arrange your work for a few days. I'll take care of the money. When it gets hotter—how does that strike you? I tell you, he's an old man and he respects me. . . . I can't stand the heat any more."

She locked herself in the bathroom and almost immediately I heard the sound of the shower. I thought of an elusive summer rain on a night of my adolescence or while lying beside Gertrudis; I thought of Gertrudis who had gone to live in Temperley, I went back to the distant days of confidence, of toughness and choice. 'You're alone again and separated, determined to forget that solitude can only serve us when it proves impossible to endure and we struggle and pray to end it. Here I am, in this bed where I can discover old mingled presences, cranky and perverse, and hear water falling on a hateful woman who is my lover and who, one of these days, will take me to Montevideo to return me—with the help of money from a respectable old man, a friend—to the years of my youth, to the friends who cherish it, to the corners where I was with you; to Raquel, perhaps. At this moment you will be performing the ritual of wretched love in the afternoon or on a Saturday night, or clearly seeing in your mother's face the only sure thing the future promises you. You will see yourself in the covetous nose, in the subdued, sighing mouth, in the phrases of petty cynicism and tolerance; you will foresee yourself living for a body that no longer serves you, for sudden saltless tears. Meanwhile, here we are. Life has not ended; there is the possibility of forgetting; we can recognize the smell of morning air, we can review the day, fall asleep ignoring the antecedents of each memory, and smile when we awaken just separated from the happiness of the absurd.'

21

The Wrong Figures

Díaz Grey passed the night in an armchair opposite the narrow hotel window that admitted a cold gray glare. For hours he looked at the shape on the bed, solid and without detail, trying to imagine what the woman's head was expressing, awake or asleep, as it lay against her hair and the pillow. It was already dawn when, furtive and in silence, he began to move around the building in the semidarkness, searching for anyone who might give him something to drink and trying at the same time to avoid the watchman who was smoking on the veranda, leaning on an elbow, facing the river in shadows. Later he threw himself across two wicker armchairs near the entrance to the dining room, feeling, as if he could verify it with his fingertips, that the cool breeze was once again becoming part of the irritation in his shrunken eyes and in the weariness stiffening his cheeks.

When he had finished bathing the night before—he had been snorting in the water, playing in it like a child, several times modeling his body with the soapy lather, dedicated to amusing himself, to not guessing what gestures and words already waited for him in the bedroom—when he had finished bathing and entered the room, vigorously rubbing his skull with the drenched towel, he saw, drawn with exactitude in the shadowy room, the same smile with which the woman had contemplated the wall partly hidden by the folding screen, as she sat for a quiet moment in the office armchair. She had not looked at him, perhaps could only distinguish him vaguely in his trousers and shirt, rubbing himself with the towel, hardly separated from the bathroom door and the sound of the dripping faucet. There it was, the immobile vague smile, letting him know that anything could happen and it wouldn't matter to her; that the same indifference—not even contemptuous, not even taking him into account—would always subsist in the depths of the woman, in her complacency, in her collaboration, whether he decided to embrace her or to stretch out and go to sleep. She didn't speak; a half hour later she had turned off the small bedside lamp. In the armchair at the foot of the bed, Díaz Grey thought about the impossibility of consciously and willfully entering into the woman's atmosphere, her world; not only because he would lack meaning there—and her womb was offering him an identical destiny—but also because his presence was condemned to be ephemeral and offensive.

Thus he preferred to leave the bedroom without hating her, sad—nothing more—at the necessity, at the madness and the enslavement that were just palpable, suddenly alive, and now all-powerful. Surrendering to his fatigue in the open air, the cold, and the tides of sleep that dragged him down at times only to yield him up immediately, he looked at the black patch of the little harbor, trying to distract himself by recalling the shapes and colors of small boats, intuiting my own existence, murmuring "my Brausen" with annoyance; he was choosing the dispassionate questions that would have to be put to me, were he to meet me one day. Perhaps he suspected that I saw him; but, needing to place me somewhere, he was mistaken in looking for me in the black patch of shadows under the gray sky. He slept, and woke up returning to his fixed idea, reviewing the infinite and improbable forms of abjectness he was willing to fulfill, if then he could implore, in exchange, that just once, for just one moment, she would passionately throw herself into his arms. He did not think about the woman when he was calling my name in vain. He slept, and was startled on awakening. He moved his legs and arms to warm himself, searched for a cigarette, and considered his obsession, the need that filled him, that had him in its grasp and provoked him—the theory of small suicides he was anxious to offer. He was not remembering Elena Sala's body; he measured his painful desire as something concrete, more real than the woman herself, born of her but separated, alien, like the odor of her body, the marks of her shoes in beach sand, the words people said when they spoke of her. Certainly the desire was child of the body, but the latter was no longer enough to satisfy it. She could not modify anything, allowing herself to be used or using him like a faceless man; nothing could be substituted for the impossible initiatives and conquest, the sensation of domination.

Awake and asleep in turn, he perceived at last the moment when things began emerging from the night. A man in white clothes crossed the landscape, picked up a watering hose, and was motionless, lost against the paleness of a whitewashed wall. 'The part of my obsession that I can distinguish, calling it love, isn't really mine; I don't recognize myself in it, it's only possible for me to represent it with alien, ordinary words. All my life I waited for this moment, without knowing it; her eyes were veiled but triumphant; in the depths of the madness a sweet peace is beginning to spread. The part of my obsession called hate is equally strange; it is as if I were searching to take revenge and annihilate her by sending her newspaper clippings in the mail with police reports or photographs of murdered women; to make her know, to prevent her from forgetting that the act I will never commit is already happening, and will go on happening in the world for a long time.' The darkness still engulfed even the small inlet, condensing the totality of beach and river, the shore that Díaz Grey had looked at the previous day; to the right, between the slanting trunks of lemon trees, a single motionless cow represented country life itself.

She came with her wet hair, her smile matching the last smile of the previous night, and lighted the first cigarette as she leaned against a tree. Díaz Grey called the waiter to order breakfast, exchanged greetings with people entering and leaving, drank the large cup of boiling hot coffee. The air became stifling and perfumed. With his body contracted, exaggerating his fatigue, Díaz Grey looked at the edge of the woman's slacks, the small rolled socks, the shoes with thick soles where dampness, sand, and grassblades made a confused bucolic emblem, a little grotesque, as if deliberately exhibited. The doctor stretched his limbs, breathed the air, felt he was suffocating. 'I no longer have a nose for the smell of spring,' he thought, yawning. 'I can only touch the memory of it, the useless sensation of former springs when, perhaps, I was smelling others already past, promising myself to know it more intimately in a future April.'

Elena's voice was a little husky from sleep and sounded slow, remote, and high above him.

"Things are complicated because the owner hasn't returned yet. He'll be back for lunch. And the heat is killing me; I didn't bring clothes to change. I'll have to work out something with the maid. I had this image of leaving at dawn on safari, going away from the coast through trees and mosquitoes. I saw myself arriving at Timbuctu before lunch."

"But you can't be sure. It's not certain that we have to leave the coast. He could be near the river, either downstream or upstream from here. Why haven't you asked how I spent the night?"

"It's enough to see your face. Rings under your eyes, feverish, much younger. How idiotic! I slept all night. Yes, it could be that he went upriver. But I saw myself going away from the coast, to the jungle and negroes. Perhaps I dreamed it. But didn't you sleep at all?"

"Some . . . enough. I wasn't sleepy, it was too hot in the bedroom. I went down toward the river and I walked in the marshes," he said, as if lying might serve some purpose, as if with the lie he might refuse her whatever she wanted.

Elena carefully flattened the cigarette under the sole of her shoe and kicked it toward the edge of the sand. Having seated herself on the railing, she suddenly began to laugh, hands between her knees, legs stiffened to help keep her balance.

"Don't you want to talk?" she asked, serious, still shaking her head.

"No."

"No, or not now?"

"No," Díaz Grey repeated. "It's useless. The saddest part is that you don't feel it's useless."

"All right. You're a man. That old inability of men to check an account when they know one of the figures is wrong . . ."

"I don't understand," he said; he was looking down at the narrow riverside road where someone would walk, coming toward him without knowing it. "And if I do understand, I'll say I always thought that a feminine peculiarity."

"No, no. A woman, no. You haven't even learned that, you poor boy. A woman will go on believing there's a figure that isn't actually there but that somehow has been taken into account, so the total is correct. Still, she'll go on checking every day, at every opportunity, and she'll always know that in appearance, on paper, she's mistaken. I knew you'd be offended if I caressed your head, so I never did it. Besides, a woman knows which figure is causing the trouble."

"Don't do it," he said, without moving.

"I'm not going to do it now; only the palm of my hand grazing your hair a couple of times. Let's go to the river; there are bathhouses to the right, farther away from the boats. We could change in the room. Look how everyone goes around almost naked."

"I'm going to bathe later, around noon."

He didn't want to look at her when she jumped to the ground and began to run. 'Only with her, as if all other women were denied me, as if to make love has meant, since forever, universally, to make love with Elena Sala. I would do anything in return and I wouldn't claim my reward because she can no longer give it to me. And I can't explain it to her either; because she's right, because it's true that my account is wrong, because perhaps through her I could stop suffering and feeling dirty, because I would have to remain empty, forced to admit that I'm dead. Also it's the old inability to act, the automatic postponement of events. Will power would be of no use to me because it's a lie that from persistent prayers grace will descend. It's also a lie, this putting off, till some indefinite future, a general inspection of spring, which I could do right now and save myself, simply by walking down to the spot where that cow was motionless at dawn. And if that is not enough—although it has to be enough—to continue walking through the afternoon and evening, and to also examine afternoon and evening. To go on moving like an animal or like Brausen in his orchard, in order to inspect and name each shade of green, each false transparency of the foliage, each tender branch, each perfume, each small round cloud, each reflection in the river. It's easy: move about looking and smelling, touching and murmuring, selfish to the point of purity, helping myself, forcing myself to exist, without idiotic intentions of communion; to touch and see in this cyclical, available beginning of the world, until I feel myself this one incomprehensible and insignificant manifestation of life, caprice engendered by caprice, the timid inventor of Brausen, manipulator of immortality during the imposed exercise of love and the personal circumstances of passion. To completely know myself just once and to immediately forget myself, to continue living exactly as before but with this mouth, now open with anxiety, closed.'

22

"La Vie
Est Brève"

Gertrudis only came in dreams now, her cheeks made round and firm by the girlish laugh, recovering the nervous shiver with which her head punctuated bursts of laughter.

La Queca's invitation that I go to Montevideo had parted me from Arce, made me irresponsible about what he thought or did, filled me with the temptation to watch him slowly descend into total cynicism, into an invincible depth of vileness from which he would have to rise if he were to act through me. The invitation also helped me rediscover, matured, my old desire—so many times insinuated and denied—to reencounter Gertrudis in Raquel, to be with my wife again, with the most important part of her, through the thin younger sister, so different but the same age that Gertrudis was then, more foolish and full of the father's Nordic blood but only now, this year, truly the sister of the other.

Sucking on his empty pipe, old Macleod had whispered to Stein that he would toss me out at the end of the month; he had settled on a check for five thousand. Meanwhile I was almost not working and scarcely existing; I was Arce at the regular drunken parties with La Queca, in the growing pleasure of beating her, amazed that it was easy and necessary to do it; I was Díaz Grey, writing or thinking about him, astonished by life's richness and my power. La Queca's generous old friend now came to visit her late Saturday afternoons; fed up with listening against the apartment wall to a silence that crippled my imagination because it offered everything, I threw myself into the street. I bought a cheap bouquet of flowers and decided, defying ridicule during the long subway ride, to go offer it to Mami and watch, slightly annoyed, the indolent kindness with which Stein, in his shirt sleeves, as head of the house ministered to the old cronies, those scarred, heroic phantoms.

I greeted Mami and the immortal girls; there was also a petite Jewish man, bald, with gold-rimmed glasses—perhaps Levoir, he of the rummy games and the sorties over the map of Paris. Stein was pacing up and down, laughing with the women, his shirt unbuttoned, a glass in hand, almost deliberately shattering the ambiance Mami skillfully and patiently established Saturday after Saturday. As if, I thought, the women, the colors of their dresses, and the tones of their voices, together with Mami herself and the small taciturn Jew, were reduced to flowers she had arranged in the parlor with the identical taste revealed by the stuffed flower vases on the table, the piano, and the floor.

I would become bored thinking about the consequences of losing my job, about La Queca, Arce, and the silent old man, about a plumper Raquel and a younger Gertrudis. Mami allowed them to half open a window onto the twilight sky; she allowed Stein to light a lamp near the piano, and finally she resigned herself, winking impartially toward me and the bald visitor, to put aside her knitting and approach the piano. Swaying heavily as she walked, she pulled her girdle down; paraded before us a condescending smile; patted Stein's cheek in passing and included me in a bantering look; then bent over to whisper into Lina Mauser's ear. Straightening up over peals of laughter, Mami bore toward the corner with the piano a new smile, equally sad but more brilliant, in which indulgence had been withdrawn from the others and was directed now to herself. She waited with her head inclined against the background of red and pink roses.

"The one about the guerrillas," shouted Buggy.

"Please . . ." Mami answered, without moving, almost without altering the face with which she waited for the result of her silent invocation.

Stein went to place himself behind the immortal Helena and put a hand on her head.

"Whatever Mami wants," he said. He lifted the woman's hair and wrapped it around his glass. "The first and the last are God's."

"Always about love," Buggy complained. "And old ones that my grandmother used to sing!"

"I used to sing them, I used to sing them," Mami repeated sweetly. When she lifted her head, her smile was different, more submissive and humble; she moved it toward me. "If you would be so kind . . ." she clucked to the little man wearing glasses.

"Please," he said smiling, and moved a hand to chase a fly away. "You don't need me, really."

"It's that we're such good friends," Stein recited, imitating Mami, "such pals that we can spend a day together insulting one another without bitterness."

"The one we heard you sing at Esther's house," the little Jewish man said. "Don't you all remember?" He began to hum a tune, swaying.

"Ah!" recalled Mami. She blinked and her chin wrinkled. " *'Une autre fois,'* yes. But that one, dear sir, is not a *chanson.* . . ."

"Even so, he's right," Stein said, bending to kiss the back of the immortal Helena's neck. "It's very pretty."

"Isn't it?" the little man asked hastily; smiling, but still slightly aloof.

"It *is* beautiful, Julio," Mami agreed, kind and stubborn. "But it's not a *chanson.*"

"That's right," exclaimed Buggy. "For her, if it's not sad, it's not *'chanson'!*"

"Not for me either, dear," Lina Mauser affirmed with a dissolute smile. "Those one never forgets are always sad."

"We're waiting," Stein said. "Ladies and gentlemen, we have reached the climax. . . ."

Mami interrupted him, waving her hand as if she were fluttering a fan. Her eyes were half closed, the old face in a trance; from the unbearable perfume of the flowers on the piano, from her heart buried in the past, the words she must sing were coming to her.

"Then *'Si petite,'*" Buggy suggested. "Suit yourself. It's sort of sad."

"Yes, it has tenderness," Mami said. "But you needn't try to guess. No one can know what I want to sing or why."

"This brute is biting me, Mami," the beautiful Helena shrieked.

Then Mami revived her condescending smile, a smile appropriate to a mature, concerned individual whose goodness of heart leads her to play with a group of children; she passed the smile around the room and stopped it, at last, on the little man who was performing *"Une autre fois"* in silence, tapping his knees with his fingertips. And suddenly, as if she had just listened to the introduction, she threw her head back gently, and seemed to submerge it, as she began to sing, into a subdued nostalgic atmosphere, into a faded personal world. And then, immersed there in her puffy baby face, so solitary and so far away from everyone, Mami nevertheless revived—for us, the six representatives of the present: the three men and three women listening, as the bedecked prostitutes twisted pensive dramatic expressions under the phrases of the old *chanson*—the girl who had emigrated from the victorious Paris of thirty years before to learn the language and soul of a new country through the melancholy clients of Rosario, San Fernando, Mataderos, and the cabarets; who had stumbled upon her man, Stein, and had brought him back to Europe in a short, bittersweet excursion into the past, so similar to this one that she performed now, standing next to the piano with her fixed smile, sad, fortunate, defiant, nurturing and pampering him through the repetition of *chansons* and ancient postures.

Perhaps we who were listening didn't know it, perhaps someone might perceive it intuitively with a feeling of pity and ridicule: during the five long minutes of the song, during the pauses that faithfully coincided with the imaginary orchestra, she, stripped of fat, years, and ravages, was singing with the aggressive confidence that young skin exudes, with the love for risk and surrender that is born of a body which has been enjoyed only by whom it chooses.

I was looking at her, touched and incredulous. With the elbow resting lightly on the lid of the piano, her left arm hung arched, following the shape of her hip, while she, languid but firm, making her voice flow out of the hollow that her dismayed head was excavating from the past, sang in pain and in joy;

> *Reviens, veux-tu*
> *Ton absence a brisé ma vie*
> *Aucune femme vois-tu*
> *N'a jamais pris ta place dans mon coeur, amie*
> *Reviens, veux-tu?*
> *Car ma souffrance est infinie*

Je veux retrouver tout mon bonheur perdu
Reviens, reviens, veux-tu?

Without returning to us, she was about to begin another song, and because her cheeks were red and damp, one of the women murmured, "But she's killing herself!" Then Stein left the immortal Helena and went to kiss Mami's neck voraciously; laughing, without releasing her, he began to speak.

"You all know the game—the girls, I mean. Of course it's really better to play it at night, and drunk; and of course today these respectable gentlemen are here. It's a game that uses all the qualities that make a man proud. And not only the five senses; manual dexterity, imagination, our powers of logic and deduction come into play. Easy rules, though strict. An incomparable game, if you can count on the good faith of the players. An object known to everyone is chosen, preferably small for reasons obvious to those who have participated in such matches. Someone is designated *it*, he leaves the room, the object is hidden, and the one who is *it* returns. He has to search; he knows the first letter of the place where the object is hidden. He can look for it any place without exception, movable or immovable, animate or not, the name of which—any of its names—begins with the letter he's been told, the first initial of the great secret."

But they didn't want to; they were looking at Mami, who was still motionless, smiling with damp eyes, and the little Jewish man shook his head negatively. Stein kissed Mami on the neck again.

"They don't want to play," he complained. "Mami dear, are you crying?"

"No, it's nothing," she murmured, pushing him away sweetly. "I'm being foolish, Julio." Smiling, she bent over toward the little man. "You must pardon . . ."

"Please, madame!"

"I bet," Stein said, "he's thinking how many languages he can use to play the game."

The little man began to laugh in his chair, his hands under his legs, moving his body from side to side. Mami sighed in the first silence and pursed her small round mouth.

"If you please, sir . . ."

He went to the piano and uncovered the keyboard. Seated on the stool, the little man squeezed his fingers and made them crack; he struck two keys with his ring fingers.

"Whenever you like, madame."

"Is he Levoir?" I asked Stein.

"No," he whispered. "Marvelous. Each day I love her more. What spontaneity and delicious rapture!"

"Anything," Mami said. "Wait. Just start to play anything, ramble a bit. . . . When I feel I have the right thing to sing . . ."

"Impromptu," Stein whispered to me. "And yesterday they were here rehearsing all night. That's what I call a woman! The last one on earth."

The little Jewish man was intermingling melodies, moving his hands in front of his chest. He guessed that there, above him, between his shoulder and the large flower vase, Mami's head was beginning to bend back; then he began to play with remarkable clarity, smoothly, almost inaudibly.

> *La vie est brève*
> *Un peu d'amour*
> *Un peu de rêve*
> *Et puis bonjour.*
> *La vie est brève*
> *Un peu d'espoir*
> *Un peu de rêve*
> *Et puis bonsoir*

sang Mami.

The Macleods

Cordial, still flushed, old Macleod welcomed me with an elbow on the bar in the café where he had chosen to say good-by to me. 'To endure him with patience, with grace, the irresistible congeniality that attracts friends and contracts; interesting myself in his problems, making optimistic comments about them, without ever being indiscreet. I can't guess by his eyes if he knows he's going to die, or if he believes the story of nicotine irritation.'

"A little whisky?" asked the old man, smiling. "Or would you dare join me in a personal concoction? A very famous concoction."

He no longer had a voice, or had only the small voice of a child aged in debauchery, a whisper that never attained confidentiality. The bartender was waiting with his thumb raised on the cocktail shaker. I said yes; the old man flattened one lip against the other, satisfied, raised his empty pipe to sniff the bowl. He put a hand on my shoulder.

"It wasn't pleasant for me to speak to you in the office. Nor here either, for that matter. You understand that it's difficult for me. But here . . ." He pointed to the bar, to a couple of chilled glasses, the base of each wrapped in a silky napkin. "It's become necessary. As I said to

Stein, Brausen is different. *You are my friend,*" he said in English. "An old friend whom I'd like to have known better, to have talked to more. But you know, that's my life. I'm tied to my accounts like . . ." He looked around, raised a hand to help himself, and failed; he let his hand fall and offered me the drink. "Tied to the accounts—an old horse pulling a cart."

He kept on wagging his head from side to side, the empty pipe between his teeth. I could not discover death in the small, bright, tired eyes, in the varicose veins in his cheeks, in the loose skin between his jaw and starched collar; only years of alcohol and folly. I wanted to help him out, and thought, while smiling at him, 'Bound like Prometheus to his rock, like a dog to a bitch, like our immortal souls to divinity.'

"Cheers, pal," he said. "Tell me if you like it."

'I don't understand a thing about it, I only learned how to drink gin a few months ago. It could be a Manhattan with any old thing thrown in; in any case, it must be cheaper for him than whisky.' But I had already taken two swallows from the glass of eternal friendship; the past and the long undeclared war remained buried. Docilely I clicked my tongue without achieving the perfect dry sound that the old man let me hear as an example; I looked straight ahead, absorbed in thought, and quite effortlessly I imitated Macleod's jubilant expression.

"Very good," I said, marveling, "excellent. You must give me the recipe." 'Maybe age and hierarchy impose the duty on me to slap him on the back, nudge him in the ribs, and pull his hat over his eyes.' He listened to my opinion modestly, winked at the bartender, and devoted a moment to his face in the mirror. 'What does he see when he looks at that old man of sixty, condemned to die soon, with the patches of gray hair under his hat, reddened skin, and tired blue eyes, sucking air through his pipe?'

"Excellent," I insisted, servile, putting the empty glass down on the bar. "Perhaps it's too strong—for me, who's just tried it." 'To show and exaggerate my fears for life's ambushes under the protection of the robust Macleod, to force the consolations of the wise old man, our leader, protector, pillar of strength.'

"No, no." He abandoned the mirror in order to pat me. "It's not very strong. It's just strong enough. My famous masterpiece, right?" He winked at the bartender again, confidently demanding his approval.

"It's very good," the bartender said, mixing again. "A lot of people ask for it. And not only the gentleman's friends; now there are customers who ask for 'a Macleod.' Excuse me."

"Take care, be very careful," the old man said. "Top secret. Nobody gets the recipe. They can drink it, if they pay; but no one gets the recipe."

"Right!" said the bartender. "That tire salesman the other night insisted the secret was in the bitters." He joined the old man's sudden murky laugh.

"Bitters!" Macleod repeated. "Psh . . . Strange idea. Bitters!"

He turned to look at me and we both marveled at this, shaking our heads.

"Bitters!" I murmured, beginning the second drink.

The old man was musing, turned toward the mirror; he pressed his lips together, the small eyes narrow and attentive. 'Perhaps he knows, perhaps he's asking himself what part of his face will show the first of the final ravages. There he is, buried in the mirror, surrounded by the colored rectangles of labels, like a mosaic, trying to guess how this mistress he keeps—almost conjugal—will like him tonight, how he'll look when he's eaten by worms.'

It was seven o'clock and the bar was starting to fill up with noisy, confident Macleods, slightly contemptuous. They were arranging themselves in a restless line against the bar, pressing on the gilded footrail, touching shoulders and hips, offering quick apologies, exaggerating intimacy with the bartender, chewing salted peanuts, crunching the celery that invigorates, helps, and preserves. Talking business, politics, families, women, as sure of immortality as of the moment they occupied in time. The heat was increasing, agitated by the noise of voices, orders, dice striking against tables. Slow and apparently wandering about under the neon light, a few women were going from their beers to the ladies' room, from their sweet fruit drinks to the telephone.

Macleod tore himself away from the mirror, greeted someone with his hand and a smile, and drew his head closer to mine; there were drops glistening on his lip, and a slight apprehension in his blue gaze. 'Now he's going to begin talking; it's all been said already, but he has to talk. Man to man, heart to heart. Why not chat about slogans and publicity campaigns, since we have to pass the time some way? No one could, for example, say no to an intelligent campaign regarding the social, hygienic, and patriotic duty of opening the scrotum each spring with the famous Unforgettable Scalpel adopted worldwide, preferred by the United States Army, by old associates of the Mayo Clinic. When lilacs bloom. This is the moment. Don't wait for summer. Cut your scrotum cleanly and allow the spring breeze . . .'

"But I've known it for a long time. . . ." the old man was saying; his smile was now destined to make him forgive himself, to forgive his dying body and the mistakes life had forced on him. "I don't want to kid myself. So many others, eh, would never admit it. Through vanity. I know that I'm not . . . I mean to say that I'm not my own man. Not totally free. I'm whatever New York decides. I can fight, yes, and you must know from Stein that I'm not afraid to. I was never afraid. Ask Stein: I fought for you for more than two months. Until the ultimatum. We have to economize, economize. They don't understand the explanations, the truth, the right thing to do. They don't take it into account. Nine people sit around a table, five minutes for Buenos Aires, for that fellow Macleod. Economize. And if I don't? Out goes this Macleod and in comes another. Eh? That's how it goes. Did Stein give you the check? He has it; as high as I could go. Another? Good—me neither. I have something to do tonight. Well, I'm not going to deny it: basically, I like this work. Buenos Aires, the B.A. branch, was dead. I made it what it is. In New York they should compare the accounts of three, four years ago with the present ones. But I'm not complaining, I'm explaining how things are. A man will accomplish nothing if he can't forget himself. I have no complaints against you; we wouldn't be here if I did. But I give you this advice: if you can't forget Brausen and devote yourself completely to business . . . It's the only way to work, to get things done. What do you say, let's have a last Macleod. We didn't have more than eight yet. Listen to this, it's very good: Stein knows who said it." While waiting for the drink, he made a short dive into the mirror. 'Something very good. Stein knows who said it. He's not going to pay me the difference between the check I was hoping for and the one he signed, and he'll cite some infallible formula of Plato Carnegie, Socrates Rockefeller, Aristotle Ford, Kant Morgan, Schopenhauer Vanderbilt.' The old man emerged, refreshed, smiling, overflowing confidence. "That's how it is. For years, you know, art was a by-product of religion."

"Art?" I asked with my glass in the air.

"Art. Music, painting, books. In the Middle Ages everything was in the service of the Church." He enjoyed my admiration, shaking his head to confirm what he had said. "That's how it was. Now, not yet, but we're going in that direction, art in the service of advertising. Music for the radio; drawings, paintings for advertisements, posters; literature for slogans, brochures. Eh? In Paris and New York advertising's already been done with first-class poetry. So it's not only a matter of getting accounts and making money. There are many other things—it's a complicated business."

Resplendent and serious, old Macleod was affirming his words with forceful nods that I repeated less vehemently. Friendly, he again put a hand on my shoulder, anticipating and preventing my exaggerated attempt to pay the bill, then led me toward the door, sighing now, lamenting about New York's incomprehension, the shortage of paper for magazines, what the future had in store for men in publicity, those who weren't lucky enough to find themselves free and with a good check in their pocket, boy.

He hailed a taxi on the corner and I saw the last wave of his hand, I saw him move away in the beginning of night, toward the poetic, musical, plastic world of tomorrow, toward our common destiny of more automobiles, more toothpaste, more laxatives, more paper towels, more refrigerators, more clocks, more radios; toward the pale silent frenzy of putrefaction.

The Trip

On opening the door, I saw the note fall; I whistled, La Queca wasn't there. The hot air had been locked in all afternoon behind the lowered shades. I put the lights on, took off my clothes, and stretched out on the bed with the note. Scarcely one line: "I'll call you or come at nine. Ernesto." I was smiling, as if that were the best possible news, as if I had been waiting a long time with the absolute certainty that I would meet him again, as if my relations with La Queca, the same necessity that bound me to her and to the air of her room, were no more than pretexts, useful pastimes while I waited patiently for the moment when I would look again at his white impassive face without a forehead, as it advanced toward me. I discovered the hate and the incomparable peace of surrendering myself to it.

I took the gun out of my trousers, I played at examining the load of bullets in the drum and the light that was visible in the barrel. I put the gun under the pillow, brought the gin in from the kitchen, and lay down again. It would be nine o'clock in an hour's time; I understood that everything depended on La Queca, that I was forbidden to force events, that it was necessary to wait like at a gambling table—that number yes, that number no. I got up to leave the note near the door and kept my eyes fixed on the white rectangle outlined on the floor—drinking and evoking phantoms that had preceded me in that room, demanding equitable and unprejudiced treatment from future ghosts charged with inventing my history—until I heard her arrive and listened to the key rattling in the door. With my eyes half closed I saw her stop and look at me, pick up the note, and come nearer to greet me and smile.

"Someone knocked," I said. "He got bored and went away."

"What do I care! Were you sleeping? I wasn't expecting you so early. I was with La Gorda and time flew. I'm crazy with the heat. Why do you have everything so closed up? No wonder you're so sleepy, if you drank half a bottle. I'm going to wash up."

She opened the balcony and noisily breathed the air as I wasted an infinitesimal part of my hatred on her stupidity, on the clumsy steps of her enormous high heels, on the dry, short, quick sounds they made when she walked. I was afraid to stop wanting her, and turned over on the bed in order to summon the image of La Queca naked, subdued, her small mouth open and thickened, without seeing her back, her height, her wash-and-wear dress.

"I'm dying of the heat," she repeated. "Excuse me a minute. I can't imagine who knocked."

She went to bathe, she wanted the privacy of the bathroom to read the note. Alone, I thought that Ernesto's face had been haunting me from the beginning, since the March night when I wiped off the filth from the cuspidor as I sat in the corridor and guessed fleetingly that the newly arrived Arce epitomized the sense of life.

La Queca came out from the bathroom naked, with a towel wrapped around her head, bringing the comforting odor of soap to me on the bed.

"I don't know," she said. "I've got the idea something's going to happen tonight. Do you feel it, too?"

"Yes. I feel it."

"What's going to happen? Good or bad?" She turned off the ceiling light; with her open hands she was flattening the drops of water against the skin of her stomach. She kneeled beside the bed and began to kiss me; subterranean, her voice insisted, "Is something good or bad going to happen?"

"I don't know—I can't. But something."

"It's strange," La Queca said. "You and me, the same idea. Crazy world . . ."

On the clock I measured the distance separating the minute hand from nine, and I evoked memories of the first sensation—still elusive, hazy, remote—of La Queca's hard, small body, the round legs and arms, the curve of her hips. I measured my diminishing fury and increasing need; I was amazed on considering the thousand features and new meanings with which intimacy and habit had almost covered the first naked La Queca. I thought something important was going to happen, that the two false omens we had formulated were capable of provoking destiny.

"How are you getting on with 'them'?" I asked.

"Don't talk about it. They come; when you're not here, they come. You have to understand that it can't be explained. They're not people. I know it's a lie, that there's no one. But if you could just see them, all tiny, moving their mouths when they speak and going from one side of the room to the other, and having conversations that I know I really heard sometime, though I can't remember when. And everything gets mixed together, things from when I was a little girl and things from now. They make jokes, too, saying things I never said, that I only thought of saying. Give me the gin."

Her loose damp hair was hiding her face and the hand holding the drink; I began to feel alone, abandoned by all reason, dreading the beginning of hate and the fundamental contempt that bound me to her, to her voracity and vileness, and that might end at any moment that very night. I invoked the peace and joy of being alive that had always descended upon me from the ceiling of that room. I calculated the movements necessary to rest on top of La Queca; as I was caressing her, I heard her murmur and go on repeating the tremulous habitual laugh that would end in sobs without tears. She sprang from the bed; standing next to the table, she shook her head no, fiercely, silently.

"Yes?" I asked; I knew immediately she was lying.

"It's horrible, horrible . . ."

I saw her, writhing, small, imbecilic to the marrow, her head in her hands. I filled my glass and was about to drink when the telephone rang; she let her arms fall and stopped with a foot in the air, looking at the clock; it was two minutes after nine. With glass in hand, I brushed against the heat of her body as I passed and went to lift the receiver. It was the same voice, the same amorphous face, the round white patch.

"No," I said. "Not tonight. She isn't here for you. She isn't here. . . ." I said again, turning to look at La Queca who was advancing, open-mouthed. "She isn't going to be here, even if you come."

I put the phone down and drank a few swallows, looking at the little doily, the pictures on the walls, the familiar peeling furniture, the greenish stain on the wall and ceiling, known by heart.

"Some man," I said. "Maybe Ernesto. Remember Ernesto?"

Her face began to tremble; it was filling with unfamiliar wrinkles as the rage mounted.

"Who was it?" she asked to gain time.

"No one, someone, he didn't say."

"Why did you say I wasn't here?"

I shrugged, breathed deeply until I felt happy. I thought absent-mindedly that perhaps I desired her because she was smaller than Gertrudis, smaller than me. It pleased me to sigh and smile, to look down at her from my height.

"Why did you say I wasn't here?"

But that wasn't really what she wanted to say; her right foot was forward, her toes barely touching the floor. Leaning against the table, her chest inclined back slightly, she seemed ready to leap or to scream.

"I told you I had a feeling—very curious, not good or bad," I explained to her slowly. The air became lighter and more casual; the objects on the table suggested movement; a dirty pincushion bristled on the arm of the chair. "Something was going to happen, I told you. It occurred to me that Ernesto would call you at nine. If he has a key, maybe he'll come. Do you think he's going to come?" She couldn't talk yet; she was breathing, making a hissing sound with her half-opened mouth, looking at me and lowering her head. When she raised her eyes toward me, she seemed desperate to hear or remember something: her dry lips, her amazed eyebrows, a soft tremor near her temple. Each piece of wood, each bit of metal in the room was vibrating, contracting and expanding, gathering from the air its small tribute of irresponsibility; a lazy wind, a slow whirlpool was rising from my bare feet and tightening around me. Excited, shaking from happiness, I stammered, "It'll be good if he dares to come."

Then she relaxed her head and body, went into the bathroom again, and came back wrapped in the bathrobe with the wide colored stripes. I saw her tremble against the wall and fumble tying the sash.

"Who are you to say I'm not here?" she began, and suddenly stopped to catch her breath. She hadn't said this to me or to anyone, she was only trying to get worked up, to lose consciousness, to throw herself aside in order to make room for the insults. "Bastard, you bastard!" she shouted from her guts.

I walked back and forth, showing one flank and then the other to the thin silhouette, to the vertical greens and pinks joined to the wall, receiving the coarse insults on my back as I moved closer to the door and balcony, and presenting my chest to them when I turned. I understood the air of the room as one understands a friend; I was the prodigal friend of this air and was returning to it after a lifelong absence, I persisted in celebrating the return, in enumerating all the times when, in the past, I smelled it and refused to breathe it. I heard her choke and interrupt herself, mix her furious weeping with gasps, insults with definitive regrets. Tireless and prophetic, assisted by unexpected revelations, insulting Arce, life, and herself, she was analyzing men and women, establishing surprising parallels, reviewing old opinions on love and sacrifice. Denying and affirming the usefulness of experience, she eulogized other ways of life while disregarding distinctions between good and evil; over and over she ended her sentences with her nihilistic "crazy world." I stopped beside the table and filled my glass.

"And to think I'd sacrifice it all for a bastard who's a born sucker! I'm not supposed to have friends. As if he was enough . . ." She was saying it for Arce's sake; I drank next to the balcony, watching beside the curtain for the darkening night, the rectangular fragment of night where a memory was distinguishable in the distance, a hope without anxieties. Behind me she used her weeping to rest, to blow her nose.

'And this isn't the end, I have to keep that in mind; when she's worn out, we'll make up. Ernesto isn't going to come, I never really believed he would.' I saw some stars and some street lights; for a few minutes there was a sound like rain and wind on the balcony. La Queca broke a glass or an ash tray on the floor; I heard her laugh and walk toward the bed.

"Sucker," she said, repeating it, making me turn my head; she smiled with the bottle of gin held between her breasts. "Sucker! What a sucker . . . You're a born sucker!"

She was panting, weak and self-satisfied; she stopped laughing and talking to drink from the bottle. I began to get dressed, whistling *"La*

Vie est brève," remembering the grotesque, pious face that Mami had flung back to overtake her past and rest on it. La Queca was talking, laughing, smacking her lips as she parted them from the bottle.

"Now your little shirt, sucker. Don't forget your little tie, sucker. Fix your lapel, sucker. Don't you want to know how many times I made a sucker out of you? And now I'm going to Montevideo. I never made a sucker out of you in Uruguay. I'll call him and we'll go tomorrow."

When I reached the door, I heard her run and fall, then sob in starts, as if between dreams.

"Tomorrow, first thing," she said. She had a cheek against the carpet, her legs bare, one hand raised to keep the bottle from spilling; she was crying and making little bubbles with her spit. The air began to fan out from her body shrunken on the floor. I approached slowly, my hat on my head, the revolver weighing down my trousers; I sat on the rug to look at her flushed face, the steady trembling of her mouth.

"I'm going away with him tomorrow. I'm going to die now. Damn the day I met you! I'm going to vomit," she whispered, rubbing her lips against an arm.

I took the bottle away and lifted her up. I shoved her until she was stretched out on the bed, face up. I knew my hatred was dead, that only contempt remained in the world, that Arce and I could kill her, that everything had been arranged so I would kill her; I examined my elation, the vigor that almost made me smile as I bent over the muttering, inhuman face making grimaces on the sheet. 'I can kill her, I'm going to kill her.' It was the same sensation of peace that I had felt entering Gertrudis' body when I loved her; the same fullness, the same swollen current that appeased every question.

I soaked a sponge in the bathroom and squeezed it over La Queca's face, in her eyes and mouth, until I had her awake, leaning back on the wall, swaying. I waited in silence, I never stopped looking at her as I brought a knee closer to support her; until she murmured, until she could remember the word and insulted me again. Then, my anger gradually building up, I began to hit her face, first with open hands, then with fists, until I tore from her an astonishing infantile cry and two small threads of blood, always holding her fast with my knee so she would not tumble down.

On leaving, I scorned the precaution of going down in the elevator and furtively creeping up the stairs. I drank a glass of water and threw myself onto the bed, resolved to think only about that which could be thought, certain I had to kill her, knowing it was not appropriate to decide when. I spent the night examining the possibilities that someone might be able to identify me with Arce; I recalled each moment, starting from the afternoon of Santa Rosa Day, when La Queca had come to live next door. At dawn I slept, tranquilized. On the following day I went to visit her and brought her a bottle of perfume; a wound remained on her lips and enough dignity to postpone a reconciliation, to utter a short series of sentences that went on about her merits, the injustice and meanness of life.

That weekend we went to Montevideo, she and her friend by plane, I by boat; we met there in the morning near the harbor, and she made me put my head on her chest to prove that she was using the perfume I had given her. Intimidated by the waiters and the clientele of the small café, I smelled the perfume on La Queca's dress and temples, unsuspecting that from a certain moment on I would have to remember it forever. It was a tranquil aroma that had no relationship to her and did not remind me of any flower.

Part Two

1

The Proprietor

Elena Sala and the doctor lunched under an arbor with the owner of the hotel, a heavy-set man of about fifty with a conceited light in his eyes and in the shine of his cheeks and chin, ruddy and sunburned.

"And I'm so concerned," the woman explained, "because I know he was desperate."

The proprietor did not know where the fugitive was; he was unable to refer to him without insinuating a smile, without frowning, amused and at a loss to understand. Since the pickled fish and the first glass of wine, Díaz Grey had discovered that the owner of the hotel was old Macleod: a Macleod without the recent shave, stripped of the starched collar and expensive clothes, stronger and less intelligent, perhaps more ingenuous. Relaxed in his chair, not seeking to participate, ignored, Díaz Grey was observing the man's movements—more abrupt—and heard his words—more direct and frank—and recognized the small blue watery eyes. Old Macleod in shirt sleeves with an unbuttoned collar, gray hair, reddish skin, legs stretched out under the poetic convention of honeysuckle vines.

"Of course I remember," the proprietor said. He cleaned his teeth, removed the toothpick to look at it, hopeful, relapsing into habit. "I'll never forget it—I can still see him. Lying on the beach, sitting on the porch, wandering about across the way. He almost never spoke, I called him 'the sleepwalker.' And it's not that he did anything special; he's just that kind of man who's hard to forget. Also, it's the way I met him, the first time I saw him. Nothing strange, don't worry, Madame, don't look at me that way. . . ." He had that same smile of Macleod excusing human frailty, letting you know that, in spite of everything, life is worth while or deserves to be lived, and that a scattered legion of vigorous Macleods exists who possess the key and are capable of providing courage; they were put on earth for that reason. "The hotel was almost empty, though the days were getting nice; on weekends some couple came or a group of friends, almost all people from Santa María. I don't want to gossip, but these Swiss of today aren't the ones who made the colony, believe me. I'm almost sure it was a Monday and everyone had gone, when I sat down to look at the road and some boats in a race down the river. The launch had passed without docking, so it wasn't likely any travelers would arrive. It didn't matter to me because here one lives off the summer; but if they come in any other season, I assure you I don't mind." He didn't smile but trailed between them, through that dry distance, an empty, candid gaze. "That afternoon I sat where you were all morning"—he looked at Díaz Grey with derision, communicating that he understood and was able to rise above all that he understood—"and although I was drowsy and always took a nap, I couldn't fall asleep. I had the presentiment someone was going to come, a couple, a traveler alone; someone was going to come up from the beach, walk down the road. And it wasn't because of the money—one guest more isn't going to make me richer. Well, it was he, your friend, who came. Of course you both know him; but maybe it's for the best that you never saw him as I did that afternoon. He was just over twenty. Am I right?"

"Twenty-two or twenty-three," Elena whispered; she smiled only with her eyes and this same brightness was barely polite, yet cooperative, fearful of interrupting.

"That's what I said. Just over twenty. I've traveled a lot in this world, I've seen it all, there isn't anyone who doesn't remind me of someone else I've met, and it's been a long time since anything surprised me. But I never saw a better-dressed man than that boy. It always gives me a laugh to see a fellow who wastes his time worrying about what clothes to wear, which tie, what the latest fad is; but not this one. When I saw him, I thought it was as if he had gotten all decked out to take a walk down Calle Florida in Buenos Aires, or to go meet a girl at a party, and that suddenly, miraculously, he appeared on this road. He was dirty, of course, covered with dust; he had come by boat and walked from Santa María, and though it wasn't windy, a passing car, or maybe a horse, was enough to do it. I was on the porch. Your friend came walking fast, his hands in his pockets, no suitcase, no package, nothing; he walked with his body so erect, his head so upright, I was sure he would go right by, I can't imagine where; I thought he was crazy or that I was dreaming."

Perhaps the proprietor suspected something, or simply responded to an old distrust, because, after filling his mouth with a plum, he bent directly, with deliberate exclusiveness, toward the woman who avoided his eyes and who had shaped a smile of affected disdain on her lips.

"It's as if I were seeing him again," he went on, "as if he were right here in flesh and blood. Without looking to either side he walked to the big staircase, turned, and began climbing as surely, as naturally, as if he came every day. Do you understand? As if it were customary to take a walk around here out of season wearing a five-hundred-peso suit, a silk shirt, and those fancy shoes just right for a ride in a car. Yes, the way one would take a stroll through the capital, down Calle Florida, for example, and suddenly decide to enter a café. He had a face too serious for his age, and later I saw that he was thin and pale; not sick, but as if he had been sick, although not any longer, and was coming here, without baggage and wearing those clothes, to recover his health. I wish you could have seen him. Very serious and tired, almost as if escaping from something, I thought, but without fear. I thought a lot of things, but I didn't move. Because I had an even stronger impression—you're going to laugh—that there was something of a joke in all this. I remained quiet, as if asleep, but I never stopped looking at him as he climbed the stairs whistling and then halted there to the side with his hat back on his head, hands in his pockets, legs apart."

"Yes," she murmured. "Go on." She was biting her lips, as if she were remembering and couldn't bear it.

"Well, that's how it was. I was waiting to hear him make some rude or derisive remark, and I was wondering which step he'd land on when I pushed him down head over heels. He wouldn't have been the first, you know, especially in summer when I have to have the hotel full of all kinds of people. But no, it was no joke. I knew it as soon as I looked at his eyes. He was quiet and kept waiting, as if he believed I really was asleep and didn't want to bother me. I got up and we spoke; he wanted to stay in the hotel for a while, but he didn't know how long. I got the impression that everything depended on something that might or might not happen and that he didn't explain to me. He didn't ask the price and later I found out from one of the maids that he had more than five thousand pesos in his wallet. We talked and I became more curious, especially since he didn't have any baggage. But afterward, when we became friends and had a drink together, I was glad I hadn't asked him anything. All this is strange and I don't know how to tell it. You both know him, of course, and besides no one seems the same to everyone. I would say that very soon after I met him, I thought that nothing he could do—the wildest thing—would surprise me. There are people who always know what they're doing and why they're doing it, and others that don't, though they believe they do. More than once the thought occurred to me, excuse me, that the boy was crazy; but he knew what he was doing. I think so. He knew it all the time, in the smallest things—and mind you, at times we're all absent-minded. He knew it when he had one drink too many, or when he'd spend the day sleeping, or when he got the crazy idea to dive in the river at dawn and turned purple with cold. He always knew why he did what he did. I know people: it was enough for me to take one look at his eyes, the way he walked, how he'd stay in a corner of the dining room listening to the same record a hundred times. And when you had to tell him something he wasn't going to like, he sensed it immediately and smiled as if he were thinking of something else—something that I as a man also had to be aware of, even if I didn't know what it was at the moment. And I wouldn't say anything to him, I'd shut my mouth and ask him if the service was to his liking, if the place seemed pleasant to him. When he told me he was thinking of leaving . . ." He poured the small glass of grapa into his coffee and leaned back on the arbor post with a sigh. "Four hundred pesos, more or less, he spent the month he was here."

"No!" Elena exclaimed. "He was here a month?"

"A long month."

"Then I don't understand." She turned to ask for Díaz Grey's help.

"Why not?" the doctor asked.

"Yes, of course," she said. "It must have been."

"A long month," the proprietor repeated. "I can show you my register."

"No, I was confused, it's not necessary. How was it that what he did seemed natural? And his way of smiling?"

"I just told you," the owner said, cold, without hostility, like Macleod abiding by the clauses of a contract.

"Yes, and you told it very well, he's just like that," she said coquettishly.

"I'm going to have another grapa," Díaz Grey announced. 'So he was first—the proprietor—to usurp my place, seated on the porch, optimistically looking down the road with the presentiment that something was going to happen, that someone would faithfully arrive in order to change my destiny.'

A ray of sunshine penetrated the wine in the glass; Elena had lit a cigarette and was smoking, her legs crossed, determined not to beg, saying with her bored expression, 'I'm alone, neither of you are there, I don't hear anything you say, I don't assume to know what you're thinking.' The owner wanted more coffee, a cicada began to sing, drawing at intervals for Díaz Grey the silhouette of the motionless cow seen at dawn. 'And then,' the doctor thought, 'the other one appears; this one also robs me; I understand now that it was I who should have walked down the road wearing dance shoes, taking long strides, head erect, as if mere determination were pushing my hat back on my head. I, quiet, legs apart, looking down at this pig who was pretending to sleep.'

"Yes, he was here more than a month," the owner said. "And he didn't even say good-by; through one of the maids he let me know he was leaving only the day before. And if I knew he went to the Glaesons', it wasn't because he told me. He was rather strange."

"Then it's been a week since he left?" Elena asked.

"Friday. The day before yesterday he was still at the Glaesons'. He'll keep getting drunk with the Englishman and his daughters until he feels like running away again. Because it seemed to me he was running away from something, although without fear."

"It's possible," she conceded, and could not control herself. "Do you remember the name of that record he listened to a hundred times?"

"That's not how it was," the owner said quickly. "I'll explain. I didn't mean he put on a record until he wore it out, always the same record. No, he listened that way to records he didn't know, anything. Not always the same record because it reminded him of something. He walked around here and there, or stayed in his room all day. Sometimes content, sometimes serious and almost rude, as if he could walk between people without seeing them. That one wasn't sad or happy for any reason, but rather because he felt like it, though I let myself be fooled like an idiot. But he had nothing desperate about him, as you say."

Elena stood up and showed both men a happy smile; she looked at the hotel proprietor as if she had to thank him and preferred to do so in silence.

"The road to the Glaesons' is very bad," the owner said. "You'll have to cut through the woods. But since you both want to walk, you'll get there in less than an hour. After a little nap I'll point out the road to you. You can't get lost."

Díaz Grey went out of the arbor behind her, almost touching her, smelling her, as if he were at last making the delayed inspection of spring and would move on to experience the small joys of the fragrances of resin, flowers, the river, and manure; he was smelling the world, desire, his own life in the air surrounding the woman's blouse, the aroma of her freshly bathed, perspiring body that was mingling with the faded perfume of her hair; he was lost and renewed immediately in the next step, in each swaying motion of the walk. They crossed through a gloomy, empty lounge, went up the stairs, and entered—both aroma and nose—the bedroom. She sat down on the bed and began unbuttoning her blouse; she did not want to lie down or look at him, she was expecting Díaz Grey to do something or to leave, waiting confidently for the first false move of the small, frail man, reddened but not tanned by the trip to the country, and who had retreated until his back almost touched the dark patch of a sealed-up door.

"It will be better to sleep an hour," she said. "Later we can go there. Lock the door and close the window. I don't want light."

"Yes, we're going to go. Listen, I have to tell you something. Don't ask for explanations—you know why. I want to tell you that you're a filthy bitch. Do you understand?" She had turned to look at him, almost smiling, attentive; Díaz Grey felt that ridicule was spilling over him as if it were pouring out of the transom. "The filthiest bitch I've ever known. The filthiest I can imagine."

She buttoned her blouse again and lay down on the bed, her legs dangling, one heel touching the floor.

"And I knew it all the time," he persisted, "from the first moment I saw you. With no possibility of deceiving myself, without wanting to either—get it?"

"But you're crazy," she said with candor, exhausted. "You don't want to go on with me? Is that it?"

"I knew it when I saw you, from the moment you appeared in the office with the first farce. All the lies, so unnecessary, so inevitable for a dirty bitch. And here I am, helping you to meet the well-dressed fugitive, ready for anything to get your body—not even for that, for nothing, for the need of something I don't really want, that can't help me."

"I asked you if you wanted to discuss it and you didn't want to," she said. She put her legs up on the bed and lit a cigarette.

He continued talking, slow and without passion, incapable of leaving the doorway or the palpable zone of ridicule that was hardening against his body and obstructing the movements of his mouth. 'Like a soldier in his sentry box,' he thought, 'a saint in his niche, Saint John in the shadows of the cistern.'

2

The New Beginning

The storm began when the train left Constitución: thunder, a sudden downpour immediately interrupted, the unpredictable clamor of wind snapping branches, coming and going, indecisive. It was later, on the terrace of the house in Temperley, when I saw Gertrudis' back as she prepared coffee wearing a nightgown with a lace border that touched the floor, that the real storm hit and I allowed myself to be drenched and pushed by the wind, feeling how quickly my early phase of drunkenness was disappearing. I breathed the first smell of wet earth, heard Gertrudis' laugh in the room.

I went inside, almost exhausted, as if returning from an unresolved crisis, drying my hands on a handkerchief, with a small dead leaf stuck to my cheek.

"All that I can bring from the mountains," I laughed, throwing myself into an armchair, lifting my mud-stained feet to place them on the cold, smudged hearth. "I don't know what would happen to you if you went back to Montevideo. It's a pity you can't know. Could it be this—nothing, or worse than nothing? To have to be convinced that one was not there, that absolutely nothing of yourself remained in the streets, in friends. To read the newspapers and not even find yourself in the typography, the misprints."

"Don't shout," Gertrudis said. "The coffee isn't very hot. That must have happened to you because you went looking. I'd never do that. You said Raquel was the same."

"She'll become a Gertrudis in time. I'd spend five years looking at her, then finally see her serving coffee and flirting through habit, wearing a nightgown that looks like a party dress. But those who are the same don't help me, and those who have changed don't help me. Because I have nothing to do with them, I'm not there in them."

Gertrudis rested her hands on top of the coffeepot and turned to look at me, studying me and failing to recognize me; her smile, however, was received with joy and approval by the unfamiliar man, wet and absurd, who was resting his shoes on the fireplace and lightly rubbing the little rose leaf stuck to his cheek, afraid it might fall off.

"I don't know," she said. "There's something going on with you; you're different. Something happened in Montevideo."

"Nothing," I said. "If something had really happened, I wouldn't be here. Everybody there is the same, and yet . . . It isn't that they've changed, only that they've decayed a little more—five years more. And I decayed apart from them, with a different style."

"It seems one is compelled to decay."

"So it seems," I said. I drank a cup of the lukewarm coffee. I felt my excitement revive, impetuous, without purpose, the way a spurt of water might spring from a broken pipe.

"You shouldn't have gone," Gertrudis said. "Mama is better." I looked at her tall body doubled up in the chair, heavy and agile, her elbows on her thighs. She let a tranquil gaze fall on her cup, a little sad, a little childish, which nevertheless, as it touched her cheeks, seemed to brush away an imprudent disdain. I looked at her, asking myself what was going on, not in her or me but rather in the room, in the distance separating us. "The doctor is pleased. Mama doesn't want to talk about us, the subject was exhausted at the beginning; I don't know what she would think if she knew you were visiting me now. Everything is so absurd! I work all day, she tries not to bother me. Sundays are spent with her. She knows I'm happy and she doesn't hate you. But she can't accept understanding it because she's old; she's not going to give in to that part of herself that stubbornly says such things aren't done, don't have to be done, and aren't decent."

She wasn't looking at me; she had put down her cup, but she remained sitting there with her eyes lowered; the scorn in her eyes had changed now into a smile prompted by some memory. We spoke or did not speak, placed there like delicate figurines, like paper silhouettes against the dense background of rain, the overbearing noise of wind in the trees. 'Just as I went to look for her in Raquel, I can get free of Raquel through her.'

"In short, everything is all right," I began.

"Everything is all right, today is all right. You didn't love me."

"No," I said. I brought my body close to the sound of the rain, I believed that I was going to understand the five years spent with Gertrudis, the dead Brausen, the story that began in the house in Pocitos when she closed the door and unfastened her bathrobe. Now that I was free from the past, a stranger to all the circumstances that Brausen had experienced, my life with Gertrudis became separated from mystery and destiny. From the first night until this one, when we spoke or were silent without conviction as the storm roared around us, she had chosen me, she had taken me. And for years she had continued choosing and taking in each one of the ways that shape the days, in each one of the two thousand days we lived together, in each one of the nights when she undressed her enormous body or obliged me to undress her, without need of words, without looking at me, perhaps only thinking of the mating, only seeing her face in the bathroom mirror before coming into the bedroom. Even though she might not have suggested it, even though she might not have desired it, even though she might have preferred another man's energy, a different code of initiatives or responses. Maybe it wasn't she who had taken and chosen, but the large white body, the bones and muscles, from the reddish heels to the firm, broad neck; the large hip bones and the roundness of the arms, the processes clearly visible through the taut skin, the sensation of the weight that the legs carried.

"I can make more coffee," she said, yawning. "What were you thinking about? There's always a bottle here, too, of something. If the rain continues, you can stay and sleep on the couch. Everything is all right and nothing matters to me." She looked at me, smiling, upright in her chair and at peace, a touch of drowsiness slipping from her eyes to her lips.

'I could tell her how I seduced Raquel without touching her, how it was enough for me to know it was a sure thing, and explain to her how much fear and power there was in the impulse that made me run away. I could describe her sister's slender body beside the café bar, and the joyless gesture with which she showed me her teeth before vomiting; perhaps Gertrudis would acknowledge how things were and come to understand. The big body under the nightgown, conscious of the ease, the vigor and equilibrium of its movements. She isn't going to do it, she isn't going to ask me to kiss her and to unfasten the lace, and if she did, the presumable frustration of my right hand wouldn't matter to me. As it ought not to matter to the other, or others (who knows?—such is my humility). But she won't do it; and because she did it on another not-so-distant night—strange to me, but in no detail forgotten—because she did it then and kept on doing it, the truth is that I didn't really love her ever.'

"It makes me happy that everything is all right, as you say," I continued. "For me, everything was wrong; but I see it only now, when I have nothing to do with you, with anyone, not even myself. The man called Juanicho loved you, he was happy and suffered. But he's dead. As for the man called Brausen, we can confirm that his life is lost; I say it as if I were giving my name to the police or declaring my baggage at customs."

"At your age?" she asked. I wondered why she couldn't understand, then remembered she no longer loved me.

"It's not that; it may be failure, but it's not decadence. Now I'd like to have that bottle of something."

"Perhaps that's what it was, Juanicho. Perhaps it wasn't because of the breast they took away from me, or your lack of love, or the inevitable end of all things."

"No, it's not a question of the defeated man," I said. "It's not a question of decadence. It's something else, it's that people believe they're condemned to a single life until death. And they are only condemned to a soul, to a manner of being. One can live many times, many more or less long lives. You should know that. I'd like to have that drink of something. But if I'm bothering you, I'll leave."

Now—while Gertrudis' long white body was disappearing beyond the curtain that separated us from the dining room, that submerged into shadows the points of reference I needed to reconstruct her nudity—the wind was rising in a tremulous simulation of fury, and the rain, seen in the pale light of street lamps, seemed compelled not to touch the gardens or the streets, pausing and curving as it fell in order to strike against windows, leaves, and the bark of trees. Now—while Gertrudis moved the nightgown out of the darkened room and approached swaying and humming an unfamiliar tune, the bottle against her chest, a dreamy smile serving to announce and mock the comedy she was presenting: docility, patience, tolerance that does not aspire to understanding—now the wind was stretching out horizontally in all directions, like pine branches, shaking and creaking.

"A drink, then," Gertrudis said.

I raised my eyes to look at the smiling face over which expressions of sympathy and concern were straying, almost impersonal. I saw the bare feet again, the veins that crept toward the ankles, the toenails that were losing their nail polish. I thought that she had been barefoot from the beginning, since she came down to receive me on the entrance tiles, stepping on the fallen leaves and rain. She put a large cushion on the floor and sat in front of the fireplace, hugging her legs, which supported the good nature of her smile.

"Then just one of your lives has died," she whispered. "Is that it? And what are you going to do with the other one that's beginning?"

"Nothing," I said. I wasn't interested in talking to her, and hesitated before getting up to kiss her. "I'm going to live, simply. Another failure, because presumably there's something that has to be done; each of us can fulfill himself in suitable work. Then death doesn't matter, not as much, not like definitive annihilation, because the man with faith is supposed to have discovered the meaning of life and to have followed it. But for this small life that's beginning, or for all the previous ones that I might have to begin again, I don't know of anything to help me, I don't see the possibilities of faith. Yes, I can enter into many games, almost convince myself to play—for others—the farce of Brausen-with-faith. Any passion or faith makes for happiness, insofar as it distracts us and offers us unconsciousness."

"But we're alive," she whispered. "You spoke that word *happiness*."

"Is it really so important?"

Then she tightened her arms and began to rock herself, resting on her buttocks, while she laughed in silence, tender and defiant.

"In the tone used to ask for an address, a street, someone who's supposed to know it. Well, I don't know where the street is, it doesn't matter to me, I don't want to tell you."

The wind was advancing, damp, stirring the fringe of Gertrudis' hair; the rain was beating on the dark landscape of crevices, moss, and soaked earth. With the elaborate nightgown, she could have been sitting in any of the old weeks that followed the first night in Pocitos; younger than Raquel, as much in control of her enthusiasm and joy now as she was then; as sure of the domesticity of the future as of the domesticity of the austere Brausen whom she could imprison with her legs. 'We can't go back to the beginning; in two nights all curiosity would be satiated. But I could modify the beginning. Her big white body is always tempering a ritual; that feminine gift of constancy, that lack of individuality, that relationship with earth, eternally new and stretched out face up under our sweat, our footsteps, our brief presence. I could modify the beginning, forcing it to happen this time in a different way; only in order to supplant the memory of the first beginning with that of tonight, and to trust that the new beginning would be enough to alter the memory of five years. Only so that I, closer to death, might evoke a profound intimacy, suitable to our best qualities, without temptations of revenge.'

"I'm going to turn off the light, I'm going to kiss you," I said to her; her face didn't change; she smiled drowsily, displaying her sleepiness. I got up surrounded by the noise of the wind and by the wind itself; I felt the coolness of the rain on the back of my neck. I turned out the light and waited to distinguish Gertrudis' form, huddled up, swaying.

"Don't move," she said; I could tell nothing from her voice. "Everything is all right. But I don't desire you. . . ." I knelt down to kiss her; she made the point of her rigid tongue appear between her lips. "I don't desire you," she repeated without moving away.

Covered and excited by the moving mantle of moist air, I tried to blend with the distant sound of the wind, solitary and conscious on top of the large body that was lending itself, without surrender, motionless. When I had to recognize my failure, when I was on my back next to her, knowing myself forgotten, I thought again of her death. I listened, felt in my eyes and cheeks the renewed fury of the storm, the spiteful noise of the rain, the howling wind filling the sky and striking against the earth; the force of the storm capable of continuing through dawn, of invading the new day, sweeping me away and ignoring me as if my deadened exultation did not weigh more than the tiny leaf that I had fondled and kept pressed to my cheek; as indifferent and alien as the woman who was resting, tranquil and silent, arched on the cushion.

3

The Denial

"This is the hour of fear and the humble, 'Lord, why hast Thou forsaken me?' " Stein had said while we were eating.

"That's right," Mami agreed, misunderstanding; distracted, she smiled toward the entrance door, almost sleepy.

"And if we pause a moment," Stein pursued, "if your salvation can wait, I'd say that very probably the Other rubbed his hands and murmured into his beard, 'my designs are inscrutable, my son.' " He burst out laughing as he clapped Mami on the shoulder. "Isn't that great? Today I feel Jewish. When you quote me, don't forget the 'my son' at the end. It's indispensable, concentrate on it and offer it as I offer this asparagus tip. Not as good as the former, but notable. If I could just be someone else and astonish myself listening . . . In any case, there's something to do, something concrete. I don't know what's going on with you, I don't force confidences, you'll come to good Porfirio without Sonia pushing you. You'll come to good Porfirio without Sonia pushing . . ." he recited, listening to himself. "Perhaps there's one syllable too many, it's not important. You seemed young and nervous. I thought you had excellent news or the money from

174

Macleod multiplied by a hundred. I saw you again, and you were changed; I saw you were beginning to have that type of baldness invented by remorse. I suspect that you're a big enough idiot to worry about your job; I proposed setting up Steinsen Limited to you, you said no. Well, whatever happens, there's something I've been saving for myself for years. The true way to salvation and the perfect crime. But Mami and her charms keep me from despair, time passes, and my formula isn't used. This is how it goes: the penitent rents a room in a hotel, he sends someone out to buy clothes. A complete wardrobe, including shoes, hat, and handkerchiefs. Nothing can be saved when we sweat misfortune. The old clothes must be burned, it's necessary to destroy them; not for love of a fellow man, but because the old suit will drag its new owner along and pursue us. I know of impressive and indisputable examples—vengeful clothes that have crossed continents in order to return their venom. One touch is enough. The old clothes destroyed, the brand-new suit and accessories at our command, it's necessary on this occasion, if you'll pardon the expression, to drink a glass of Epsom salts and take a very hot bath. Although variations are permissible, consistent with particular idiosyncracies. The penitent sleeps, wakes up with a smile, decks himself out, and begins to live fresh as a newborn, as alien to his past as to the heap of ashes he leaves behind. I pledge my word."

But I didn't want to scrub myself, or rid myself of stains, or conceal the dirt with whitewash. I didn't want to deceive myself, I wanted to keep myself vigilant and alert, to nourish Arce with my will and money in allotments of the many peso notes that I had hidden in a small steel box in the basement of a bank, together with the revolver, screws and springs, and bits of glass. I went on knowing I was destined to support Arce in the same way that, after death, my decomposition would feed a plant; I sustained him with the hundred green bills, frequenting La Queca and in the nights and dawns pressing against the wall of my room to listen to her entanglements with men or women, and to her lies to them, too, as she chatted hurriedly with sudden force, drunk, sobbing, when "they" invaded her solitude. I would keep Arce alive by means of Díaz Grey and the woman exploring the territory I had constructed and peopled. Money, La Queca, Santa María and its inhabitants. But I knew, without fears about food or future shelter, that the essential source of Arce's life was the money hidden in the bank, the bills I had to save and spend in the dark until the inevitable moment would arrive, a moment impossible to defer or to hasten, when Arce would stand back to contemplate the motionless La Queca.

It was I, my contempt and my self-denial, who descended the bank stairs on the hot mornings when I needed money or needed only to see it, to touch it with my fingertips. We entered into the coolness of the subterranean corridor; a man with a holster on his belt approached to attend me, to guide me between gratings and thick walls into an ambiance of laziness, of tamed expectation, where another man, bored, was sitting on a bench, his black hat tilted to one side of his head. I entered the room, shut myself in with the box on the table, and turned the little key. I bent over the bills without avarice, like over a mirror that would reflect my face fleetingly, inadvertently. But I didn't trust my eyes alone; I closed them before lowering the lid and moved my fingers among the papers and accumulated objects, trying to recognize Ernesto's note: "I'll call you or come at nine." I believed the edges of the note were charged to give me advance notice that Arce's moment had arrived; I grasped it and encouraged it between my fingertips, thinking, 'Crazy world, crazy world,' remembering La Queca's face smiling, talking, lusting, lying. My fingers did not receive the information. I managed to see La Queca's face with a reality so astonishing, with expressions so intensely personal and never exposed, that sometimes I went back to the bank to be closeted with the box in order to see her gesticulate, to surprise looks she had never shown me, to believe that during the space of a minute I would come to know her and make her mine without passion, like food.

Then something threatened to destroy it all. I was knocking at her door and I had her, I was breathing the air of the room, it was possible for me to see and touch objects one by one, to feel them alive, intense, suitable to construct the irresponsible atmosphere in which I could be transformed into Arce. But in some way the old order had been altered; something was missing or was interposing, or was dead. 'This is all there is, fool,' I thought, going on with a scornful smile, trying to excite La Queca's fury and her past.

Changeable in mood, she was either pleased to see me or taciturn and enraged. I moved around, examining furniture, books, pots and pans, the way a technician might examine a machine to find its failing part, trusting deduction and chance in turn; knowing she was immobilized in some part of the room, directing a tired, ironic grimace toward me until I looked at her, her narrowed eyes trying to seem mysterious and pretending to judge me. And not only judging me myself—I who entered cordial and crude, rattling keys, mumbling without faith, 'Crazy world, crazy world'—but my destiny, humanity, the differences between her and others. She waited until our eyes met, then turned her back to me and threw herself on the bed, or dusted furniture and the books she would never read.

I kept on searching for the lost harmony, evoking the old order, the atmosphere of eternal present where it was possible to lose one's self, to forget the old laws, to not age; I kept on compensating for the false intelligence of La Queca's expression with the lie of my implacable cordiality; I moved along the walls, offering bribes to the unknown element that refused to act. Like a victor on conquered territory, unable to deceive myself, I suffered the vague unseen opposition of its resolute and silent inhabitants. 'When my fingers in the box at the bank know the moment has come, the room will be the same as before, the rebellious mechanism will slip into place again; but it will happen only once, for a day or a night, and won't last more than twenty-four hours.'

I greeted her and set out to kiss her with a distracted lust; occasionally, La Queca's face and voice reproduced with exactitude the urgent joyous surrender of the first weeks. I suspected that what had died in the room was inside her and could be resuscitated, or that it obeyed only her will. So I was not totally insincere when I lay down on her bed to listen with interested eyes to the torrent of unimportant events, unimportant people, the everyday cynicisms that La Queca's anxious voice poured over me between caresses and some laughter, unexpected, abruptly cut off; not insincere, because my eyes were dilated with hope, because I was bound to believe that return to the painfully remembered lost world was imminent.

I remembered that I had discovered, almost sensed, the miraculous air of the room for the first time on a night when La Queca was not there; that the particular atmosphere of a brief life had come to me from a confusion of wineglasses, fruit, and clothing. 'It isn't her, she doesn't do it,' I convinced myself. 'It's the objects. And I'm going to fondle them with such an intensity of love that one by one they won't be able to resist me; I'll be so sure and confident that they will have to want me.' I began my attempts at seduction by silently reviewing the names of things; I decided they were divided into two categories: those that were decisive, and those that could do nothing for or against Arce's existence. The hardest thing was to find the right spiritual attitude in

Encounter with
the Violinist

The door, under the hanging blaze of fuchsias, was opened by a young girl; she had a face inured to terror, stiff braids, a blue tie. She was small, and later Díaz Grey thought that this one was a dwarf of the other, the counterpart on a smaller scale of the violinist, the girl they found playing next to the enormous piano in the parlor when the now-and-for-all-time dwarf ushered them in, sucking distrust and apprehension like tears, one for each eye.

The dwarf announced that Mr. Glaeson was sleeping, and tried to smile. "Oh no," said the life-size girl. She held the violin and bow at the sides of her body, and bowed in the timid greeting appropriate to courteous applause before the start of a concert—a slight greeting imposed by good manners, and that could eventually be tossed off and easily forgotten by both parties if the young artist's gifts did not reach the distinguished height anticipated through hopes and precedents.

"Oh no," she repeated, like a refrain rising again at the propitious moment. "He's taking a little nap, though it's time for him to wake up.

If you wish to wait a bit . . . I practice at this hour every afternoon, and he doesn't wake up, he doesn't hear me. But it's about that time, if not later. Papa's used to it. We must see if he's awake and tell him he has visitors. Won't you sit down? Where you'll be comfortable." She smiled, separating the violin and bow slightly from her body.

The permanent dwarf copied the girl's smile; she cast a covetous look—not at them, not at any of the three, not at the parlor overwhelmed by the magnitude of the piano, but rather at the dramatic possibilities of the situation she had to leave—and went out without a sound.

Alone but fortified, the girl bowed again, her heels together.

"Madame, sir . . ." she said. "Would it disturb you to hear me play?"

Elena and Díaz Grey answered "no," mutually sweeping the question away, shaking their heads to dispel any doubts. She again faced the music on the stand, steadied herself on her legs, on her delicate ankles, and with the violin now set under her chin and the bow held motionless, suspended midway, waited, falsely disinterested, for Díaz Grey to imagine an obscure introduction corresponding to the piano part. (Someone treads, a stranger, on the fallen leaves in the forest; we bury without pomp the last rose of this rainy summer.) The violin raised a furious supplication too soon, stopped immediately, repentant, and resigned itself to wait. Díaz Grey thought about the tattered words of the piano while the girl waited patiently, almost turned backward now, her big buttocks massed—her body's only amplitude. She answered the piano's reticent discourse by saying, by trying to say, the inexpressible; she understood her new mistake and resolved to aspire with no ambition other than an approximate, attainable precision. She phrased it as best she could and endured without exasperation the piano's skeptical grumble, the music Díaz Grey was imagining with his eyes fixed on the girl's hips, transferring to them the desire engendered by Elena Sala, who, ironical at his side, scarcely curious in the hot afternoon's drowsiness, awaited the apparition of the desperate fugitive or Mr. Glaeson's denial, pretending to listen, nibbling the thickest bead of her necklace.

The girl made the violin sound an interminable nostalgic phrase that tried to impose the prestige of a memory without forcing it; then immediately, without waiting for a reaction or a response, she screeched two notes of joy, allowed time for the piano, screamed again, and yielded a passage to the piano's silence; then suddenly, paying no attention, mingled with the keyboard's voice that of the violin, compromised enough to be heard, and went on phrasing—together with slight hesitations, and cunning, friendly questions, opinions about the weather, best wishes for the sick—what she was determined and condemned to say. Next she believed, or went along with believing, that it was possible to arrive at understanding through the rhythm of old folks' prattle around the fire. Díaz Grey was looking at her hips, so wide that they could surrender to childbirth with just the help of a smack; taking advantage of the pauses, he studied her asexual profile, the straight nose, the blinded eyes under the crown of pale frizzled hair, the slight and tragic sensuality that filtered through the corner of her mouth.

She allowed the piano to speak with the hope of harmonizing, of being able to express herself by imitating the notes entrusted to the imagination of the unknown little man with large glasses and scanty hair, seated next to the disagreeable woman. But neither the piano nor the stranger—with his eyes fixed on her substitute buttocks—understood anything. So the girl ended by pressing on the violin strings and rushing ahead—her attitude of flight always compensated for by her conspicuous hips, which Díaz Grey's obsession and cooled-off suffering endowed with confessions and reticences—attacking, with her chin resting on the violin, and rising effortlessly to recite her resolute and impudent passion. And while she was slowly soaring in the big music room, she even came to scorn being heard and understood by herself, she who had known by heart the passion that she proclaimed and that was eluding her now, coming and going, speaking and ringing.

Díaz Grey thought the stuttering notes matched the defeat and awkwardness of the piano; his eyes were moist—'at least in dreams I can see the face of what I don't know,' she repeated—from the security and joy in what he heard, from the confidence, the posthumous quality of energy in the phrase, the silhouettes and groups of mourners and flowers on his tomb that the phrase was insinuating.

The girl stopped flying with two brief cries and stood upright again before them; she bowed, legs together, cheating him of her buttocks.

"Thank you," she said with ease. "The other part is smoother." (She meant to say "more resigned.") "Much prettier, perhaps." (She meant to say "melancholy.") "Papa is coming now. You'll have to excuse me for the way I received you."

Mr. Glaeson, with a thin cloth jacket over his undershirt, looked at them while squinting his sky-blue eyes, the only brightness in his face, the only part that seemed to have been washed to clear away the dreams of his siesta and the bad humor of his waking. He announced that the fugitive, desperate, had left for La Sierra the day before. He had gone in search of a bishop, he had a letter for him; or the bishop was his relative—he couldn't be precise.

While his daughters were whispering in English in the shadows surrounding the piano, he contemplated the room with a vigilant sadness, as if estimating the damage done to the air by the violin music, the traces of wrong notes; he looked at the open shutters, imagining the details of the dry, burning landscape, its meaning.

"You should have had something cool to drink," he commented now, without looking at them, stroking the gray hairs revealed by the open undershirt, letting them know that the moment of cool drinks had passed forever. "A bishop from La Sierra, madame. I don't know which one."

5

The First Part
of the Wait

It was a time of waiting, sterility, and disorientation; everything was confused, everything had the same value, identical proportions, equivalent meaning, because everything lacked importance and was happening outside of time and life, already without a Brausen to assay events, still without an Arce to impose order and sense.

The room was saying no, and I was beating La Queca, more disinterested each time, my repentance more tempered, with less hatred and contempt, less need that she be drunk.

The city had reached the heart of summer and all of us believed that it would remain forever in the middle of the unmoving heat, stretched out and panting from the red dawn until the pitch-black and exhausted night, when each of us tried hard to save the last breath in order to be prepared for the indefinite event, the realization and beginning of which was promised by the metallic leaves on the trees, the large expanse of avenues and squares, the furtive irritating trickle of sweat down the skin.

I, the bridge between Brausen and Arce, needed to be alone, understanding that isolation was essential to me in order to be born again, that simply being alone, without will or impatience, I would come to exist and recognize myself. Thrown across my bed and hearing La Queca's life with a wall between us, or next to her, horizontal and impassive under the monologues she unleashed and paraded through the room, I kept on waiting—indeed, I thought I had waited all my life without knowing it, and that if I had been conscious of this wait I would have shortened it, perhaps by years—and I preserved also the abandonment, the slightly feminine and shameful sensation that someone was providing for me. I ignored the objects and began to suspect that "they" were the ones mutilating the air of the apartment so as to harm me.

"But what are they?" I asked in friendly moments. "If you had to draw them, if you'd seen them in the movies . . ."

"They just exist—I never saw them," she said. During all our months together, only in talking about "them" did she become an intelligent being. "They exist and I feel they're here. I could tell you I see and hear them, but I'd be lying. Because I don't—not the way I see you or any other person. Once you asked me if they spoke very fast, and you made me wonder if you'd guessed or if you knew them too, because that's what really drives me crazy. They talk and talk, sometimes at an impossible speed, and yet I understand them perfectly; and sometimes so slowly that they seem silent, as if they can't say things slowly. But I always hear them, I know what they think up to bother me. One begins from a corner and then all of them are moving around on every side, calling my name and then ignoring me. So very softly at first that I have to strain to hear them and see them. And as soon as they realize I know what's going on, they start full speed so I go crazy and run all over the place trying not to miss anything."

"Are they people you knew—memories, familiar faces?"

"No, they aren't—can't you understand me? But no one can understand me. . . ." She was incapable of lying if she was speaking of "them"; only then did I believe truth was more important to her than the miserable fantasies with which she misrepresented everything she told me. "I don't know. What does it mean to you if I tell you that the other night this place was full to the ceiling, and all because I remembered something naughty that I did to mamma when I was a girl, and also because I was afraid of dying in my sleep? But I almost never know who they are—as if I'd lived two lives and could only remember this way, don't you see?"

Perhaps it was "they" who kept me removed from Arce, "they" who were denying me the completeness of that irresponsible air, of the atmosphere of a brief life. Lying in one bed or the other, my inertia keeping me outside of summer, the street, and the world, I waited, occasionally distracting myself by speculating about names, faces, and memories, thinking about Gertrudis, Raquel, Stein, my brother, streets and hours in Montevideo, as if I might evoke someone else's past, ghosts condemned to pursue someone else. Bits and pieces of Arce and the truth were falling on my laziness: I knew that these were not the leftovers, but everything one gets by accession; that what I succeeded in obtaining through my own efforts would be born dead and stinking; that one form of God or another is essential to men of good will, that it is enough to be unmercifully loyal to one's self in order that life may put together opportune acts at the opportune moment.

Free from anxiety, renouncing all I had searched for, left to myself and to chance, I was preserving the everyday Brausen from an indefinite debasement, I would allow him to end in order to save him, I was dissolving myself to permit Arce's birth. Sweating in both beds, I was saying good-by to the prudent, responsible man putting up an appearance based on limitations that others had placed on him, limitations that had preceded him, that were still not he himself. I was taking leave of the Brausen who, in a lonely house in Pocitos, Montevideo, had acquired—along with the vision and gift of Gertrudis' naked body—the absurd mandate to take care of her happiness.

I also had to think about La Queca, because the endless monologues in which she piled up unvaried insults and reproaches had now become customary, filling almost all the time we were together, and it was almost impossible—even in the subterranean room of the bank—to imagine her silent. I was returning to her through the scattered dirty phrases she compelled me to hear, the new offensive tone she had in her laugh now; looking at her, verifying her existence, I remained sure I could kill her, that in the game the two of us were forever playing, she was beginning to have a presentiment that I would kill her, that she hurled her filthy vociferations to provoke the moment. I was sure also of having thought of it before, sure that an irrevocable future had unsealed itself when she came to live in the house, when she brought with her—like a piece of furniture, like a cat, a dog, or a parrot—the

air that nourished and determined the men and women who were
obliged to follow her, like a court that moves its setting. (The air that
was simultaneously created and maintained by the very men and
women who were inhaling and exhaling it; by the breathing, the words,
and the movements of men and women, by the cigarettes they
consumed and put out, by their enthusiasms and fears, by the
rudiments of ideas they couldn't avoid.)

Then—and I had something of Arce in me—I invented Brausen
Publicity. I rented half an office on Calle Victoria, ordered business
cards and a letterhead, and stole a photograph of La Queca in which
three Córdoba nephews and nieces were trying to smile with grace. I
put the photo in a frame and placed it on top of a desk that someone
lent me, and there was not a single day when I forgot to look at it with
pride and the certainty of death conquered by my triple prolongation
in time. I had Stein, Mami, and Gertrudis telephone me each day, and
I played my part with energy and healthy ambition, starting at ten in
the morning, ready to struggle tirelessly to attain a place in the sun.
Stein called me punctually close to noon. We discussed possibilities for
obscene campaigns and vied in perfecting drawings, copy, and slogans
with which to palm them off. I dreamed up meetings and business
lunches, I would go from café to café on Avenida de Mayo, or I would
sit on a bench in the square throwing food to the pigeons. Never was the
sky bluer; little by little the men who crossed the square began to feel
the fraction of friendship I disinterestedly offered them without seeing
them, yawning and smiling, scratching myself, my eyes lost in the trees
that were then changing color, in the façades of buildings, in magazine
and flower stands. Sometimes I wrote and at other times imagined the
adventures of Díaz Grey, approximated Santa María through the
foliage of the square and the roofs of buildings near the river, wondered
at the doctor's growing tendency to wallow over and over again in the
same event, at the need—which was infecting me—to suppress words
and situations, to attain a single moment that might express it all: to
Díaz Grey and to me, therefore to the entire world. Other times, after
lunch I would go down toward the port and pick up screws, bolts, and
nuts, dazzling pieces of glass that I substituted in the metal box at the
bank for the money that I was forced to take away with me.

On the desk the photograph was between the inkstand and the
calendar: the heads of La Queca's three repugnant nephews and nieces
forcing their smiles to wait for the moment when the man who had

rented me half the office—his name was Onetti, he didn't smile, wore glasses, and let it be divined that he had time only for vague scatterbrained women or intimate friends—might succumb at any time, in the hunger of noon or late afternoon, to the stupidity I thought him capable of and accept the duty of taking an interest in them. But the man with the bored face did not come to ask about the origin or future of the photographed children. "Nice looking, eh?" I would have said. "The little female is delicious." And I would have looked unblinkingly at the young girl with a huge ribbon in her hair and eyes without innocence, the upper lip raised for all eternity. There were no questions, no symptoms of any desire for intimacy; Onetti greeted me with monosyllables that he infused with an imprecise vibration of affability, an impersonal disdain. He greeted me at ten, asked for a cup of coffee at eleven, attended to clients and the telephone, looked over papers, smoked without nervousness, and spoke in a grave, unchanging, lazy voice.

The days were growing hotter; my money was dwindling; sometimes I met Stein for a meal and before him succeeded in imitating his humble old friend Brausen. He never suspected anything and our meetings were pleasant, with or without Mami. The money was dwindling, and the old pieces of iron and glass deposited in the box were not enough to calm me. I saw Gertrudis occasionally and tried to guess from her laugh, or the ripeness of her beauty, what good or bad luck she was having in love, calculating the time that would have to pass so that being with her might really mean deceiving another.

6

Three Days
of Autumn

Always the same, one day and the next; a gesture repeated in pantomime and the waiting, an imitation of Brausen and the waiting, unsettled, as if vibrating out of me into the air and objects, manifest suddenly in the slight trembling of my idle hands.

Perhaps this was already ending when the idea began to pursue me that the summer would be followed—in a September or October that could only be imperfectly imagined—by three shivery cold days racing through the streets like fear-crazed horses. Three days I wasn't going to see, a false blizzard that would pass me by, vexatious dawns and afternoons when other inhabitants of the city would be able to take a girl to bed without dreading the splashy sound of sweaty breasts, trusting that cold feet and knees would generate the need for closeness without desire. Moving through streets, looking at buildings from my house or office window, abandoned to the vague dream of love at first sight that would be born on the first of the three days of cold in the autumn of the city I would not know; I imagined the drizzle and the sweet sadness, the meeting, the mutual urgency; I saw the man smoking near the hotel window, the girl waiting huddled up on the bed, her knees against her chin; I saw the man look anxiously with a lone circling glance at the wet landscape outside, the signs on stores and cafés, the Frenchified architecture, the vehicles and cyclists, the umbrellas and raincoats, the policeman's traffic box, the confusion of footprints and leaves at the edge of sidewalks. Standing up for only an instant near the window curtains, I listened to discover what was inside the abundance that this first rain of autumn could offer to new love, the richness provided by layers of memories that the bad weather was stirring up.

I saw the faceless man, the form of the young girl's body on the bed; already I was beginning to distinguish the design and colors of the hotel wallpaper. The three days of dampness, cold, and wind were moving around me incessantly, dogging my steps, agitating and confusing everything I tried to say. Until one Sunday afternoon when Díaz Grey came to free me from the obsession, when he did for me and for himself what I could not do: he skipped a year of time, he left Santa María as if he had cut off an arm, as if it were possible for him to get away from the provincial city and its river, leaving Elena Sala in a past that was never going to happen:

'The taxi comes through Avenida Alvear toward Retiro, toward the Bajo and the first coolness of night; the swirling air that vibrates in the small side window of the cab hits my face, increasing my body's bliss so much, so perilously, that I fear happiness may end and I turn around, without desire, to look at the girl. She was waiting for me and she smiled; the light from street lamps enters, flashing and fading in her eyes; I do not want to look twice at the dark swollen mouth. I abandon myself against the back of the seat, against the girl's shoulder, and I imagine moving away from a small town made up of motels; from a silent village in which naked couples amble through small gardens and mossy pavements, protecting their faces with opened hands when lights are turned on, when their paths are crossed by pederast butlers, when they ascend the museum's high staircase to pass through galleries flanked by almost invisible pictures, sleeping statues, the row of opened beds, spittoons, night tables, towels, and mirrors. "Here we are, here I am," I tell myself, "again." The girl strokes my hand, moves her finger forward to trace in my wet palm a drawing immediately forgotten.'

"Darling . . ." she says.

"Yes . . ." I reply.

"Deegee . . ." she murmurs—a name she made with my initials.

"Yes . . ."

I smile at the air touching my teeth; I don't want to think, I don't want to know what made my happiness or what can destroy it. I remember, I would measure precisely the liquor left in the glasses.

"Darling," she says. 'I should have gotten a little drunker,' I think.

"Yes," I answer. I bend down to kiss her head, I smell her.

"If I could only tell you . . ." she begins, and interrupts herself.

"I know," I say. I rub my cheek against her head and she sighs and draws closer; I feel that soon I can kiss her.

"Could something happen to me?"

"No, no, I don't think so," I say to her.

"Nothing matters to me. I know that nothing's going to happen, Deegee." She raises her face so I can kiss her. "Nothing's going to happen, but everything has importance. Everything!" she insists. I realize that for some time now both of us are thinking with attenuated desperation of the uselessness of words, of the insurmountable clumsiness with which we use them. From above, with the eye not covered by the girl's somewhat disheveled hair, I look at her face, I recognize the short nose, the wide space between the eyebrows, I see the sad, sensual shape of the lips, the roundness of the temple.

"Here, or do you want me to turn around?" the driver asks.

I help her to get out, we remain on the corner a moment, uncertain and vacillating, we go walking down the street toward the air coming from the river. I look at her, separated from me but at my side, her eyelids lowered; it amazes me to see her walk in the same way she did before, her body leaning to one side, an arm swinging back and forth exaggeratedly to help her walk, the pelvis thrust forward and graceless. I remember that an hour before I was sure of forever modifying her steps, her smile, her very past: I am ashamed when I recall the pride inspired by the strength of my arms, the precision and happiness with which I opened my way into her. 'Perhaps I also believed I was changing the way she looked in her baby pictures,' I reflect with scorn.

I guide her unnecessarily between the café tables and we go to seat ourselves near a window. I ask the waiter for something, the shot of liquor I needed; she nods agreement, raises her shoulders, decides to direct her mysterious smile at the street, at the world. I think of Elena

Sala, my wife; I count the hours she has waited for me, I examine the solidity of the lie I will tell her.

Now the girl takes my hand, directs her smile to me, silently enumerates the joys of life, soothes me by revealing that it is normal to encounter difficulties when we return to it, to reconcile comfortably the length of our legs and the philosophy we have constructed for ourselves in a foreign land. Everything will be all right, she affirms with her smile and the pressure of her fingers; not only will we remember the native language, but also the idioms, the capricious pronunciation, the omissions and abbreviations that made us young, that will make us young again.

"Deegee . . ." she says, and sips her drink and interrupts herself to cough.

I think about Dr. Díaz Grey, immobile at this table, against a side of the stormy autumn night, looking at the laugh, the interior rose color of a girl's mouth, proud of being capable of every injustice. She looks at me, brings close to my face the expression of a fury without destiny, the bitter corners of her mouth with that short curved outline that each side wants to reproduce in the other, as if to cast it into a mold ineffaceable until death, still visible years after the end of lóve. Everything is possible, we can think; or think without sadness that we will not get anything of what is possible and that this fate does not worry us. 'Now you smile at me again, play with your empty glass, put the memories of the night in order. I try to fortify myself by silently repeating, like a woman, that love is more important than ourselves; I fortify myself imagining the curses of the porter who came in to change the bedsheets. I love you and I say nothing. I reproduce the movements of your fingers caressing my hand, intent to discover in your eyes a trace of the healthy obscene look that I saw only one or two hours before, and that also fortifies me and makes me believe in you. I do not find it and it's not important to me, because I think about Dr. Díaz Grey, quiet on this side of the table; a man, any man, this man, labeled with the words *in his forties*, already dragged down by the need to protect himself. A man of forty on the other side of the table, who opens his wallet to pay the waiter, who perfects the first alibi, who feels with a gentle dizziness, with a pleasing uncertainty, the return to life.'

7

The Desperate Ones

That part of the history of Díaz Grey was never written in which, accompanied by the woman or following in her steps, he arrived at La Sierra, was received in the bishop's palace, saw and heard things that perhaps he has not understood to this day. The visit had many variations, but in each case they had to walk with feigned resolve between two lines of halberdiers of short stature, hardly martial, conscious of the bad condition of their uniforms, the faded colors of the cloth. They were always received in the anteroom by a smiling laconic giant wearing white stockings, who led and delivered them to the bishop's aide, a cassocked clergyman with a hooked nose on which slyness crept upward until it was consumed by his hair. There were no further delays in any one of their visits. They arrived at the dining room where the bishop was lunching, and he would rise, swiftly and joyously offer his ring to brief kisses, and invite them to eat. She declined with the exact smile, never seen, that Díaz Grey had dreamed of provoking; the doctor appreciated the indomitable ridiculousness, regretted it, and remained silent as he looked at the boiled chicken and red wine. There was only a servant behind the bishop; the noon sun and the ringing of bells hurried to die in the depths of the enormous corridor.

The bishop urged them only once, parting his hands toward the dishes; then he wanted to know whether they had noticed the unique quality of the city's atmosphere, those characteristics of antiquity and mildness given it by the uninterrupted piety of its inhabitants. Yes, they had noted it; perhaps a little baffled at first, with an inquisitive wrinkle on their brows, then clearly smelling it as they oriented their noses toward the center of town. The bishop went on agreeing while he listened and ate; the reddish area of his face and the irreducible shine of his eyes were increasing.

"Time, faith, so many exemplary deaths," he explained.

He almost immediately acknowledged having seated the fugitive at his table; he raised his hands, adding that he did not know the man's destiny since the last cup of coffee of that not-so-distant lunch.

"Is he your relative?" he asked Elena Sala.

"His mother was a close friend of my mother. I never knew what was going on with him; that need to run away. It worries me that he was desperate."

"He will find grace, that boy. . . ." His Most Reverend Excellency said, pushing the chair from the table. "Yes, he was desperate. We talked a great deal on that occasion. In your place, I wouldn't be worried."

"But he wasn't well," Elena Sala ventured. "Why would he want to run from everything? It was like a quiet madness, a furious melancholy, as if he were being summoned for nothing and nevertheless had to go."

Dressed in mourning, starched, Díaz Grey was taking advantage of the seat he had chosen behind them to look scornfully at the woman, to despise himself, to try to understand himself, to compare Elena Sala's thighs with the innocent, martyred face that she raised toward the bishop. His Most Reverend Excellency was washing his fingertips with a distracted air of benevolence and calm rejoicing; he lit a cigarette, sucked on it only once, and let it fall into the water jug; the sputter of the hot ash decisively divided the two silences.

"Desperate," pondered the bishop. "The pure desperate man exists, that I know. But I've never met him. Because the motive doesn't exist that would cause the path of the pure desperate man to cross mine. And if it were to happen, more than likely we would rub shoulders without recognizing each other. And sometimes I don't believe I'm worthy, even, to know . . ." Here he laughed confidently, without malice, showing himself to be young. ". . . to know the reason for our apparently fruitless meeting." He frustrated the trace of protest from Elena Sala with his powerful humble look, enveloping her in it as if to protect the woman from what she was thinking or about to say. "We are not worthy of knowing it, we weren't since the beginning of time, and so it was planned for our good. Many sins would be impossible if we eliminated the sin of vanity. There are problems, but let us not seek explanations and there will be no problems. Later we'll go to the library," he informed them, with only his eyes directing the phrase to one and then the other, dividing the implicit promise with equity; the servant bowed and moved away, walked close to the large curtained windows, then suddenly disappeared in the softness of the shadows. "It is God's will that I must reject the pure desperate man. In the past I have asked often for the grace of such a meeting; I had the presumption to believe that there was in me all the strength necessary for his consolation and salvation. I don't know him, yet even now I am tempted; I imagine him dispossessed of everything, overwhelmed by what he calls misfortune, incapable of standing up with pride to the demands of his trial. Without enough intelligence to kiss the stone on which he scratches his scabs and sores. At other times I imagine him having in abundance both what men call gifts and the true gifts, but equally incapable of rejoicing in them and being thankful for them. I am not going further. One type or another of the pure desperate man. Only occasionally do I stretch out my arms to summon him, to receive him, to give form to the impulse of pride that makes me believe I would be adequate refuge for him. I ought not to do it, perhaps; or maybe I'm still in the world only for that meeting. But don't believe what you hear or read, mistrust your own experience. Because apart from what I will now describe, there is nothing more to the weak or strong desperate man: one is subordinate to his desperation and the other, without knowing it, is above it. It is easy to confuse them, to mistake them, because the second, the impure desperate man, passes through desperation but is strong and superior to it; it is he who suffers the more of the two. The weak desperate man shows his loss of hope with each act, with each word. The weak desperate man is, from a certain point of view, more lacking in hope than the strong one. Hence confusions arise, and it is easy for him to be deceived and perturbed. Because the strong desperate man, although he suffers infinitely more, will not show it. He knows or is convinced that no one can console him. He does not believe in his ability to believe, but he has the hope, he, desperate man, that in any unforeseeable moment he will be able to confront his desperation, isolate it, see its face. And this will happen if it suits him: he can be destroyed by this confrontation, he can reach grace by it. Not holiness, because such a state is reserved for the pure desperate man. The impure, the weak desperate man, on the other hand, will proclaim his desperation with system and patience; he will crawl, anxious and falsely humble, until he finds whatever is willing to sustain him and convince him that the mutilation he represents—his cowardice, his negation of being fully that immortal soul imposed upon him—is not an obstacle to a true human existence. He will end by finding his opportunity; he will always be capable of creating the small world he needs so as to curl up and get drowsy. He will always find it, sooner or later, because his perdition is inevitable. There is no salvation, I would say, for the weak desperate man. But the strong one—and I hasten to say that the son of your mother's friend is a desperate man of this type—the strong one can laugh, can walk in the world without involving others in his desperation, because he knows he must not expect help from men or from his everyday life. He, without knowing it, is separated from his desperation; without realizing it, he awaits the moment when he will be able to look it in the eye and kill it or die. Your friend is not rich in gifts, nor has his patience been subjected to repeated and apparently insufferable tests. Unfortunately there are no sores eating away at him from the soles of his feet to the top of his head; he is not seated on ashes, nor has he been given the opportunity to kiss the stone on which he scratches himself. There is no woman at his side to tell him, 'Bless God and die.' He will not reach the touching verbosity of the pure desperate man in the presence of a predestined Elijah the Tishbite. Any unimaginable circumstance, any person can come to embody desperation for him. He will then have a crisis, he will be saved or lost by killing himself. Perhaps we are qualified, both of you or me, to confront the pure desperate man, to struggle with him and against him, to save him. But the impure weak one cannot be saved because he is petty and sensual; and the strong one will save himself or perish alone."

He got up, anomalous and violet as a stain of wine, and waited, inviting, smiling; he was growing obese, covered with an indifferent patience.

"Although there are shades, subgroups, causes of confusion . . ." he added, when they began to walk; he was smiling as they went toward the library, excusing himself on touching Elena Sala's shoulder to guide her. "Can the impure strong desperate man be converted into a weak desperate man? Or, if he does so, will he not always have been that at heart? I've passed sleepless nights thinking about this."

He shook his head, confessing only once, energetically, without expecting a reply; touching them with his fingernails, he conducted them toward the library, where the servant withdrew the lectern with the bound journals, and brought the table with the coffee service, the glasses, and the bottle of cognac.

And this always happened, with small inconsequential variations; time and again, pretending to work in my half of the office, carefully watching Onetti's back, I placed Elena Sala and the doctor in the white light of a mountain noon, moved them from one servant to another, from the familiar to the bishop, from the discourse about desperate men to digestion and the pause in the library, where His Most Reverend Excellency imposed frivolous themes on the conversation, and Elena tortured herself reviewing questions about the fugitive that she did not dare ask. I had discovered a rare happiness in detaining the three of them in the empty drowsiness of the library, in making them believe that the interview would be restricted to what had already taken place. 'She and he have time to remain here and yawn, for the rest of my life; a minute before my death I can think about them again, I'll find them as young as they are now, equally tiresome, and the same serene maliciousness will vibrate in the bishop's voice, sparkle in his eyes without their noticing it.' But I finally took pity on them, recognizing indebtedness, imagining that by taking them out of that pause I was shortening my own wait; I then rewarded the woman and the doctor with the carving of the pensive angel, with the recitation that rejuvenated the bishop, with a frightful profile, with a heavenly and lilac-colored radiance.

And here, independent of my will, the never-written episode had to branch off. Because if what the bishop was reciting under the angel's shadowless height was nothing more than admirable buffoonery, Díaz Grey and the woman would have gone to sit in the rear of the library and rub their backs against travel books, dictionaries, the complete works of Jonas Weingorther. They would then have been in the shadow, on a lower level than His Most Reverend Excellency, and a chalk stain could have substituted for the angel. But if what His Most Reverend Excellency was saying—watching for assent or disgust in the angel's unique profile—constituted, even if only for them, truth and revelation, it was imperative that the doctor and Elena Sala arrive by chance at the scene. In this case they appeared in a part of the palace serving as a music room in winter. Many notes still hung in the air, more perceptible around the sides of the room, like the stains on the heavy curtain that they both parted; then, in the second version, they rubbed their hands and held their breath in order to be terrorized as they looked closely at the beauty of the angel; they were coming to believe its beauty attainable, they were spreading it like light on the scene before them. They were resolved to listen, possessed by that curiosity which, in dreams, shows itself stronger than the fears born of any circumstance, and which prompts us to go along to the always ambiguous endings and the awakening.

The profile of the angel maintained the curled smile when the bishop's discourse proceeded without errors; when His Most Reverend Excellency chose the wrong words, the only visible eyelid blinked violently, undismayed, weakening the light in the room. Upon the parchment where the monologue was written, the victorious mouth of the angel was stretched, hard and horizontal, like an accusing finger.

"If they did not exist before, they will not exist afterward," the bishop was saying with premature emphasis. "Time past or not yet arrived, it is as if nothing had been, as if they had never come to be. And yet each one is culpable before God because, mutually helping each other from the blood of birth to the sweat of death's agony, we maintain and cultivate our feeling of eternity. Only God is eternal. Each of us exists for scarcely a fortuitous moment; and the debased conscience that permits them to accept the capricious, dismembered, and complacent sensation they call the past, that permits them to cast off lines of hope, and to correct mistakes in what they call time and the future, is only, even admitting it, a personal consciousness. A personal consciousness," His Most Reverend Excellency repeated, an arm raised toward the ceiling, calming himself with a glance at the angel's smiling profile. "Which is to say, exactly that path most removed from the goal they have pretended to seek from the beginning. When I speak of eternity, I allude to divine eternity; when I mention the Kingdom of Heaven, I limit myself to affirming its existence. I do not offer it to men. Blasphemous and absurd: a God with memory and imagination, a God who can be conquered and understood. And this same God, this horrible caricature of divinity, would take two steps back for each step forward that man might take. God exists and is not a human possibility; only by understanding this may we be totally men and conserve in ourselves the grandeur of our Lord. Apart from this, where do we go and why?" In his shining, moist face the eyes acknowledged the downsweep of the angel's eyelid; he corrected himself: "Where? And if someone finds a direction that seems plausible, why do we have to follow it? I will kiss the feet of he who may comprehend that eternity is now, that he himself is the only end, that he must accept and strive to be himself, simply that, without need of reasons, at all times and against all opposition, living in abject poverty through passion, forsaking memory and imagination. I kiss his feet, I applaud the courage of he who accepts each and every one of the laws of a game he did not invent and was not asked if he wanted to play."

Elena Sala let the curtain fall, she opened her purse and began to powder herself; with difficulty, opening a path through the crowd in the vestibule, she moved toward the door. A brisk wind tempered the warm air of the square, blowing down toward the neighborhood around the station.

"Did you find him interesting? I did," she said, hanging onto the doctor's arm. "Naturally, I don't believe I understood everything. No, I don't want to go into a coffee shop. He's that way, just like the bishop said: a man who wants to be himself and who accepts the rules of the game."

They were walking along one side of the square, smelling the nocturnal perfume of the trees, barely united by the rustle of the reddish sand on which they were stepping; they looked at movie posters unheedingly and drifted effortlessly down the sloping street toward the hotel.

"I don't know why," she said. "It's idiotic, but I'm sure that he's here; if I'm lucky, I'll see him in a café or stumble upon him at any moment."

"Why don't you stay at La Sierra?" he suggested.

"I can't, I have an appointment with Horacio in Santa María, at the hotel by the river. Besides, it wouldn't help to stay here; nothing helps. Only if by chance . . . I shouldn't have run after him. I'm sure I'm not going to catch up with him. I talked to Horacio on the phone; he has business for you."

In the half block separating them from the sign and the round lights of the hotel, Díaz Grey decided to escape on the first morning train, to return to the office and the hospital, to rest a while in the imbecilic atmosphere of friends; to forget the woman and the promises without the possible fulfillment she had implied; to row up the river some morning to the creek by the wooden hotel, to climb the staircase and surprise the drowsing owner, to return to Mr. Glaeson's music room, to look at the violinist's thighs and rectify the myth of the dwarf.

"I'm sending you up to sleep," Elena said, stopping at the entrance to the hotel. "It's finished for me." She let an ashamed laugh be heard as she crossed her arms and looked around, omitting him. "It's all over. I don't know how long ago, I've just realized it. But perhaps you want to do something else. I always behaved badly with you. What would you like?"

"I'd like to hold you close," Díaz Grey murmured. "For a little."

"All right, let's go," she said, taking his arm.

When they passed in front of the porter's desk, she bore—high and detached, like a fragile object—a calming smile, the drowsy remains of a long intensity in her mouth and eyes. Díaz Grey did not dare speak to her, nor did he say a word as they went up in the elevator, feeling that he—the man whose arm Elena Sala was pressing until it hurt—had for her the same meaning as the expression of wonder that she paraded through the corridors and then lay softly on the bed: nothing more than a precarious symbol of the world and her relation with the world, unimprovable because of the circumstances, indispensable for the charitable act.

8

The End of
the World

The three days of bad weather came while I was still in Buenos Aires; I forgot the farce of the publicity agency and was at home every possible hour, contemplating the gray air, the puddle of water that was growing larger next to the badly fitted balcony door, sensing how sweetly the solitude was extending itself toward the moment when I would be obliged to look at myself, isolated, naked, and without distraction, when it would be ordained for me to act and to convert myself through action into another, perhaps into a definitive Arce who could not be known in advance.

Stretched out on the bed or walking around in the disorder of the room, I was helping myself to stop being, to extinguish myself, pushing or isolating Brausen in the humid air, stirring him like a piece of soap in water so that he would dissolve.

In the afternoon, with the wall between us, I listened to La Queca's weeping. I hadn't heard her come in, but I was sure she was crying alone on her bed, turning her open mouth into the pillow. Perhaps she, too, had allowed herself to be overwhelmed by the failures that the rainy day symbolized, or the humidity might be multiplying "them," or she might have a presentiment of Arce's emergence and her own destruction. She could be guessing the end in the sudden, domineering presence of memories, sensing how they came one by one and went on expanding until they were intolerable, until they became hard and massive, then melted and disappeared, this time forever, each face, each episode, each one of the feelings already lived; so that she, like me, would not be engulfed again in the plot of previous days, would not deduce the future from this, but would end by recognizing herself for the first time in her life, forced to change the expression in her eyes, to feel in her fingers the true, always surprising, always discouraging meaning of the shape of flesh and bones. But above all—I was listening to the sound of her crying—on the other side of the wall "they" were there, assured and jovial as on a first date, like simple children of the rainy afternoon.

Perhaps La Queca had lit the red-shaded lamp across the room from the bed where she was crying and trying to escape. She would light that lamp in order to attract them like insects, to lure them away; they would hover there or remain motionless, heavy, surfeited, soft, making fun of the fact that they couldn't be counted, stirring up for her, their generous mother, cause and effect, sweet totality, a single grimace suitable for all their faces or the fluctuating zone that she imagined as the setting for those faces. I will die without knowing them. They might be grouped as if they were in front of the fireplace at an inn one stormy night, forming a pyramid with the diversity of their statures, grateful for the refuge and life granted them, demonstrating their gratitude with the grimace, unique and uniform, that stretched and contracted the soft fat of their faces, making the small round hole of their snouts tremble.

And only when she leaped out of bed to try to drive them away with swats and slaps, when they saw her stop, defeated and impotent, in the middle of the room—her fists clenched against her thighs, rigid, as she ordered herself to smile—only then would they begin to talk to her with the monotonous and indefatigable persistence of voices that do not solicit understanding or response, but sound only for the gratuitous joy of being.

There they were, calling her with the s's they hissed next to her ear or howling her name from remote places, from frozen stars, from the submarine pit where the first bone was buried; calling her with indifference, with tenderness, with urgency, with supplication, with mockery, with need, separating the syllables of her name as if warbling it, repeating it until it sounded like a rattle in the throat and then transforming themselves into the name. 'They are my name, they are Queca, it's me,' they would end by making her think, disappearing as she felt herself become tranquil and smiling—'I am they, there's no one else, they aren't here'—only to run and wait for her on the bed and touch her body rapidly, imitating the rhythm of the rain with the tips of their forefingers, softly, with no intention but to keep her awake and terrified.

Night had come and she continued weeping on the other side of the wall—the noise muffled by her tears, by the curtain of hair stuck to her mouth, by her bitten knuckles—when I decided, on one of those three days of bad weather, to get up and chew a crust of bread and another of cheese in the kitchen; I flattened a black banana between my fingers and drank a bit of water over the funereal odor from the refrigerator. 'Maybe it'll be tomorrow, perhaps I shouldn't continue to trust in the superstition of a sign. But I won't be the one to kill her: it will be someone else, Arce, no one. I was all those things that no longer exist, a personal form of melancholy, an intermittent anxiety without purpose, peaceful and useful cruelties to wound me and make me know I'm alive.' I went to search among the perfumes of the chest of drawers for a packet of letters from Raquel; I burned them one by one in the kitchen sink, without unfolding them, reading aloud the phrases that passed before my eyes, not understanding what I saw or what I was doing, interrupting myself occasionally, in vain, to evoke the sadness: "Days when Mamma hardly spoke to me. Exactly the same, my pleasure in being with him and my desire to be alone. He had been in Brazil and he talked to me about the friend he was in prison with. After the 'conversion' I always remember myself trying to give Mamma those things. Superior and much more intelligent than me, but Gertrudis will never understand. Then the atmosphere changed completely and there was some happiness. To be cornered in a meeting and pay the price for something I didn't . . ."

I turned on the faucet and helped destroy the carbonized paper, the incomprehensible words that had remained intact, bordered in mourning, strengthened and ominous. I walked toward the balcony and stepped into the rain water with my bare feet; I forced myself to think about my trip to Montevideo, to see myself holding Raquel's forehead to help her vomit, sneaking into La Queca's hotel room and performing the comedy of jealousy that she expects, that she considers one of my duties.

La Queca was crying sporadically between snores, between the absurd phrases of Raquel's letters. 'It would be the same if I had read them slowly before burning them, if I were to find myself now at the end of five years of living with her. The stream of water over the brittle, hardened remains of the paper, the grave, merry sound of water, the black fragments pulverized and spinning in the bubbles over the drain. She isn't crying any more, she must be asleep with one leg under the light from the lamp that she'll still discover still lit only at noon.'

I returned to my bed, not sleepy, resolved to suppress Díaz Grey, even if it were necessary to flood the provincial city, to put a fist through the glass of that window where he had leaned, in the docile and hopeful beginning of his story, in order to contemplate without interest the distance between the square and the barrancas. Díaz Grey was dead and I was agonizing from old age on the bedsheets, listening to the whisper of water softly exuding from clouds; I had begun to get wrinkled on the night when I accepted embracing Gertrudis for the first time in Montevideo, with the help of Stein's pimping, in a two-story house whose wood was impregnated with decency or forms of decency, which had absorbed respectability and the unwavering idea that "my home is the world" through twenty years of domestic rituals and family reunions; I had provoked old age in the moment that I agreed to stay with Gertrudis, doing the same things again and again, welcoming the anniversaries, the security, rejoicing because the days were not preludes to conflicts, choices, new compromises. I was dragging into my decomposition Díaz Grey, Elena Sala, the husband, the ubiquitous desperate man, the city I had erected with an inevitable incline toward the friendliness of the river.

It was dying with me, that conflict barely sensed, dying amid the tiresome, energetic, austere inhabitants of the Swiss colony and the settlers of the city; amid the idle rich of Santa María and those who kept it alive, shopped in it, visited it in crowds on the important holidays (not those that they, their parents, and grandparents had brought from Europe along with hope and determination, prayer books with broken spines, and dull photographs with dates on the back; but instead someone else's important holidays that they half respected and tolerated sharing); inhabitants who then passed across the square, apprehensive, with repressed excitement, going down the walk near the river, past the movie house, through the streets dedicated to business that they called downtown and against whose walls men with slick hair leaned their backs, making jokes with a light, romantic envy as they watched them as they passed, slow, dressed in Sunday clothes, in family groups that announced the quality of indestructibility. The conflict born from mutual and well-hidden contempt scarcely showed in the smiles and ironic intonations of the dark men, smiles and voices that the blond men succeeded in changing into obsequious attitudes—these blond men who were worried, close to doubt when they exchanged money in business, buying automobiles and harvesters; who left exaggerated tips on café tables without kindness or conviction, tips that only strengthened the disdain of the others.

All had disappeared without pain or the possibility of nostalgia: 'Here we are, here is this recently born man whom I only know at present by the rhythm of pulsations and the smell of a perspiring chest. La Queca sleeps and snores; if she remembers her dream, if she wants to tell me about it tomorrow, she will say, "Then 'they' rose up like a wave in the sea to overwhelm me before I could speak, because we guessed at the same time that if I named them I'd kill them, if I called each one by name . . ." When the rain has ended, the wind enters through the balcony and strikes against the nose and nape of the neck in Gertrudis' photograph on the wall. Tomorrow will come—it's astonishing to know it with such certainty. The sky will be clean and this man will sally forth into the street. I'm going to sleep and I'm going to wake up; I will attempt to discover myself with a sly glance in the bathroom mirror, surprising and settling upon the movements of my hands; I will try to know what to depend on, as if it were necessary, asking myself with cunning and feigned disinterest about God, love, eternity, my parents, the men of the year 3000; with a twisted smile indicating only the small shame of being alive and not knowing what this means, I will sit down to breakfast, I will verify that nothing of importance has happened since someone wrote versicles from the preacher's words that the forgotten Julio Stein recited when drunkenness caught him without a woman, and while he looks at the new sun in the street, I will substitute for them phrases that allude to condolence cards, to the heads of children, and the lust of loved ones.

'I will walk toward the south and allow myself to be tempted by the idea of excluding Díaz Grey from the end of the world begun tonight, perhaps definitively realized tomorrow. (Women with purses and baskets, ill-tempered and driven men will be crossing the light of morning without suspecting that they were killed by my death, that the streets they walk have disappeared under lava, under oceans.) Around Constitución I will again sit in a café near the square and buy cigarettes in order to let one hang motionless from my mouth, so that the smoke can extend between my eyes and the clump of trees, the movements of porters, travelers, taxis, and merchants, making all the activity I watch incomprehensible. Then—and it will not be necessary that I move a finger or my face—Díaz Grey will wake up in the hotel room at La Sierra, he will discover that the woman at his side is dead, he will hurt his heel crushing the empty ampules, the syringe on the floor; he will understand with humiliation and an admirable sense of justice why Elena Sala said yes the night before; he will submit to the power of a melodramatic sensation, he will imagine a future friend destined to hear his confession—"She was already dead, do you understand, when I held her in my arms. And she knew it." In the gray shadows he will retreat a few steps to move away from the dead woman and contemplate her form on the bed. When the light grows stronger, he will be able to look at her face, he will see it tranquil and affable, back from its excursion to a zone constructed with the reverse of questions, with the revelations of daily life nobody ever understood. Dead and returned from death, hard and cold as a premature truth, abstaining from shouting her experiences, her defeats, the conquered spoils of war.'

9

Raquel's Visit

A little blood was coming out, perhaps the nose was swelling, moment by moment, visibly; La Queca was surrendering to the dull, methodical blows without any attempt at rebellion or defense other than her almost continual laugh, whose origin of hate was revealed by the care and tenacity with which she separated it, sound by sound, from the background of weeping where it was born, the care and attention with which her laugh went on cleansing itself of delicacy and tears.

From the pillow, stifling her laugh at regular intervals in order to touch her tongue to her lips and stop the tickling sensation of blood and sweat, her eyes, brilliant with enthusiasm, followed me around the room.

"Yes," she said after a while. "I'm a drunken bitch. Crazy world . . . I'm a drunken bitch."

She laughed and repeated the phrase when she went into the bathroom to wet her face, when she was getting dressed, stuffing cotton soaked in cologne in her nostrils; her nose was red and shiny despite the powder.

"A drunken bitch," she said from the door, and smiled. "I don't care if you stay or go. I'm going to look for them and bring them here. In every color."

I dressed and walked around the room, examining my pockets, shaken by the need to give her some gift, to leave something as a symbol of the superstitious love that began to bind me to her violently as soon as the door slammed and I found myself alone, as suddenly as the slammed door agitated the air and the atmosphere stirred, moved toward me from the corners, permitting my face and chest to again feel the miraculous climate, gone so long, denied. Under a handkerchief in my hip pocket I found a rusty hexagonal nut; I bounced it in my hand and let it roll under the bed.

Futilely I listened alongside my apartment wall; La Queca did not return that night. During the dawn hours, impelled by my sudden growing love, needing to add mementos to the bit of iron I had pitched under her bed, I found a razor blade and made a slanting cut on my chest facing the bathroom mirror, as I recalled the smile she had flung at me before slamming the door; then I could sleep, consoled by the thin burning where only isolated drops of blood had appeared.

But during the following days and nights La Queca came up from the street accompanied by men; and with each new, unknown step, with each repetition of the sound of the key in the lock, I felt increase that grateful, pious, implacable form of love that bound me to her. I listened to her struggle against the preliminary minutes of timidity and clumsiness, then hasten the coupling on the bed, and eject her visitor almost immediately, heading him toward the door with lies and promises. I heard her repeat the old voice and laugh, the sounds that would stop abruptly like an air brake. I listened to her verifying the man's footsteps in the corridor, the passage of time necessary for him to leave the building and get into his car or go into a café for a strong drink, the time necessary for him to weigh the pleasure greedily, to fear its consequences, to yield to elated pride, to work eagerly at fitting what had happened into everyday life, caught between transitory youthfulness and old distrust. Because she alone in each case had accepted a dirty, greenish, dark gray, symbolic peso note; and when I entered to visit her she was smiling, looking at my eyes that quickly glanced at the pile of wrinkled bills on the blue tablecloth to appraise its gradual growth.

"I'm a drunken bitch," was all she said, showing me her teeth a little, almost with affection.

I imagined her powdering her face between each man, tightening her thin lips thoughtfully, meditative, and then renouncing this mood with a shrug; I listened to her open the door and close it with a bang, as if she suspected that I could hear her, as if the noise were indispensable to keep count, as if it might add to the previous numbers, might underline the amount.

I arrived at the door of the bank a little after noon and joined the group waiting for it to open; I sidled between shoulders and necks and turned my head to look at the whiteness of the sun on the Diagonal, the monument in the small square, the etched lines of buildings inscribed onto the clear sky, perhaps the last blue of summer. After my eyes slid over the ill-tempered, arrogant expressions, over the immobility of the faces around me, as if I were groping for a gun, I moved my fingers inside my pocket to touch the slip of paper where I had written the schedule for the day, the letters and numbers representing each one of my next movements and the hours when they would be executed, directing and setting my course until the end, until at nine-thirty I would walk away from La Queca's body and begin to breathe audibly, pacing back and forth, transformed into a void, into an impatient curiosity, waiting for the consciousness of having done it.

I wadded the bills neatly and put them in my pockets without counting them; I closed the strongbox and called the attendant. 'What will they think when the quarterly rent is overdue and they open the box and find screws and bits of glass?'

Nothing had changed in me or the city when I walked on, indifferent to the sun, a hand in my trouser pocket, through the Diagonal Norte toward the obelisk; for the two blocks going toward Esmeralda, nothing distinguished me from the tired noontime pedestrians; I looked at my sweaty face as I passed the polished shopwindows, carrying from one to the other an imprecise, fleeting memory of the new youthful expression that moved with my face, an air of confidence and challenge, a face of indifferent cruelty. Prudent, afraid of driving away the newborn apparition that floated in the air, accompanying me behind the glass, from time to time I directed a quick oblique glance at shopwindows, stopping in front of them, barely raising my head to recognize and study myself, never getting past the jaw, the strange lips that were protruding in order to imitate in silence the attitude of whistling.

I ate some sandwiches, taking refuge in a corner of a café. Against the background of Elena Sala's death, I was imagining a jubilant Díaz

Grey, a jovial and resolute Horacio Lagos privileged to order dance music from the violin of Miss Glaeson and to slap her on the nearest bulge of her body, a desperate ex-fugitive who had discovered the need to languish next to the dead woman's husband. The violin case traveling loaded with morphine ampules, dance slippers that picked their way through the streets of a city in fiesta—one foot then the other, a quick turn—toward a sudden and foreseeable ending.

The itinerary I carried in my pocket scheduled lunch for one-thirty; I was eating twenty minutes late. The next move—shave and shower, choose the best white shirt in the wardrobe—had to be executed at two; I left some coins on the café table and went out into the street to hail a cab; for a moment I suffered racial hatred for those crowding the sidewalks. 'Perhaps it's preferable,' I thought in the cab, 'to give up the schedule; perhaps it would be best to take a bath and wait, stretched out on the bed, to look for Gertrudis' old metronome in the bottom of the closet, to try to make it play larghetto and to let myself go, without acting or thinking, only obsessed by the eternity that the device will keep on dividing into small parts until it's six in the evening. Then reinstate the schedule, go down into the streets, find a prostitute, leave her at eight-thirty and come back to Calle Chile, look through the windows at the loud, languid fellows in the Petit Electra, stop to talk with the doorman, go up to La Queca's apartment. She'll have returned and will be alone; I will know who I am, who this other is.'

When I walked out of the elevator, I saw the woman's body from behind, her hand raised toward the bell of my apartment; I didn't recognize her until she turned and I understood at the same time that there was something about her that inhibited emotion and astonishment.

"Hello," she said. "How are you? You don't seem happy to . . ."

I shook her hand in silence, smiling at her, searching to find, in the face and in the alien, unpleasant body that Raquel had brought, what the grotesque thing was, unconnected with me and my remembrance of her, that she was isolating in the dark corner where the door of my apartment almost joined at a right angle to that of La Queca's. Perhaps the new man I had become did not recognize her, perhaps that pale, bony face was not the same one that I had seen and evoked, the one that suited Raquel, the one that had to be in its proper place under the small hat cutting a crescent on her forehead.

"Finding you here is a big surprise," I said. "Gertrudis isn't living with me."

"I knew that," she said, nodding; she was separating her lips until it was impossible for me to doubt that she was smiling, until I saw, close to my face, a kind, impersonal smile shaped to expand the tolerance. "It's the third time I've come; I was here in the morning, as soon as the boat arrived. I called the office, but they told me you weren't there any more."

"Yes," I said; I opened the door and let her in. I was sure of La Queca's absence. 'I'd like to tell you what I'm going to do,' I thought as I advanced behind her walk, the tapping of heels that stopped under Gertrudis' picture. "That story's finished, and it's a subject that doesn't interest me. But that isn't why you're here; nor to comment either on the last time we were together."

"No," she replied without turning, her nose brushing against her sister's picture. "I know why you left me like that, I understand all you suffered then. I want to thank you."

She turned suddenly, dramatic, the indefinable unpleasant thing spreading over her and gathering intensity in her face. I went to sit down, arranging the bundle of money in my pocket; something emanating from her was menacing me, from the moment her ridiculous hat had touched Gertrudis' photograph; she was going to leave something unpleasant behind her like a skin blemish, a kind of remorse.

"No," I said, "I don't believe you understand. I knew you were vomiting in the café bathroom, that you'd need me when you came out. But I didn't feel sorry for you. Perhaps it was cowardice; in any case, the desire to free myself, to not compromise myself. Nothing more."

She smiled again and came close to me with short steps, dragging her feet a little, paying attention to the friction of each step on the floor; she looked for a chair and sat down very slowly, bracing herself with her arms.

"No one knows I'm in Buenos Aires." The words crossed the ecstatic smile without altering it; her eyes were anticipating my surprise. "Neither Gertrudis nor Mamma. I didn't even speak to them on the phone. I wanted to see you before anyone else."

I smiled at her in silence, I was sure of having repeated with precision the old expression of understanding, the look of wonder that I always had for her.

"I've wanted to see you and talk to you. I've wanted to from the moment I understood why you did it. It became a necessity, and here I am."

The unpleasant thing she had brought was filling the room, it was already more solid, more real than we were ourselves.

"Yes," I said. "I understand."

I composed a prayer that she take off her hat and I repeated it mentally; I needed to see her bare forehead, her loose hair. I would have paid all the money in my pocket to love her again.

"It's quite possible you're no longer suffering," she went on. "But I want to erase the pain you suffered then."

I stopped praying and began to play with the word *suffered*, I squeezed its ridiculousness, I let it fall. Suddenly I had to hide my face because I understood what it was that had changed her, I discovered the significance of the slow steps, the body swaying in its walk, the care she had taken when she sat; I saw the stomach that came forward to a point over the thin parted thighs. The repugnant sensation and the enmity had issued from the belly someone had given her, from the fetus that was growing larger, negating her, that was expanding victoriously to transform her into an anonymous pregnant woman, that was condemning her to vanish into a strange destiny. She held her body upright against the back of the chair; the loving smile was raised, constant, directed at the universe. 'She should be thinking, word for word: now an interior glow lights up my face.' From the little hat stuck on her head to the shoes trying to meet at the tips, failure and extravagant happiness continued to flow from her like a bad smell.

"And that necessity reached a climax," she was saying, "when some ten or fifteen days ago I received a letter from Gertrudis. She told me about the two of you; of course I already knew. But in addition she talked about you and me; not in a direct way, but hinting at it with a joke."

"What difference does it make?" I said dejectedly.

"It's not that, I want you to listen to me. What does Gertrudis know about us? What did you tell her about me?"

"Nothing. When I returned from Montevideo, I didn't say a word to her. Before that, I'd have told her that I loved you." I smiled at her frankly, I forced her to look at my eyes, fastened on her stomach. "That you were marvelous, that you were absurd, that unlike anyone else, you were part of life's rapture and mystery." 'She's as old as Gertrudis; the belly growing on her is equivalent to the breast they cut from her sister.'

"Weren't you like that? Could Gertrudis prevent you from being that way and prevent me from admiring everything you were?"

"It's not that." The smile moved patiently from one side to the other, rejecting discord and sudden attacks. "I'm concerned about us—the need to end this."

"This?" I exclaimed, bringing closer to her—unintentionally now—my old face of wonderment and candor.

"When I got the letter, I understood it was necessary; I went through a crisis and finally I felt relieved, I knew I had to come see you. I know we have nothing to regret. But it puts us on a level . . ."

'Maybe she's gone crazy, maybe—thank God, then—she laughed at me from the beginning and she's laughing at me now.'

"Are you going to have a child?" I interrupted. The jubilant way she savored pushing the *yes* through her teeth was enough to make me furious. "Damned if I know what it is that must end!"

"Don't get angry," she whispered.

'If I tell her I'm going to kill La Queca without any motive that I can explain, she'll advise me sweetly, "Don't do it"; and she'll lower her eyes, she'll bathe in that fountain of kindness and tolerance that is swelling up her uterus.'

"Don't get angry, dear. I know most of the blame is mine. I never should have . . . Alcides knows all about it and was able to understand. I loved you a great deal. I'll never know anyone as good as you."

I got up and went to the kitchen to look for something to drink. I changed my mind and slowly turned in the direction of the fixed smile, stupid and placid.

"I have no reason to get angry," I said. "But it happens that I don't know you, I don't know who you are or what you're doing here. I don't understand a word you're saying."

"Yes, of course," she agreed readily. "I was blind or crazy, as you wish. I always loved you, since the time you came to Pocitos to see Gertrudis. I was a child and at fifteen—I'm not just saying this for your sake—one may fall in love with anyone, from the most likely to the most impossible. Perhaps I loved you for your kindness, your understanding, your intelligence—so special, so human. I blame you for nothing. Now this time, when you returned to Montevideo, each of us did something to aggravate the mistake. Without realizing it, I'm sure. You weren't happy with Gertrudis and I was confused, going through a period of trial. Spiritually we needed each other."

"But I went to Montevideo with a woman; one who paid for my trip and not with her own money, but with money she got from another man I don't even know, in exchange for sleeping with him. Understand?"

"It doesn't matter, we all make mistakes."

"But we kissed each other," I said, laughing. "I embraced you, I touched your tongue."

She blinked, made the interrupted smile reappear, practiced on me the look that she was planning to use on her child.

"Certainly we kissed. But what troubles me is that you persist in that night's state of mind and think that I do, too. I was blind, now my eyes are opened. The events aren't important, what we feel is. Each unworthy, unjust sentiment, each act of selfishness, feeds our imperfections. And it doesn't affect only us, but those who are in contact with us, and the evil that we pass on, they continue passing on to others. Do you understand?"

'She's crazy, she has no right to do this, to turn into a grotesque ruin, to deform the Raquel I thought about when I was sad. I have to tear her hat off. I have to see the round head and loose hair, to try to see Raquel's face before it's impossible. Because just as the beltless, shapeless dress is the uniform of every imminent mother in the world, the small unadorned hat, tight-fitting as a helmet, is the public announcement of resolute purity, contempt for life's sensual possibilities, its adherence to duty and arrogant stupidity.'

"Perhaps you don't understand," she continued. "Don't worry, it took me a long time. I remember having refused to understand; I remember that when I began to see clearly, there was something in me that became irritated, that resisted unreasonably."

"It's best that you don't talk any more," I said, and I sat down on the bed; I looked at her, soft and heavy in the chair; I was stirred by the quality of the smile that puffed up her cheeks, as previously some unexpected happiness had puffed them up, immediately separated from its cause. "Don't talk."

"You don't want to talk?"

"No, not about anything. I don't know you. All this is sad and stupid. I see you as sad and stupid."

"Sad?" she said mockingly with a sigh, without hurting me. "Perhaps I did wrong to come and chat so directly. I thought of writing you and then . . . I knew I had to see you."

I stretched out on the bed and closed my eyes, chewing mints, listening to Raquel's sugary voice and the silences on the other side of the wall.

"We were wrong, dear. Now I can call you 'dear.' I know we didn't want to hurt anyone, neither Gertrudis nor Alcides nor ourselves. But evil can lurk in feelings we believe most pure."

"Raquel, I want you to shut up. I want you to take off your hat."

"Oh yes! I don't want to give you the feeling that I'm here . . . I had forgotten my hat. Is that better?"

"Yes, thank you," I said, without wanting to look at her.

"We wouldn't have been happy," she said softly, and stopped talking. 'She's taken off her hat and it's possible that her hair has fallen free and that I could recognize her in a glance; it's possible that she's undressing and in a moment will come toward me, preceded by the mass of her womb and the same unforgettable, transfigured face she had in Montevideo when she sang "The Hut" or "No Other Land in the World" in a chorus at Party meetings in Stadium Uruguay; possible that it may occur to her to save me by cutting my throat, and my only revenge would be to exaggerate the scorn in the corners of my mouth as I let her do it.'

"We would have been embittered, who knows for how long." Again the slow, sticky murmuring, uncontrolled, sounding for no one, as if she were condemned to talk, talk, until death closes her mouth and makes her double over in the chair, pressing her belly against her legs. "You're going to know happiness, not sensual happiness but another, forged from obligations, from love, my dear."

Twice the *dear* buzzed around my head on the bed, touched my smile like a dull, fatigued insect.

"I want you to shut up," I said, "to leave, I don't want to see you or hear you any more."

I didn't want to look at her; I imagined her rigid, with the hat pulled down to her eyebrows, putting an end to the expression of pardon that she directed toward the door and the smells from the kitchen, toward the rest of the world, toward the slick fellows of the Petit Electra, La Queca, La Gorda, the past, and the inevitable mistakes men would have to go on making. I shouted at her again and in that way strengthened the silence; I imagined her getting up, hesitant, fluctuating between disenchantment and confidence; I could hear the weak sibilance of kindnesses and excuses returning with reluctance to again become part of Raquel. I listened to the tapping sound of her body's course as it progressed, swaying in the direction of the door; I was afraid a phrase free of bitterness would come at me, oozing faith, a phrase that would be like offering the other cheek.

Alone, drowsy, I came to think that Raquel's visit, her pregnancy, and her tedious lunacy had been mere elements of a dream; I forgot Raquel until at the end of the afternoon I heard La Queca arriving and a man's voice; I raised myself up from the bed and my eyes found a little printed card on the table that said in English:

THE NEW INVOCATION
From the point of light within the Mind of God
  Let light stream forth into the minds of men.
    Let light descend on Earth.
From the center where the Will of God is known
Let purpose guide the little wills of men
The purpose which the Master knows and serves.
Let light and Love and Power restore the Plan on Earth.

At the foot of the card there was written in pencil: "I'll be at Mamma's house; come there tonight without fail."

I understood almost all the words that began with capital letters, I tried to pronounce the last line and did not oppose its sentiment. I thought it was incomprehensible to have loved Raquel, that perhaps I had never loved her and that my determination to not touch her stemmed simply from the fear of discovering my lack of love for her.

I undressed and until nightfall paced up and down the hot room, convincing myself that I had chosen that month, that week, that day, because now the summer, refusing to die, was elevating with itself—to a level scarcely discernible, but unmistakable on the stone of time—men and things; convincing myself that the heat could be sensed through the eyes and that it broke in colors on the walls and around my moving body, divided into stripes that crossed without becoming entwined, yellows and ochers, dark yet vibrant greens, the green of a lawn in afternoon shadow.

From behind the wall there was silence; the man had already left.

10

Ernesto Again

It occurred to me that I was unable to act because my feelings were faltering—anxiety and hope, fears equal to the prospect of what I was going to do. To squeeze her throat and kiss her while upon her, my arms pinning hers to her body, her legs blocked by mine—this had become a task I regularly performed, an understood business, an indifferent way of earning my bread.

I began to dress, immediately transformed into the pitiable man wrested from sleep by the alarm clock that instantly restores consciousness of duties and responsibilities. I moved quietly, pausing now and then to sense the silence on the other side of the wall, imagining "them" floating over the drowsy La Queca, chatting and agitated without reason, perhaps simply to keep themselves alive and not be caught off guard when she woke up. Clustered, moving their viscous mouths, alternately infantile and aged, they swallowed and regurgitated the dead, unbreathable air of the room.

I put on my best shirt, distracted myself by playing with the gun barrel; I heard a radio signal give the time as eight-thirty. It was the moment when I was to have left the prostitute, exuding frustration and respect as I pressed her cheek and smiled, the unrenounced homage to love's impossibility.

I closed my door without a sound, I rang for the elevator, opened it, and slammed it so it could be heard. Before putting the key into the lock of La Queca's door, I knew everything was going to be easy, that she would come close to me so I could stun her with one blow; afterward, when she was stretched out on the bed, whether she heard me or not, I would try to tell her everything that can be told to another person, I would rest my grave voice against her ear without the pressure of time, not caring whether she understood me, sure that a few minutes would be enough to empty myself of everything I had had to swallow since adolescence, all the words choked by laziness, by lack of faith, by the feeling that it was useless to talk.

I opened the door and entered the disorderly room, I looked at the rearranged furniture, the jumbled clothes; each thing seemed to have shaken itself awake in order to celebrate the reconquest of the air. I breathed it again, thanked it with a smile. Under the lamp next to the head of the bed—the only light on—La Queca was naked with a twisted sheet across her belly, her hands joined on her chest, one leg stretched out, the knee of the other raised.

A spurt of water sounded in the kitchen sink, heavy and brief, cutting in two the noises that rose from the street; I didn't understand immediately; laboriously I pulled my eyes away from La Queca and made a hand slide over the hardness of the revolver, verifying that the world was mine. Legs apart, without interrupting the circular movement of the finger playing with the key, I looked toward the sound in the kitchen; there was a silence; from a distant radio came the high pitch of a violin, like a shuttle. Although the kitchen door was not pushed open by La Gorda—I was sure it was she, I saw her leaning over the sink in an evening gown, her bare arms large and heavy as thighs, the low-necked gown giving off the odor of a violent perfume, long pendants trembling from her ears—I remained motionless, full of the same confidence, adapting it immediately to the substitution. The man—I knew he was very young, almost a boy; I saw him bent over, I saw the prominent bones of his face, the jet black and recently wet hair growing close to his eyebrows—pushed the door with his shoulder, half erect and twisting his head over the rocking, deaf moan of the door, and rolled his eyes around. He was in shirt sleeves, shaking his wet hands toward the floor, while shadows collected in each depression of his white face, immobile, as if condemned to maintain a dull, inexorable expression through the next hours. He moved forward without hesitation, always a step behind his smell of jasmine, with his eyes directed toward me but unseeing; he stopped when he was about to touch me; the perfume flowed from him and with it an infinite incomprehension, the loud breath that was rapidly absorbing the capacity for oblivion from the air.

She did not move, she did not speak. The rings on the fingers against her breasts, the skin of her knee, and the crescent of her teeth emerged with equal intensity from the dim light around the bed; suddenly they began to repeat idle explanations.

"Yes?" Ernesto asked, but not looking, scarcely opening his dark, blind eyes toward the place my head occupied. I didn't want to smile or show him any kindness; he twisted his mouth in the direction of the bed, slowly raised a hand, and rested it on my shoulder. "Is she . . ." he said; he seemed to wait for something and did not become discouraged by the silence. "Is she . . ."

He clenched his fists over his stomach and began rubbing them, one against the other, alternately; he backed away from me and began to walk around the room in a circle, looking at the floor, determining the speed of his shoes with his eyes. I went toward the bed and touched La Queca's raised knee; I slid my hand over her naked skin until it touched her shoulder.

"Yes," I said, when I had straightened up.

Ernesto was walking in a perfect circle, remote and insular, his fingers rapidly fondling themselves. I looked at the spots on La Queca's neck and bent over again to smell her mouth. 'I knew it the moment I opened the door,' I lied to myself. Seated on the bed, I prayed my weight would not disturb her as I watched the boy circling the dirty rug. I touched the cold, flat belly, I tugged at the sheet to cover it better.

"Let's go," I said. Little by little he came to a halt and stood with his back to me. "We'll talk later, away from here."

He turned without seeing me, stared at the place from which my voice had issued; he made a movement with his shoulders and resumed walking, bent over, his hands together, wringing them. I picked up his hat and jacket and walked until I stepped into the circle he was treading.

"Let's go," I said. "Don't be an idiot." He raised his head, but not toward me, and his lips were moving in silence; the circular walk had made his face more frail and wan. His eyes stopped at my hat and he continued putting on his jacket; the jasmine perfume was fading like a memory.

"Is she . . ." he repeated, almost daring to question.

I picked up a garment from the floor and spread it across La Queca's face.

"We have to get out," I said; I put his hat on him and pushed him. "We've got to get out immediately—leave the light as it is."

In the corridor I heard the silent house; I let the slam of the door die, its echo reverberating down the staircase. Without releasing him, I extended an arm and opened my door.

"Go in, I live here."

I felt that I was waking up—not from this dream, but from another, incomparably longer, that included this one and in which I had dreamed I was dreaming this dream—when I had him inside, when I saw him move forward, brushing against the foot of the bed, colliding with the glass balcony door, and standing there like a lump, then turn with an astonished face, unintentionally revealing the touching determination to sustain himself on pride alone; when I saw him bend over clumsily, sit down, and deposit his short square hands on the table, quiet, without looking, but with his eyelids raised, pretending a failure of memory, hard, weary, and secretly waiting.

I woke up from my dream without happiness or displeasure, standing, backing up until I touched a wall and looked from there at the shapes and colors of the world that silently presented itself, a vortex from chaos, from nothing, and that was suddenly quiet. Now the world was before me, ready for my five senses, wonderful before it could be recognized, incredible when memory began to function again. Standing against the wall in the shadow, smiling, I contemplated the immobility of the other. I credited myself with the stamina necessary to go through dawns and journeys looking at this man rigid in his chair with his hands resting on the table, and who was beginning to sweat under the light as if in the hottest spot of a summer night; who was shaking his head gently to deny the desire to let it fall against his chest. I surrendered to the illusion that I had the strength to look eternally at the damp white face, bony, where youth was nothing more than a vicious quality; to look at it understanding that the man who was shaking it back and forth with defensive persistence was, simultaneously, separate and part of me, an action of mine: to look at it as a memory, the remorse of a guilty act. I might have wanted the boy locked up there till the end of time, like a child or an animal, caring for him and consoling myself for all possible misfortune with the conviction that he was alive and remembering.

But as soon as his eyes—motionless in his face, as if only the neck muscles could give them direction—were aimed toward my body against the wall, I came forward smiling, raised a hand, and touched him on the shoulder. I lingered in the pleasure of lightly rubbing the cloth that covered his shoulder, the muscle in repose; I thought no former sensation was comparable to this joy and this contempt.

"Coffee?" I asked him. "Or a drink?"

He shrugged, I protected the movement with my hand; I got the bottle of gin and two glasses. When I returned, he was raising his fingers to inspect them, all at the same time, without lifting his palm from the table. He took a long drink, his mouth hung open for a moment to catch his breath, and then he looked at me, relaxing his body in the chair, saturated now with the resolution not to speak. I filled his glass again; I was cleaning off a mint that I had found loose in my pocket. 'If I could get him to think now about the life that continues to go on around us, about his buddies and the women to whom he'll be lying, envied, telling dirty jokes. If I could get him to feel that the acts and sensations he calls life are going on uninterrupted, that they are serving rum on ice at the Novelty, that the guys are chalking up their billiard cues leaning on the pool table, that María is practicing poses and trying clothes on in front of the mirror, that idiots by the hundreds, their brothers, are arriving at Corrientes from the suburbs, going toward the movies and cafés and dance halls, toward the taste of heroism and stale stew at dawn. If he could understand that I am here, looking at him without need of sympathy, bound to him, pledged to divine the nature of his misery . . .'

He emptied the glass and made a sound like a snore; he moved his fingers to unloosen his tie, then contorted his face to show me the first smile, to convince me he could smile. He had white teeth, long canine teeth, two lines of white saliva on his lips, and cold, cowardly eyes.

"Don't worry," I said to him, "we're going to take care of it." He closed his mouth, kept his eyes on my face, not wanting to answer. 'Dead, on the other side of the wall.' "Are you sure you didn't leave anything there?"

"I didn't leave anything. I didn't bring anything to leave." He smiled again as he gripped the bottle. "Isn't what I left enough?"

"Think about it. In any case I'm going to check. We have to go away. Perhaps no one will find out tomorrow. But if two days go by . . ." 'The only thing missing now is for him to believe himself intelligent, to act on top of what he's just done.' "And even tonight; anybody who has a key could get in."

He looked as if he couldn't understand, sweating again, unable to stop his face from melting before my eyes, from changing into a white mass defined only by the gray shadows filled with anguish.

"Who has a key? I didn't forget anything." He opened his hands and showed them to me. "I didn't bring anything, I only took off my jacket."

"You can't be sure. I've got to take a look. Have another drink, but no more. Have you thought of something?"

"I was thinking . . ." The dark eyebrows slid toward the hollows of fear and sweat. ". . . about how to get away."

I passed in front of him and his terror, made an effort not to stroke his head. For a moment I waited next to the balcony for the sounds of the door slamming, the steps, the husky voice on the telephone, the laugh that swelled and then was immediately stifled. I placed myself again behind the head that had resumed its soft denials.

"Nothing happened, right? You didn't want to do it. It's better this way. You think you can stay in Buenos Aires?" I repeated the question, laughing, and saw him stop shaking his head and shrug his shoulders. "You don't know, but I'm sure you think it's possible to hide here. You must have some friend, some woman who can hide you in her room. And you're going to lock yourself in there until they get you. Because they will get you. You'll read the papers, get drunk, die of fear, and in the end—a week or two from now—cops will be banging on the door. I can see it. And don't you also have a friend, someone who used to clean a lawyer's office, and who'll give you advice?"

"Ah!" said Ernesto; he began to get up, his fist on the table, without turning his body.

"In addition, there must be that brother-in-law of a friend who worked in the Police Investigation Department. . . ."

"And what the hell does it matter to you?" he exploded, keeping his back to me and giving the table a punch. I looked at the scruff of his neck, as confident as if I had the gun in my hand. "What does it matter to you what I do or don't do?" Now he hit the table lightly, without conviction.

"Don't forget," I said quietly, "someone might be listening."

He sat down again, his body stiffened, obdurate as it had been at the beginning, his hands still and resting; the smell of jasmine seemed to come now from the protruding ears. I turned to the table and filled the glasses.

"Things have to be thought through," I said. "Not beforehand, of course; if so, they don't get done. But afterward you have to think about what to do. It's none of my business, you're right. I could go find a cop. But when you've gotten over your fright, we'll reach an understanding."

"That bitch," he said finally.

"Yes. Do you want to die in prison because of her? That must be it. Because in Buenos Aires they'll catch you within ten days."

"Why did you bring me here?" He again showed the smile, the cowardice. "Do you want to keep me from escaping?"

"You'll soon get over your fright. Do you have a place where you can hide?"

"That's my business. When I want to, I'll leave without your permission."

"Of course," I said. "When you want to." I touched the note in my pocket: 'I'll call you or come at nine.' "Do whatever you want. I'll be back in a second. Don't be frightened, I'm going to see if you forgot something. If you make up your mind to leave Buenos Aires, I can get you out of here and help you cross the border—it's easy. Think about it."

"Don't go in!" he shouted when I opened the door. I paused to see him leaning over the table, to look at what remained of his face, the whiteness and the imperfect circle, the obvious dank fear directed toward me, the simple habit of fear. "Don't go in," he repeated, copying the previous shout with a whisper.

I slowly opened and closed La Queca's door; under my lowered eyelids I carried the image of the fear-stained head, until my thighs collided against the table. I let the key fall onto the tablecloth and I walked away to turn on the ceiling light. I saw the yellow towel rolled up on the floor. I withdrew the paper from my pocket and looked at it again; I was searching for just the place where La Queca might have dropped it at the end of an afternoon frequented by strangers, by the fight and the reconciliation. I decided to leave it folded next to the key on the table. Slowly I turned my neck to make out the painted toenails, the curled-up toes, the foot stretched over the edge of the bed, the other one resting on the wrinkled sheet. Then there were the legs and their down: one extended rigid and horizontal; the other, its knee resembling a child's head, doubled under and lowered toward her belly, toward the twin curves of her flattened buttocks, toward what was transformed in shadow, depression, and hair. I leaned over in order to make the lewdness incomprehensible, in order to examine a senseless complication. "Crazy world . . ." I mumbled, seeing it as one long foreign word.

I straightened up and stepped back; I remembered that there was someone on the other side of the wall, I admitted the obligation to call him so he could see what I had been looking at. "They" were no longer here; they had totally filled La Queca's body in the decisive moment, trickling out like sweat after her death, vanishing now, merged with the dust and fuzz in the corners. But the room's air, with the freedom and the innocence, was rising like mist at dawn; happy and silent, it recognized the shape of my face.

I moved aside the bathrobe covering her head, and her face—little by little, sure of the infinite time it had at its disposal—first showed death, and then the two wide teeth that were protruding, biting the air. Her eyelids almost covered two curved, watery lines. We were alone; I began to share the discovery of eternity. I took a step back in order to observe the stiff and unknown woman occupying the bed, that woman's body, never seen, that was just being introduced to the world. The folded arms, the shrunken open hands poised to separate her breasts, to make a path for her breathing. The face suggested death, and death like a liquid slid from her loose hair to her contracted feet.

But I was no longer looking at La Queca or the absurd attitude that legs and arms shaped, encrusting themselves in the bold air; I wasn't looking at the cold body of a woman abused by men and women, by certitudes and lies, needs, the concocted and spontaneous styles of incomprehension; I wasn't looking at her closed-off face, but rather at the face of death, sleepless, active, pointing out absurdity with two square frontal teeth, alluding to it with the fallen chin in search of an unpronounceable monosyllable. And the body was that of death, intrepid, lit by faith, preserving the obvious foreshortening of revelations. Dead, transformed in death, La Queca had come back in order to

11

"Paris Plaisir"

In the hotel—attached to a vaudeville house whose laughter and music entered the room like an oceanic noise, like a yellowish light, phosphorescent and undulating, like an expectation always born before or after the appropriate moment—I waited for Ernesto to undress, I listened to him stammer the plan for a meeting that would reveal many phases of the human adventure on earth; I heard him, watched him as he knelt next to the toilet bowl, invoking his mother. The room smelled of wine and gin; he imitated, adjusting his hairy white body, an attitude of rebellion, a brave and almost provocative defiance of destiny; I waited for him to sob and throw himself onto the bed; I covered his legs and did not deny him the hand needed to cool his cheek. Perhaps the incomprehensible phrase he murmured before falling asleep and snoring had decisive importance.

His face was no longer sweating; it was pale, again shapeless in the shadows, extending across the pillow and toward the headboard as if it wanted to rise, straining the tendons of his neck. 'I have to suppress the hate and vanity,' I thought, as with my calm I helped him to sleep; 'I have to know beyond doubt that he is no more than a part of me, sick,

225

which can kill me, and which it is prudent to take care of. I'm the only man on earth, I'm the measure; I can caress him without pity or disdain or tenderness, with only the feeling that he's alive. I can pat him, gently hum a lullaby, confirm that he is falling asleep and ceases to hurt me while I think he's handsomer than I, younger, stupider, more innocent. The hand that strokes him goes on wearing out the memory of the night when he beat me up in front of La Queca's cowardice, the memory of his imagined ardor in bed, of his power to change her into a woman unknown to me and who would be denied me even if she had continued to live. He's no more than a part of me; he and all the others have lost their individuality, they're parts of me. Men, and this light, this wood grain, the music rising and falling, the same sensation of distance that separates me from the place where they are playing it.'

He was sleeping with his mouth open when I gathered up his clothes and went on packing them in the valise. Without examining them, I separated the papers, medal, pencil, lighter, and money in the pockets. I switched off the light and left the room, repeatedly banging the suitcase against my knee, calculating where I could hide or burn the clothes, where I could meet Stein to lie to him with my silence, to deride him unaggressively while thinking of all this and comparing it with his happiness, his intelligence, his dirty avidity for life that kept him restless. I convinced myself that it was necessary not only to find Stein, but to do so on the first attempt; in the cigar shop at the corner of the hotel, I failed when I tried to get information from Mami on the telephone.

"I haven't seen him since yesterday, you know how Julio is. I'm worried because he's sick, he shouldn't drink. He doesn't take care of himself, as usual. Brausen, you have to come hear me; I have some twenty *chansons* from the Resistance. Julio is bound to be at the Empire, but don't tell him you know it through me. You understand, Brausen. Remind him I'm alive, convince him that he should call me without telling him you spoke to me. I hope to God he's not drunk already. Don't let that woman get money out of him, Brausen. You know how he is with money. . . . If he's not at the Empire, look in that smaller place on Maipú, near Plaza San Martin. I'm all right alone tonight; I'm poring over the map of Paris—you know about that through Julio. Ask him how long it's been since he's seen the poor old woman and he'll

get up and call me. Look after him—he's too good and everyone takes
advantage of him."

I decided to continue on foot toward Corrientes and then walk down
toward the Empire, glad of the weight of the suitcase, measuring the
significance of what I could leave at any corner, at a café urinal, next to
a subway grating, by only bending over and opening my hand. I
walked in the warm night without hurry, benevolently reviewing the
details that were shaping this night made for me, promised me since
always. I smiled at the theater posters, breathed the sluggish air stirred
by vehicles, greeted with my eyes the faces and newspapers spread out
behind café windows, the almost motionless groups in the movie house
lobbies, the arrangements of journals and flowers, the stout, grave
couples, the solitary pedestrians and quick women who were going
toward a moderate ecstasy, a fugitive brush with mystery, the sigh of
abandonment, the perishable matter it is possible to mine from the
veins of a Saturday night.

I went down Corrientes step by step, alternating the fatigue of each
hand holding the suitcase, finding everything fine, everything appropriate to the values, the needs, what people were capable of dreaming. I
crossed the circle of the obelisk with the decision to reconstruct a night
of my adolescence in which I would have declared positively, alone or
before the deaf, that the period of perfect life—the rapid years when
happiness grows inside one and overflows (when we surprise it like
weeds sprouting in every corner of the house, in every street wall, under
the glass we raise, in the handkerchief we open, in the pages of books, in
the shoes we force on in the morning, in the anonymous eyes that look
at us for an instant), the days made to the measure of our essential
being—that this period of perfect life is attainable, and cannot happen
any other way, if we know how to abandon ourselves, to interpret and
obey signs of destiny; if we know how to despise what has to be obtained
with effort, what does not fall into our hands through a miracle.

'All the knowledge of life'—I was in the coat room of the Empire,
determined not to be separated from the suitcase—'is in the simple
delicacy of accommodating ourselves to the gaps in events that we
haven't provoked with our will, in not forcing anything, in simply
existing each minute.'

'Yield as to a current, as to a dream,' I was thinking when I went
inside with the suitcase, into the darkness of the ballroom, listening to

the unfamiliar tango, the solo of the concertina above the distant piano. I could not see Stein on the dance floor or at the tables, I put the suitcase down next to my leg and ordered a drink; I knew it was impossible for me to get drunk, I realized how weary my body was when I leaned back in the chair. I began to imagine the expression that each of the faces I was looking at would assume in death; I divided them, at first glance, into the ceremonious and the ingenuous, into the group that would become taut, hard, dry, adequate to the human interpretation of death, and the group that, inexpressive, would submit docilely.

All the lights were turned off, a spotlight fell on the empty dance floor, a woman in a bullfighter's costume bowed, blowing kisses, and began to dance. I could not make out Stein. Like a blind cow, the big slack udders resting on the table next to the telephone, Mami would be lowering her dyed yellow head close to the map of Paris, *itinéraire pratique de l'étranger;* she would be swinging her long skirts in accompaniment to the indecisions of her shoes, her bust small and corseted, uncertain—she was coming from Sacré Coeur through the Rue Championnet and had paused (that day and the world were hers) on the corner of the Avenue de St. Quen—uncertain about whether to take the Boulevard Bessières or the Avenue de Clichy in order to go down the Boulevard Berthier toward the Porte Maillot, in blue letters and just a step away, as it were, from the Arc de Triomphe. Mauve, the mild afternoon was beginning to dissolve evenly on the Rive Gauche and the tiny bistro located between the Jardin des Plantes and the Gare d'Orléans (. . . or d'Austerlitz?), and the dark, unventilated little room that had not been occupied for months, that might just as well be on the other side of the world in Buenos Aires—in any case, off the map. The ease of the afternoon was also coming to an end through inertia, the recent past, and compromises; Mami could dedicate—facing the Porte de Clichy, sinking her youthful eyes into the discreet mist rising from the curve of the Seine opposite Asnières, as she struck the pavement and the toe of her boots with the tip of the parasol that she had never opened after inspecting it in the shop where she had bought it with the money Julio had forced her to accept and on whose golden waterproof silk some butterflies seemed about to take off on wings of a paler gold, their bodies embroidered in the vivid pink color of mucus—she could dedicate the beginning of the night to rambling along the Quai de la Conférence; and from there she would embellish her walk by swinging her parasol, by swaying her shoulders and her hips very slightly to the rhythm of "Katie, the Ballerina" (hadn't Julio told her, as the music played, that they were forever joined by something more than love, something men didn't even know the name of and that was beyond love?), and it would be possible with the help of the map to linger over the Eiffel Tower and St. Pierre, and maybe the Invalides, too, if she were lucky, if it were not overcast.

But Mami also could use the hours before her meeting with Julio to go on a sentimental pilgrimage to the Rue Montmartre, so difficult to find and not to be confused with the Pont de Montmartre beyond the Boulevard Ney, beyond the marble warrior standing guard against the green background marking the fortifications. On the Rue Montmartre she had danced with Julio one whole night and while they waltzed to *"La Demoiselle des Collines"* he found new words to tell her of his desire; Mami had not answered, had made no gesture until they arrived at the darkness of the table, until she extended a bare arm and begged Julio to burn her with a cigarette. But inexplicably the Rue Montmartre could be found on the map only by accident, perhaps immediately, perhaps when sleep overtook her before the telephone would ring. So that she abandoned—in the relative peace that decisions bring—the corner of the Rue Championnet and the Avenue de St. Quen and ascended, her attention prolonged by a knitting needle, into the always gray, always luminous sky of the City of Paris (*Gravé par L. Paulmire, Impr. Dufrénoy*, 49 Rue de Montparnasse) and continued, gliding with moderate speed from left to right, from east to west, with a pronounced inclination toward the south; from Puteaux—black letters on a green field, between two small villages—to Alfortville, where the Seine seems three-forked next to the Pont d'Ivry and disappears, cut by a line in 8-point type that reads *Stations des bateaux T.C.R.P.* From the mauve or gray sky, soaring to a height of 700 or 1200 meters, according to the scale, Mami contemplated buildings and recognizable streets, memories that stuck to her like bandages. She saw the Petit Palais and the Jardin des Tuileries, the Quai Malaquais and the Rue de Tournon, the Musée de Cluny, the Boulevard St. Marcel; already in motion, she passed over the railroad crossing of the Orléans and Ceinture lines and suddenly—a stroke of luck, when the smile was fading from her lips over the Ivry church tower—she shifted her eyes to the left toward the green patch of the Cimetière du Montparnasse, between the Observatoire and Notre Dame des Champs and Notre Dame de Plaisance.

Confirming that the inexpressible sense of life was kept true and ardent—although Julio might not call her all night, although recurrent bladder pain might strike with fury in the early hours of the morning—she pecked with the knitting needle at the neighborhood of the Rue Vercingétorix, where, a half block from the Avenue du Maine, the last hoot of the train whistle could be heard; where, in a room in the center of which a heater stood that neither of them had learned to light, Julio had slapped her suavely before murmuring an obscene phrase, lavish and low, that all proper women need to hear before dying, a phrase to be engraved on the heart forever and whose immediacy would be real consolation in difficult hours: "I've never known such a bitch of a bitch."

The applause died down, obliging the lights to come on again, returning the dance floor to the dancers. I searched again for Stein at the tables, in the faces that went spinning by; without stopping her dance, a woman raised two green hands to the height of her head; the straight hair covered her profile. I drank and put the glass down with disappointment, sliding my leg against the suitcase. As, definitely outside the conflict and Santa María, Díaz Grey was putting up with the girl—she made visible now her tendency to appear on the corners of a city in spring bloom, almost always turning her back on the first man who spotted her, with her irresolute masculine steps, with one of her shoulders higher than the other to offer the left breast or protect herself from the unexpected attack—he was putting up with her and handling her body coarsely, suppressing her and consuming himself in her, and sometimes managed to stop time, only to be convinced that nothing can possibly happen in eternity. I saw him enthusiastically repeat the useless game of permitting the girl's more agile legs to overtake him at intersections, to surprise him with a timid hand on his arm, with the smile and the silences; I saw him condemned to feel that each meeting was a prologue to the weekly scene in the motel, to the abandonment, the oblivion, the dubious victory of ceasing to be, that was attained in bed. And always—later—the waiting, the provocation of remorse. As if they were objects in his pockets, the doctor would touch her movements in order to keep them hidden from lights, waiters, other couples; the odor of disinfectant in the pillows clung to the girl's hair; the new odor, opaque, dull, of disinfectant mingled with the familiar cheerful perfume; the impossibility of kissing her or talking as they waited for the porter to come collect a tip and announce the taxi. And as each of these memories—these hard, sharp objects—marked and asserted their clandestine nature, Díaz Grey was forced to stop loving the girl in order to put her aside, to separate his love from the clandestine, from the tacit acceptance they both gave to sordid, filthy things from the moment they practiced them. He stopped loving her then, until the separation; the signs of the clandestine became distinct, vigorously alive, afflictive, alone in the world—alone in the night, in the automobile that carried them like two strangers—but they were already incapable of hurting his feelings for the girl, of wounding a love that did not exist. And in the dawn, next to the sleeping Elena Sala, the doctor slowly deposited near the bed—like the wristwatch, the cigarettes, the matches—the sharp objects he had received in secrecy; he was isolated, without ties to the girl, living only for the symbols of sordidness, the memories that he had brought with him and that kept an impassive vigil. Until dawn of the following day would make it impossible to live in the small frozen inferno of shunned lights, embarrassments, porters' looks, the smell of bedsheets rising again with the sweat. He had to save himself, and was saved punctually by the recovered intensity of his love; he repented each repentance, each backward step; the objects became soft, they yielded amicably to the pressure of his hand, and Díaz Grey rearranged them, transformed into symbols of his love, in exact suitable places; he was illuminating walls with taxicab headlights and the girl's face in their reflection; he returned the morbid curiosity to waiters' eyes; he crowned the girl with the touching aroma of disinfectant and perfume.

12

Macbeth

"This Lady Macbeth of hands stained in chlorophyll . . ." Stein said suddenly. I had returned to the Empire, after searching for him in three other cabarets. He was standing next to my table, with the woman of the green gloves. He introduced her by an absurd name, had her sit down, and kept looking at me with a smile, as if he were about to hear important good news, as if I had come out of exile to be near him and tell him how right he was.

"Lady Macbeth soaked in chlorophyll . . ." he repeated upon seating himself; he pressed my hand as he smiled, slightly drunk, sparkling. "I'm the one who'll always be found waiting in the right place, for better or worse. Maybe I had a presentiment: I was talking to her about you." He turned to the woman, who was inserting a cigarette in a holder. "This is Brausen, dear—my friend. But tonight, in order to belie me, he's here and drunk."

She raised her mouth, merely changing the place her thick dark lips occupied in the air; she seemed to look with them, observing us placidly.

"You're drunk, too." The voice was slow, husky, distracted.

"Me, too," Stein agreed. "And with each glass I intend to intensify my drunkenness to celebrate my friend's visit. I'm going to get drunk according to rites of welcome, respecting conditions of the ceremonial. Brausen the ascetic, fed on lobsters and wasp honey, forsakes the wilderness. He's drunk; and yet I'm not sure it's right that I rejoice."

"If one comes here, it's to get drunk," the woman said; she raised the cigarette holder with a green hand so Stein could light her cigarette. "Both of you, at least. I'm here for something, too, but I'm not going to drink any more. What's with you and my gloves?"

"Nothing," I answered. "I like them. I was wondering if you didn't feel too hot in the fingers. But that's your business."

"Bold ideas," Stein said, "dead ideas. All these animals think the same: gloves, plush gloves in this heat. But we're also able to think about Macbeth, harvests, the felling of trees, beating the woods for game. And I was thinking about the dampness that changes her into a web-footed creature and that I'll have to kiss at the end of the night. I'm going to celebrate your return to the world of the living. But should I be happy? Where's the treachery, the trap?"

"There is no trap," I said. I looked at the woman's face and divided it into two parts; I recognized Gertrudis and Raquel in the area that went from the hairline to the base of the nose, but saw the mouth of Díaz Grey's girl, soft, mulatto, shaped to adapt itself to each of love's limited audacities, the line of her lips incapable of holding sadness, protruding from the round firm chin that alone revealed the unconscious will to live. "There's no trap or treachery; it's all right for you to feel good."

"I feel good, too," the woman said, tossing the hair that hung down straight to her shoulders. "You don't notice that in me, right?"

"I'm going to remember the poems," Stein said, rubbing one of the woman's gloved hands against his temple; he had had a bottle brought to the table and she protested, emitting hoarse syllables toward the tablecloth. 'You like them to rob you, it seems. As if you couldn't wait until they closed.' "She's marvelous. I went looking for her one night, I fell in love with her when I discovered the green gloves wrapped around a glass at the other end of the room. But there's something that's not your style, something aggressive, something confident, something definitely anti-Brausen. I have to remember the poems, the smell of blood is still here."

"Why aren't we dancing?" the woman asked.

"You said you were tired," Stein said. "Or was the tiredness for me and the invitation for my friend?"

"I don't feel like dancing," she replied; exhaling, she made the cigarette fall onto the tablecloth, then put it in the ash tray. "But you both came to dance—"

"We're not going to fight," Stein interrupted. "We always talk this way."

"You're friends," the woman said, snapping the cigarette case shut; she inserted another cigarette in the holder. "I know you're only joking. But when one's had a few drinks, one doesn't know what one's doing."

"No," Stein said firmly. "We only talk, and not about everything, because he doesn't reveal himself. He thinks no one will understand him, he doesn't care whether they do or not."

"If you're going to pay for a whole bottle, I'll have another," she said. "You two talk, I'm not bored." She filled the three glasses and looked toward the dance floor.

"I never deceived you," I said, looking at Stein.

"How come they let you in here with a suitcase?" she asked.

"I said I had a lot of money inside. I never deceived you; it makes me weary to discuss and correct what others think of me."

"But something's going on with you," Stein insisted. "Because tonight, I'm sure, it doesn't tire you to make explanations."

"I'm not bored, I'm drinking," the woman said. "I'm listening to you, I understand some of it, and think my own things."

"Why not tonight?" Stein asked. "I'm going to kiss her, finger by finger. There are nights of revelation. You heard the husky voice; were you able to recognize it? I toast to the immortal soul of old Macleod. It's two weeks today. How did you happen to look for me here?"

"I was here twice, and once in three places like it. I wanted to find you, I called on Mami mentally. No, I didn't talk to her; it's been months since I . . ." It occurred to me that I would find it impossible to stop lying through the entire evening and that in this way, disinterested, I was transforming the world only for the pleasure of the game.

"The passing away of Mr. . . ." Stein said in English. "An efficient formula to whisk away putrefaction. Bad odor in your house? Make putrid flesh disappear like magic, selecting your own personal formula from the vast stock. . . ."

"The word," I agreed, "the word can do it all. The word doesn't smell. Transform the dear corpse into a discreet poetic word. The best necrologists . . ."

"Is it getting to you?" Stein shouted at the woman. "That phrase, that joke, that way of talking . . . This is not Brausen. With whom do I have the honor of drinking?"

She entwined her fingers, twiddled her thumbs, and began nibbling on them.

"Don't be serious," she said to me. "I don't intend to be bored all night."

"That's how she is—marvelous!" said Stein, laughing. "From the wet depths of a dungeon she'd swear she was free. I don't knock myself out to give her what she deserves, the vigor and repetition of youth, the experience of maturity."

She turned her head and smiled at Stein, made him light another cigarette; for a moment she directed an expression of reproach at me in which the intelligence in the upper part of her face dominated the mouth, changing the thickness of her lips and the roundness of her chin into an animal melancholy.

"I'm going to kiss the tip of every finger without help from the swan transplanted to the pronunciation taught by the Jesuits," Stein bragged; I never knew what he meant to say. "Juan María Brausen—to say it in Gertrudis' style, to whom I would propose a toast if not paralyzed by the deepest respect—do you believe in passion?"

"You're friends and you're not going to fight. The three of us are friends tonight. But there's no need to be deceitful; if you deceived him, you should explain it to him now."

"I, you, he," Stein said. He raised the bottle and asked for another. "We're no one, isn't that so? Or does an exception have to be made for you?"

"I, you, he," I confirmed. "Who is Brausen? The man who married Gertrudis; and everything they knew about me had to be made to fit, had to be adjusted until it would fit in with the basic idea, with the precluded definition. I'm talking for the sake of talking; I should think about leaving."

"No," Stein corrected. "I say: my friend surprises me, suddenly I see my friend on the offensive, animated by an absurd desire for revenge. My friend holds his legs around a suitcase in which he carries black

Bibles. My friend drinks cautiously, not wanting to look at the woman who is with me, he smiles at me as if I were a child."

"Don't leave," the woman said. "In a little while, they're closing. Then we'll go to my place and have a few more drinks. Would you both like that?"

"Yes," I answered, and I looked at her eyes for the first time; her mouth had reached the maximum of softness and it protruded more, revealing (again, like a glance) the small hole at its center, the opening her lips could not suppress. "It's very easy. He who has married can be translated as he who has to pay the price. Except that she was extraordinary and marrying me was not a means but an end. I needed five years to understand truly, one by one, each of the things that made her extraordinary. One night would have been enough for someone more cynical, who thought he understood; to another man she would have posed a different problem, or none."

"That's the way," Stein said, "I like it. Not taking into account that very likely it's oneself who has to invent difficulties, has to confuse and mix up the issues. But why must you begin with Gertrudis in the story of this faith in passion?"

"Gertrudis is your wife?" the woman asked.

"She's no one," Stein exclaimed, rapid, polite, shamefaced.

"I was asking him. Is she?"

"She was," I answered. "A long time ago."

"You're drunk and grouchy," she murmured, touched. "You must love her very much."

"Because it began with Gertrudis," I said. "It began when they believed in my paying a price. But when I really got to know her big white body—when I knew it by heart and felt I could draw it in the dark without even knowing how to draw—I only thought about certain things, an investigation of the new situation was beginning. The key to the mystery was someplace else, the mystery wasn't symbolized by the big white animal in the bed."

"I'll order a small bottle," Stein said; he bent over to kiss the woman lightly on her mouth; she stopped looking at me and smiled at Stein peevishly, as if she had been awakened. "I can't recognize you; I mean, I recognize myself in what you're saying. Again, in a certain way, you're Stein tonight. I'll have to convert myself into that unforgettable Brausen in order to contradict you, even if I only disagree with my silence, so there can be a discussion, so as to extract every advantage from this moment. But it's not disgraceful to hear myself speak with your mouth."

"There's no system that can be used to know someone; it's necessary to invent a technique for each person. I was creating it, modifying it during the five years I tried to know who Gertrudis was. I had to know it to attain the security that she was mine."

"Attain the security . . ." Stein repeated, smiling.

"Five years, and later I had to return to the bed. But there's no contradiction, only then did I know something about what I was embracing. I can exercise the same patience, the same respect each time it's necessary."

"His left hand is under my head, and his right hand doth embrace me. But I no longer hear myself in what you're saying. I'm not like that. All right, agreed: you weren't the man who paid a price."

"I wasn't he, in that sense. And I wasn't the one searching for ways or things, the desert dweller on the side of life. I was the witness; I was, furthermore, he who had made a pact with time, the compromise of not pushing ourselves to act quickly. Not he me, nor I him. I always knew that everything I agreed with was waiting for me on the back of a day of a week of a year whose date was of no importance to me. And I, the one giving testimony, was filled with pity when I saw others content, needing the misery of induced labor. Because each one accepts what he comes to discover of himself in the glances of others, he becomes shaped in the act of living together, is confused by what others assume about him, and acts in accordance with what is expected of that nonexistent person."

"I don't understand," Stein said. "I mean I don't believe that."

"Tonight they're going to close later," the woman predicted. "They say that when there's a lot of action, it's worth paying the fine."

"That husky voice," I commented, "reminds me of Macleod. Examples for children: Macleod, for many years, was no longer himself; he was the position he occupied. He was determined by what they had believed he was; before thinking, he thought about what would be suitable for a transplanted North American to think, one with similar profession, age, and salary. Before desiring, he thought. Is that clearer?"

"Now I see," Stein said. "But it doesn't work. Why was Macleod what he was, and not a band leader or a gold prospector? Why do others have to suffer for our mediocrity?"

"It's not fundamentally a question of mediocrity, but one of cowardice. Also it's a question of absolute blindness and oblivion; not to have awake in each cell of our bones the consciousness of our death. We could talk the rest of the night; everything's peaceful, everything's quite removed from me."

The woman looked toward the dance floor and searched on Stein's wrist for the time.

"Not yet, dear. You know I can't get out of here early.

"Not only lying to me all these years in a direct way," Stein clarified, "but with each gesture, each attitude, each phrase you didn't know I'd understand. One Brausen; and suddenly with the same voice, the same tilt of the head, with Jack the Ripper's suitcase between his legs, that Brausen or another, out to contradict and correct, to oblige me to rethink a long past, to rub in a thousand sensations until I discover his true face. I don't know if it's worth the trouble."

"Always ready to pay the price," I said. "But not to buy things—instead he pays to deserve them after God or the devil gives them as gifts. Not in advance, like you, like everyone. Now there's a woman; I'm going to Montevideo with her, I'm going to see Raquel again, my brother, all of them. I came looking for you so I could tell you. I don't know for how long."

'I'm leaving on the morning plane,' I went on lying. 'I believed how important it was to go back to Montevideo, to see them after all these years. But now I understand what counts is to be on the move, far from Buenos Aires, from the "Macleods," from Gertrudis, from you, from that time. Because that time has already ended, although not entirely; as corpses confirm, the beard and fingernails continue to grow. Now it's finished, as definitively as if it were a dream dreamed by someone else. I wanted to deceive myself and I thought about the city, and the café on the corner of the square, and nights in that street descending between two others, and the grass borders—you must remember—at Ramírez or Punta Carretas; those things and a thousand more, and Raquel, my brother and Lidia, Guillermo, Marta, Suárez; all of them and everything that was protecting my youth and that is retrievable simply by going there.'

"Don't forget to look at her from the front when she comes back," Stein said. "Her legs, her dress between her legs when she walks. It drives me crazy. But that doesn't happen; and if it did, if they had preserved the Brausen of five years ago, you wouldn't know what to do with him."

"It was a lie," I replied. "The important thing is to finish—with this past and the previous one. Perhaps I'll spend a month there and go on to Brazil. I promise I'll write you."

The woman arrived at the table before I could look at her; she opened the green fingers on the tablecloth, and alternated the direction of her laugh. Now she was placed in the world to wait for something that she had never lived but could imagine with exactitude, in each detail, in the importance and consequence of each detail.

'They must close at three. Ernesto is still sleeping in the hotel room, I'm sure. He can escape, of course, but he'll always be bound to me by the note they'll find next to the key; what interests me is that he could escape and may not feel encouraged to do it, that he may feel the impossibility of parting from me. And you? I, whatever they want; I took pity on him, I thought the adventure was worth the risk. There's the note, there's that desire to tell everything, poor boy. I'm not drunk—hardly this excitement, against an interminable background of peace and indifference. Now I have nothing to talk about with Stein.'

"Just a moment, dear," Stein said. "I also was the past for those Saint Joans; they reduced me to a symbol of their ignominious pasts and then left me, they always went off with a man who had long hair and a pronounced Adam's apple, a convict of physical filthiness, a frenzied man of twenty odd years who fell out of military service the way a thistle falls, always landing—damn my soul!—on Buenos Aires, Federal Capital. And hardly recovered from the blow, he would discover that God was pointing him out with a finger, pursuing him with an eye enclosed in a triangle so he would make the world revolution. A task which, as is known, cannot be fulfilled without the support, proximity, and inspiration of a desirable girl capable of earning a living. So I had to endure those unvirginal Maids of Orléans reviewing my *petit bourgeois* acts, passing judgment with prejudices (that really were not long-standing prejudices, as they had been acquired a week before, without my famed masculine intuition suspecting the process of politicization imposed by the current damnable long-haired favorite), judging each one of my actions and opinions, demonstrating to me with generosity and hopeless pity that I was the creature of a moribund society, the death rattle and hindrance. And the paratroopers, those suspiciously abundant untarnished adolescents, did not hesitate to make clear—aside from the good established condemnations and summaries in ABC magazine on which their affirmative speeches rested—their ethics of sacrifice and violence. And furthermore, aside from the broad, monotonous hybrid homilies of Christ and Zarathustra, they insinuated that the succession of infidelities also obeyed the obvious circumstance that I was closer to my forties than my thirties."

"Let's go," the woman said. "I can leave now. You're drunker than your friend."

"I'm yawning, but I'm not bored," I replied, smiling, and I raised the last drink. 'I will have to be absolutely alone and in a durable solitude to remember the dead La Queca, to make another attempt at comprehending the hardened, impersonal body, to enumerate everything that has become quiet, the things that for some hours now have ceased to exist, erased from the past, and that I can pledge myself to revive.'

"Separated from my lethal influence in order to cohabitate revolutionarily, to advance proudly between abstinences and abortions. I insist, for my egoistic tranquillity, in evoking them clutching to their breasts the kind of consolation they found."

Two waiters were approaching, gathering up the tablecloths; maneuvering in the center of the growing silence, the musicians finished packing their instruments into cases. Slowly she turned to show me the persistent similarities that I had discovered shaped her face; desperate, she showed me freckles, roughness, blemishes, like confessions that might add to our intimacy.

"Did you get paid yet?" Stein asked, as he put his money away.

"I'm going," she said. "It's better if you wait outside, in the café across the street. I have to go upstairs for my coat."

"Let's smoke a cigarette," Stein suggested to me. "There's still something left in the bottle. Let them wait. Are you in love with that woman you're going away with?"

"No," I said, and I leaned back in the chair, restless, suddenly lucid. It was as if I had just been told of La Queca's death. Behind Ernesto's transparent gestures in the hotel room, I could only see her head, hard, dry, and wrinkling, with the pair of wide teeth protruding, pursuing the lower lip. I understood with horror that I had forgotten her, I imagined that the interrupted memory of the cooled body was enough to remove the dangers. While I might think of her—with a certain tenderness, a certain weak quality of fear, a moderate love—La Queca, more powerful than the living, would be protecting me: one leg doubled under, the other extended, the black mouth, two moist curves on the eyelashes; dead, definitive, with a solidity denied to the living and on which I could rely.

"But you're sad," Stein said. "Would you like to take her with you?"

The woman was standing at my side with a shiny gray coat hanging from her shoulders, pulling the green gloves toward her elbows; she had flattened her hair against her ears and I could see the friendly, pensive smile, the meekness with which she acknowledged the baffling attitudes of beloved beings.

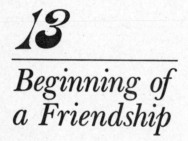

13
Beginning of a Friendship

It was three-thirty in the lobby of the hotel and I was crossing the carpet noiselessly, my feet pointed toward tomorrow, toward a time that I had accustomed myself to think of as impossible. I smiled at the night watchman, but he gave me the key without looking at me; I partially maintained the smile, directing it, expressive, exaggerated, at the young elevator operator who couldn't avoid it and who didn't know what to do with it. 'If only it were possible for me to understand myself, to bring it together and understand it all, and give it to this fellow in a short, unemphatic sentence.'

The room was dark; I put the suitcase in the closet, turned on the light, and went to look at sleeping Ernesto, curled up now, a hand under his cheek, a lip puffing up and then collapsing with each breath. Later I discovered the corner with the writing table, the lamp with its silk shade, the stationery, ink, and pen. I remembered the letter I had promised Stein, I was tempted to will him Buenos Aires and my past, to play the comedy of posthumous confessions. I yawned all my sleepiness

242

at once and made myself friend to my weariness as I resumed the bent position in front of the table. I lit the lamp and placed a handkerchief around the shade; Ernesto, the woman with her hardness and her cold, dark smell of death, were at my back, dissolved in the shadow. I began to draw Díaz Grey's name, to copy it in block letters and put before it the words street, avenue, park, walk; I drew the plan of the city I had constructed around the doctor, nurtured by his small, motionless body next to the office window; like ideas, like desires that would lose their strength if fulfilled, I sketched blocks of houses, the outlying woodlands, the streets that sloped downhill to die at the old pier, or lose themselves behind Díaz Grey in the still ignored rural landscape interposed between the city and the Swiss colony. I struggled for a bird's-eye view of the equestrian statue in the center of the main square—there was another, earlier and now abandoned, next to the market and visited only by children—the statue raised by the voluntary contribution and grateful memory of his countrymen to General Díaz Grey, second to no one in feats of war or the abundant battles of peace. To indicate the river, I drew an S for ripples, then parentheses for sea gulls, and felt myself tremble for the joy, for the intense illusion of riches over which I had made myself imperceptibly the master, for the compassion that the destiny of others inspired in me; I saw the statue of Díaz Grey pointing with his sword toward the fields of San Martín, the greenish stained pedestal, the sober and suitable inscription half-hidden by the ever renewed wreath of flowers; I saw the couples at twilight on Sunday in the square, the girls who approached along Avenida Díaz Grey after a walk under the enormous trees of Parque Díaz Grey, where the majority of them had followed in their mother's footsteps, breathing the anxieties that a fixed idea had provoked in their mothers twenty-five years before; I saw the men leaving the Díaz Grey Coffee Shop with feigned ease, their hats tilted, a freshly lit cigarette between their fingers; I saw the cars of the settlers climbing toward Santa María, moving a round cloud of dust smoothly along Camino Díaz Grey in the fixed beginning of the night.

I signed the map and slowly tore it up, until my fingers could not manage the little bits of paper, thinking about Díaz Grey's city, about the river and the colony, thinking that the city, and the infinite number of people, deaths, twilights, fulfillments, and weeks that it could hold, were as much mine as my skeleton, inseparable, free from adversity and circumstances. Further beyond the hotel blinds the day was shaping itself and I was going to introduce myself into it, secure and privileged, moving before hostile or indifferent presences, before the same imagined face of love, Santa María and its burden, the river that I could dry up, the Swiss farmers' stolid, determined existence that I could transform into disorder simply for the pleasure of injustice.

I cut off the hotel letterhead from the stationery, again reassured myself that Ernesto was tranquil and breathing, then began my letter to Stein, dated Montevideo a week hence; I started to tell myself the story of the days spent in Montevideo months before with La Queca, from the first sight of the dirty port streets to the final image of Raquel, the one I had set aside from others and decided to keep and protect through future years, in spite of herself, of what she might do, of the altered Raquels that life might oblige her to choose and express.

It was already morning—I could see the moist, aggressive light of the sky, hear the sounds of cleaning in the corridors and on the staircase, the increasing enthusiasm of the call bells—when I stopped before the last sentence of the letter, put the written sheets into my pocket, and crossed the smoke-filled room to sit on Ernesto's bed, to wake him, to show him with my tired, nervous face the face of dead La Queca, to place it and fear again in his memory. He sat up in bed quickly— mouth open, arms defensive—then stretched out again; the preoccupied, disconsolate look that returned to his lips, to his eyes, to the unshaven skin, to the lock of hair between his eyebrows, was less powerful than on the previous night, and almost familiar now through its presence in a nightmare.

"What time is it?" he asked the ceiling.

"I don't know, six-thirty or seven. We have to leave soon."

"I fell asleep. Have you a cigarette?"

We smoked, I opened the window facing the sun shining on rooftops, and tossed out my cigarette; the air was already warm, it smelled of some new thing that I had never experienced.

"There are quite a few matters to take care of if we want everything to go well," I said, turning around; I examined the hatred that Ernesto was beginning to revive and that was spreading, attenuated, over his face, over his sprawling body, one hand under his neck, the other slowly moving back and forth with the cigarette.

I reflected about the need and risk of talking, about the brief common destiny that depended on my words. "We're going to take a train. But not the one they expect you to take to get away. I'm going to go out, and meanwhile you can bathe and ring for breakfast. Don't say good-by to anyone, don't use the telephone. Forget everything, leave it to me, and things will all work out."

"Where are my clothes?" he said without moving.

"It occurred to me to get others, but . . ."

"Where are my clothes?" He sat up in bed and threw his cigarette to the floor; I moved my foot to put it out. "Tell me where you hid them. They're not in this room."

I felt fatigue rushing up my legs, I hesitated before the obligation to construct sentences in order to establish a future that only partially interested me. Lack of sleep was burning my eyes, the movement of my mouth to smile had become a complicated labor.

"I thought about changing them so they wouldn't recognize you." I looked at the muscular white body shrunken in dismay on the edge of the bed, the cautious grin the young man raised toward me; I knew fear was inside him, not far below the surface of bravado, settled forever. "Your clothes are in the closet, in the suitcase. I thought I'd go buy others."

"Money thrown away." He shrugged and began to look at me with serious eyes, with a restrained sneer, as he rubbed his chest with his fists. "Too much to carry, I don't want to lose time. I thought about that already."

"And later we're going to take a train," I continued. "And other things, cars and maybe boats. It's all arranged, don't worry." I went to the closet and took out the suitcase. I swept the last bits of the map of Santa María into the wastepaper basket.

"Listen," Ernesto said with a calm voice. "Bring those clothes here, give them to me. We'll leave together, I'm not going to escape." He was in bed again, looking at his foot outside the sheets. "Nobody saw me come in; any suit is all right."

"You're sure?" I asked from the door; I was trying to maintain my resolution of someone beginning to live again according to Stein's prescription: the unknown hotel, sleep, a bath, a physic, new clothes. "You can't know if they saw you. Besides, a lot of people know how you were dressed when you disappeared." I began to laugh and put the suitcase down so my limbs could shake. "We've got to think about everything, there's no other way."

"I thought about it," Ernesto said. "And the best thing is for me to surrender and show my face. She began . . ." With a meditative grimace, he raised his head to look more closely at his foot. I didn't take notice of him: he was only searching for contradiction or consolation, or trying to annoy me. "And the papers? The ones I had in my pockets?"

"I'm going to put everything in the new suit. A cold shower will do you good."

"But listen a minute. Don't go away. After all, who killed her?" He put his head on the pillow and turned to look at me. "You see, I admit it. Talk or don't talk. . . . Last night I thought you didn't want me to escape. I woke up and couldn't find my clothes. But I didn't let it bother me and went to sleep again. The police will wake me up, I thought." He began to laugh, looking at the ceiling; a stripe of sun was growing in the window, sliding slowly toward the floor. "Why didn't you bring them? If I killed her, if we had that scuffle, I don't understand why you're getting involved in the mess and want to help me. I don't understand. Anyway, I'm going to give myself up. Or can't I?" He was smiling without aggressiveness, almost without scorn; he looked at me a moment and moved his eyes away. "Do what you want, whatever you feel like doing. Buy me two suits and a tuxedo; buy me a raincoat."

"I'm not coming back," I said, and pushed the suitcase with my foot. "I'll wait for you in the Central coffee house, at Retiro. I'm paying the bill when I go down and I'll be waiting for you one hour from now at Retiro. At eight, in the coffee house."

"That's the way it is, then?" He made an effort to sit down on the bed and was shaking his fallen head. "But I don't like it. And am I supposed to go to Retiro naked?"

"There's the suitcase with your clothes."

"Wrinkled, for sure. But didn't they see me come in? Weren't there a hundred guys who knew how I was dressed?"

I heard him laugh—the laugh rebounded against his chest—while I went to put the suitcase on my untouched bed; when I turned around, I met his small, shining eyes that were trying to stay on my face, offensive.

"What's the matter with you?" I muttered; the back of my hand grazed the hardness of the revolver over my buttock. My hatred was limited to his round, muscular shoulders, to his laugh and his glance, to the lock of hair dangling on his forehead.

"Why all this talk about their seeing me or remembering my suit? Why all this giving orders and sticking your nose—"

"What's the matter with you, you son of a bitch?" I moved a leg, trying not to let him see my hand on the grip of the revolver. "Why don't you get up? What are you laughing about?"

He blinked, showed me his teeth, stopped smiling; on his open mouth weariness began to appear, suddenly, like a tongue.

"Which one of us is crazy?" he grumbled.

I waited until the hate abated; I felt the morning on my left cheek, felt again the need to establish with words a common and absurd destiny.

"Listen to me," I began. "We have to be calm. We're going to take a train, we're going to get out of here. I know how it can be done, where there's a place to hide, where to go so we're not captured. You killed her. I'm not going to explain now why I'm helping you, why I'm involving myself in this. I'm going to wait for you at Retiro; you can come or not, you can surrender or try to get away alone. At eight, in the coffee house. We'll take any train; we won't have difficulty crossing the border, but we will in getting out of Buenos Aires. We'll get to Bolivia, but I don't know when; we have to go back and forth a lot, east and west; we must zigzag, come and go. But everything will turn out all right if no one acts crazy, if you get over your fear and learn to go where I tell you."

On the way to Retiro, I went into a café to write the end of the letter to Stein, a sentence that had been on my mind for months: 'And I think she suspected something, because she stopped and spun around to look at me from the corner of the bar, with eyes of fear and an expression that bared her teeth but was not a smile; and while I called the waiter to pay him and went out into the street, while I ran in the drizzle to catch a bus and escape to any other place, I still saw her, thin and half leaning next to the tin curve of the bar, her head twisted and irresolute, looking at me, her lip raised to show her teeth clenched with decision.'

At Retiro I put the letter in an envelope with Stein's address, wrote a few lines to my brother asking him to mail the letter without reading it, then studied train schedules and resolved to make two transfers and arrive in Rosario at midnight. It was about twenty minutes to eight when I entered the coffee house and tried in vain to find La Queca's pleasure in a glass of gin; I distracted myself looking at the blond, boyish girls who were arriving for breakfast in school uniforms, carrying tennis rackets and hockey sticks.

Letter to Stein

'Here it comes, as promised, the story of the trip, the legend of the man who returned to rescue his past, written by the same man who aspired to protect it from oblivion. I am animated by the idea that you can stop reading me when you wish, but that no one can prevent its being written. I reread this and find it perfect: I can be certain you won't believe I'm writing in earnest.

'There is a bar in the harbor, next to Dick's; the second room has an enormous round table and a painting in dark colors. You ask for a bottle of *tostado* wine, the specialty of the house; it is set out on the table next to the painting and one sees: a sky of excessive blue, palm trees and mountains, sailboats carrying fruit, people in clothes of no particular period. No one will disturb you between nine and ten o'clock at night. One begins to understand with the first glass of the second bottle; one begins to distinguish with clarity the curve of the rugged coast, the row of slanting trees, the round bay where a scow is mooring and that a boat approaches, its smokestack fuming, a big paddlewheel to port. The men of the coast wear tight pants and short jackets; others with handkerchiefs on their heads are busy unloading crates. The first group of men do not speak, talk, chat, or discuss: they converse. There are women in full skirts, maids and ladies, these protected under shade trees. The location of the landau with white horses is central: it is there for those who debark at nightfall to distribute money among the boatman and the Negroes, then to move rapidly across the picture in an angle to the upper left. The chestnut mare is close by and breaks into a gallop toward the slope of the mountain; at night one has to cross through the sleeping village of wooden houses.

'Occasionally the speed of the beast cuts through the confusion of a stampeding herd and a man who is trying to halt it. A wooden bridge is crossed and the plain is reached; there the mare's hooves slip and destroy ant hills. Always toward the north now, until coming upon small adobe huts with palm leaves on the roofs and bamboo fences. And far beyond, after the mountains, after marshland and a new village, the boat that blends into the foliage is discovered; it is rowed with caution around rocks, it rams the other shore. Between trees, guided by a taciturn Negro, one reaches a clearing, in the dawn light one sees a log cabin surrounded by four others of adobe, conical. It is necessary to advance without waking the dogs or beggars who are lying in front of the door; and immediately, upon stepping over the threshold, one distinguishes someone rising in the back of the room, tranquil and proud, metals and shells ringing on arms outstretched in welcome. The bar is next to Dick's; no other bar has a large round table in the second room. Perhaps this—and the lies that I finally resolved not to write—is what is most important about this letter, come what may in the following pages. It is Brausen who writes, I could not fake the handwriting for so many sentences.

'The night was like others there; my brother and Lidia, Raquel, Guillermo, Marta; occasionally talking about Stein and Suárez. Horacio smiled at me while handling the bottles and the cocktail shaker. "Scotch Manhattan," he jokes. "You can drink it," Guillermo insists. "But you shouldn't offer it," my brother says rapidly, with a short bow. Without asking, I am informed that Alcides, Raquel's husband, is not in Montevideo. I go next to the table on the upper floor, in the room they call the library, where Raquel is bending over magazines; I greet her again and she smiles, I inspect her long bony hand, tobacco-stained, fingertips a little dirty. I deposit the bottle and glasses near the hand. She puffs up her cheeks and the saliva makes a swishing sound as it rolls from one side to the other, then she swallows it. She doesn't resemble Gertrudis, I can find nothing of Gertrudis in her face. "It's better this way," I say. "Am I immoral?" she asks. "Would you say I'm immoral? I like being with you again. You couldn't understand me, I know, after so many years. Don't I have clear eyes?" I examine the inexpressive green eyes; I move my head a little to search in her eyelids and mouth for the old sensations of candor and impudence. "None of them matter to me," she says firmly. "Only Alcides; I want you to stay until you meet him. Give me a little drink."

When she stands, her reddish hair reaches her breasts. "I hope you're not going to stay up here all night," Guillermo says before going downstairs. "Friends also have rights." Raquel drinks again, smiles in silence with the glass dripping in front of her mouth. "I want to know if you were sick," she says. "After that you stayed alone. You used to have a serious illness and sometimes it made you afraid and other times it didn't matter to you. Just this one little drink. I want you to say yes, that you were sick and that no one came to take care of you, even if it's a lie. I only want to know if it was summer or winter. But it couldn't have been winter." "Yes, it was summer," I answer; then she smiles again and lets go of my arm. The same marvelous smile, intelligent and eager, appears as I explain to her why we only fulfill our destiny in what is unalterable, in what does not express us, in what can be fulfilled by anyone else. She is not convinced; she fondles her hair and bites it with the now saddened smile.

' "But I've done things that are really me," she asserts. "I can go on doing them. I can." I touch her hair and withdraw my hand, I free myself from the temptation to confess to her that I am full, not of love and homesickness, but of patience and cunning. I want to use her like a handkerchief, like a towel; furiously, I need to use her like cotton, like a bandage, a brush, a swab. I want to change her look forever. "This can never end," I say to her, "because never, whatever happens, will I discover your secret. I don't have enough time left to trace the centuries of blond people, snowy winters, the traditions that are behind you."

' "Gertrudis is my sister," she says. "It's the same and yet it's finished." "It's not the same. Gertrudis doesn't resemble your father. Your father was the foreigner." "It could be," she says, smiling. "If I tuck my hair in, I look the same as Papa's photograph. Give me a little drink. I want you to tell me something that you wouldn't say for anything." I do not say it to her, I bend over to look at her as she pretends to sleep, and I think that if I were to live with her every night for many years, I would always feel a difference, cool air, distance, an untranslatable word. She has ruddy skin, weather-beaten, dry, and without make-up. "No, please," she says on moving away. From below, there is a whirlwind of voices, a trembling burst of laughter at its center. "We can imagine orders," my brother says, "a general order that presently makes the rounds from anthill to anthill. Taking possession of the planet must not be improvised." I remember now that Raquel raised her hands to her eyes and that she didn't stop looking at me from between her fingers. Leaning against the wall, she begins to cry: "I want you to swear we'll spend all day tomorrow in the sun." I kiss her drenched face, I don't interrupt the negative movement of my head; I understand, without joy, that it is no longer possible to retreat, that the memory of not doing what she asked would be unbearable. When we go downstairs they look at us or refuse to look at us, no one speaks to us. With her body stiff, inflexible, she advances, presents to each one her unhappy smile, the brave set of her head; I watch her move, passing between chairs, turning toward me with obedience and pride. They are looking at me when she raises her eyes to wait for what I may approve and order; Guillermo smiles in his chair, waves a hand to say good-by to us.

'I have the taxi go downtown first; she is not crying, she is silent and leaning on my shoulder. As I do not want to repent, I attempt to contain all my pity and shame, I caress her and desire her again until she moves away. "If you could know what I feel when I look at you," she says. "What I feel now, when I look at you, this way, with my mouth open." In the hotel she lies down and closes her eyes; she is growing pale and I believe that she can become totally white, transparent, and disappear. She gets up and walks, one hand in her mouth, the other toward me, open, to prevent me from coming close. I support her head so she can vomit, I make myself see and smell everything that comes out of her mouth, it occurs to me that I love her and that everything can be true. I help her get into bed, I surrender a hand so she can kiss it and hold it pressed between the sheet and her cheek. She falls asleep and wakes up, murmurs, and falls asleep again. Dawn is already in the window when I begin to say good-by to the city and to each of them. I have no security other than being here in bed next to Raquel, who trembles and allows a thread of saliva to fall into my palm.

'We leave the hotel at ten in the morning; the car moves cautiously along the wet street, its horn echoing in the fog. "Some day I'll come to Montevideo," I think, powerless to console myself. In spite of the drizzle, a woman sells flowers near the café; I clean the window so I can see her, fat and motionless, wearing a dark apron. We go on arranging our faces and we look at each other again, anxious and empty, Raquel's hand under mine. I search for things to give her, I believe in my need for what I can find in her tired eyes, in the complicated network of veins. "Don't look at me," she says. "We don't have to talk, ever. Last night I didn't have this ring on." The finger rises to show me the greenish stone, falls with a light thud. "We did nothing bad," she murmurs. "Nothing," I say. Encircled, she and I and our gazes, in an absolute solitude, timeless, we would end by finding the necessary words, born from us, wet and bloody. Raquel moved and made her teeth chatter; her head was getting sick, it seemed to become smaller and older in order to nourish the gaze. I inspected it with the thorough spirit of conquest with which the face of a dead person can be observed. Every bit, every harsh, taut split of the skin, attacked by time, corroded by each minute; each confused feature of the face only capable of looking, transformed into nerves and muscles of the eyes fixed on me. "Will you swear?" she asked. "Yes," I said. She sat up slowly, incredulous. "No use," she said. She was standing, leaning on a chair; the waiter was looking at her from a column, a man put his white drink and his newspaper down on the bar to look at her. "Nothing you say or do helps," she said; she contemplated me with surprise and pity. "I'm sick, I'll be right back. Also, I want to cry a little." I felt ashamed that everyone was on my side against her: the waiter, the heads turning to look at her as she stammered and swayed, my brother and friends, Gertrudis, the envy and scandal, the years separating me from Raquel, the sign of autumn in the sky and street, the perfume of her clothes that burned, dwindling, near my face.

'And I think she suspected something, because she stopped and spun around to look at me from the corner of the bar, with eyes of fear and an expression that bared her teeth but was not a smile; and while I called the waiter to pay him and went out into the street, while I ran in the drizzle to catch a bus and escape to any other place, I still saw her, thin and half leaning next to the tin curve of the bar, her head twisted and irresolute, looking at me, her lip raised to show her teeth clenched with decision.'

"The Englishman"

Díaz Grey recognized him as he opened the window, certain of who he was from the moment he could distinguish him seated in the garden with the iron table between him and Lagos; he was in shirt sleeves, holding a small unlit pipe in his hand, his face thin and lively, with an expression of conscious satisfaction that seemed immutable. It was a face deliberately and patiently assembled, and although the arrogance was by now very deeply ingrained, it seemed incapable of consequence, without real meaning or object other than to show itself.

Lagos got up with his arms raised high to greet the doctor.

"A very good day, doctor. All this time and events . . . Is that how you take care of the sick? Sleeping until ten? And on a truly admirable day, a day that deserves to be remembered, as I was saying to my friend. This is Mr. Owen, of whom I have already spoken to you; you know many good things about him."

The man stood up, his long body indecisive between adolescence and maturity, resolute and languid; he bowed with a smile and then, again haughty and distant, extended his hand to shake that of the doctor.

"Owen," Lagos said. "Oscar Owen, O.O.; or the Englishman, especially now that he won't stop chewing on a pipe. In time you'll decide what to call each other. I was telling him that the finest day of the year should be recorded the same way we record the warmest and coldest. Each season has its perfect day; a committee would have to select it, don't you think? And don't tell me, like Oscar, that we can't know if there will be a better one. One always knows."

Abruptly Lagos took a step back, and the enthusiastically animated face became grave, accusatory; his eyes were now directed toward Díaz Grey's knees and something in the attitude of his body, stiff, bent forward with heels together, forced Díaz Grey to observe the black necktie and mourning band.

"I haven't extended my condolences," the doctor said. Free from the spell that was paralyzing him, Lagos showed an approving smile and stepped forward to take Díaz Grey's hand and hold it against his chest.

"You too have suffered and remember her, I'm sure. That conviction in some way . . . I know you will do everything possible. Now we're three friends, remembering her." He smiled again, his head tilted, infantile and feminine, grotesque. "Pardon me. Sometimes I want to know the details and other times I absolutely refuse—it would be terrible. In time we'll talk about it." He released the doctor, cast a look of distrust at Owen, and went to his chair. "Sit down, doctor. Let's talk about everything; we three must come to be very good friends. The same bond joins us."

The Englishman was smoking his pipe; the vanity and defiance were directed at the landscape and the sky; one side of his mouth mocked the chatter that reviewed the past, the memories—always slightly ridiculous—that Lagos chose to glorify over the iron table between aperitifs three times refreshed.

"I've spoken at length with the owner," Lagos said during lunch. "A very congenial person. Through him I found out that you had the decency to accompany her and to lavish on her all the attention, the patience necessary. Don't apologize. Elena was extraordinary and only people like us could understand her. When I received your telegram from La Sierra . . ."

"It wasn't mine," Díaz Grey interrupted. "They held me for ten days. The police must have sent it."

"It doesn't matter, it's the same thing. If you reflect, you'll discover that everything comes together; she hasn't died, apart from no longer being alive at my side; the telegram was sent by you. Later we'll talk. When I received the telegram, I thought it useless to move a finger, useless to go on living. Why did I react? From the habit of acting, from the years of being schooled in learning the appropriate move for each occasion. I went to La Sierra and had her buried without so much as looking at her; nor did I wish to search for you. I assumed you had explained to the police, and I confirmed what you said; I told them you were charged with accompanying her, to treat her. I know my statement led to decisive results. I was dead, I could act only on reflex, couldn't I? But later, suddenly, everything changed and I understood. Believe me, I forced them to stop the train (it's dreadful to think that I was on my way to Buenos Aires, that at that moment I could be in the very place where it would be impossible for me to find her), and I traveled miles by car to come to Santa María and talk to you. Just to be with you—not to ask you questions. How well I know that only a mistake or a cruel moment of depression could have been the cause. And you weren't in the city; I made inquiries, I spent two days and some money, and finally came to this hotel. I met Mr. Glaeson, a gentleman, and his two daughters; I found a great deal of understanding and friendship in that house. I knew you both had gone on to La Sierra after Oscar; there was no reason for me to return there. I needed to visit the places where Elena had passed; to see them, to live them, you understand, as she had lived them. Then I could stop and lie down to die. But things happened—I'll explain to you later; I knew that she needed to be avenged. And everything coincides, everything confirms that it is Elena who guides me, she directs our steps: Oscar's, yours, mine. Why should Oscar—the great friend she pursued with only the intention of saving him—appear in the hotel exactly on the night when I conceived that form of revenge which is an homage? And how does it happen that you yourself arrive, doctor? No, don't say a word; presently we'll talk, there's no hurry; Elena will be patient, she always was."

The Englishman filled his pipe and stood up; thin and muscular, he bowed to the doctor and turned to Lagos. "I'm going to sleep a bit," he said, as if he were asking a question. "You have a date with the violinist; it must be very soon."

For the first time Díaz Grey saw a tranquil, imperious look on Lagos' face; he also saw that the entire face was composing itself and that the shifting mask of deceit and distrust had disappeared. The man—looking from his chair at Owen, with an open hand on the armband, with an interest so persistent that Díaz Grey wondered about insanity—was older now, saturated by varied and plentiful experience, as secure, invincible, and patient as if the sum of his life had been dedicated to a calling.

"No," Lagos said. "Before sleeping . . ." He bowed toward the doctor, once again ingratiating, restless, and cordial. "Everyone wants to sleep on the day that I declare perfect. You must talk to the doctor; our revenge has to be explained to him, and all his questions answered." He got up and adjusted his tie. "I had thought of talking to you myself; but he will introduce the subject to you along general lines, the invitation it honors us to give you. Later we can discuss whatever you wish, doctor. I ask both of you to excuse me."

He walked toward the hotel, erect, with smooth, sure steps; seated again, the Englishman followed him with his small gray inexpressive eyes; he made the moisture in the pipe stem rattle until there were clouds of smoke encircling his face.

"He spoke to me about you," the Englishman said. "Before you arrived; therefore I believe you two are in accord and all this is a farce. But it doesn't matter to me. In any case I'll tell you what he wants me to tell you. The truth is, he thinks he can make a killing—use you to stuff himself with money. I don't know why he needs me; perhaps it's the habit they always had of using everyone. Also, I think both of them were always mad."

With his hat and cane, Lagos approached the table with undue speed, and smiled at Díaz Grey.

"Doctor . . ." He bowed, with his mouth cordial and curved, one hand next to his leg, the other holding the cane handle and straw hat against his chest. "In only a moment—a half hour—I'll be with you. I have to make a call on Mr. Glaeson—something indispensable for our plans."

He bowed again, heels together, and headed for the pale, indistinct path between the trees; he walked with his body rigid, handling the cane in time to his step, his head tilted to the side, his stooped shoulders suggesting sorrow. The mourning band cut across the light-colored sleeve of the jacket, the hatband stood out against branches and shrubs. Díaz Grey watched him recede; and it was as if the small silhouette interrupting the siesta hour were ending once and for all the feelings of mockery and contempt it had inspired in him in Santa María. 'Just as he was the perfect husband during office visits, and at night when we met again in the hotel on the corner of the square and went up to see Elena—he who never yielded to the temptation to forget, never pretended he had forgotten anything of the ludicrous and the abnormal that clings to the condition of husband—with the same astonishing perfection, he goes on creating, as he walks between the trees, hasty and inconsolable, his widower's personality.' The Englishman also watched Lagos until the trees hid him, until the shrubs brushed by his body or cane had stopped moving.

"That's it," Owen said, smiling. "He's crazy, and that's his only virtue. But I don't care about him, her, or you. He didn't go to visit the old man, but rather the girl who scratches the violin. I saw him cry with his head in her skirts. Well, I want to go to bed; in two words I'll tell you the plan, the revenge, the homage. He wants us to go to Buenos Aires and have you sign as many morphine prescriptions as there are pharmacies. I drive the car; we do all our business in one day and disappear. In each pharmacy, ten pesos for what can be sold later for fifty. Or a hundred. How much were you charging them? He and she had lived years of that life. Perhaps eventually he'll find a buyer; or he may decide to hide it and then sell it off little by little. In that case he'll make as much money as he cares to ask. If you accept, name your price. This is the homage, the revenge he was speaking of."

At nightfall Lagos knocked on the door of Díaz Grey's room, holding it half open as the doctor sat up in bed and turned on the light. The widower's head showed a smile, made a list of excuses, beginning and interrupting different versions of a preamble. While the doctor lit a cigarette and covered himself to the throat with the sheet, Lagos stepped to one side so that the violinist could pass; she dragged her feet along the floor until they touched the iron rung of the bed, then gradually she lost her shyness as she extended a smile of recognition and greeting, and finally sank her fingers into the loose blond hair that covered her head like a helmet.

"Here we are again," she said. "You came to the house with the lady. I never played as badly as that afternoon."

Lagos moved forward suddenly, giggling and bowing, as if the doctor might not know he was there; he had the violin case in one hand, the cane and hat in the other, but deposited them all on the floor and straightened up.

"Doctor . . ." he said, eyes raised, mouth thin and protruding; he looked at the ceiling in ecstasy; slow and sad, the voice came. "I knew you were resting, I confess it, that was the first thing I wanted to find out when I got back; and yet, as you see, I dared to bother you. Because the moment has come, without my provoking it, spontaneously. When revenge inspired me, I needed Oscar and you, and both came. I needed the purity and faith of this child, and she is coming with us. Now I know that it must be immediately. Oscar is waiting for us in the car, doctor," he said with a smile, eyes half closed, hands on his stomach, shifting his eyes from the doctor to the girl, certain the word and gesture summed up everything to be said.

The girl remained quiet, observing Díaz Grey's face, with her hands locked around the horizontal bar of the bedstead, her thick, unpainted mouth almost black, offering to Lagos' voice the measured attention that learned and indubitable things deserve.

"You . . ." Díaz Grey said, and she agreed with her head, smiling, anxiously desirous; but the doctor had only wanted to refer to her.

"Her name is Annie," Lagos intervened. "Now, the four of us, united as we are, ought to call each other by the names our mothers gave us, familiar names."

Díaz Grey gave the widower a small smile of compassion and looked at the girl again. 'We are separated by everything that we lived through together and of which she is ignorant; and the word "you" keeps this separation sensible, prevents her from coming to know and forget. We are separated by three days of cold or wind, by the minute when I went close to a hotel window to look out at the rain in the street, while she was waiting for me huddled up in bed; we are separated by the return in a taxi from the motel in Palermo, by the voice saying Deegee, by the vertical vision I had of her face as she leaned on my shoulder, by the gracefulness with which she advised me that it is natural to encounter difficulties when one returns to life; separated by my certainty that an exact phrase existed to define the sensation of her naked body. Because all this that we lived together—all this intimacy with which she is unfamiliar—could go on having value for me only if I keep the "you," if I do not call her by name, if I do not permit the birth of a new intimacy that would make the former one disappear.'

"You . . ." Díaz Grey repeated.

"Doctor . . ." Lagos murmured.

The doctor looked at the girl's face, the eyes that were bulging expectantly, passionate and comical, the dramatic curve of her lips; he sat up to toss the cigarette through the window.

"Doctor . . ." Lagos insisted. "It is the moment; this child is abandoning everything for me, for our mission; she is abandoning her home, interrupting her artistic career for what is evidently destined. To make her resolute, it was enough for her to know that I am suffering and need her; her innocence permits her to understand the holiness of our revenge and our homage. Oscar is waiting for us in the car."

"Yes," Díaz Grey said. "Wait downstairs, I'll be right there. But I don't want explanations; don't try to convince me of the holiness of what we're going to do. It's essential that I not know why I'm doing it."

"Ah!" murmured the widower with kind dismay. "The same as Oscar. You will understand each other perfectly."

Then she relaxed the muscles of her face and those of her hands encircling the bar; she allowed tears to fill her eyes and fall, she smiled again while drawing close to Díaz Grey's head, and dampened it as she kissed it. Her mouth smelled of hunger and anguish.

"You . . ." said the doctor with naturalness, on parting from her.

16
Thalassa

Perhaps ever since that night in Pergamino, Ernesto had had the caressing, teasing smile without my noticing it; he might have listened to the explanations of each step of the retreat, the numerous brief lectures on psychology and strategy that I made during after-dinner conversations, my face crossed by that tolerant smile; perhaps he had not been able to hide it when he observed my movements, my taciturn crises, the proud excitement with which I got up in the middle of the night to resume conversations with hotel managers, chance acquaintances, drivers of the cars in which we climbed the roads. It is probable he had smiled that way on my restless dreams and as he watched me grow thinner, as I passed from suffering to peace, annihilated in the fulfilled happiness I succeeded in prolonging, moving my lips silently for hours to shape my name. Perhaps he had perceived since Pergamino—next to the cement pillar of the service station, in front of the attendant in shirt sleeves who was sleepily rubbing the fuzz on his chest, where I alternated the comedy of need that knows no laws with the comedy of resignation to misfortune—that the entire trip, which I called a retreat and thought of as escape, lacked an explicable purpose, and that he, the roads, the intersections, the towns, the dawns and delays, were only necessary propitious elements in my game. Perhaps today he smiled that way whenever he thought of me.

When we arrived in town, at the bookstore I bought an Automobile Club map, a notebook, and pencils: during the last week I had felt the need to do something more for Díaz Grey than simply think about him. Often I saw him in the La Sierra Hotel, moving forward in the dark with a belief in premonitions, approaching to touch Elena Sala's arm and to step back, cutting his foot on the emptied ampules—not to contemplate her instantaneous incursion into death, or to first resign himself to her quiet and reserve, to attribute a significant meaning to them, but rather to step back with the idea that he was seeing and touching death for the first time, struggling furiously against memory in order to go on believing it.

I wanted to write what the doctor was like in the darkness of the hotel room, in hospital corridors, in the emergency room where he would drink coffee; I would begin to answer each one of the foreseeable remarks—remarks that different mouths would repeat for more than a week, sometimes with the smoothness of distrust, sometimes with the smoothness of the committed believer—I would acknowledge his profession and vacillate between the cynicism and premature dismay of the faint-hearted as he tried to explain. But it was not Díaz Grey or his reaction and difficulties in the presence of the dead woman that made me buy the notebook and pencils; in recent days I was only interested in thinking about the hospital room, I wanted to describe minutely, until I was in it, the tiny room of the emergency doctor, its white walls, the desk with the telephone and neat stacks of papers, the photograph of a fat Minister of Public Health on the wall, the radio on a table from which a small woolen doily hung in a triangle, the smoking spout of the coffeepot on the hot plate between tubes and narrow pitchers. I wanted to be there, to hear the mumblings and dutiful pauses, to be Díaz Grey myself, timid and hesitant next to the desk, to be the young emergency doctor with the long reassuring hands, the cold, animated smile; to be in the room and to be outside it, to pause in the solitude, in the yellow odor of iodine in corridors through which there moved, always remote, the creaking wheels of a hospital stretcher; to contemplate the corrugated glass of the emergency doctor's door in order to distinguish the scarcely moving shadows inside, to guess at the meaning of phrases and glances, to guess what each one of them was assuming and dreading.

Ernesto was trying to swat flies on the curtain of the café window, and smiled in silence when I opened the map on the table; my finger touched or went hopping over towns, highways, and railroads, over irregular blue spots, meaning unknown; mute, concentrated, without paying attention to the idiotic tune he was whistling and repeating with his happy face turned toward the window, I established the time and roundabout course necessary to arrive at Santa María by crossing through isolated areas with ugly villages and dirt roads, where it would be impossible for a Buenos Aires newspaper to fall into our hands.

I drew a cross over the circle on the map that designated Santa María; I was debating the most convenient way to get there; I examined the several possibilities, the advantages of approaching from the west and those of taking a winding course and entering Santa María from the north, crossing through the Swiss colony and appearing suddenly in the square, in the restless and musical agglomeration of a Sunday afternoon, walking provocatively and slowly, dragging my defiance amid men and women.

But I decided to stay in Enduro and send Ernesto ahead to go into Santa María and look the city over; the idea that he might read the newspapers no longer worried me. Enduro was a small village so close to Santa María that one had only to climb up onto a flat roof—both the store and the inn had one—to spy on the activities of the people in the city; one had only to go up and then down a steep narrow street of dry clay to come to the first buildings of the colony, mingle with the population, and discover, under its animated but timid demeanor, that implacable will that sees good or evil in simple duties, the conviction that truth is held in safekeeping under vests and corsets, a certainty passed on like a torch from headboards of dying fathers, grandfathers, and great-grandfathers, candid as a frown or an index finger, yet complex as an artisan's secret.

I waited in Enduro for Ernesto's return, facing the southern entrance to the city five blocks from the church wall and vineyard, ten blocks from the Town Hall tower. In any case I was still outside the city, in a populated neighborhood of fishermen and cannery workers, amid miserable huts of wood and zinc, badly painted, with masts of wooden slabs bound by wires and mended nets on the roofs, with dirty, ugly children, taciturn men, women who changed their clothes at dusk—and one saw that it was for nothing—and began marching off to the store clutching peso notes that absorbed the sweat of their fists, carrying wine and soda bottles, their curly hair still dripping, with odors of badly ventilated kitchens under the perfumes of soap, with a need for revenge ready to shine in the indolence of their eyes.

Near the city and outside it, it was possible for me to stretch my legs under the table at the inn, to leaf through some old issues of *The Liberal* from Santa María, to despatch Ernesto like a postdated letter that would bring me—without his knowledge, clinging to his expression and his voice like qualities—answers to my curiosity, advance news that would be obvious a moment after it was made known. It was possible for me to examine, to crumple and smooth out the last hundred peso note left me; and to make comparisons between Elena Sala and La Queca, both dead, to imagine biographies for the headlines of obituary notices I found in the newspapers, to discover that love must rapidly lose its identity when it merges with death.

Old yellowed newspapers were stretched in the window of the inn, protecting me from the sun; I could tear them and look toward Santa María, I could think again of all the men living there to whom I had given birth—men whom I could make conceive of love as an absolute, and recognize themselves in the act of love and accept this image forever, transform it into a river bed through which time and its burden would run from the definitive revelation until death; and I could think, finally, that I was capable of giving them each a lucid and painless death, so they would understand the meaning of what they had lived. I was imagining them breathless but peaceful, bound by the contradictory impulse to push away and to preserve what was reflected in the damp faces of kin, full of generosity and humility, knowing nevertheless that life is one's self and that one's self is the others. If any of the men whom I had made did not succeed—through some unexpected stubbornness—in recognizing himself in love, he would do so in death, he would know that each instant lived was himself, as much his and untransferable as his body, he would renounce the search for sound accountings and efficient consolations, for faith and doubt.

I pulled out the center of the newspaper stuck to the window and contemplated the parched ocher earth, the houses of Santa María, the bell tower of the church that must have resounded over the square, over the heavy men who walked up and down there on Sunday afternoons, arm in arm with their apathetic, resolute women, holding vigorous children with crew cuts by the hand, deeply and unenthusiastically engrossed in the absurd day of rest, fearlessly challenging the demons lurking in the imposed laziness, comforted by the vision of a Monday that was promised them, the big copper sun that would rise punctually over the colony to illuminate and bestow a gift of eternity on the transactions of trading, delivering, and storage.

The lights of the square were coming on when we arrived in Santa María; amid the trees, the iron railings that bordered the grass and the pedestal of the statue, I looked at the façade of the hotel on the corner, the church and the sign where the road turned off to the colony; I turned around to look at the quiet surface of the river, and we began to descend a tree-lined street to the pier. The slope was gentle, a reddish light flashed in the middle of the waters; what I remembered or had imagined of the city was there, present at each glance, exact at certain moments, less evident and more elusive at others. There they were, the inhabitants of the colony, stiff, with distrust and an offer of cordiality on the flushed faces, parading by; the girls walked arm in arm or holding each other around the waist, moving along the edge of the wharf that rose like a tide, that was rising now—according to custom, they all strolled the wharf from north to south as far as the dock of the rowing club, then returned along the rail of the walk, leaning into the wind—so that the rail seemed to reach first to the calves of their legs, then to their hips, their chests, and finally above their heads.

I was going step by step, Ernesto forgotten, trying to discover the habit of piety and resilience in the fair profiles; these were women and could be understood. The men were proceeding in straight lines, remaining silent or making comments without moving their heads, until the dark hats—pulled down to the eyebrows without any slant, as if incapable of being tilted; stuck to the skull and substituting forever for the yellow, red, or gray hair that they almost hid—first rose above the level of the dock, then descended, diminishing the stature of their owners. The strollers stopped in the curve of the narrow port, for a moment directing indifferent eyes toward the small boats of the club; and the women imitated this pause, repeating the same slow inclination of the head, the braids of the oldest bound at the nape of the neck, those of the young ones straight over the temples. I asked myself to what degree I was responsible for the pairs of bright eyes glancing at the bows, the sails, the capricious names of the boats. Then the eyes turned away and tried to orient themselves toward the dark green of the grass lining the walk. With them we went up toward the square, moving along in the current of men with arms at their sides, large women, girls wearing long dresses of bright colors. I looked at the storm clouds that were rushing the night, I searched for vestiges of presentiments, hopes and fears accumulated year after year in the changeable shadow of trees, around the greenish stains that had dripped down over the statue.

"Let's look for a hotel," I proposed. "But I don't want to eat there. We'll get a room and go out."

I sat on the first empty bench; the gravel was scattered where the band musicians had been, and there were tracks of music stands and footprints surrounded by peanut shells and paper cups; collapsed on the bench, I counted the faint distant streaks of lightning over the river.

"Tell me why you never want to talk," Ernesto said. "You know what I want to say. It's been more than a month. I did it, just me; I don't understand why you've involved yourself, why you've helped me escape and come along with me, spending your money, for more than a month."

"For nothing," I said, "it's not important. It seems unjust to me that they should put you in jail for having done something that I myself would have done."

I was tired, wishing that the indecisive storm above the river would arrive, wishing for any ending that would rid me of the responsibility of ascribing a meaning to the month and a half of flight; I was thinking about the single hundred peso note, guessing at Ernesto's reaction when I told him that the retreat, the game, was over.

"I can't understand," Ernesto continued, grumbling. "I've got nothing against you, I'm asking you again to forgive me for that night. I explained to you already how she was, I told you that I'd been crazy for a long time. But I can't see you choking her, I don't believe you could kill anyone. And not on account of fear, but because of the way you are. Why did it occur to you to come to this city? And to sit here on a bench, wide open, as if there were no danger. When every town turns out to have too many people for you, and you're afraid that a bird might see you. I don't understand you; it's as if we were lifelong friends; but when

I set myself to thinking, I know I'll never get to know you, that I can't touch bottom. Sometimes I think you like me and other times that you hate me."

I was allowing him to express his feelings, at times I smiled at him or touched his shoulder, agreeing with a nod; I was thinking of Juan María Brausen, I was assembling slippery images to reconstruct him, I felt him close by, likable and incomprehensible, I remembered that I had felt the same about my father. I saw Ernesto shrug, take out a cigarette, and light it.

"You never want to talk," he repeated; the threat and bitterness were quickly dissolved in the silence. Nothing now; the back of my neck rested on the bench; the thick, twisted trees, shadows of the last pedestrians materializing under the light of the street lamps, momentarily, over the murmur of crushed gravel. "If you'd tell me the truth, why you're doing it, then we'd be friends for life and I would be glad to be escaping this way."

Now the silence was spreading into the dark sky, like the prelude to a storm. Only a hundred pesos remained, there was nothing to lose, but I was determined not to speak.

"I told you a hundred times," I answered. "I wanted to help you because it seemed unjust that you might go to jail for something I myself would have done, that seemed right to do."

"Could be," Ernesto said. "There's a guy on that bench, near the gas pump. I saw him this morning; he seemed to be following me."

I didn't look toward the corner where the gas pump was; before me stretched a section of the square that Díaz Grey had contemplated from some of the surrounding windows; I remembered that the first storm of spring had shaken the trees and that under their damp leaves there rose the perfume of recently opened flowers, the heat of summer, men in overalls carrying samples of wheat, women with desire and the fear of confronting what they had imagined in the stiffness of winter cold. They were all mine, born from me, and I felt pity and love for them; I loved also, in the flower beds of the square, each unfamiliar aspect of the land; and it was as if I might love in any given woman all the women of the world, those separated from me by time, distance, failed opportunities, deaths, and even those who were still children. Next to Ernesto's prattle, I discovered myself free from the past and the responsibility for the future, reduced to an event, strong in proportion to my capacity to be abstract.

The hotel was on the corner of the square, and the construction of the block of houses coincided with my memories and the changes I had imposed when I was imagining the doctor's story. We rented a room in the Travelers' House in the middle of the block; they gave us a large room with two separate beds, and two windows overlooking the square. After we bathed, Ernesto looked out toward the stormy night and began to smoke; he was in shirt sleeves, rigid, erect, and from the bed I saw his motionless, inclined head, the forehead and nose almost submerged in the weak light of the window. I saw the composure of his face rapidly disintegrate without resistance, the truth that he believed he told himself in secret. As if on a return trip to Buenos Aires, to Calle Chile, he went on reviving and setting aside—station by station, town by town, day by day—the expressions that had gradually ennobled him, the periods of transition toward the clear, gentle countenance that for an instant he had shown me on the bench in the square; as if that indolent smile, the friendly voice, the loss of the feeling of ridicule, the renunciation of bitterness, insolence, and solitude, marked the highest point he could reach, and now, swiftly, he was obliged to descend to the fact of the white, drowsy, vicious face that he had brought close to me in the first encounter, step by step, escorted by La Queca's proud cowardice.

"I told you there's a guy," he said, and he repeated it almost shouting. "The one dressed in gray. I saw him this morning; he was talking with a policeman and now he's walking back and forth or sitting on the bench so he can watch the door. No, you know I've never been afraid—I'm not seeing things. Let's go eat and I'll show him to you."

I went close to the window, I saw the man who was walking along pushing a stone with the tip of his shoe; perhaps Ernesto was right, perhaps the gray figure moving under the trees might signal the end of the retreat. I saw a last bright gleam on the river, a church the same as any other, a deserted provincial square. A noise of automobile horns was moving nearer and then suddenly stopped to my right, close by. The man in gray paused to look toward the corner of the hotel, touched his forehead with an open handkerchief, and folded it in quarters before putting it away.

"There's one thing I can't stand," Ernesto said. "Are we going to eat?"

While I finished dressing in the corner of the room to which I had allotted a folding screen, a clothes rack, and a mirror, I contemplated Ernesto motionless at the window, bent toward the coming and going of the man; I used his body to measure the space that was filling this other air, dead, all this strange emptiness of undefinable quality.

"They're hanging little paper lanterns in the square and on the street to the pier," Ernesto announced. "The carnival is Saturday. A dance here must be fun."

He was serious, with his dreamy eyes, with the old face of loathing and disgust. He must feel himself trapped, yet be unable to understand how; neither could he understand that the last chapter of the adventure had been waiting for us there, in the large room with the two windows that overlooked the square, the church, the club, the market, the drug store, the coffee shop, that overlooked the turbulent night in which music from the conservatory was swelling, in the space Díaz Grey had once occupied and where I imagined I had arrived too late.

We passed by the indifference of the man in gray who was cleaning his nails as he leaned against a tree; I saw his round Mongol face, the full, cheerful lips with which he was blowing on the blade of his penknife. After crossing the square, we arrived at the broad street that began at the pier.

"There has to be a restaurant here," Ernesto said. "A few blocks ahead, to the left, I think I saw one. Swiss people . . . The guy isn't following us; I guess you're right, I'm seeing things."

But if the air of the rooming house was coarse and implacably hostile, this stormy wind that came from the river and curled around our backs was the same savage air, and without history—scarcely altered through hundreds of anecdotes of heroic intention—that had circled around the episodes of Díaz Grey, that had prevented all communication between the solitude of the doctor and the solitude of others.

"These people are celebrating carnival already," Ernesto said, when we advanced toward the middle of the restaurant, toward the voices, the smoke, the heavy-set man who was playing the accordion. All the tables were occupied and those eating at them looked at us with hostility while they swayed from side to side singing.

"There are tables upstairs," the waiter said in passing.

A garland of paper flowers ran across the ceiling, and red and white bouquets hung from the walls around photographs and small flags with crossed staffs. When the music ended—the man, fat and old, put his instrument on the floor and began to stand up, hands on his chest, shaking his bald head up and down in thanks for the applause, without smiling, with pale, very open, sad eyes above his fleshy ears of a drunkard—Ernesto mounted the platform where the musician was and looked around, observing the small antipathies confronting him on the faces over the tables; his dirty hat was pushed back, he had his hands in his pockets, an unlit cigarette dangling from his mouth, defiance in his raised chin. He heard the individual silences that moved toward him and became stronger on uniting and surrounding him; he looked at the faces again, slower now, dispelling their provocation with the expression of dread and curiosity that he passed around in a semicircle, from the rusty stain of light at the foot of the stairs to the impassivity of the owner leaning his elbow on the bar. I saw him turn around to ask the accordion player for a match, and voices began to swell at the sides of the room, mounting again toward the curved timbers delineated by the hanging, hardening flowers.

The musician was seated, with the accordion between his legs; behind his cloud of smoke, Ernesto smiled and winked at me. No one was looking at him from the tables when a tall young waiter placed himself at his side, waiting for Ernesto to turn his head and see him; another waiter, shaking a napkin in front of my face, said, "There's another dining room upstairs."

Separated, each one followed by a waiter up the middle of the aisle, we were moving toward the staircase and beginning to go up it as the accordion again sounded and the patrons again sang incomprehensible phrases in chorus.

From the dining room above, narrow and almost dark, where lame tables and chairs with broken seats were gathered, and where we were alone, we could see, to my right, the entrance to the restaurant and the far end of the bar, with the proprietor leaning on his elbows, motionless in front of an overflowing glass of beer, his quiet interrupted when a waiter came close to disturb him or he had to smile and shake his head—one could guess, then, the heels placed together, the conscious attempt to cover his belly—in order to wave good night to groups that were leaving. To my left, below, separated from the room by a fringed curtain, was a private dining room that filled up after our arrival.

Ernesto ate the first dish quickly and gave up on the second almost without trying it; he consulted me with a glance and asked for two bottles of Moselle, "So the waiter won't wear himself out going up and down the stairs."

"What I can't stand is fear," he said without looking at me. "Not even the idea that I'm going to be afraid. It doesn't let me think or remember, as if I were nobody."

"Yes," I said to help him; but he began to smoke and drink with his freshly shaved face resting on his fist, he did not explain himself, and I could not guess what he meant.

It was as if we were seated at a table following our first encounter at La Queca's apartment and I marveled to discover in his vague white face the revelation of a world of fear, avidity, avarice, and oblivion, the incommunicable world where they lived, he, La Queca, La Gorda, and their friends, the owners of the voices and footsteps I had heard through the wall. He had struck me because of fear, he was joined to me through fear.

"Anything except that," Ernesto said, when the singing ended in the dining room to my right; under the sign "Bern Brewery" with the painting of a crowned king raising a glass, the owner was looking straight ahead, expressionless, his double chin very close to the foam of his beer. "I'm not afraid any more, but it's going to come back. You never saw me drunk? Sometimes I get that way. You were always the one who was afraid and wanted to hide and make a run for it, and now I'm like that, too. I can talk about what happened, I feel better if I talk, I like to think that I killed her and say it to you and think that now she's dead. No, I'm not going to scream. Since I saw her dead, I no longer know why I did it."

From the private dining room to my left, cigarette smoke was slowly rising, murmured monologues could be heard, some brief, scattered laughter. I filled Ernesto's glass and placed the bottle at his side; below they were singing again, enveloping the music of the accordion.

"During the war . . ." Ernesto said, straightening up with a smile. "Ever hear it? They played that in the Loeffler."

I moved my chair close to the railing so I could observe the private dining room comfortably. There was a woman dressed in a tailored gray dress, with a full body but not fat, dark, about thirty-five; her fingers were dipping in and out of a plate of grapes, she held them in front of her eyes until they stopped dripping and submerged them again into the water with ice; the other hand was on the table, held by a young blond boy who, serious and on guard, kept looking at the other faces, very erect against the back of his chair.

"But these people are Swiss and the war is over," Ernesto said.

Below, with his fragile hand open on top of the woman's fingers, the young boy was drawing on a cigarette, raising his head in a graceful, touching attitude, with his golden uncombed hair curled at the temples and the nape of the neck, and falling straight over his forehead. To his left was seated a small heavy-set man, with his mouth half opened, the lower lip trembling when he took a breath; the light fell yellow on his round, almost bald skull, it made the dark fuzz shine, and the solitary lock of hair plastered against an eyebrow. Closest to me, exactly under my chair, was a pair of thin, moving hands, and weak shoulders covered by dark blue cloth; the head of this man was small and the hair was damp and neat. Another, invisible, must have been standing next to the curtain, behind the man with the blue suit; I heard his laugh, I saw the glances of the others toward him.

"I'm only asking," the small, fat man said (he had a slender, curved nose, as if his youthfulness were conserved in it, in its audacity, in the imperious expression the nose added to his face; he hooked his thumb into his vest, and moved his body toward the table and then toward the back of his chair, in rhythm, as if shaken by a car jolting him across bad roads)—"I only want to ask if it was legal. Whether or not we were working with a municipal official. Two thousand one hundred twelve. Did the council unite to revoke it?"

"Maybe you yourself wrote it," the invisible man said, kidding him. "The order is from the governor."

There was another man next to the curtain at the entrance, an old man who advanced limping, with his hat on.

"But let's see, everything in its place." He had a Spanish accent, with an ironic manner of delaying words in his throat; he walked behind the pensive fat man, who was continuing to rock himself. "With your permission," the old man said over the head of the young boy with the childish hand opened on that of the woman. He served himself a glass of wine and drank it in one swallow, made a harsh sound as he touched his gray mustache, then again filled the glass, making the wine fall in a long, thin, resounding stream. "Let's see," said the blind man. "You, Junta, have already said all that *ad nauseum*; you're tiring the lady and the doctor and it doesn't help at all. That the council . . . that the law . . ." He saluted the woman and the man in blue with his glass, he looked toward the curtain. "And this friend, who so many times honored the achievements of the enterprise that in turn honored him, is now doing his duty. Don't knock it, Junta, with the reasoning of a petty lawyer that he can't answer. . . ." The man standing next to the curtain laughed again and reached forward. "Don't torture the lady, Junta. All those complaints . . ."

"You needn't call me 'lady,'" interrupted the woman, freeing her hand to light a cigarette; the boy seemed to wake up and looked around restlessly. "I'm María Bonita to my friends."

"Thank you," the old man said, touching his hat; he looked at the woman through and then over his eyeglasses.

"As I was saying to the boy," she continued, patting his cheek, "the whole point is that the priest went crazy. As if someone could teach me to respect God. . . ."

"That could very well be," the old man said. "Perhaps, as the doctor will have guessed, all that may be no more than a stage of the age-old struggle between obscurantism and the light represented by our friend Junta."

The small fat man raised his shoulders and the hand that was resting on the table; his large, bulging eyes were directed toward the woman and the man dressed in blue.

"Why doesn't the council give up their vacation?" he said with a smothered, trembling voice. "The prestige of the council is at stake."

"What can one do? Orders from the governor . . ." said the invisible man.

"You see, doctor?" the old man asked. "Junta hasn't struggled just for birthrights, civilization, and honest trade. Among other things—but who can remember them all? Also, he was constantly preoccupied with respect for constitutional rights. I believe everything is documented. But madame, not just the priest is to blame. The angered priest reflects the spirit of this city of Santa María, where we are for our sins. Happy are you who leave it, and distinguished by the escort of the friend . . ." He was not entirely the clown when he took a step back and began to recite with his glass held high, *"Ave Maria, gratia plena, Dominus tecum, benedicta tu . . ."*

Only the man in blue laughed, gently, interrupting himself to cough. The old man touched the fat man's back, absorbed in thought, grave, and disappeared again near the curtain.

"And now," he said, "to trot off to the editorial rooms. I'm sorry I cannot publish the farewells you deserve. The fourth estate speaks muzzled."

"Go to sleep, old Spaniard," said the fat man without raising his head, without ceasing to sway.

"To work, to move pounds of lead and stupidity. I might have wanted to record these Hundred Days that shook us. From the return from Rosario, slattern city of shopkeepers, to the embarkation for Saint Helena; from which it is also possible to escape, Junta, it is possible. My respects, madame."

The fringes of the curtain were moving, and the invisible man murmured a good night and laughed again.

"Drink something," María Bonita said toward the curtain.

"No thank you," said the man. "Whenever I come in, the owner makes me drink. I'm grateful to you. I'm going to come for all of you at one and we'll leave for the station."

The fat man interrupted his seesawing to look toward the curtain; his bright, bulging eyes were gyrating, without expression, like glass balls; the curved nose moved forward like a ship's prow, triumphant over the oiliness and decrepitude of his face.

"Are you going?" the man in blue asked.

The young boy lifted his body against the back of the chair and remained there, blinking with a thin smile that moved the cigarette toward the corner of his mouth.

"On the first train," he said.

The woman turned around, chewing a grape. "What are you thinking, doctor? All night you looked at the boy without opening your mouth. Do you think I convinced him to come to Buenos Aires? You don't know me; I'm a woman and I'm thinking only of his mother. Not to mention the responsibility for Junta and me."

"I can go in another car," said the boy, angry and blushing. "If you don't let me go with you now, I'll go tomorrow; I'll take the first train I can get."

"Listen to him," the woman said. "He's made it very clear. It's not because of María Bonita that he's leaving. How does it look to you?" She buried a hand in the boy's uncombed hair. "Sixteen . . ."

Ernesto was staggering on the stairs when we went down to the large, almost deserted room, adorned now with posters announcing carnival dances. Through the wet streets, dark and windless, walking arm in arm with Ernesto, I thought that Díaz Grey had died long before that night and that his solitary meditations in the office window and his meetings and adventures with Elena Sala would have to be situated in another era, at the beginning of the century. No one was strolling in front of the rooming house; a deafening noise of horns and motors wounded the night at the corner of the hotel, went along the square, and moved away toward the river, then toward Enduro, and died in the dirt streets and zinc houses of the neighborhood around the fishermen's wharves.

Ernesto took off his shoes and sat down on his bed to smoke; very far off, the timid, constant rattle of rain began; the brightness of lightning lit up his motionless, contracted body and consumed the cigarette's red glow.

"Are you asleep?" he asked; I stopped sleeping and arranged my pillow so I could look at the sky. "Excuse me. I'm not going to bed tonight. Too bad we didn't get a bottle. I'm not afraid any more." He tried to laugh and he coughed; I remembered the hands, the question, the blue color of the suit of the man whom they called doctor in the private dining room. "You have every reason for bad feelings. But even if you don't believe it, I'm your friend. Forgive me for waking you."

"All right," I said.

Almost noiseless overhead on the roof, but with a sensation of being remote, the rain continued in the morning; Ernesto was dressed, standing next to the window, smoking; the bed was untouched. 'There he is, lost, existing only in fear; obliged first to kill for me, now trapped in the void left by the disappearance of a country doctor invented by me; now he is discovering the story that I assigned to Díaz Grey, he is thinking the jaded thoughts I made him think.'

He believed I was asleep and came to my bed to put his fingers on my arm and to sigh with the morose and hapless sound of someone unaccustomed to sighing. In the same way he had left the note for La Queca—"I'll call you or come at nine"—and in the same way I had placed the note in the room where the dead La Queca was, Ernesto, before leaving, wrote a sentence in the margin of a newspaper and put it on my pillow: "Take it easy, I'm going to keep you out of this." I went close to the window to watch him walk away; I finished dressing as I looked through the window at the drizzle in the square, the men in raincoats conversing without moving; one stood leaning against a tree, the other two were seated on a bench, legs crossed, arms folded. I saw Ernesto cross the street slowly with an unexpected dignity that transformed him; he paused facing the tree and the man, his arms hanging as if broken, as if he would never be able to raise them. The other assumed a smile, and with the water-stained newspaper that he had kept under his arm, signaled toward the door of the rooming house, toward me, without seeing me. Ernesto, motionless, was leaning toward the smile, protecting his eyes from the drizzle; the man brought his head closer to him, moved it in the direction of the bench, then took a step backward and smiled again. Separated by distance and the rain, I thought I discovered the absence of joy and distrust. The man walked toward the bench and Ernesto followed behind him; the other two men were standing up, touching Ernesto's arms and letting go of them; before leaving the window, I looked at the four pair of arms, fallen, hanging like empty sleeves.

The man was once more on the edge of the square and again had the newspaper folded under his arm. Across the street, without moving, he greeted me with a smile and remained there when I paused, when I walked toward him. 'This was what I was searching for from the beginning, since the death of the man who lived with Gertrudis for five years; to be free, to be irresponsible before others, to master myself without effort in true solitude.'

"You're the other," the man said. "You're Brausen."

Looking indolent and bored, as if water were not falling on him, as if he were sheltered from the rain and waiting for it to clear up, Ernesto was moving his foot back and forth, seated on the bench between the two men. I recognized the voice talking to me and closely watching my eyes: it had sounded on the previous night next to the curtain in the private dining room, directed to the made-up woman eating grapes, to the blond boy beginning life, to the aquiline profile of the fat, defeated, retreating man. Ernesto was now to one side of the smiling man and was opening his eyes to seek mine; I didn't want to look at him; the men on the bench had gotten up but were not walking.

"Brausen?" the voice asked.

I looked in silence at the man, I understood that it would be possible for me to say nothing, neither affirming nor denying. Ernesto struck the face of the man and made him crash against the tree; he struck him again as he was falling and the body remained motionless in the mud, face up to the drizzle and open-mouthed, the newspaper folded on top of his throat.

Mr. Albano

When I get up to telephone—once more Pepe answers, "Mr. Albano has not arrived yet"—I can study the profile of the man with the straw hat pushed back on his head, who is drinking at the bar. Perhaps he has not noticed me all morning, maybe he is not interested in the table where, between the Englishman, who is drinking another large cup of coffee, and Lagos, who rests his face in his hand, you are looking at your finger, compelled to spin the ash tray on the tablecloth.

I return to my table and light a cigarette; without moving, scarcely shifting his eye, Lagos understands I have no news. Oscar, the Englishman, turns his face toward the door, disinterested, in no hurry to shorten the time that separates us from disaster. You abandon the ash tray and point, without conviction, toward the March morning beginning to unfold in the window. I leave my coins on the table and take a last look at the man in the Panama hat near the bar; I see that the clock on the cash register reads seven-fifty, and I go out onto the street. I walk under the trees from corner to corner, waiting for the store to open, looking at you through the café window, quiet and pensive, as if weighed down by the heavier silence of the two men. Above, from behind some open balcony doors, they are already preparing for the last day of carnival, and the music of a piano comes down, intense, recedes with a watery ripple; it seems to divine and follow the direction of my steps.

The store is opened now and sunshine brightens the noses, the mustaches, the silky fabrics in the shop window. I see the three of you leave the café, you in the middle, Lagos with his cane on an arm, the Englishman biting the pipe and with his hands in his trouser pockets.

"Good morning," I say to the little man who brings his old, blinking face near me. "We need costumes. Something very special, very good."

"For the dance," the Englishman adds, and laughs during the three words.

"Yes," the man says, despondent; suddenly he shows his teeth and turns to look at you.

You are at my side and smile at me; Lagos places a wig on his fist and raises his arm toward the shadows still remaining on the ceiling.

Sadly the Englishman insists, "Costumes."

"Yes." The man does not move. "For this afternoon?"

"For now," you say rapidly.

"We need to take them now," Lagos explains; he inclines his fist, and disappointment shows in his face when the wig slides and falls onto the glass counter. "To be returned tomorrow; first thing in the morning, their mission of deceit without malice fulfilled, the costumes will be in your hands, ready to go back into mothballs."

"It will have to be first thing in the morning," the owner repeats. "And you'll have to deposit security." Lagos makes a bow and shows a fistful of bills; the old man raises his forearms, his elbows. "I didn't mean to say . . . It's the policy."

Oscar, with the pipe between his teeth, laughs at him, obliging the old man's face to demonstrate the marvelous ability to endure anything. The owner raises a curtain and allows us to pass, one by one, touching our shoulders lightly as if he were counting us. We enter the gloomy corridor where we face two large shelves covered with cretonne curtains that he begins to pull back; then he leaves to turn on the light.

"Men's and women's," he says, moving his small hands toward the shelves.

Without understanding, we look at the colors of shoulders, skirts, flaccid stockings, shoes with buckles, a rapier that draws us around it. We take down hangers with costumes and bring them to the narrow courtyard with the skylight. You inspect the dresses, make them float in the air, bring them back to the shelf, take others down so quickly that the colors dazzle my eyes. Suddenly I imagine that everything—escape, salvation, the future that joins us and that only I can remember—relies on our not making a mistake in choosing the costumes; I look fearfully at the clothes the Englishman spins round on the hangers, those that Lagos stirs slightly, nudging them with his cane. I hear your laugh, see your hand touch the nape of Lagos' neck, I listen to the old man try to enter into your merriment; but I cannot take an interest because I am trembling before the danger of making a mistake; I crouch down, as if this might bring me nearer the truth.

"I'll wait for you in the front of the store." It is your voice, your steps, your silence.

Lagos' cane passes over my head, touches a costume, skips to another. Suddenly I stretch out my arm and take down a costume. Lagos has lowered his hand with the cane and takes a step backward.

"Take that one out for me," he says without enthusiasm.

You are alone in the front of the store and you smile at the street; I look in vain for the outfit he has just chosen; I step in front of you, almost brushing you with my costume, almost blinding you with the reflection from the spangles; but I do not succeed in separating your eyes from what they are looking at.

"Yes," Lagos says as he arrives. "All the girls will want to dance with me. There's no doubt; your remark has been happy and prophetic."

The owner laughs next to the curtain behind the showcase, and out from under his arm and his hoarse voice the Englishman appears, his body bent over, and joins us. Lagos drops his costume on top of mine.

"Halberdier," says the Englishman.

"It's a very original costume," the owner says. "Don't you think so, miss?" You agree with a nod of your head and it seems adequate to all of us. "Original and very beautiful. And yours! A king."

"Splendid, no doubt about it," Lagos replies. "Tonight, this afternoon, my popularity in social circles will increase and be established. Perhaps something could be done about the stones in the crown and the whiteness of the ermine, but it's not worth the trouble."

He has spoken in profile to the owner without looking at his costume, and ends with a sigh. In spite of the ironic expression, I imagine he is afraid, I suppose he is repentant that he so little resembles the Horacio Lagos who in the early morning hours, in the private dining room of

Pepe's café, gave us orders, almost making me believe in the sincerity of the revenge and homage undertaken for Elena Sala's sake: 'We are here at the carnival and we have to hide ourselves in it. They're looking for a short, heavy-set man dressed in gray; a fair, thin one wearing a dark brown suit; and a good-looking one who smokes a pipe. They're looking for a girl of average height, light eyes, straight nose, and no visible marks, apart from subtle professional ones left by practice of the violin. Right? Very well: let's abolish them as if we were blowing out four candles, let's substitute a Madame Du Barry, a Cossack, a Son of Zorro, the Last of the Mohicans; let's turn them loose to wander through dances and places of honest amusement suited to these four.'

"All the costumes are pretty," the owner ventures, bothered by the silence. "Silk . . ." He touches Lagos' outfit, lifts a corner of it, then removes his hand.

The Englishman comes close to me drawing on his pipe, the halberdier costume slung over his shoulder; he picks up Lagos' costume and breathes the smell of mothballs; then Lagos smiles as he looks at my costume on top of the counter, he laughs in my face and walks toward the door shaking his head. Oscar waits for him, motionless, with the halberdier's costume still on his shoulder, the king's jacket over his arm. Happy and excited, the old man turns toward you and begins to talk to the back of your neck.

"But where is your costume, miss? You chose well, very original, something in very good taste. And it's not a costume, it's a real outfit. It's a secret. . . ." He looks at me and winks.

You touch your chest with your thumb and murmur something when Lagos returns; he touches the tip of your chin as he passes and comes over to me and my costume.

"Bullfighter," he says, "eh, doctor? Yellow and green . . ." He takes the suit and holds it up for a moment. "Bullfighter," he repeats as he puts it down next to my elbow; then he takes the cloth cap and jams it onto his fist, as he did before with the wig. "I don't remember having seen it in the back room. It's a complex, you'll say, doctor, but I've always wanted to have a bullfighter's outfit, to wear it on some occasion and have my picture taken. If you, doctor, would add to your already innumerable kindnesses . . . If it would not inconvenience you to accept an exchange . . ."

"*I* chose it," I say dryly, without knowing why I want revenge. "You took it out and put it back again." I plant my elbow on the costume and look at Lagos with humility and sadness. "Now I want to wear it."

"I won't argue. But you must admit, Díaz Grey, that on the hangers all of them looked the same. Perhaps I saw it, perhaps I took it out and examined it; but in point of fact . . ."

He rotates his head to search for the Englishman's eyes, continues the movement to smile at you, then darts a sideways look at the old man's yellow teeth.

"No," I say when he looks at me again.

"All right, it's not important. How much do I owe you?" He leans on the counter at my side, watching the sun's progress in the street; I hear another flash of sound from the piano overhead, outside, behind me.

You and the owner raise the curtain and disappear into the corridor; you return and whisper into Lagos' ear.

"No," he says. "It's marvelous, but impossible. Ask him to rent us a suitcase or to wrap them up for us."

I wait, walking up and down while the tottering old man packs the costumes in a suitcase, while Lagos pays and Oscar tries to whistle without taking the pipe out of his mouth. You overtake me under the trees and explain to me, quickly, without looking at me, that we're going to René's house to change clothes. I turn to Lagos, I permit him to come close—now he has an affected strut to his walk, an expert way of looking at things, almost vain—and I begin to realize how much I love and respect him. The Englishman carries the suitcase, he moves ahead with long steps, he comes abreast of you.

"We're going to René's," Lagos says to me, patting me on the back. "A great fellow. But it would be best if you call Pepe again. Excuse me for everything, and especially for these small annoyances, doctor."

Perhaps he was teasing, perhaps he had been teasing all along; his eyes show nothing but friendship and an old man's sadness. I go into the drugstore, smile into the telephone, make the call, and inquire as to Mr. Albano's whereabouts. Last night, following the gunshot, Lagos turned into a giant to halt and organize the column in retreat; the resignation and skepticism he felt in us made him invent, in the private dining room of the café, the phrase "Is Mr. Albano there?" as a code to telephone for news being transmitted through Pepe. A useless precaution, a virtuoso's touch. Mr. Albano—"I've got it!" shouted Lagos with his index finger extended, bending toward us an expression of triumph and secrecy—was born from the label of the bottle we had on the table. But when I telephone Pepe, I feel my interest increase in the impossible presence of Mr. Albano in the small café, in the shadow of his body, dressed in white, on the stained floor; in his unheard voice, cut short in rhythm to the movement of his heavy jaw; in the gesture of his greetings; in the patient and malevolent quality that I ascribe to his posture.

René was wearing a silk bathrobe, gray and with black circles, as he stood there letting us into his apartment, after having appeared briefly behind the windows of the watchmaker's shop and drawn back the bolt on the small metal door. While we were entering crouched over, he ran upstairs to wait for us in the door of the apartment, erect, laughing with the teasing tone which, one guessed, was habitual to him, while taking off his glasses for vanity's sake or to see us better.

Now, moving swiftly and effortlessly, he removes books and papers from the desk; he doesn't hear the joke the Englishman repeats; he shrugs when Lagos makes excuses.

"They're here," he says. "Do what you like, you can stay a couple of years. That's not the problem, from my point of view. But if you don't leave Buenos Aires soon . . . Who did it?" he asks with a suddenness, a fiery excitement in his eyes.

"All of us," says Lagos.

"I did it," Oscar says; he bends over to put the suitcase on the floor carefully, he straightens up, drawing smoke from the pipe. "All this is idiotic, a game. I'm going to kill someone else and give myself up; they can disappear."

You begin to walk back and forth from the open window to the niche with St. Christopher and the Child on his shoulder, as we sit down, carefully choosing our seats and the order in which we will occupy them. Immediately weariness climbs up to me from the leather armchair, it is entering into my pores; I look at you and think that you are forcing the return of that happiness, that annihilation in silence and solitude that you revealed at the costume shop.

"Discussions don't interest me," the Englishman says. "I'm not going to listen to them." He settles a leg on the suitcase, shelters the pipe between his fingers. "We don't have the right to stay here, and I don't see the point of it. I'm going to the bedroom to change, if there are no women there. I want to die in the uniform of the Swiss Guard. Does René know the story of the costumes?"

"You can all stay two years," René repeats; he shows me his medallion profile, the thin cheek, the high hardened wave in his hair.

"I don't have to know anything, if that's what you're worried about. I'm just welcoming some friends who want to have a carnival party in my house."

As if led by your own smile, you pace back and forth, here and there. I relax into the armchair, into weariness and drowsiness; I resolve to forgive you, to renounce revenge in homage to this, your tenacious tracking down of a reason for joy, in homage to that will to believe which you accept and cultivate now, in this moment when the future can be calculated in minutes, when every situation seems compromised.

The Englishman gets up, bends over to pick up the suitcase, walks to the bedroom behind the curtains.

"Pardon," Lagos says. "But you, my dear friend, are not answering me. I can't think why you shouldn't let me know exactly how long you've known. Supposing, for a moment, that some part of this story may be true."

"As you like," René says; seated on the table, he removes and examines his glasses with a smile; the feminine tracery of his mouth is attenuated by an ascetic slenderness of the lips. "It's amazingly simple. I never knew about it, I don't know about it now. I swear, I don't know about it. Of course the radio has been blaring it every fifteen minutes since the morning. I can hear it and imagine anything, make my deductions, and carry them with me to the grave."

He laughs, always bantering and full of love. To relieve the awkwardness, he pretends to be interested in the transparency of his glasses.

"Who is René?" I ask.

"René," he answers, shrugging his shoulders, separating his hands woefully.

"He's my friend," Lagos says. "And you'll never know how much I love him. Very well; deductions . . ." There is no impatience or fatigue in his face; perhaps everything is false, we may even be in the hotel next to the river, the Englishman may not have killed anyone. "Technically unobjectionable. And we, dear friend, swear to respect your secret, your reticence."

"Then," René answers, "we agree. But I beg you to accept for a moment the supposition that you did it and that I know it. If only for the sake of talking for a moment, until Owen returns. Lagos, you and I have played chess."

"I'm grateful that you remember it; you might not be a very skillful player, but you could be considered among the world's most elegant. We may assume that, then."

On the edge of his chair Lagos is caught now between the husband and the widower, between polite lightheartedness and implacable despair. You continue walking back and forth, faster and more resolved now; perhaps there never were any problems, and it is enough to choose between the image of St. Christopher and the daylight in the window, or to waver between the two.

"Halberdier," the Englishman says on returning; he sits down and searches for a match to light his pipe. We try to avoid his catching us looking at him in his disguise, we are thankful to him for being the first. I look at your ankles to escape the small dread emanating from this man sunken in his armchair and caressing the wig, his rigid horizontal arm leaning on the ridiculous weapon wrapped in aluminum foil.

"Well then, technically perfect," René says. "But the carnival ends today. As soon as the sun rises tomorrow, you won't be able to move a finger disguised. I can only say you're losing twenty-four hours; I can only repeat that I myself would use them to get to a border."

"Exactly," Lagos says. "You and everybody would do that."

He makes a light sound with his fingertips against the arm of the chair and bends his body toward René, not so rapidly as to prevent my knowing, even before the movement ends, that he is lying. "And they, the police, will think the same thing. Everybody; men with Mausers in the roads, inspection of automobiles and trains. So obvious . . . At this very moment they are waiting for us at every border. But who are they waiting for?" He turns toward the place I occupy; I know that he is talking for you, nothing more, in order at each step to pour into your ears in turn the conviction that *tomorrow* holds a meaning, and that he is infinitely more vigorous than his age. "They all have, they all should have, we may presume, descriptions of us. But will they ever find anything like this halberdier, the king into whom I will transform myself?"

"Yes," René murmurs with sadness. "I understand."

"All this, my dear friend," Lagos says, standing up, "within the broad limits of the initial supposition." He smiles and approaches the table with quick steps, pressing René's shoulder. "My poor friend, there is the sudden, seemingly enraged brief unhappiness; there is also the other, gray, daily, without a foreseeable end. Yours. Dear friend, my time has come, I'm going to be a king." He pauses next to the bedroom curtain, I feel he suspects that he has left fear and distrust behind him. "If I were to direct a retreat . . . Yes, it's true, the carnival is ending. But I'll have already won the absolute security of twenty-four hours, I'll have strengthened my army's morale, and during the time so gained I'll have organized an approach to the border."

"That's true, too," René says. But Lagos is not convinced; he turns smiling toward the center of the room, seems to collide with you, taken by surprise, and gently holds you against his chest.

"I, the king," says Lagos, beside the table. "Would it bother you to come with me a moment?"

He bows, heels together, and goes into the bedroom with René.

You have turned to walk to the other side of the smoke from the Englishman's pipe; I discover that the zone of tranquillity and indifference extending from the frail knees of the halberdier, from the wrinkles of the white stockings, persists in destroying what you construct. You struggle and persevere, but you finally stop, you smile toward me without seeing, you come near and fall into a chair at my side.

In costume Lagos seems simultaneously fatter and taller; I watch him advance, increasing the dignity of his manners. He is probably testing the recently acquired gifts when he bends over to whisper in the ear of the Englishman, who is sitting motionless in his chair, the straight angle of his arm supported on the short lance that he calls a halberd. You look wide-eyed at René, who is wearing street clothes and carrying a straw hat and a black notebook in his hand.

"We're leaving," Lagos explains; he looks at me, then smiles toward you. "I don't think we should linger. René has a magnificent idea; it's possible that everything can be arranged in a couple of hours. There's a telephone in the bedroom, doctor; I beg you, from time to time concern yourself with our friend Albano."

"There's no problem in using the telephone," René adds. "But don't answer if it rings and don't use the business phone."

There is something unfathomable in his courteous smile, I have a presentiment of loathing that frightens me, of something that will be grotesque and mournful in the group when they turn their backs and walk toward the door; the king, the halberdier, and that man accompanying them or leading them, like a keeper of a madhouse with his patients.

I go toward the bedroom so I will not see them leave; I make the call as they softly shut the door, I have more than enough time to perceive the growing silence in the first room, the solitude beginning to surround and isolate you. It is Pepe's voice on the telephone, projecting over the noises to be expected at noon, the restless clamor of vermouth glasses, siphon bottles, plates of olives, money, and chips. Mr. Albano has not arrived yet; I thank him and, fully awake now, throw myself onto the bed and scarcely sink into the blue quilt. I think about you and forget you, I accept my will to forget you, I forget the unrealizable future that united us, I forget the insignificant portion of what we did together and what awaits us. With my hands under the back of my neck, surrounded—almost impaled—by the blue, rose, and cream stripes of the wallpaper, I lapse into memories of some faded, happy past. I evoke Mr. Albano with no result other than some badly distributed jet-black hair above dark, oily skin; I guess that I will be obliged to suddenly know his anecdotes, his face, his voice, and his mysterious temperate habits in the same moment when Pepe may substitute the monotonous negative for the explanation of recently emerged complications, enumerating developments of the blockade that will end by trapping us. I remember Lagos' grandeur when he assessed possibilities in his inevitable infantile language, when he demonstrated his capacity to anticipate everything, except the smooth gesture with which the Englishman pressed his pistol against the man who approached the automobile and wanted to stop us. I return to Mr. Albano and imagine our meeting in a private room of the café or next to the bar—the interview in which, holding each other's arm, we will tell one another, without haste, the tedious confidences a dead man can exchange with a ghost.

I think that I am going to fall asleep and I jump up from the bed; I discover you asleep in an armchair, I imagine the totality of animal life in your body, from your shoes to your eyelids lowered to protect your sleep. Under the staircase I cross through the periphery of the watchmaker's workroom, the shop; the street light enters almost vertically, outlining the gilded letters of the shop sign on the glass window, the metallic squares of the alarm system. In a corner café on the other side of the street, seated next to the window with an elbow thrust forward in the damp, hot morning, there is a man in profile wearing a Panama hat, bent over a newspaper.

I remain motionless, looking at him; I listen to the uneven ticking of a score of clocks at my back, over my head, vibrating in the showcase near my stomach; I invent a constant throb of machines I do not hear, those in the safe, in the showcase, in the greenish light of a small aquarium; I am powerless to escape the beat of clocks measuring and gradually wearing away this and other times that I can remember and take for granted. The air of the place suddenly recedes, it becomes silent and subsides; from all sides noon bells strike, carillons hammer and sing. I walk backward until I collide against a standing clock; trembling, I devote myself to sweating all the fear I had accumulated since yesterday without knowing it, while the deafening noise continues, while the last sounds of the clocks agonize in my memory.

I go to the narrow workroom and sit on a stool next to the table; I adjust a watchmaker's lens in my eye, I light a cigarette and examine with a cold one-eyed glance, through the glass of the partition, the light from the street settled on the front part of the shop. I listen to the battalion of ticktocks that attack the splendor of noon, drive it away, consume it; I listen to the punctual carillons and bells that go on celebrating partial victories. Without thoughts, without intervening, alien to time and light, I witness the struggle until it ends, until the metal and glass of clock dials begin to reproduce and fragment the reflection of the first lamp lit on the street. I leave the black lens on the workshop table, sigh the fatigue of the day, and go up the staircase with my body aching, a hand on the small of my back.

In the dark I walk slowly between the pieces of furniture in the apartment, I hear you murmur or laugh; I am confused when I see you separate the white patch of your dress from the wall. You run, quick and silent, stop next to the couch; I slowly recognize your face, your body that seems smaller in the ballerina costume. I sit in a chair and we begin to talk about your costume; I answer docilely, accepting whatever you say or imply, I begin to believe in the hesitant story of a similar costume, a young aunt, two or three sentiments imparted with the improvised bloom of youth and that could interest only you. I discover that your legs have been made amazingly strong and I understand that you were dancing without rest as night fell, that you were running from one side of the room to the other, making a timid leap to the niche, another close to the window.

When you finish your story, I assent with a reflective tone and I sigh. Noise reaches us from very far away, shouts and automobiles, and in the contiguous silence, feeling a little nervous, I have a presentiment that our life in common is going to begin; I realize that we do not fully understand each other and that it will be necessary to fill many gaps with ignorance and good will.

The door opens and the three men enter, they emerge from a background of ringing bells and musical prologues. Someone turns on a light.

"Everything is all right. Almost arranged," Lagos says.

"Tomorrow. At dawn," the Englishman adds.

Lagos' face seems firm and happy; that of the Englishman discreetly shows resignation and failure. I realize that both expressions are part of the same countenance, that they have agreed to share confidence and discouragement. I ask no questions; I place myself at René's side and help him clear the table and open packages; I uncork the bottle of wine.

When someone deposits the last chicken bone on the platter, René smiles toward the ceiling and says quickly, "You can all stay, if you like."

"No," Lagos answers. "Now less than ever. There are many things to do."

You, alone at the far end of the table, raise hands shiny with the grease of the meal, look at your fingers one by one, and bring them together and apart in an unexpected gesture. In the bedroom I discover that the sash of the bullfighter's suit is only a broad padded belt held fast with a metal hook in the back; I cannot remember why I wanted this costume and was ready to fight for it. I am in front of the mirror, ridiculous and sad, I do not dare stand up straight or look myself in the eye.

Perhaps Lagos himself has begun to see men in Panama hats, distracted Mr. Albanos with broad jaws, as we walk two abreast down a main street, pressing into the crowd, offering unmasked faces. You touch me on the shoulder, I turn my head toward you and the Englishman.

"Enter here, doctor," he says. "Please. We're going to go in here."

We do not ask questions as Lagos goes into the theater lobby to buy tickets to the dance. You laugh, hanging on to the stiff arm of the Englishman, head turned toward the sound of the music. Step by step we try to reach an empty table; too late, Lagos advises me, "We're not going to dance yet."

You press the Englishman's chest with your forehead, the two of you move into each other's arms and by dancing arrive long before us at the empty table.

"One moment," Lagos says; he looks at you with a sudden tenderness, almost impudent, and both of you laugh; then as on another night that has not yet arrived, you conceive the expression of a fury without target, a dark and bitter mouth, you seem to be leaning your chest against the warm air, the perfumes, the smoke. "One moment," Lagos says. "Let's have a drink, let's make a toast."

We toast to nothing, raising our glasses a moment toward the colored streamers hanging from the ceiling. When you go off with the Englishman, I watch Lagos' eyes closely as he tries not to lose sight of your round, stiff skirt and the naked triangle of your back amid the dancers; I fill my glass, relax, and go on pursuing in Lagos' face the turns you make, held in the Englishman's arms. I would not say he is old; I would say he has just arrived, this very minute, at the onset of becoming old.

You return to the table, rest the fingers of one hand on a corner of the table, take a drink, smile at me as if you could give me something; you raise your arms to receive Lagos and you both move away, dancing.

The Englishman presses my arm without speaking; I wait, determined to ignore any confession. He empties his glass and fills it again with what remains in the bottle.

"It was only this morning," he says, "that we almost fought over a costume. And it was yesterday afternoon when I shot the guy and left him stiff, face up in the drizzle. I didn't think about it until I saw myself doing it. But deep inside I must have decided to do something like that ever since the hotel on the river. But I don't know if I have the right to involve a man like you in this."

"Thanks," I say. "And what about the girl?"

"The violinist?" He is surprised, banters a little, waves a hand in the air. "To that kind of woman one should give anything but peace. The exciting thing, *exciting*," he said in English, "is her motto. They were born to live, I respect them, they're so rare!"

You dance in turn with me, Lagos, and the Englishman; you dance with me again and I remember the telephone. I walk around the edge of the dance floor, wind up at the bar. I ask for Mr. Albano, I learn they've been to the laundry already and found your violin case, full of vials, on the shelves under the counter. Alone with Lagos at the table, I watch you raise your smile toward the Englishman's face as you dance together, and I recall the skill with which the Englishman had hidden the case under clothes in the laundry, and the small pride he had felt when he straightened up and looked at us; I recall the odor of hot dampness and soiled shirts.

"They were in the laundry," I report. "At ten o'clock."

"Thank you," Lagos answers; when he spies your dress near the orchestra, he smiles again. "We're going," he announces, when you and the Englishman arrive at the table; he puts money on the tablecloth, offers no explanations, nor does he look at us; perhaps he imagines he can extract a final prestige from arbitrary acts and mystery.

With inflexible speed he crosses the dance hall and the lobby; only when he stops at the sidewalk curb does he understand that he is desperate, and he turns to face us with a smile of amazement. We climb into a taxi and cross through the carnival in the city without talking to each other; we get out beside a long wall with political slogans painted in tall white letters.

"What happened at the laundry?" I ask Lagos. "Does it mean that . . ."

Lagos takes me by the arm and holds me until you and the Englishman walk down an ill-lit street into the night.

"Who knows, doctor? Would you say all is lost? Excuse me for answering you with a question. My plan remains, our plan; we continue to hide in the carnival, we do not exist until morning. I have the greatest respect for your equanimity. Do you reproach me for not having spoken to you of Elena in all this time, these days? Look over there, doctor, look at that white figure at Oscar's side. It's Elena. Nothing is interrupted, nothing ends; although the shortsighted might get lost in changes of circumstance and character. But not you, doctor. Listen: that trip you made with Elena pursuing Oscar, isn't it exactly the same trip that they're taking this dawn in a launch from Tigre—a ballerina, a bullfighter, a guardsman, a king?"

He lets go of my arm and continues walking in silence, modest and majestic at the same time, determined to plant his last phrase inside me like a cutting so it will take root and grow.

"I'm not going to any dance," you say at the corner. "To go now would be like killing every dance in the world—what it is, what a dance should be. But I'll go any other place you wish, wherever you say. That I'll do."

When the Englishman gets a car and I am again seated next to the driver, rolling toward the west without a precise destination; while Lagos changes plans, disappointed on arriving at intersections named by him, and we try another route that doesn't satisfy him either; as we pass through streets we do not recognize, through laughter, music, and lights, I suppose that Lagos and I will add to our remorse by leaving unanswered the greetings of dozens of Mr. Albanos who smile by simply slackening the jaw and who wave their Panama hats as we pass; they wave from balconies, café tables, other automobiles.

Now, with the carnival all around us, I am next to you in the small arbor of dry, dusty branches from which streamers and paper flowers hang, where initials, dates, and graffiti are blazoned that we scan, moving our lips in silence. We look for the waiter; a guitar preludes interminably.

"I make a toast," the Englishman says, raising his glass, the other hand hanging over the lance; he drinks without waiting for us. "A toast to the hairdresser's shop with one lonely chair, a mulatto, a jagged mirror. To one hour of siesta, and me sweating in the shadows, leafing through magazines. At this moment I can't think of a more significant memory."

"There's nothing new," I announce on returning to the table, after finding out by telephone that Mr. Albano is not in the café, after passing close to the guitarist preluding in the courtyard facing four silent friends, three women almost asleep.

"They've been to the laundry," Lagos says. "Dear doctor, I must confess there is no boat." He raises his glass, shows a smile that fails to separate his lips; he allows us to see that he is old and loves no one.

I lightly touch the hand you hide under the table, I hook a fingernail in the ridge of a bracelet, and suddenly I understand life, I recognize myself in it, I experience a final disenchantment without complexity.

"I would now toast," the Englishman says, "a very old man. He used to feed himself on tiny, unimportant mysteries. When death came, he thought he could save himself by saying he was sleepy."

Going to the telephone, I see the deserted patio, the tables piled up, a lunar brightness already dissolving in the foliage. I ask for Mr. Albano and Pepe speaks with his monotonous voice, without a pause, as if he were reciting his information for the hundredth time and still couldn't discover its meaning.

"Thanks," I say. "I don't know if I'll call again."

When I return to the table—there is a distinct glimmer over the arbor—I sit down impeded by the ridiculousness of the costume, I am ashamed of the silence of my shoes with a buckle on the red tiles, on the dirt floor of the patio where you and they wait for me.

"They've been to René's and the watchmaker's shop," I say on seating myself. "He himself warned Pepe when he heard them pounding on the door."

"Thank you," Lagos says. "We can also toast to that."

You straighten up as if awakening, you nudge my leg with yours; for a long moment laughter prevents you from speaking.

"Do you mean that the clothes . . . that we won't be able to change?"

"Excessively hidden in the carnival, it seems," says Lagos, and he tries to make me see him smile.

You raise your arms to look at them; you look at the bodice, the short stiff skirt that seems to rest on your knees; you laugh, smoothly now, each time slower, as if you were moving away.

"Not only the clothes and documents," Lagos says. "The money was also at René's."

"Let's toast with empty glasses," the Englishman proposes.

Then a silence begins in which the last street sounds are only sensed, sinking and disappearing into it; a silence in which it is possible for me to pick up, unintentionally, the thoughts of Lagos and the Englishman, and for a moment to think their thoughts for them. I can see you ten years earlier, hiding a pair of little dance slippers under your pillow; I can look over your shoulder at the pictures you go on clipping from thick old magazines, see the shine of scissors on the glossy paper; I can see you dancing to what they make you play on the violin. And here in the arbor, above the table—while the sound of birds starts timidly, with no other purpose but to cover and protect the silence—I can see the Englishman's youthful and dispassionate face, his eyes squinting at the bowl of the empty pipe in his teeth; I can see Lagos growing old between vigorous sighs, as if he were applying all his will, all his pride, to advance in years, imposing dates and seasons on himself without any fear but that of a premature death.

Flanked by smiles, sighs, restless heads, we are moving toward the great farce of tomorrow morning; we advance behind Lagos, trampling on the last vestiges of the carnival, persisting childishly in our ignorance of the streets and through noises rising like vapor; led by Lagos' will, which we fail to understand, believing in him for the last time. Burdened with our immortal silence, we advance.

I do not take your arm when we cross streets, I do not intend to protect you or remember you. In the streets the weak wind mingles and entangles traces of the defunct carnival, and dawn is imposing new limits on the world when Lagos stops leading us and the four of us sit on a backless bench in a little neighborhood square without statues or iron gratings, with an enormous central pine tree that offers us midday shade. There we wait, rigid, clumsy, shaken by the wind while we enter the morning and draw close, motionless, to clarity and the end. But when I succeed in distinguishing—between the trees, stepping lightly on the grass—the fleeting image of men who wear straw hats and venture vague greetings, I prefer irresistibly not to wait on the bench for Mr. Albano, and stand up. A moment later you and the Englishman get up.

We contemplate Lagos' sunken mouth, the half-closed eyes where the mounting daylight sinks, the lock of his hair graying and slipping out from under the wig. The Englishman shakes his head with alarm, as if discovering ghosts that multiply patiently above the stone borders of the grass, partially hidden behind tree trunks. Then he begins to walk back and forth in front of Lagos, in front of the body on the bench, collapsed and august; he comes and goes, the lance on his shoulder, with the steps and right-about-face of routine.

I can go away in peace; I cross the small square and you walk at my side, we reach the corner and go up the deserted tree-lined street without running from anyone, without wanting to meet anyone, dragging our feet a little, more from happiness than fatigue.